SKINNER'S ORDEAL

Also by Quintin Jardine

Skinner's Rules
Skinner's Festival
Skinner's Trail
Skinner's Round

SKINNER'S ORDEAL

Quintin Jardine

HEADLINE

Copyright © Quintin Jardine 1995

The right of Quintin Jardine to be identified as the Author of
the work has been asserted by him in accordance with the
Copyright, Designs and Patents Act 1988.

First published in Great Britain in 1996
by HEADLINE BOOK PUBLISHING

10 9 8 7 6 5 4 3 2 1

British Library Cataloguing in Publication Data

Jardine, Quintin
    Skinner's ordeal
    1. English fiction – 20th century – Scottish authors
    2. Scottish fiction – 20th century
    I. Title
    823.9′14[F]

ISBN 0 7472 1465 4

Typeset at The Spartan Press Ltd,
Lymington, Hants

Printed and bound in Great Britain by
Mackays of Chatham PLC, Chatham, Kent

HEADLINE BOOK PUBLISHING
A division of Hodder Headline PLC
338 Euston Road
London NW1 3BH

This book is dedicated to the people of Gullane, where most
of it was written.
Yes, Cameron, even you!

ACKNOWLEDGEMENTS

The Author's thanks go to

Dr George A Bell OBE
The hypnotic Inverdarroch

A ball of fire, unspeakable searing heat, pressure, breath forced from the lungs, the sudden awful realisation that Death is not around a distant corner, that the corner has been turned and that, too soon as ever, He is here.

Cast out from the safe, warm environment of the aircraft into the rushing winds of the morning sky, some torn, some burning, some screaming, all unable to acknowledge or believe what has happened.

Many still strapped inside the flaming fuselage as it plunges earthwards; some tearing at seat-belt buckles, standing upright, being hurled to the back of a craft that has become a coffin; others clutching at their neighbours in the last human contact they will ever know; wide-eyed, self-soiling, thinking as they fall of wives, husbands, sons, daughters, lovers, thinking of things done badly, of things unfulfilled, of all the dreams that will never come true, never, never, never, as the dark, purplish land draws nearer.

Upon some, death lays His hand at once; to a few He grants oblivion; but for most, He reserves the ultimate horror of awareness, of the moment of impact, of the tearing, the rending, the sudden, blinding light.

Finally for them, it is over. Now the horror of grief will begin.

I

There are few things in life as stomach-tugging as the ringing of a telephone at an unusual or unexpected hour.

Professor Sarah Grace Skinner lived with the phone in a state of watchful neutrality. For years, in medical practice in New York and in Britain, and more recently as a policeman's wife, it had been her constant companion.

Yet, even in the few weeks since she had taken up her new post at Edinburgh University, she had come to regard her small study in the old building as an island of peace. No one bothered her there. In all that time she had received precisely three telephone calls; one, internally, from the Principal to wish her luck with her first lecture, and the others from her husband, warning her that he would be late for dinner.

Now, when the phone rang in the second that she hung her overcoat on the tall stand in the corner of the room, she jumped involuntarily. She glanced at her Giorgio watch. It was 8.17 a.m., on the last Friday in October.

She stared at the flat cream instrument in surprise, and in apprehension. As she took the three paces from the coat-stand to her desk, fingers of fear ran through her. The baby had been asleep when she had left him, twenty minutes earlier, in the nanny's care, lying in the recommended position, the one which was credited with such success in the reduction of cot deaths.

Her husband had left home half-an-hour before her, bound for a snap and unannounced inspection of the CID office in Hawick, where there had been a consistent decline in detection rates over the previous six months. He would still be driving, down the fast, sometimes difficult A7.

Her step-daughter, only ten years younger than her, at twenty-one, had been back at university in Glasgow since mid-October, pining for the recently discovered love of her life. He, in his turn, was at an anti-drugs liaison meeting in Cambridge.

Her father? He had just turned seventy-two, and his health was far from robust, although he had declared himself hale and hearty when she had called him the weekend before.

She steeled herself and picked up the phone.

3

None of her personal-disaster scenarios had come true, but as she listened to the shocked voice on the other end of the line, she felt her hand shake, and the blood drained from her face.

'Of course,' she said, very quietly. 'I'll cancel today's lectures and tutorials. I'll be there within the hour.'

2

He was on the outskirts of Galashiels when the car-phone's trembler sounded over the droning voices of *Good Morning Scotland*.

'Bugger!' he said aloud, annoyed that the call had interrupted an item on the Radio Scotland news magazine reporting on the contrast in drug-related fatalities between Glasgow, where the previous year's record high had been surpassed before the end of the tenth month, and Edinburgh, where the incidence had fallen yet again.

Deputy Chief Constable Bob Skinner tolerated his car-phone as a necessary evil, something that went with his job. But every time it rang he resented its intrusion. He valued drive-time as an opportunity to think, away from interruptions, or as he was doing on the journey to Hawick, to catch up on the news of the day. Just as his wife enjoyed the sanctuary of her office, so he regarded his car as a place of peace.

Frowning, and with a slight shake of his steel-grey mane, he pushed the button to take the call. 'Skinner,' he snapped into the microphone clipped into the panelling above his head.

'Bob. It's Jimmy here.' Chief Constable Sir James Proud's voice was distorted by static, but still Skinner could hear the tension in his friend's tone. 'Where are you just now?'

'Just coming into Gala. Why?'

There was a pause. Uncharacteristically, Skinner felt anxiety grip him. He glanced at his car clock. It showed 8.19 a.m.

The silence extended, and Skinner realised that the connection had been broken in his hilly surroundings. For a second or two, as he drove on into the small Borders town, he fretted about whatever it was that had shaken his imperturbable boss.

But then the presenter of *Good Morning Scotland*, her voice sounding as unsteady as Proud Jimmy's, overrode the drugs story. As the woman read the newsflash, the DCC drew his car to a halt at the side of the road, and sat there, listening in horror.

By the time the phone rang again, he had turned the car around, and was heading back north up the A7, filled with fear of what awaited him.

3

'Mario, enough! Okay, the boss is away today, but that makes it worse. It means I have to shift all the crap in the in-tray myself, and sort out for him only the things I reckon he has to see.'

The grin on the big, swarthy face widened into a broad smile. 'So this is the reality of marriage! When we were living in sin you wouldn't have said "no" to a spot of morning glory.'

Maggie laughed. 'Dream on, Detective Sergeant McGuire. Sunday, maybe, but not through the week!'

She stood up from the breakfast table and dropped her cereal bowl into the dishwasher, holding out her hand for her husband to pass his across. The smile was still there, full of mischief. He caught her wrist, drew her to him gently and kissed her, ruffling her red hair. 'Okay then, Inspector Rose, let's go and put in another day towards our pensions.'

She chuckled at his sudden sombre tone. 'You really are up for the job this morning! Has Superintendent Higgins been rattling your cage?'

'Alison? No, she's fine. It's just the way things have been since we got back from our honeymoon. On this shift I've been catching the shittiest, most boring shouts, that's all. I feel more like a roadsweeper than a CID man. I'm thinking about putting in for a transfer to Andy Martin's outfit.'

His wife's eyebrows rose. 'Drugs and Vice? Indeed, you will not! That might be all right for Neil McIlhenney, but I'm not having you mixing with all those whores and junkies!'

The last traces of McGuire's grin vanished. 'I'm serious. Car thefts and shop-lifting, that's all I'm doing these days. I've been in that office long enough.'

Maggie straightened his tie, and kissed him, quickly. 'Maybe you have. I'll let you into a secret. There's an acting Dectective Inspector vacancy coming up in Special Branch. The Boss asked Brian Mackie yesterday if he'd like you posted to him. And the Thin One said "Yes please". I wasn't going to tell you, but . . .'

He looked at her, incredulous. 'Are you serious?'

'Never more so. But just you remember, when the Boss Man tells you, it comes as a complete surprise – okay? I like being the DCC's personal assistant, and *I'm* not after a transfer, except on promotion.'

He nodded, the customary smile back in place. 'Trust me. I'll give Big Bob my best "bewildered Italian" look. When'll he tell me, d'you think?'

'At the beginning of next week, probably. The vacancy's there already. It's Joe Brady's job. Remember, he won a million or so on the pools. Now, McGuire,' she said firmly, 'let's go. I do not like being late.'

Mario gave her rump an affectionate squeeze and picked up his jacket. 'Okay. You go and run the world. I'll go and stamp out shop-lifting.'

He was about to close the front door behind them when the phone rang. Maggie looked up at him in surprise. 'Yours or mine, d'you think?'

'Who knows?' he said. 'Let's find out.' He stepped back into the hall and picked up the phone.

'Hello,' he said. 'You're connected to Mario and Maggie's answering machine. If you'd like to leave a message, please speak after the tone. Beep.'

Watching from the doorway, Maggie saw him stand suddenly bolt upright, to attention. 'Sorry, sir. Yes, she's still here. The radio? No, we didn't have it on.' He fell silent and as he listened his face grew grim.

'Oh my God.' His left hand went slowly to his mouth; with the other, he held out the phone. 'It's Mr Skinner, Mags, for you. It's . . .'

She grabbed the instrument from him, consumed with anxiety. 'Yes, sir. What is it?'

'It's the Shuttle, Maggie – the seven a.m. flight to Edinburgh from Heathrow. It came down just after eight, away up behind Gifford, on the Lammermuir Hills. The thing just fell out of the sky! The disaster that we've all rehearsed so often – it's happened. I'm on my way there now, and so is the Chief. Jim Elder's heading for Fettes, but he won't be there for a while yet.

'I want you to alert Charlie Radcliffe at Divisional HQ, then to call out every available officer to assist him. If they can walk, I want them there. Tell Radcliffe to close off all the roads to the Lammermuirs to everything but emergency vehicles. I want a helicopter over the site if you can dig one up. Call the RAF at Pitreavie, and see what they can give us. Get on to Air Traffic Control after that, and make sure that they declare an exclusion zone. I don't want TV cameras buzzing around our ears up there.

'Call Brian Mackie too, just in case there are foreign nationals on board. Oh, and you might as well tell Mario he's on Special Branch duty as of now. He's to report to Brian this morning, as acting DI.

'Remember, Mags, every available officer. By God, we're going to need them!'

4

The spinning blue light in his rearview mirror snapped him out of his trance, breaking the fearful thoughts which gnawed at his stomach.

In his quarter of a century as a police officer he had attended so many scenes of carnage, that sometimes he had the strange feeling that the bulk of them had fused together in his mind, into a single bloody experience. Some had not. He recalled a bomb outrage in an auditorium in the heart of Edinburgh, where many had been killed and maimed, torn apart as they had watched an innocent entertainment. He recalled the aftermath of a fire-fight, where four people had been shot dead, and one of his own men badly wounded. He had walked in the aftermath of these bloody occasions, and of many others, not coldly, but professionally and objectively.

Yet there was something unnameably dreadful about this call, something that had him trembling behind the wheel of his BMW.

Skinner glanced at his speedometer as the siren's whine sounded behind him. He was doing 85 m.p.h. down a straight stretch of the B6368, just past Humbie. He had been so wrapped up in his thoughts that he could not remember overtaking the patrol car. He slowed down and waved an acknowledgement behind him, but the vehicle overtook him at speed and pulled in, stopping unnecessarily quickly in his path, and forcing him to brake hard. Two bulky officers jumped out of the white Peugeot and headed back towards him.

Hissing with annoyance, the Deputy Chief Constable pressed his window button. The two uniforms were both Constables, in their late twenties.

'Who the fuck d'you think you are,' shouted the driver as he approached. 'Michael bloody Schumacher?'

When Skinner felt his temper go, he always began counting to ten, but he rarely made it past six. He swung the door open and stepped out of the driver's seat to face the man and his partner, staring at them, unblinking, with deep blue eyes. His features were set hard as he moved to meet the policemen.

'*You* tell me who I am, Constable,' he said, with something in his tone that made the driver freeze in mid-stride and his passenger edge backwards towards the patrol car.

The officer's truculence seemed to drain out of his boots. He stared at Skinner, his mouth hanging open, trying to say, 'Sorry sir,' but struck speechless.

'What's your name, Constable?' Skinner snapped.

The man recovered control by standing rigidly to attention. 'PC Reader, sir.'

'Very good, Reader. At least that's something you know. Listen, I don't have time to fillet you in the way you deserve, but let me tell you this. From now on I'll be watching you like one of those things . . .' his right index finger jabbed upwards at a kestrel hovering in the still morning air above the hedgerow on the opposite side of the narrow road, intent on its prey '. . . and if I ever hear of a complaint against you of incivility to a member of the public, I'll make you wish you'd joined the Brownies rather than this police force. Now tell me this. Have you two been called to an emergency near Gifford?'

Reader nodded. 'Yes, sir.'

'Okay, here's something else you should know. That takes priority over everything, especially over hassling your DCC. Now get back in that car, keep that blue light flashing and lead me to the scene, just as fast as you can.'

5

The door of Yester Kirk was open as the two cars swept through Gifford village, their speed moderated.

People stood on the pavements of its wide main street, in groups of two or three, some in deep conversation, others staring at the sky, as if awaiting a slow-motion replay of the disaster.

A white-collared minister waited outside the Kirk. Skinner thought that he looked stunned, as if trying to reconcile his faith with the reality of what his Saviour had allowed to happen on his doorstep.

The cars swept up the hill out of the village, climbing towards the moors. At first the road was lined with trees, clinging to the last of their autumn colours in the wan morning sun, but gradually woodland gave way to cattle-dotted fields as the slopes began to level out.

The transition from farmland to moorland was almost instantaneous. The cars rumbled across a cattle grid, and past a final copse of trees; suddenly, the pasture grass had been replaced by acres of brown and purple heather, rolling and undulating in a strange alien landscape. Skinner looked ahead as a mottled valley opened out before him. On the far side, in the middle distance he could see three, no, four thin columns of black smoke rising towards the sky.

The smoke grew nearer, the columns thicker as they drove on over and through the bumps and hollows of the otherwise featureless moorland. At last they came to a fork in the road, with twin signs each pointing to *Duns, via Cranshaws*, and *via Longformacus*.

A uniformed Sergeant stood by the signpost, as if on guard. Skinner flashed his headlights at his escort car, and pulled to a stop himself. The officer approached as he climbed out. Skinner recognised him at once. 'Hello, Sergeant Boyd,' he said, but without his usual affable smile of greeting. 'Where is everyone?'

The whey-faced, forty-something policeman gave him a loose, wavy salute. 'Chief Superintendent Radcliffe took the rest of the lads up the Longformacus Road, sir. He left me here to divert the traffic and to direct. So far there's only six of us here.'

Skinner grunted. 'That's a start. But in just a few minutes this place is going to be like Princes Street at the Fireworks.' Footfalls sounded behind him. He looked over his shoulder and saw PC Reader and his partner approach from their parked car.

'You two,' he said, not unkindly, beginning to feel guilt over his savaging of Reader, who, after all, had been only doing his job, if a little over-aggressively. 'Stay here with Sergeant Boyd. Use your car as a road block, and divert any traffic from Gifford down the Cranshaws Road. As our people and the other emergency services get here, send them on up the road.' He jerked a thumb over his shoulder. 'Others, and especially the press and telly, hold here. Don't let them past you, and don't let them head on down the other road where they can get round behind you. I don't want cameras all over the scene, at least until the rescue operation's well under way . . . Sergeant, get on your radio and make sure that this road's being blocked at the other end too. I'm off to find Mr Radcliffe.'

He folded himself back behind the wheel of the white saloon and headed off down the narrow roadway, towards the four columns of smoke. They were beginning to spiral on a light morning breeze, which Skinner guessed would have been triggered by the turning of the tide in the estuary a few miles distant. On either side of him, the heather was thicker than ever. The Longformacus Road was steep and twisting as it plunged and climbed in and out of a succession of featureless gullies. At first the smoke beacons were dead ahead of him but as he grew ever nearer, they veered round to his left with the curving of the road.

As he drove he was concentrating more on the smoke signals than on the road, and so, when his eye was caught at last by the shapeless, mangled body he had to brake hard, throwing himself painfully against the restraining seat-belt.

The thing lay across the roadway, blocking most of it, only a few yards short of the crest of a steep climb. At first, Skinner registered only a red, torn mass beyond the bonnet of the BMW. Breathing heavily, he squeezed his eyes shut as he composed himself. Then running his fingers through his steel-grey hair, he braced himself and stepped out of the car.

6

It was a sheep.

As Skinner stared at it, shuddering in spite of himself, he could see, protruding from the carcass, the long, jagged piece of metal which had caught the animal as it plunged from the sky, eviscerating it and hurling it, in a trail of gore and entrails, from the heather in which it had been grazing across the road. It was almost wholly red, looking for all the world as if science had produced a new strain of pre-dyed wool. His nostrils were filled with the smell of it, the almost palpable reek of blood and guts and faeces, and he turned his head away, staring back down the slope where the rest of the flock had gathered together as if for security, against the terror which had seized one of their number.

Suddenly his senses were caught by another odour, one which overcame even the stench of the sheep. It was an acrid smell of burning, of the reek of ignited aircraft fuel which still hung over the fields. He looked up the slope, to its crest; his dread returned as he realised that he was very close to the disaster scene. As he stared, a faint voice reached his ears, borne on the breeze.

With an effort of will, he switched off his revulsion. Seizing the dead sheep by its bloody forehooves, he dragged it from the roadway into the heather, ignoring the slithering sound it made as more of its innards were loosed into the light of day.

Wet tendrils of vegetation tugged at his calves, soaking his woollen trousers, and he swore softly. Leaving the animal to the attention of the huge black crows which were circling above, he jumped back out on to the tarmac and opened the BMW's boot. Rummaging inside he found his trusty old black Wellingtons and pulled them on, discarding his black Loakes. He had carried his rubber boots, and their predecessors for as long as he could remember, all year long in successive motor cars.

The pedals were awkward under the heavy, ridged rubber soles, and so he eased the car slowly up the last few feet of the climb, pulling it off at the summit into a flat grassy area, beside a navy blue police personnel carrier which had been parked there. Inside, there sat a man, his face buried in his hands. Skinner looked at him and decided, quickly, that he could wait.

The long shallow valley spread out before him, like a sub-division of

12

Hell. The closest of the four smoking columns was perhaps thirty yards away. The heather around it was burning and its heat reached out to him, yet not even the high octane fuel could make much progress through its thick growth, saturated as it had been by the heavy, almost continuous rain of one of the wettest Scottish autumns on record. Beyond the fire, as if contained by it and the other three main blazes, hundreds of yards away in the far slopes, a great black slash, perhaps half a mile long and fifty yards wide, had been scorched into the valley floor. Here and there, isolated flickers of flame and tendrils of smoke drifted upwards. At the head of the valley, lay the plane's twin engines.

Skinner closed his eyes. As vividly as if he had been there, he saw the plane's belly crash into the ground, exploding in a white-hot blast. He saw the engines cartwheeling on. He saw the deadly rain of jagged metal plunging from the sky.

He opened his eyes to escape the vision, and felt a renewed trembling wrack his body. The sheer scale of the disaster seemed almost too much to take in. As he looked down into the valley, he thought of his own recent flights, and felt the guilt as an involuntary surge of relief swept through him, that others were lying there, not him nor his own.

Standing out against the dark scar, and around it, against the purple of the heather that remained untouched, Skinner saw a sea of myriad spots of colour. There were reds, blues, greens, yellows, whites, hundreds of them, scattered in a great circle all over the walls and floor of the valley. Some lay still on the dark ground, others flapped on the breeze. Skinner knew what many of these coloured markers represented, and his eyes moistened at the realisation. Among them were more than a few Day-Glo splashes. He guessed that they might be life-jackets donned in some last fair hope.

The aircraft had blown apart on impact. All around Skinner, and all around the crest of the site, pieces of shrapnel, like the one that had slaughtered the sheep, were tangled in the undergrowth, or sticking into the ground. The only part of it that remained more or less intact was the tail section. It lay, recognisable but upside down, at the top of the southern slope.

For a second the DCC felt that he would be overwhelmed by the immensity of the thing, but suddenly looking down, he saw five small figures moving among the wreckage. They were all in uniform, and all wore Wellingtons. The officer closest to him, who was perhaps 300 yards away, wore a cap heavy with silver braid.

'Charlie!' Skinner shouted. The man looked up, and the two headed towards each other through the heather, one down the slope and one back up, each of them looking not at the other, but at their feet, as they walked.

They were fifty yards apart when Skinner's eye was caught by something away to his left. A grey line showed just above the stubby, thigh-high shrubs. He veered towards it, motioning Radcliffe to follow, but not looking at him. As he drew closer, he saw that the grey shape was at the centre of a deep circular depression in the ground-covering plant. A fist of apprehension grasped at his stomach.

He was still almost ten yards away when he knew for certain that it was an aircraft seat. It was lying on its side, its back towards him and it was impacted into the ground. As he closed the distance, he realised that the seat was still occupied. He stepped around to the other side.

The body strapped into the chair was that of a man. It was intact, but the head hung at a grotesque angle, and the legs were broken and bent back under the chair. The face was bloody and unrecognisable, and the blue business suit was torn to shreds. Skinner guessed that while the heather might have cushioned the impact as the seat hit the ground, it had taken its toll too.

Chief Superintendent Radcliffe's footsteps sounded behind him and then stopped. Skinner heard his colleague's heavy breathing interrupted by a sudden sharp gasp as he caught sight of the victim.

'God, sir,' he said. 'We've all rehearsed this often enough, but it doesn't really prepare you, does it?'

Skinner turned to face him. 'No, Charlie. Nothing ever could.' He nodded towards the valley. 'What's it like down there?'

'Carnage, Bob. Sheer bloody carnage. Bodies all over the place, and not all of them in one piece. My lads are being thorough, but there's not a cat's chance of finding anyone alive.'

'I know, Charlie, but we've got to look. We owe it to them: to them and their families.'

Suddenly in the distance, they heard the sound of sirens. 'That'll be the reinforcements. Let's get back up the hill and set up some sort of a command point.' Skinner turned and retraced his steps through the thick heather, leading the way. 'Who's the bloke in the van?' he asked Radcliffe as they walked.

'An eye-witness. A shepherd. He was up the hill there when the plane came down. We found him shambling along the road. We'll get nae sense out of him for a while though.'

Radcliffe winced as they trudged up the hill. 'Are you up to this terrain, my friend?' asked Skinner solicitously. 'I mean, it's not that long since your operation. And you're not as young as your men.'

'I'm fine, sir,' said the uniformed officer, although his pale face belied him. He was in his late fifties, and earlier that year he had undergone major surgery. 'It just gives me a twinge every now and again.'

'Aye, well; just you look after yourself.' The DCC paused. 'You made good time getting here.'

14

Radcliffe nodded. 'Just luck, sir. I happened to be in at Haddington early this morning. When HQ put through the message from Air Traffic Control, I grabbed five of the six people in the station, piled them into the bus and came up here. But you've made pretty fair time yourself.'

Skinner glanced at his watch. It was a minute after nine a.m. 'Right enough. Mind you, I was stopped for speeding on the way.' Radcliffe smiled tensely, not suspecting for a second that the other man was speaking the truth.

They stood together on the brow of the hill, looking to the north, where two red fire tenders were winding steadily onwards. Just behind them came an ambulance with a police car in its trail.

'A drop in the ocean, sir, that's all they are,' said Radcliffe grimly.

'Don't I know it, Charlie. Let's find out what's been done.'

He took his mobile phone from his pocket, switched it on and dialled the number of Police Headquarters in Edinburgh's Fettes Avenue. The call was answered as quickly as ever.

'DCC Skinner here. Get me ACC Ops, wherever he is.'

'Very good, sir,' said the telephonist. 'I think he's in the Command Room.'

When Jim Elder, his colleague in charge of force operations, came on the line Skinner could hear the babel of sound behind him. At first the Yorkshireman had to shout above the din, until after a few seconds it subsided.

'Bob, it's good to hear from you. Where are you?'

'I'm at the crash site, Jim. I was south of Edinburgh when the Chief called me, and I burned rubber getting here. Tell me, how were we alerted to it?'

'Air Traffic Control,' said Elder. 'They called us to say that the seven a.m. Edinburgh shuttle had vanished from their screens at eight minutes past eight, over the Lammermuirs, at a height of eight thousand feet. It just turned into a shower of sparks on the VDU, so they said.'

'What's been done so far?'

'As you know, the disaster plan puts me in charge at HQ. The Chief's on his way out to you. When I got in, I found that your Maggie had started things moving. She's got units from all services heading out to the scene.'

'Aye,' said Skinner. 'Some of them are here already. But it's not fire engines we'll need, Jim. The flames will go out of their own accord. And it's not ambulances either. You can stand down the emergency centres; they won't be having any patients from here.'

He felt his voice crack, and paused.

'No hope, Bob?' asked Elder, quietly.

'No, Jim, none. What we'll need up here are experienced people

15

with the stomach for what has to be done. I'll send the fire and ambulance people away. They'll have other calls, where they can do some good.'

'What d'you need then, mate?'

Skinner paused again, gathering his thoughts.

'First of all,' he said eventually, 'I'll need stretchers, blankets and bearers. And I'll need some sort of a field mortuary. This place is the middle of nowhere. We'll try to find a hall as close as we can to here that'll be big enough to take all the bodies. But God, man, I doubt that Meadowbank Stadium would be big enough!

'No, I need tents, large ones, and the people who can get them here in a hurry and have them operational. I need the Army, Jim. Will you get on to Craigiehall and ask Scottish Command if they can help us. Ask them if they can get choppers up here with a full battlefield set-up, and as many men as they can spare to help our lads with the dirty work.'

'Okay, Bob, I'll do all that. What about the Civil Aviation Authority – should we tell them?'

Skinner thought for a second. 'The airline will have done that, for certain. But you might want to ask them what they'll be doing and whether the people they send up here'll need assistance.'

'Right. Speaking of the airline, I've already asked them for a list of all the passengers on board, seat by seat, and all the information they have on each of them. Once you confirm that there are no survivors, I'll get the next-of-kin operation geared up. Mind you, we're getting calls already. The switchboard's lit up. Royston's people have acquired an emergency number, but it hasn't been flashed up on telly or radio yet.'

ACC Elder gulped. 'God, I almost forgot – there was a call for you a couple of minutes ago. Your other office in London. They said they wanted you, urgently.'

Skinner scowled. In addition to being Edinburgh's second most senior policeman, the big DCC was Security Adviser to the Secretary of State for Scotland. As such, he was a member of the MI5 network. Scotland, with one notable exception, did not have an extensive history of terrorism, and so the job was not onerous, but by its nature it could thrust its way unplanned into the busiest of working days. And this one promised to be one of the most hectic of his career.

'Bugger it,' he said. 'This overrides them. If they come back on, tell them what's happened, then put them on to Special Branch, and ask Brian Mackie to speak to them.'

'I'll try,' said Elder, 'but they might not like it.'

'Tough shit. Right, what else do we require? For a start, although one of our mobile HQ units will be coming up here under the plan,

16

we're going to need two. There are no buildings for miles around, and Alan Royston will want somewhere separate to handle the media.

'I'd like you to send Maggie Rose up, too. In our rehearsals, she's played the part of co-ordinator at the disaster site, so it makes sense that she does it here. Normally it might fall to Charlie Radcliffe, who's standing beside me, but I need him out in the valley directing the troops.' He paused, as Elder grunted agreement on the other end of the line. 'Anyway, I can think of no one better than Mags. She's rock steady under pressure.

'I'll stay here until everything is in place, and the recovery operation's under way. Then it's over to you, Assistant Chief Constable Ops. I don't mind telling you, Jim, I wish it had been you who was closest to the scene this morning. Times like this,' he said, grim and earnest, 'I'm glad I'm just a simple thief-catcher!'

Still gripped with tension, he looked back once more down the hill and to the north. There, several police vehicles were making their steady way towards him. And behind them he saw a blue Vauxhall Frontera.

'Jim,' he said sharply. 'Which medics have been called in on this?'

'Didn't the Chief tell you?' replied Elder. 'He called Sarah, straight away. Then he called the Health Board and asked them to implement the disaster plan.'

Charlie Radcliffe, standing nearby, caught the change in Skinner's tone. He saw his eyes narrow and his jaw clench. Involuntarily, he backed away.

'The daft old sod!' Skinner shouted. 'Surely to Christ one of us up here's enough for him. Surely there are enough doctors in Edinburgh. Surely he could have spared her this!'

At the other end of the line, Elder flinched also. 'Come on, Bob. Who else would he ask?'

'Just about anyone! Anyone but my wife!'

7

He punched the 'end' button and put the phone back in his pocket. He stood framed against the sky and watched the Frontera as it wound its way up the hill, watched as it pulled off the road and drew up beside him.

Sarah looked at him uncertainly through her big, dark-hazel eyes as she reached her foot down from the driver's seat. She was around five feet six inches tall, but the car rode high off the ground. She wore a long Barbour jacket over her university suit, and blue rubber boots, tied at the top. In her right hand she carried her medical bag.

She ran a hand over her auburn hair, in an unconscious gesture. 'Bob?' It was a question.

'What are you doing here?' he said softly. He was unaware of Charlie Radcliffe sidling off towards the valley.

An edge to match his own crept into her voice. 'You're asking me that?'

'Too right I am.'

'It's my job, remember!'

'No, it isn't. Not any more. Your job is in the University. There are other people to do this.'

'I'm still on the strength as a Force ME. You know that.'

'Sure, as holiday cover, and for police emergencies. Not for this!'

'And what the hell is this if not an emergency?' It was the first time in her life that she had ever raised her voice to him in real anger.

His eyes flared at her shout, but his voice dropped to a whisper. 'This is a disaster. There's nothing you can do for anyone down there.'

'Oh yeah – and which Med. School did you graduate from? Can you say for sure that there's no one alive down there? Can you say for sure when someone's dead?'

'I can when his head is thirty yards away from his arse. Look, go back to University, go home. Go anywhere, just don't go down there.' His desperation broke through his anger, and she was touched, seeing how much he cared for her.

'I'm sorry, Bob, but I took an oath that says I have to.' She turned away from him and strode towards the valley. He started after her, stretching out a hand to hold her back . . . and then his telephone sounded.

8

'Dammit!' He kicked a stone in frustration and tore the instrument from his pocket. He jerked out the aerial and pushed the receive button. 'Yes!' he snapped.

'Bob?' The man on the other end of the call sounded taken aback. 'Z'at you?'

The DCC was so surprised that for a moment he forgot his argument with Sarah. 'Adam? what the bloody hell do you want?'

It had been over a year since Skinner had seen Captain Adam Arrow, although the two were close friends. The little soldier had stood by his side during some of the most dangerous moments of his life, and the very sound of his Derbyshire tones was enough to lift the policeman's spirits.

'That's a fine 'ello for an old mate,' said Arrow.

'Sorry, chum,' Skinner replied sincerely. 'You caught me at a bad moment. In a bad place, in fact.'

'It's all right, I know where you are. I tried to get you at Fettes a few minutes back. Your mate Elder told me.'

'Eh? But Jim said that my London office was looking for me. I thought you weren't attached to Five any more.'

'I'm not, Bob, but it was easier to tell him that.' Suddenly Arrow sounded uncharacteristically serious. 'I'm back with the MOD. I'm Head of the Security Section. I'll leave you to guess what that covers.'

'Look, mate, the fookin' shit's going to hit the fan just directly. The plane that came down on your patch this morning had two VVIPs on board: Colin Davey, the Secretary of State for Defence, and Shaun Massey, the American Defence Secretary.'

Skinner whistled softly. 'Jesus! That's all we need. What were they doing there? And why wasn't I told that they were coming on to my territory?'

'There's a NATO exercise on this weekend in Scotland – off the west coast. Davey and Massey were going to look in on it. As for telling you, they weren't going to leave the airport. Our people had arranged for a private plane to pick them up from the general aviation terminal and fly them on to Oban. Bob, you're on the ground. What's the score with survivors?'

The big policeman sighed. 'Forget it, my friend.'

'Ahh. I expected as much. Do we know anything about the crash?'

'There's a witness here. I'm letting him calm down before we talk to him.'

'Well, do it as quick as you can, will you? I need to know fast.'

'Oh, yes?' said Skinner, intrigued. 'Have you had—'

Arrow cut him off in mid-question. 'Yes! There've been threats, and a bloody serious one among them.' He paused for several long seconds as if thinking something over. 'Bob, d'you mind if I come up there?'

'Of course not. Even if there's nothing sinister here, you have to satisfy yourself. Anyway, suppose I did mind . . .' He let the sentence tail off unfinished.

'Okay then. I'll be with you as quick as I can.'

Skinner switched off his phone and put it back in his pocket. Chief Superintendent Radcliffe had returned from his strategic patrol. 'Everything okay, sir?' he asked tentatively.

'Oh no, Charlie. It sure as hell isn't.' Quickly and tersely he told him of Adam Arrow's telephone call and of his news.

The veteran policeman drew in his breath. 'Bugger me!' he gasped. 'That's all we need. Your man doesn't really think this was sabotage, does he?'

'That's what we're all paid to think, Charlie, until we know for sure it wasn't. Adam's got me thinking now, and I'll tell you, there's something about this crash scene that isn't right.'

'What d'you mean, sir?'

He led Radcliffe back towards the start of the downslope. Below him, he could see Sarah making her way among the wreckage, kneeling every so often, then standing up and moving on. He put his annoyance to one side, at least temporarily, and stretched out a finger pointing along the length of the shattered valley.

'There's something missing. Look, there's the tail; there are the remnants of the wings; there are the engines. The fuselage, okay it's blown to buggery. But the nose-cone, Charlie – where the hell's the nose-cone? I don't see a vestige of it down there, yet there it should be.'

'But wouldn't that have been blown apart too, sir?'

'No, I don't think so. It's not as if the thing went nose-first into the ground. Look at the mark – it shows you what happened. If anything, it came down nose-high. See the way the tail is? That was ripped right off on impact. The engines? They were too, and flung ahead of the rest of it. The fuel left in the wings ignited, and that, together with the impact, blew the fabric of the cabin all over the place . . . But the nose-cone would have survived, at least something recognisable would have. Think of all the air-crash scenes you've ever seen on TV, or in person.'

'I've never seen anything like this before, Bob,' said Radcliffe softly. 'Thank Christ!'

'Well, think back to that crash a few years back. The body of the plane was shattered, but the nose-cone remained in one piece. Not that it helped the people inside, though.' He shuddered violently. 'Down there, though, there's nothing that looks remotely like the sharp end of that plane. And we have to find out why. Come on,' he said sharply. 'Time we talked to your eye-witness in the van, whether he's ready for it or not.'

He led the way across to the blue minibus. The man was sitting in the second row of seats, staring over his shoulder away from the valley, down the hillside to where a flock of sheep had gathered dumbly around the body of the slaughtered ewe. Chief Superintendent Radcliffe opened the passenger door and leaned inside.

'How are you feeling, sir?' he asked.

The shepherd shrugged his shoulders, helplessly.

'There's someone here who has to speak to you. Is that okay?' The man nodded. Radcliffe backed out of the vehicle and allowed the DCC to climb into the front seat.

'Good morning,' he said. 'My name's Bob Skinner. What's yours?'

The man looked at him as if he was trying to remember. Seated, he looked short, but stockily built. He had thick, black, matted curly hair, and wore a dirty tweed jacket over a heavyweight check shirt. His hands were in his lap. Skinner was shocked to see that they were stained with blood. He looked at the man's face properly for the first time, and saw a red smear by his right temple.

The shepherd blinked. 'Ronnie Thacker. My name's Ronnie Thacker.'

'What were you doing up here, Mr Thacker?'

'Getherin' in the sheep. It was time tae bring them back tae the ferm.'

'Mr Radcliffe said he found you running down the road. You didn't have a vehicle, then?'

'Lost ma licence!' The man glared at him, as if he should have known. 'The boss dropped me off on the hillside, then went back for his breakfast.'

'So. Let's talk about the crash, Ronnie. Take your time, now, and try to remember everything. When did you see the plane first?'

Thacker knitted his brows. 'Ah dinna ken really. Ah just looked up and it was there, comin' towards the ground.'

'Was there anything in particular that made you look up?'

The shepherd paused, as if struggling to express himself. 'Ah dinna ken for sure. At first, Ah thought Ah heard a shot, far away, like. Ah thought tae myself, "Wha's out wi' a twelve-bore at this time o' day?" It was then Ah saw the plane.'

'Can you describe it, as it came down?'

'It . . . It . . . It seemed tae be in slow motion at first. It just sort of drifted down. Then the closer it got, the faster it seemed tae be goin'. Ah couldna dae a thing, ken. Ah thought it was goin' tae hit me, but Ah couldna move. Then it went past me and crashed intae the valley. The tail tore aff and then a'thing just blew up. Great big dods o' metal goin' up in the air, and fallin' all about me. Yin bit just missed me. It hit wan o' ma ewes, though. Turned the poor bugger inside out. Ah've never see a mess like yon, outside of a knacker's yard.'

He held up his bloody hands to illustrate the point. Skinner winced.

'That's when Ah panicked. Ah just had tae get away from that thing. Ah never thought where Ah wis goin' other than just down the road, away frae here. Ah walked and walked . . . Then Ah met your lot, and the buggers brought me back!'

Skinner smiled at him gently. 'You're an important man, Ronnie. You're maybe the only witness we've got.'

A light seemed to go on in a dark recess of the shepherd's brain. 'D'ye think I might get money, like? Frae the papers?'

'Don't book your holidays on the strength of it. Now, let's go back to the crash. I want you to think carefully. When the plane hit the ground, what happened to the nose-cone?'

'The whit?'

'The bit at the sharp-end, Ronnie. Where the driver sits.'

The shepherd's brow furrowed again. 'D'ye ken, that's a funny thing. And it never occurred tae me till you said. The bit at the front. It wisna there!'

'You didn't see it at all?'

'Naw. It wisna there, Ah tell ye. The front was open. There wis smoke and some flames comin' out. But Ah never saw the bit at the sharp end. Not at all!'

Skinner sat and stared at the man for several seconds.

'Honest!' said Thacker, plaintively.

'Okay, okay. I believe you!' He stepped out of the car, and beckoned to Radcliffe.

'Charlie. I want you to put this boy in a car and send him up to Brian Mackie. Tell him he's to give him a statement, repeating everything that he's just told me. Then get word to Brian that no journalists are to be allowed within a mile of the bloke. Got that?'

Radcliffe looked at him, wide-eyed. 'Got it, sir. Every word of it!'

9

Sir James Proud rarely used a police driver if he could avoid it. 'Policemen are trained for policing,' he said often to Bob Skinner, 'not for driving pompous sods like us around, just so that we can be seen in our big cars.'

On the other hand, the veteran Chief Constable was rarely seen out of his impressive uniform on public occasions. 'The boys and girls on the beat like to see their Chief wearing the silver braid, Bob. It makes their uniforms feel that bit more important. Besides, it makes *me* feel that I really am in command of this outfit. When you drive a chair for as long as I have, you need to reassure yourself on that score.'

But, on this day, when Proud Jimmy's car crested the rise and pulled into the impromptu police carpark, he was in the back seat. When he stepped out, Skinner saw that he was clad in a heavy, navy-blue pullover and baggy old flannels, their legs tucked into thick grey woollen socks worn inside tan hiking boots.

For a moment, Skinner's anger over Sarah's involvement threatened to burst to the surface, but it evaporated as soon as he saw his friend's shocked, drawn face. 'I came to help, Bob,' said the Chief quietly. 'But on the way, I received this over the car fax.' If Skinner disliked his car phone, he loathed the very idea of a fax on wheels, but in the official vehicles reserved for chief officers they were standard equipment.

With an impression of distaste he took the sheets of paper which Proud Jimmy held out to him. 'What is it?'

'It's the passenger list, row by row. D'you see the name against Row 1 seat E?'

Skinner glanced at the first page and saw the name of Colin Davey MP. 'I know about him. Wee Adam Arrow called me a few minutes back. He's flying up here.'

'Mmm,' said the Chief. To the DCC's surprise, he sounded almost uninterested. 'Now look at the fourth page. Row 28, seat A.'

Skinner thumbed through the pages until he found the reference. He stared at it, and as he did so he paled, and his shoulders sagged. 'Oh Jimmy, no. Surely not! Not Roy Old. Not nice, amiable, easygoing Roy.'

'I'm afraid so,' said the Chief sadly.

'What the hell was he doing on that plane? I spoke to him yesterday. He was going to the conference dinner last night. It was a black-tie do, port and cigars and all that. A real "AlkaSeltzers at Oh Nine Hundred" job. Why the bloody hell did he have to be so damned conscientious that he dragged his hangover on to the seven o'clock shuttle?'

Detective Chief Superintendent Roy Old was Head of CID, Skinner's immediate deputy in the criminal investigation hierarchy, and once upon a time Detective Inspector to his Detective Sergeant in the Gayfield Police Station. He was a quiet, self-effacing man, to the extent that he had been in a backwater job in West Lothian until Skinner's accession to Chief Officer rank. One of the first acts of the newly appointed Assistant Chief Constable had been to install his former boss as his number two – the ideal man, he had thought, to maintain stability while he formulated his long-term plans. Those plans were in place. Now their implementation would have to be brought forward.

Skinner turned his back on the Chief and leaned against the roof of his car. 'I put him there, Jimmy!' It was almost a howl. 'I could have gone to that bloody conference, I should have gone. But I sent Roy instead. And why? Because I looked at the programme and thought, "Christ what a bore! A three-day inter-Force conference on fraud! No way I'm sealing myself up in that. Roy can go. Good old Roy. It'll help him while away some time till his retirement."

'Now good old modest Roy's lying in bits down in the heather, because the great Bob Skinner was too self-important to bother with the mundane parts of his job!'

Sir James laid a hand on his shoulder. 'Bob, son. There's no reason for you to think like that. Delegation's the name of the game. You and I could each spend eighteen months of every year at conferences if we went to them all.'

'No, Jimmy, that won't wash. I can't get away from it. *I* put Roy on that plane. And I did it for a laugh. I did, man! I looked at the programme and I said to Maggie, "Old can go to that one. He's just the guy to sit on his arse for three days listening to a team of accountants droning on about corporate misbehaviour!" So I filled his name in on the form and sent it through to him. It was a joke, really, but he didn't get it. He just booked himself in and went.

'And he never came back! How am I going to tell Lottie that, or look in her eye at the funeral?' Skinner, desolate, bowed his head.

'Bob, Bob,' said Proud Jimmy quietly. 'It wasn't a joke, and you know it. I sent Roy out to West Lothian for much the same reason, and I'd have sent him to that conference as well. He was the sort of copper who could sit for three days, listening conscientiously and taking notes, and then represent the Force like a trouper at the dinner.

He was a good, solid, dependable bloke, so bloody dependable that he probably decided that bad head or not, he was going to put in a full day at the office. So he booked himself on the seven o'clock flight. *That's* how you've got to see it, man, or you'll gut yourself.'

Skinner straightened up. He shook his head. 'The last thirty seconds, Jimmy. That's all I can see. But don't let's talk about that, or I really will go crazy.'

'Aye. Let's grieve afterwards. You wait till you read the rest of that passenger list. Quite apart from the Right Honourable and late Colin Davey, some of the names on there are very familiar to me.'

Skinner looked at the list again. His stomach turned over as he read the first name aloud. 'Master Mark McGrath. Oh dammit! Life's just not fair, is it? And next to him, must have been his dad. Roland McGrath MP. McGrath! Christ, he's the Home Affairs Minister in the Scottish Office. It's not three months since he paid us a visit to open the new station in Craigmillar.'

'The Defence Secretary's protection officer was in the seat next to McGrath,' said the Chief. 'That's why it's simply labelled "Male Passenger". Another lost policeman.'

'Not so likely,' said Skinner. 'More probably a soldier. Defence tend to look after their own.'

'Colin Davey himself was in the middle seat on the other side of the aisle,' said Proud. 'The people on either side of him were his Private Secretary and someone called Shaun Massey. That name's familiar too, but I'm damned if I can remember from where.'

Skinner grunted. 'Jesus, it should be familiar. He's the American Secretary for Defence. Look at Row 2 Seats D to F. Three more "Male Passengers", two of them marked "US". Another of our protection people and two Secret Service, I'd say.

'Who's this in Seat 2C, d'you know?' he asked, and read the name aloud. 'Ms Victoria Cunningham.'

'Roland McGrath's Private Secretary,' said the Chief Constable. 'She was with him when he performed the opening ceremony. I remember her quite well. A nice wee lass. She looked a bit like my daughter-in-law. Oh dear.' He shook his head mournfully.

Skinner read on, down the list. Several of the names seemed familiar to him, and four more of them were Members of Parliament. He looked up at Proud. 'Six MPs in all,' he said. 'I make it two Tories, two Labour, one Lib Dem and one Nat.'

'That's right. The first shuttle on Friday's a popular plane with Parliamentarians. I'm surprised there weren't more on board. Did you see Lord Barassie's name there?' Skinner nodded. 'He sat on the Labour benches. A spokesman on something or other.'

'You said you think you know who some of these other people are?'

'Aye,' said Proud Jimmy. 'It's well seen you don't use the New

Club as much as me. You'll need to get to know the Edinburgh establishment better, Bob. I tell you, I reckon the Club will have a right few vacancies as a result of this calamity.

'The two chaps sat next to each other in Row 5. Yeats and Bernard. They're both directors of the Bank of Scotland. I recognise three other names as senior people with the insurance companies. There could be a couple of directors of the brewery there as well.

'The business community will have been decimated here, Bob. There were eight Japanese on board, too. Possibly inward investors, or executives with some of the electronics companies.

'I counted the names on the list. There were a hundred and ninety-eight passengers and seven crew on board. Two hundred and five lives, snuffed out, just like that. And for what? Just to get from point A to point B that wee bit quicker. You can't exist in this world without flying, but I'll tell you something, my friend: every time I do it, I'm scared stiff.'

Skinner looked at his Chief. 'Do you think you're unique?' he said quietly.

They stood there in silence for almost a minute, looking down at the scene of growing activity in the valley. Eventually Sir James glanced back towards Skinner. 'Has the airline given us any idea what might have caused this?'

The DCC shook his steel-grey mane. 'They don't have a clue. I do, though. We've got a witness, a guy who saw the plane come down. God, it almost landed on the bugger. From what he told me, it looks as if there was an explosion in mid-air.'

'Oh bloody hell!' said Sir James.

'Exactly. On top of that, Adam Arrow told me there have been threats made to Davey.'

The breath hissed between the Chief Constable's teeth. 'I hate the sound of all that. Have you called in the Bomb Squad?'

'Not yet. I'd just finished speaking to the witness when you arrived.'

'Better do it, then.'

'Time enough. The first task is recovery of the victims. Then we'll have the world's biggest jigsaw puzzle to solve. We may have to try and put the plane back together again to get a picture of what happened. And before we can do *that*, we'll have to find all the bits!'

Skinner didn't need to send for the Bomb Squad. It came to him.

He and the Chief Constable were making their way through the heather and down the hillside to add their manpower to the pointless, but obligatory, search for survivors when he heard the steady drone of the helicopter engine. At the sound, he stopped and looked up, thinking at first that an over-eager TV crew might be breaching the air exclusion zone which Jim Elder would have seen imposed by now as the DCC had instructed him earlier.

The sky was still empty, but as he listened, the tone of the engine told him that the approaching craft was a heavier machine than those normally available for hire by the media. He looked back up the slope, westward, towards the source of the sound. It grew louder, forcing itself upon the stillness of the valley, until eventually it burst over the horizon and into view – a big, ugly, dark green machine, flying so low that Skinner could feel the down-draught from its heavy rotors.

'Who's that?' said Proud Jimmy beside him. 'It isn't carrying RAF markings. Naval, is it?'

Skinner shook his head. 'No, Chief. That's the so'jers. I can't tell which lot though. No. Wait a minute.' The helicopter held steady in flight hovering just in front of them, and swinging round so that they could see a man in a window to the side. He was pointing and gesticulating towards the other side of the hill.

'That's Gammy Legge, Jimmy.'

'Who?'

'Major Gabriel Legge, known to one and all as Gammy, the Head of the Bomb Squad in Scotland. You remember him, from the business last year. Adam Arrow must have called them out.'

'Oh aye. Funny bugger that Legge, isn't he? What's he pointing at?'

'I think he's telling us that they can't land here and that the pilot's going to put down on the other side of the hill.'

He waved an acknowledgement to the Major. The helicopter veered away.

'D'you want to come and meet them?' Skinner asked.

'No, Bob. It doesn't take two of us. I'll get down to where I can do some good; you go and talk to Legge.'

'Okay.' Skinner turned and headed off, not back towards the road, but following the aircraft as it lumbered towards its landing spot. As he reached the top of the slope, he saw it settle on the uneven ground on a spot 200 yards away. He covered the distance at a trot.

Major Legge, wearing a green officer's pullover with rank insignia on the epaulettes, jumped first from the helicopter. He was followed by three other soldiers – a Lieutenant and two Sergeants.

'Thought we'd find you here, Bob,' he said, in his smoothed-over Ulster tones. 'You and I always seem to meet like two comrades on a battlefield, don't we?'

Skinner gripped the outstretched hand and shook it. 'I'm afraid so, Gammy, and this is the most devastated yet. Tell me, who called you in on this one? Adam Arrow?'

'Who's he?'

'Military Security.'

'Oh yes, the little chap who was here last year. No, it wasn't him. In fact, no one ordered us here. But sooner or later, our guys are always called in to something like this, if only to make sure that there is nothing to investigate other than an accident. When I heard about this one I simply decided to anticipate the request from CAA. Anyway, why should Adam Arrow call us in on a civilian air accident?'

Succinctly, Skinner told him who had been in Row 1, Seats E and F, and of Arrow's concern about threats. Major Legge's tanned face seemed to darken.

'I see,' he said. 'And tell me, have you seen anything so far to indicate that there might be external involvement in this?'

Skinner nodded. 'A witness who says he saw the plane come down, in flames and minus its nose-cone. To back that up, although the rest of the machine is spread all over the valley, there doesn't seem to be any sign of the cockpit.'

'Sure and that's a fair indicator,' said the Major, his brogue deepening.

Skinner pointed skywards. 'Gammy, let's go up in your helicopter. Let's look at the site from the air, and then let's see if we can find the nose section.'

Legge nodded. He turned to the Lieutenant. 'Gerald – take us up again, please. Sergeant Allan, Sergeant Law, you two stay here. Have a look at the wreckage on the ground furthest forward from the point of impact. See if it tells you anything. Come on then, Bob.'

They climbed into the helicopter and strapped themselves into two seats behind the pilot. 'Gerald,' said Legge. 'Take us up three or four hundred feet, high enough for us to see the spread of the wreckage. Fly very slowly down the length of the valley, then hover and await further orders.'

'Very good, sir,' said the young pilot, in clipped training college tones.

Legge handed Skinner a headset, with built-in microphone. 'Communicate through these,' he said. 'You'll be bloody deafened otherwise. These things are built for functionality, not comfort.'

As the policeman looked at the solid plastic ear-defenders, the pilot started the engine and immediately, the cabin of the helicopter was filled with booming sound. He put them on quickly.

The clumsy craft took off with all the ease of a lumbering albatross, but like that great bird, once freed from the constraints of the ground, it displayed wondrous grace and manoeuvrability.

The pilot veered away from his landing site, turning as he gained height, back over the parked vehicles, westwards and away from the disaster valley. At last when he had reached the designated height, he swung round. Moving at not much more than hover speed, he followed the path of the doomed aircraft, towards the point of impact. As he flew, he kept the helicopter canted over, to give his two passengers the clearest view possible of the ground before them.

Staring down, Skinner felt strangely as if he was looking at an aeroplane on the drawing board. The tail and the wings, incredibly strong structures, had retained their shape through all the impact and conflagration. But the rest of the wreckage resembled some huge sausage which had been slit, unfurled to reveal its ingredients, then hammered flat. It had spread out and over the remnants of the wings, so that, taken all in all, most of the wreckage in the valley, other than the metal fragments which had showered further away, was contained within a rectangle not much greater in area than an Association Football field.

And as the helicopter moved on, he could see the players in the grim game, moving slowly through the wet heather. Where each one had been, their passing was marked here and there by small white flags. As a co-author of the disaster plan, a writer of the rules, he knew what each one meant. Already, the markers were numbered in dozens, but he knew that the count was not yet half-finished. Ahead the flags hung limp on their staves, but those close below the aircraft flapped and fluttered in the down-force of the rotors.

'Careful, careful,' snapped Skinner. 'Not too low; not too low. Don't disturb them!'

'There'll be no disturbing *them*, sir,' said the young pilot. For an instant, the policeman shot him a furious look, until he remembered that different people react to the unthinkable in different ways, some of them ignoble, but most of them understandable.

'Nonetheless,' said Major Legge. Skinner had seen the Major in other places, matter-of-fact in the face of mayhem. Now there was emotion in his voice. 'Climb a little higher and take us out of here please, Gerald. Forward, steadily in a straight line, if you please.'

The Lieutenant did as he had been ordered, easing the helicopter up by around 100 feet and moving out of the valley, maintaining his angle of flight so that Skinner and the soldier could see ahead of them.

Beyond the disaster site, the ground seemed to level off into a wide sloping plain, still heather-covered. Legge reached behind him, and produced a heavy pair of binoculars. He focused them on the ground ahead, peering through them with raised eyebrows.

'Nothing there,' he said.

'Wouldn't the nose section have dropped like a stone?' asked Skinner.

'Not necessarily,' said Legge. 'Things don't have to have wings to make aerodynamic sense. It's more likely that the truncated cabin and tail section would have come straight down. We'll go on for a bit yet.'

Skinner took the binoculars as they flew ahead, but he saw no more than had the Major. As both continued to stare at the ground below them, with increasing frustration, they were startled by the pilot's interruption.

'Body of water up ahead, gentlemen. Either of you know what it is?'

Skinner thought for a second or two. 'Almost certainly, it's the Whiteadder reservoir.'

'In that case, sir,' said the Lieutenant, 'should it have a small island in it?'

'No, it bloody shouldn't! Let's take a look.'

The craft straightened and speeded up as it made for the reservoir, covering the ground in less than a minute. 'Something there,' said Gerald, as he slowed to a hover, swinging and dipping once more so that they could see.

It lay on the far side of the reservoir, close to the bank. The water could have been no more than two fathoms deep, for at least six feet of the plane's nose section, and virtually all of the window on the starboard side still showed above the surface.

'Still intact,' said Skinner quietly, strangely unsure whether to feel relieved.

'Yes,' said Legge. 'D'you know, I think it's done a Barnes Wallis. Look at that stuff floating in the middle of the lake. I think that she impacted there, bounced across the surface, and finally settled close to the embankment.'

'Could be.' The policeman looked across at his companion. 'We've got to go in, Major – you know that, don't you?' Sombre, the soldier nodded.

'Shouldn't we wait for the frogmen?' ventured the pilot, warily.

'No, son,' said Skinner. 'It might only be a million to one shot, but like the man said, they come up more often than you think. Radio in for the police sub-aqua team, sure, but we've got to open her up, right now.'

30

'Very good, sir. I'll hover directly above, so that you can winch down.'

'Don't be bloody silly, Gerald,' Legge drawled. 'There's a rowing boat on the bank. I'm sure the Deputy Chief Constable will allow us to commandeer it! Just put us down beside it, and get ready to row, there's a good lad.'

II

There was a road about a hundred yards away from the flat area on which the Lieutenant landed. Two cars, one a sleek saloon, the other a battered farm Land-Rover, had pulled up at the roadside, and their drivers stood together on the other side of the fence, staring and pointing at the part-submerged aircraft section.

As Skinner jumped down from the helicopter, having changed from his wool worsted into a spare flight suit, his police instincts almost made him yell at the men to move on, but suddenly a thought occurred to him. He squelched across the dewy grass towards them in his Wellingtons.

'Police,' he called.

'What's happened?' the driver of the saloon asked him, superfluously. Skinner ignored him, and spoke to the other man.

'Do you have an axe in the Land-Rover? We need to get in there, fast, and it looks like we'll have to smash our way through the window.'

The man wore much the same country worker's uniform as Robert Thacker, the witness; heavy trousers, dirty old sweater, and big boots. He looked at Skinner with the calm appraising stare that farmers and their people reserve for town folk.

'An axe! Naw, sorry.' He paused. 'But Ah do have a posting hammer.'

'Even better,' said the policeman. 'Can I have it, please?' The man was already ferreting in the back of the much-abused old truck.

He re-emerged after a few seconds, lugging over his shoulder a huge, flat-headed hammer on a long shaft, far bigger and heavier than any axe.

'Here y'are then. Will you be able to use it a'right?'

'I've handled one of these before. Thanks.' Carrying the huge implement in both hands, Skinner set off across the grass once more, to where Legge and the Lieutenant had manoeuvred the rowing boat into the water, and where they sat.

He untied the mooring rope, tossed it into the boat, and climbed in beside them, sitting on a cross-bench in the bow. As soon as he was settled, Gerald pushed them free of the bank with an oar, swung the vessel around, and began to row towards the wreck of the plane.

32

He was a powerful and skilled oarsman; the distance to the stricken craft closed quickly, until Skinner had to call to the young officer to ease off his strokes. As the boat swung soundlessly against the fuselage, Legge reached out and steadied it by grabbing the handle of the starboard loading door, which showed just above the surface of the water.

'Here.' Skinner tossed him the mooring rope, which he wound through the handle then handed back to the policeman, who passed it under his bench seat and tied it off against a piece of metal which had peeled back on impact.

As he sat in the bow, Skinner's eye was level with the bottom of the cockpit window. Gingerly, he stood up, then swayed deliberately, testing their makeshift mooring. He was relieved to find that the boat offered a surprisingly stable platform.

For a second, a feeling of dread flooded through him, and his stomach turned over. But he thrust emotion away once more, and leaned across to peer through the glass.

The window was misted up on the inside. Hard as he tried, he could see nothing but blackness.

'Give me the hammer, Gerald,' he ordered, taking the great bludgeon in both hands as the officer passed it up to him.

'Now, you guys, brace yourselves against the side away from the aircraft, and try to keep this thing as steady as you can. That glass isn't going to give first whack, and I don't want to wind up in the drink!'

He took a deep breath and tried a practice swing, working out the best way to attack the window. Eventually he was ready. Remembering the principles of karate, he focused on the point where the energy of the blow would be delivered, and swung.

The huge 'Clang!' echoed across the water. Even with Legge and the Lieutenant holding the boat steady by bracing their feet against the fuselage, Skinner still swayed back. He almost lost his balance as the armoured window threw his own force back at him, but saved himself by dropping into a half-crouch, lowering his centre of gravity.

As soon as the boat was absolutely steady once more, he stood up and swung again, ready this time for the strength of the reaction. Still the window remained intact, but on the third blow a hairline crack appeared. As fast as he could do so safely, he rained huge hammer blows upon the glass, hitting the same spot every time, until at last the section split in two, and swung inwards, loosened from its frame.

He crouched in the front of the boat, breathing as hard from the effort as from his customary morning run, and still holding the huge hammer. His heart was pounding and his pulse roared in his ears, but still, the unexpected sound broke through.

A cry, a plaintive fearful cry. Not quite hysterical, but close to it. A child's sound, a mixture of relief, shock and fear. It came from inside the cockpit.

Skinner dropped the hammer and stood bolt upright. He stared at Gabriel Legge. The Major's eyes were wide and glistening.

The cry came again. Louder this time.

'Major, to this end of the boat! I'm going in.'

The policeman reached across and took the empty frame of the window in both hands. The metal dug sharply into his palms, but he ignored it, straightening his arms, taking his weight on his shoulders and swinging his right leg up and into the opening.

Straddled across his makeshift doorway he looked down into the half-submerged cockpit. One of the officers was slumped in his seat. His shoulders were clear of the water, but from the angle of his lolling head, Skinner knew at once that he was dead.

Beyond the body, the blond child crouched against the curve of the window. His eyes were wide with fear and shock, and his mouth was set in a rictus, a grotesque parody of a smile. For a second the policeman's mind swam as he looked at the miracle of the living boy, seeming to stand on the surface of the water.

In fact he was perched on the aircraft controls. His hair was wet and his clothes, blue trousers and a red polo shirt, were sodden and clung to him. He looked to be around five or six years old.

Skinner tried to speak, but only a croak came out. He coughed to clear his throat. 'What's your name, son?' he asked at last.

'Mark,' said the little boy. There was a shudder in his voice as he stared, stricken with terror, at the intruder.

'Well, Mark, my man, my name's Bob. You don't need to be frightened any more. I'm going to get you out of here. You'll have to help me, mind. D'you think you can do that?'

'Yesss,' he whispered. 'I think so.'

'First of all, do you know if anyone else is in here?'

The child nodded his wet, blond head. 'There's Mr Shipley, the pilot, and there's April, the stewardess. They're both down there.' He flicked out a finger, pointing down towards the water beneath his feet. He nodded again, towards the body in the flight seat. 'That's Mr Garrett. He's the first officer. They were showing me how they fly the plane.'

Skinner took a deep breath. 'Okay, Mark. Now let's see how we're going to get you out of here. Can you swim?'

The boy shook his head. The two, man and boy, were only two or three yards apart, but the water in the cockpit was black, silted, cold and deep. The policeman knew that if the child fell below the surface his chances of recovering him quickly enough, if at all, would not be great.

The control console rose out of the water between them. Skinner

34

looked over his shoulder. 'Major,' he called, 'I want you to stand up behind me and be ready to take a package.'

He reached into the cockpit, towards the co-pilot and felt below the water-line. Eventually he found the catch of the safety belt. Something was wrapped around it. Without allowing himself to speculate as to what it might be, he flicked up the lever. The belt came undone, and the body of First Officer Garrett rolled from its seat and disappeared below the black surface, to join his dead crew-mates.

Skinner swung his other leg across the window frame, then slid his body into the cockpit, perching on the back of the co-pilot's recently vacated seat, inching around until his position was secure.

'Okay, Mark,' he said to the boy, who was watching him, still wide-eyed but seeming to tremble less violently. 'I want you to stay crouched down and walk up the control panel towards me, as far as you can. D'you understand?'

The child nodded and began to inch along the console. 'Watch you don't fall in, now,' Skinner cautioned. When the boy had gone as far as he could, he and the policeman were still four feet apart. Taking care not to lose his own balance, Skinner held out his hands. 'Very good so far, wee man. Now if you jump I'll catch you.'

Taking a deep breath, as if he was in a play-school game, the blond boy leapt forward.

Skinner caught him in mid-air and held him close. 'There's a clever lad,' he said, words as heartfelt as any he had ever spoken.

He sat the child in the crook of his left arm. 'Now for the next bit. If I stand you across on the window frame, d'you think you'll be able to jump again, to another man this time? He's a soldier. A real one, in uniform.' The boy's eyes widened still more. 'His name's Major Legge. He's a good catcher as well, so you'll be all right. D'you want to do that?'

'Yess!' said Mark, eagerly now.

Skinner smiled at his enthusiasm, and at his child's courage. He looked across. Through the window, he could just see the top of Legge's head. 'Okay, Major,' he called. 'Mark's going to jump when you tell him and you're going to catch him. You won't drop him, will you?'

'Of course not!' said the soldier, deprecatingly. 'Sure, didn't I tell you? I caught for Ireland!'

'There you are then,' said Skinner to the child. 'Ready?'

'Yess!'

Slowly, gripping the flight seat with his legs as hard as he could, he lifted the child under the armpits and set him carefully on the window frame, holding him with his arms at full stretch.

'Ready, Mark?'

'Yess!'

'Ready, Major?'

'To be sure!'

'Right. You give the word.'

'On three,' Legge called. 'One! Two! *Three!*'

Skinner gave the child a gentle shove, throwing him outwards and away from the fuselage. In the same motion he grabbed hold of the window frame and pulled his head and shoulders through, leaving his legs trailing in the water. Just beneath him, Major Legge stood upright in the boat, holding the boy.

Their eyes met. 'Just one,' said Skinner, knowing that little Mark was too young to understand him, 'but from them all, it was him. You know, every so often something happens to make me think that there *is* a Fella up there after all, and that He knows what He's doing!'

The soldier smiled. 'In my line of work, my friend, we never have a moment's doubt about that.'

12

'Where's my Daddy?'

Little Mark McGrath, the only survivor from the Lammermuirs disaster, as it had been christened already by the electronic media, sat on the edge of a table in the mobile Police Headquarters. As Skinner, Legge and the Lieutenant had found and rescued the Scottish Office Minister's son, the articulated office on wheels had been established on a site around half a mile beyond the scene of the crash, where it could tap into telephone cables.

The child was wrapped in a blanket. Sarah Grace Skinner sat behind him on the table, squeezing his ribcage gently in search of any hidden fractures, as she completed her medical examination. If the boy had looked over his shoulder he would have seen that she was in tears.

'Doctors don't believe in miracles,' she said quietly to her husband, 'but this is one. There isn't a scratch on him. Down there, people are—' She shuddered, and stopped herself just in time.

'The water, the angle of descent, and the stewardess's cradling, must have cushioned him against the impact. From your description, I'd guess that the cabin crew all suffered fatal whiplash-type injuries. But Mark must have been curled up like a ball, and held safe. He's completely unscathed.'

'Let's hope he stays that way, mentally,' said Skinner fervently.

'Where's my Daddy?' asked the child again, more insistent this time, with more than an edge of fear in his voice. The last of his trembling had gone, but as the adults looked at him, each was torn by the haunted look in his eyes.

'Your Daddy's had to go away,' said Maggie Rose gently. 'You know that happens sometimes, don't you?'

The child nodded sagely. Even at his age he must have known the demands of a politician's life, for the answer seemed to satisfy him.

'Mark,' asked the red-haired Inspector, 'do you know where your Mummy is today?'

'At the dentist in London.' The boy screwed up his face with distaste.

'Do you know if she was coming up to join you later on?'

'Yes. We're on holiday. From school,' he added, with emphasis.

'Is this your first year at school?'

'Yess! Mummy teaches there. We're both on holiday. We have to go back on Monday morning, though. Daddy's going to take me to football tomorrow.'

'Which team do you support?'

'Celtic.' The boy stuck out his chest, proudly. In spite of himself, and for the first time that morning, Skinner laughed. Suddenly he felt Sarah tug at his sleeve.

'Bob. I have to go back.' He looked down at her. The tears had stopped, but her face was ghostly white and drawn. He guessed at the images which were before her eyes, and his heart went out to her.

'No love, you don't,' he said quietly. 'There are other doctors on the scene now.'

'But no one else to organise. There's no one else here who's been involved in the contingency planning for this sort of thing.'

'Others have. I'll get one of them.'

She shook her head. 'No special treatment for the DCC's wife. I signed up for this sort of thing, and I'm here. I have to go back.' She pulled her hand away from his and left the office, almost at a run.

Through the window he watched her, as she climbed into her car. He had never seen this Sarah before, and he was frightened by her; even more frightened *for* her.

'Sir,' Maggie Rose broke into his thoughts. He turned round towards her, and the boy, who was concentrating on liberating a four-finger KitKat biscuit from its wrapper.

'We should ask him now – about what happened?'

He looked at his assistant. 'You're trained in interviewing kids, Mags. But are you sure it's safe? Couldn't we damage him?'

'Obviously he doesn't understand what's happened. There's trauma, but he isn't able to comprehend the scale or the consequences. It's probably better that we help him to talk about it now, rather than later . . . if you know what I mean.' Skinner winced at the thought of the child's pain to come when he learned of his father's death. His mind went back almost twenty years, to a young Police Sergeant breaking the news to his daughter, even younger then than Mark, that her mother was gone for ever. He remembered her initial disbelief, then her refusal to understand him, and finally her confusion as she struggled to come to terms with a concept which was beyond her ability to comprehend. The picture was as clear in his mind as a video recording, and with it was his recollection of his struggle to keep the tears from his own eyes as he explained, as best he could, life, death and the cruelty of fate to four-year-old Alex.

'All right. You can talk to him,' he said at last, in a voice not much above a whisper. 'But stop at the first sign of distress.' Unnoticed by the child, he switched on a black tape recorder which lay upon the table.'

'Mark,' said Maggie, 'why were you in the cockpit?'

He looked up at her. 'April took me in,' he said through a mouthful of KitKat. 'Mr Shipley wanted to show me how to fly the plane, she said.'

'Was that good? Did you enjoy it?'

He nodded vigorously, chewing and swallowing.

'Do you want to be a pilot when you grow up?'

He shook his head. 'Can't.'

'Why not?' said Rose, intrigued by his earnest answer.

''Cos I'm going to be Prime Minister. Daddy says.'

The Inspector suppressed a smile.

'When you were in the cockpit: do you remember what happened?'

The child screwed up his eyes, as if to emphasise that he was concentrating. 'There was a huge *Bang*!' He squealed the word, for extra effort, and the listeners started slightly. 'From behind the door.' Rose glanced at Skinner.

'Then what?' she went on quickly.

'Mr Shipley said to put our seat-belts on. I didn't have one, but April sat down and put hers on, then put an extension thing around. Then she cuddled me. It was nice. She gave me a sweet.'

'What else did Mr Shipley say?'

'He said "We're going to do an Emergency Routine now, Mark. You have to sit with April." Emergency Routine.' He stuck out his chest once more, as if pleased by his pronunciation of the phrase.

'Then Mr Shipley started saying "Madie!" into his microphone. He told me that you have to shout "Madie!" in a Emergency Routine.'

'Then what happened?'

He looked at her, puzzled.

'What did you see?'

'Nothing. Because April was cuddling me. She was holding my head. In there.' A small hand emerged from the folds of the blanket and pointed to Maggie's bosom. 'I could hardly breathe.'

'She was cuddling you tight, in there?'

'Mmm.' He spoke through another finger of KitKat.

'Did you hear anything, apart from Mr Shipley?'

The child munched and knitted his brows. 'Nothing.' He paused. 'No noise. No engines.'

'Then what happened?'

Listening and watching, Skinner realised suddenly that he was holding his breath. He filled his lungs.

'The plane went "*Boinng!*" and bounced. There was a huge big splash, and it went "*Boinng!*". My tummy went all funny. Daddy and Mummy took me to Alton Towers, on the great big ride there. It was just like that, only my tummy went a lot more funny this time.' Mark's eyes were shining – with the memory of his terror, Skinner imagined.

'Then it went "*Boinng!*" again, and again.'

'And all this time April was still cuddling you?'

'Until she made a funny noise and let me go.'

'When was that?'

'I think it was just before the plane stopped.'

'After the water came in?'

Mark creased his brows again, his special concentration sign. 'No. Before.'

'Did the water come in all of a sudden?'

'No. Slowly.'

'Did Mr Shipley say anything else? Or April, or Mr Garrett?'

'No. I asked Mr Shipley, "Is this still Emergency Routine?" but he didn't say anything.'

'Were you frightened when the water came in?'

'Not really,' said the boy slowly. He was an unconvincing liar.

'What did you do?'

'I undid my belt, and climbed up, till it stopped.'

'Were you frightened at all?'

Mark turned his head and looked up at Skinner, shyly embarrassed. 'Yes,' he said, reluctantly and quietly. 'Most of all when Mr Bob banged on the window and broke it.'

'Why were you especially frightened then?' asked Maggie.

''Cos I thought he was a big thing come to eat me, like in *Power Rangers*.'

Again, Skinner laughed aloud. 'No chance of that, Mark. I don't eat wee boys. Just policemen!'

13

They sat in the small private area at the far end of the mobile office, a few feet away from the child survivor, who crouched in his blanket, still unconcerned, drinking Coca-Cola from a can, through a straw, and now devastating a Tunnock's Caramel wafer.

'Tell you something, Mags,' said Skinner. 'I'm going to make sure that flight crew, and especially April the stewardess, get some sort of posthumous award. I don't think I'll have too much trouble persuading the Secretary of State to recommend it.

'I saw the co-pilot. His neck was snapped by the whiplash of the first impact, and I think his seat-belt had cut right into him. That girl must have kept calm and held on to wee Mark with the last breath in her body.'

Maggie Rose looked at the boy. 'I can't get over it, sir. The only child on board, and the only survivor.'

'Don't dwell on it. Like I said, million to one shots do come up. Someone wins the lottery every week.'

'What about the mother?'

'Jim Elder phoned, while you were getting the wee chap his Coke. The Scottish Office people in London were going to break the news to her, and arrange for her to be brought up. Roland McGrath's father is on his way out here to pick up Mark. He's collecting some clothes for him on the way. D'you hear that, Mark?' he called out to the boy. 'Your grandpa's coming to get you. He'll take you to meet your mum.'

The child looked up and grinned. 'Can we go to UCI?'

'In the afternoon? That would be a treat, wouldn't it.'

'Can I come and see your police station?'

Skinner smiled, and knelt down by the boy's perch on the table. 'Very soon, you can come and spend a whole day with Maggie and me. You can be a police cadet. We'll show you all over our headquarters. You'll even meet the Chief Constable in his big silver uniform.'

'Honest?'

'Dead cert, cross my heart honest.'

He ruffled the child's blond hair, dried now but streaked with mud, and left him to his Coke. As he did so, a phone sounded at the other end of the van, but stopped on the second ring.

Skinner looked towards the sound. 'That'll be Jim Elder's fax,' he said. 'He told me that they had identified most of the passengers, by address, next-of-kin and job, and that he would send it out here.' He glanced back towards Rose. 'He said it would make our hair stand on end.'

The Inspector walked across to the fax machine and watched at the last of the five pages rolled silently from its printer. When it had stopped, she picked them up, checked the page order and handed them to Skinner.

The DCC glanced through the list, then re-read it, more slowly. He looked through it a third time, as if to confirm what he had seen.

The final page was a summary of the list. 'Jesus, Maggie,' he muttered, 'would you look at this! In that plane, we had a member of the House of Lords, two Directors of the Bank of Scotland, seven senior executives of major insurance companies, five directors of a major brewery, eighty-five administrators of various companies, thirteen civil servants of various grades, and one senior policeman – one of our own. On top of that, we had twenty-seven foreign businessmen – eight Japanese, five Americans, Four Germans, six French, two Spanish, one Israeli, and one Czech. Last but not least there were the six MPs we know about – one Nat, one Lib Dem, two Tories and two Labour.'

He laid the paper on a desk and shook his head. 'Maggie, a disaster like this is a human tragedy on an enormous scale. This one's a corporate tragedy as well. And it's a political tragedy. It strikes at the whole fabric of the Scottish economy. And with the loss of Roy Old, we suffer too.'

He looked at his assistant. She had gone chalk-white and her hands were covering her face. 'Mags, I'm sorry,' he said, realising at once. 'No one told you. Yes, Roy was on the plane. I expected Jim Elder to put an announcement round Fettes. It must have gone out after you left.'

He placed a hand on her shoulder. 'You see, kid? None of us are special. None of us are immune. None of us are free from blame. I sent him down there, and I won't be able to cut myself loose from that one for a long time. I'll tell you something though, and you remember it. If you want to get to the top in this game, you have to practice being callous. Just like you might think I'm going to be now.'

He picked up a telephone from the desk and dialled, from memory, a mobile number.

It was answered in seconds. 'Detective Superintendent Martin.'

'Andy, it's Bob here. Are you in mid-session?' He paused. 'Well, leave the room and call me back on this number.' He read from a handwritten list on the desk, then replaced the phone, to pick it up as soon as it rang ten seconds later.

'Andy? Right. I've got some pretty shocking news for you, I'm afraid.' Quickly and with no frills, he told Andy Martin of the crash and of Roy Old's death. There was a silence while the news sank in.

'Yes, I know. It would have to be Roy. Aye, and with him and Lottie right on the edge of retirement. But, terrible as it is, unfair or not, life goes on. It means my game plan goes into play a year or so early. You'll be Roy's successor as Head of CID. Pull out of the Drugs Liaison thing, right now, and get back up here. I need you.

'This my friend, will be the biggest investigation that you and I have ever tackled.'

14

'The Permanent Secretary told me that official attendance at scenes like this was one of the burdens of my office, Mr Skinner. But he couldn't help me to prepare for it.'

The Rt. Hon. Andrew Hardy MP, Secretary of State for Scotland, and his Security Advisor, walked slowly through the valley amid the wreckage and the heather, and at the heart of a forest of white marker flags. Around them the area was strewn with flight seats, some still in rows, some broken apart and lying individually. By now at least, all of the seats around them were empty.

Both men were ashen-faced.

'It's your burden, but it's a duty of my job too, Secretary of State,' said Bob Skinner, 'and of every man and woman here. I don't make political comments as a rule, but next time public sector pay, or staffing comes up in Cabinet, I hope you'll remember this morning. This is the most horrible task Society could ask any man or woman to perform, yet look around you. You'll see tens and hundreds of people carrying it out without question, although every one of them will be scarred by the experience. They'll carry it with them for the rest of their lives. And so will you. I'm sure it will make you an even better advocate on their behalf.'

The politician looked at the policeman, and nodded.

Skinner had got on well with the Secretary of State, ever since he had agreed to continue to act as his Security Adviser. However, he had been careful to deal more formally with Hardy than with his predecessor, having learned from that disastrous relationship that when dealing with Ministers of the Crown it is safest to serve the office rather than the man.

Or as Sir James Proud had put it in a moment of typical candour: 'Now you know, Bob. Never trust the bastards any further than you can throw them.'

Privately, Skinner felt that he could trust the straightforward, serious Hardy, but hoped that he would never have to put it to the test.

'Where should we go now?' asked the Secretary of State. Skinner had briefed him earlier, in the command trailer, on the disaster and on the witness accounts of an explosion. Hardy had absorbed the information calmly and without any sign of panic.

'I suppose we'd better look at the mortuary tent.' The policeman nodded upwards. Just beyond the crest of the slope, they could see the ridge of a great grey marquee which had been set up by the Army.

'Very good. Let's give these chaps a hand.' Two soldiers were walking past them, beginning the trudge up the hill with a laden, blanket-covered stretcher. The Secretary of State took a handle at the front, Skinner at the rear.

'Doesn't bear thinking about,' said Hardy quietly, as they climbed. 'This could be Colin Davey, or Roly McGrath that we're carrying.'

Skinner glanced down at a small, bare, bloody foot which showed beyond the end of the blanket, and saw red nail-varnish. 'No,' he said. 'This was a woman.' He saw no point in reminding the Minister that from the accounts of Robert Thacker and the child, Davey and McGrath had been at the heart of an explosion big enough to blow the plane's nose section away from its fuselage.

There had been no room in the Army transporters for trestle tables, and so, inside the long tent, the victims recovered from the valley had been laid on the ground, in neat, ordered rows. Each one was in a black, zippered body-bag.

As Skinner, the Secretary of State and the soldiers laid their stretcher on the ground near one of the tied back entrances to the marquee, Sarah rushed across. Bob opened his mouth to introduce her to Hardy, but she ignored him and bent beside the stretcher. Her face was drawn and her eyes were creased. She was just over thirty, but for the first time ever, her husband saw how she would look in middle age.

Without a word, she drew back the blanket covering the body. Skinner felt the Secretary of State flinch beside him, and heard his gasp as he caught a glimpse of bloody blonde hair, and of a face without recognisable features. 'That's done by the seat in front,' said Sarah, in an emotionless, professional voice, acknowledging their presence without looking up. 'The brace position gives you a chance in a low-level impact, say a crash landing, but in an incident like this, there's no chance at all. All that the doctors here are doing is certifying death.' As if to illustrate she placed two fingers against the woman's neck.

'In most cases, even with a post mortem, it's impossible to be specific about the cause. It could be a broken neck, it could be the shock as the impact pulps the internal organs, it could be, and in many cases it probably is, heart failure induced by sheer bloody terror.'

She stood up. 'Okay, boys,' she said to the soldiers. 'Bag her and place her in order.' Then: 'As we lay out the bodies, we're trying to picture the floor of the tent as if it were the valley, south this end, north up there. They're being placed in roughly the position relative

45

to which they were found. We figure it might help in the identification, that it might approximate to the seat order.'

'How many victims have you recovered so far?' asked the Secretary of State, his composure returned.

'They're coming in so thick and fast we ain't keeping a running tab.' She looked along the length of the tent. 'So far I'd guess about a hundred and forty.' She glanced at her watch. 'It's just gone eleven-thirty. Not bad for around two hours' work.'

'Will identification be a problem?'

'Not as great as it might have been. Quite a few of the bodies even have ID in their clothing. Normally, in a high-impact accident you'd expected widespread disfigurement and dismemberment, with bodies burned and personal effects destroyed. Most air accidents turn into human jigsaw puzzles. Not this one, though.'

'Any ideas as to why?' asked Hardy.

'Well, in this case the plane seems to have been well into its descent when the incident happened, so the seat-belt signs would have been on. That will have had an effect. The people on board seem to have been fairly well disciplined, too. I'm no expert, but from what I've read on the subject, in a situation like this, people often unstrap themselves, so that on impact, they're thrown about, sometimes right through the fuselage, and torn apart. Not all, but most of the bodies recovered here have still been strapped into their seats.

'Most of all though, I'd say it was the heather. It's so thick up here it seems to have had a certain cushioning effect. When the plane impacted, the fuselage disintegrated, the seats were ripped up and their occupants thrown all around. They were probably all killed instantly at that stage, incidentally. When the bodies landed again, you'd have expected dismemberment to a great extent, but the heather seems to have stopped that.'

Skinner thought of the body which he had found on the hillside and nodded.

'What about burning?' he asked.

'Not much,' said Sarah. 'The explosion of the wing-tanks and the disintegration of the fuselage seem to have happened simultaneously, so apart from a few scorched people in the central area, that hasn't had the effect you'd imagine. What *is* noteworthy, and the point that will interest you most, is that the greatest burning effect and the greatest damage to the corpses seems to have been found on those recovered from the far end of the valley, and we assume from the front area of the plane.'

'Where the Defence Secretary was sitting,' said Skinner.

She looked at him. 'Was he on board?'

'Yes. Let's look at the front of the tent.' Rather than walk among the rows of bodies, he led the way out of the marquee and walked along its side to the eastward entrance.

Three body bags, side by side, lay along the end canvas wall. 'The flight crew?' Skinner asked.

'Yes. They were brought in about ten minutes ago.'

One of the bags seemed smaller than the others. Skinner knelt beside it and unzipped it from the top. As it opened, he saw the grey, dead, but unmarked face of April, the stewardess who had saved young Mark McGrath's life. Dark, wet hair was plastered against her temples.

'I will order an autopsy on her, for sure,' said Sarah. 'As I thought, the two pilots have broken necks and seat-belt crushing injuries, but I'm almost certain that she drowned.'

Alarm flooded Skinner's face in an instant. She read his mind. 'No, Bob. She'd have been dead for quite a time before you found the boy. You can't save the world, you know.'

He shrugged his shoulders. It was a gesture of helpless frustration.

'These bodies here,' he asked, after a few seconds, 'these are the ones with burns?'

'Yes,' she said, 'but not like they've been in a fire.'

'Like they've been in an explosion? Like last year?'

She stared at him. She had been so involved in the gruesome business of certifying and arranging the dead that she had not had time to ask herself the questions which would have been second nature in a more normal situation.

'Yes,' she said softly. 'But not at the seat of a blast. Caught in its heat, but not torn by it.'

'And these are the bodies found furthest north?'

'Yes. They were still in their seats, the recovery teams said, in rows. There were none beyond them, and the whole of the northern half of the valley has been cleared. The eighteen bodies in the three front rows are the most mutilated we've recovered.' She pulled down the zip of a body bag. Skinner glimpsed a black, scorched woman's face surmounted by frizzled hair.

'We've got to do some more searching,' Skinner said to Hardy, who stood stiff beside him, teeth clenched. 'So far we haven't looked south at all. We've been assuming that the plane's tail marked the beginning of the wreckage. But none of these . . .' he waved a hand towards the lines of body bags '. . . can have been the front row.'

'Why not?'

'Because there are six of them to each row. Wee Mark McGrath was in the cockpit, so we know that one seat was empty when the disaster happened. Major Legge and I did an air search to the north of here and found nothing between the main crash site and the reservoir. And the divers had a look at the cockpit below the water.

47

They reported that it was torn off around the bulkhead, with no seats attached.

'We need to find the centre of the explosion before we can begin to find the cause. Those front-row seats, and what's left of their occupants, must be out there somewhere. I have to get the choppers airborne again.

'Once I've done that, Secretary of State, I think it's time we gave a statement to the press.'

15

'I have to tell you formally what you know already.' The Secretary of State's voice shook for a moment as he surveyed the media crammed into the back-up mobile police station.

'The seven a.m. London–Edinburgh shuttle crashed on the Lammermuirs just after eight this morning, with two hundred and five people on board.

'I have to tell you also that the passengers included Colin Davey, the Secretary of State for Defence, Roland McGrath, Parliamentary Under Secretary of State in the Scottish Office and Shaun Massey, the Secretary for Defense of the United States.' A flurry of hisses and gasps swept through his audience.

'A full list of the dead will be issued at the conclusion of this briefing. It will show that I have lost many colleagues in addition to those in Government whom I have mentioned, including fellow members of the House, and several in the civil service. Sir James Proud, who sits beside me, has lost a distinguished serving officer, and many families have been bereaved.

'However, even in the midst of this disaster, we can take comfort from one remarkable event. One of the two hundred and five people on board the aircraft, one, a young child, has survived, and uninjured at that. I will not reveal his identity, although I expect that it will become public knowledge in due course. When that happens, I hope that you will all desist from doing anything which might add to his distress or affect his recovery from an event whose nature and scale he does not yet understand.'

Hardy paused. 'In the main I will leave briefing on the details of the accident to the police and to the airline representatives, but I will take one or two questions.'

Hands shot up, awkwardly in the enclosed space. 'Sir!' 'Secretary of State!' 'Mr Hardy!' Reporters shouted over each other clamouring for attention. Alan Royston, the Police Media Relations Manager stood up, calming the throng. He pointed to a Chinese girl in the front row.

'Annabel Yi, Radio Forth. Can you give us any indication of the cause of the accident, sir. Was it engine failure?'

'Obviously,' said the Secretary of State, precise to the end. 'But the experts must confirm what caused that failure.'

49

'Was the child on board with his parents?' asked John Hunter, an ever-present freelance whom Hardy knew well.

'With one parent, John, the fact of whose death he does not yet understand. Now no more questions on that subject, please.'

'Is he still here?' asked Annabel Yi.

'No!' said Bob Skinner firmly, from his standing position at the side of the small table.

'What effect will this have on your majority?' a tabloid reporter called from the centre of the group.

'All parties seem to have suffered in this tragedy,' Hardy said curtly. 'I doubt if any of us are thinking of majorities right now.'

'How many MPs were on board, sir?'

'Six in all. You will see them on your list.'

'What was Mr McGrath's majority in Edinburgh Dean, Mr Hardy?'

The Secretary of State shook his head emphatically. He needed no reminding that his dead colleague's majority had been less than secure. 'I'm sorry,' he said, with a trace of temper, 'but I am not going to be drawn by that line of questioning. Ladies and gentlemen, that is all I have to say.' He stood up and left the trailer, with Skinner following. His black chauffeured Rover was parked outside, with its driver standing by, in grey uniform and peaked cap.

'I must be on my way, Mr Skinner,' he said quietly. 'I'm going to the airport now to collect Leona McGrath. Roland's agent's meeting me there too.'

'Good luck to you both,' said the policeman sincerely. 'Tell the lady from me she's got a great wee boy. And tell her about the girl who saved his life too, will you?' For an instant, a lump rose in his throat.

'I'll do all that. I'll tell her about you too, rescuing Mark from the plane. Jimmy Proud told me about that just before we saw the press.' His voice dropped. 'Keep me personally informed, Bob, will you, when you find the rest of the wreckage that you're after? *Personally*, you understand.'

Skinner nodded. He looked after the car as it reversed out towards the moorland road. When it was out of sight, he turned and headed away, not towards the press centre, but towards the Command unit. Suddenly a stocky dark-haired figure fell into step beside him. It was Julian Finney, of Scottish Television. The man was, Skinner knew, a real ferret of a reporter, but he knew also that he was trustworthy.

'Sorry to doorstep you like this, Bob, but . . .'

Skinner smiled. 'Come on, Julian, you *always* doorstep me like this. What is it?'

'Something I didn't want to mention in there.' He nodded towards the press HQ. 'My office had a call from a woman in Longformacus, saying that she saw the plane coming down in two parts. She said that the main cabin and tail section came down without the rest. She

50

described it very vividly. The airline guy in there, after you left, did his best to give the impression that it broke apart on impact. If I say on air tonight that eye-witnesses spoke of an explosion, would I be making a fool of myself or would I have the story of the year?'

The policeman glanced at him as they walked. Finney knew the questions to ask, all right. 'I don't hand out press awards, mate.'

'No, but if I ran that story, you wouldn't be on to the Complaints Commission either, would you?'

He stopped and looked at the man. 'Just don't go over the score, Julian. You've got one eye-witness. Stick to that, don't speculate any further and you won't have any problem with me.'

'Fair enough. There's something else you should know,' Finney went on. 'I heard the guy from the *Record* take a call from his office. I think it was a tip-off about you – something about smashing your way into the cockpit of the plane and coming out with a kid.'

There was a long silence.

'Roland McGrath had a wee boy, didn't he, Bob?'

Skinner glowered at the reporter. 'Tell you what, Julian, and you can believe me. You run any of *that*, and I really will crucify you.'

'I believe you, Bob. I believe you!'

16

As soon as Skinner stepped back into the Command vehicle, the telephone rang. One of the two uniformed Sergeants whom Maggie Rose had pressed into service to assist her in her co-ordination role picked it up on the instant.

'Sir!' he called to the DCC. 'Are you available to speak with Superintendent Higgins?'

'Sure,' he said without a second's hesitation, and took the phone. 'Ali. Hello. Where are you?'

'I'm at the St Leonards office, sir.' The normally confident Higgins sounded shaken. On another morning Skinner would have been taken by surprise.

'You heard about Roy, I take it?'

'Yes, sir. It's awful, isn't it? I feel awful. I spoke to him yesterday. He and I had an arrangement to do performance reviews this morning. When I heard he was at the conference I called to remind him, and of course, he'd forgotten. But he promised me he'd catch the first shuttle and be here on time. "Officers' careers are more important than a few extra drinks at a stuffed-shirt dinner." That's what he said. I can't help thinking, if I had just postponed the interviews, he'd—'

'Don't, Ali. I've been doing that too. You didn't put him on that plane, and I didn't. This may sound odd coming from someone who deals in fact and logic, but it was fate; a combination of circumstances. I could have gone myself, I could have sent you, I could have sent Andy. But I didn't. I made the right choice. You could have been neglectful of your responsibilities towards junior officers, but you weren't. You can't look at it any other way. You mustn't.'

There was a long silence at the other end of the line. 'Thanks, boss. I'll bear that in mind. But there's something else.' If anything, Higgins sounded even more agitated. 'I've just heard a radio news-flash. It said that Roland McGrath was on the plane too. Is that true?'

'I'm afraid so. Why – d'you know him?'

'Yes. Well, not him so much, but Leona, his wife. She and I were at school together. We've been pals since we were five. I spoke to her last a few days ago. She told me that she and Roland and their wee boy were having a week together in London, then were coming back up to Edinburgh this morning. So was she on the plane too?'

He could almost feel Higgins gripping tight to her self-control. 'No, Alison,' he said. 'She wasn't. She had a dental appointment in London. She'll be on her way up now. The Secretary of State's going to Edinburgh Airport to meet her.'

A great sigh of relief burst from Higgins, but it was cut short. 'But Mark! What about Mark? I'm his godmother. Was he on board?'

'He survived, Ali. Maybe the report that you heard mentioned a survivor. It was him, and he's perfectly all right. That's fate again. It sent Roy Old to his death, but it put wee Mark on the flight deck, in a stewardess's arms, and it kept him alive.'

As Skinner finished speaking, he heard his colleague explode into tears. 'Okay, Ali, it's okay,' he said quietly. 'Why don't you go and look after your pal. Take a uniformed officer with you too, to keep the press at bay. On you go now.' He handed the phone back to the Sergeant.

Maggie Rose was looking at him, concerned. But all he could do was shrug his shoulders and turn away. 'On days like this you have a surfeit of emotion, Maggie. Not just in you, but all around you.' He forced himself back to business. 'What have you done here?'

'My role is co-ordination, sir, and that's what I'm doing, but I'm determining priorities as well. Chief Superintendent Radcliffe is directing the recovery of victims – that's objective number one. Once it's complete he'll move on to gathering in personal effects.

'The CAA people are on the scene. Their first job is looking for the flight recorder, the Black Box thing. They say it's in the cockpit, in the reservoir, so our divers are going down again to bring it out.

'I'm focusing on identification. Look here: this is what I've done.' She led him across to a large pinboard, on the wall facing the door. Several sheets were fixed to it. 'This is the full passenger list, in seat order, and the crew list.

'I've got three constables – two old-stagers and a lad who volunteered – moving between here and the mortuary tents, checking each body as it's brought in, then coming back here to enter details on the lists. Those with the wee stick-on dots beside them have been identified by possessions found on them: driving licences, credit cards, that sort of thing. If the dots are yellow, that means that the bodies will be visually identified easily by next of kin. If they're red, we may need dental records.

'This big sheet here represents the floor of the mortuary tent, where the bodies are laid out in rows of six. Each square blue sticker represents a recovered victim. Where they've been identified, their seat number is written on the sticker. Obviously, the body bags are being labelled in the tent as well.'

'That's important,' said Skinner. 'The last thing we want to do to a distraught relative is to show them the wrong body. What about photography?'

'Taken care of, sir. We have six photographers here. Every body is being photographed where it's found, and is given a number as it's bagged. Then it's being photographed again inside the tent.'

'That's good work, Maggie. With about two hundred or so bodies lying about, we have to move them as fast as possible. But this is looking like a murder investigation, so we have to cover every detail. When this thing gets to court, we don't want to wind up in the witness box with our shirt-tails flapping in the breeze.'

He peered at the list again, and pointed to Roy Old's name. There was no dot next to it. As he looked the door opened, and a Constable entered, a young man whom Skinner recognised. His face was drawn, but his expression was determined and composed. He carried a clip-board with a sheaf of papers. The top sheet was a copy of the mortuary plan. The DCC guessed that the boy had aged three years in three hours. 'Afternoon, PC Pye,' he said. It was twelve minutes past noon.

The young officer stood to attention. 'Sir!'

Skinner smiled. 'Stand easy, boy. You volunteered for this duty, did you?'

'Yes, sir.'

'Well, good for you. I'll remember that. You have more details to enter?'

'Yes, sir.'

He stood back, allowing PC Pye to approach the pinboard. The Constable looked at his notes and placed six blue stickers on the master plan of the mortuary. On four of them, he wrote numbers. Skinner read the first number and tensed. It was 28A. Silently he watched as Pye unpeeled a yellow dot from its sheet and placed it beside Roy Old's name.

The young man placed yellow dots against two more passenger names and a red against the fourth, then turned, and with a final salute to Skinner, left the Command vehicle.

The DCC looked after him as the door closed. 'That boy, Maggie – I want him on my team. Andy will have CID officers on his personal staff. He'll want McIlhenney, I know. Make sure that Pye's another. Anyone his age who volunteers for that task deserves looking after.'

Rose smiled and nodded. 'Very good, sir. Will you tell Mr Radcliffe or will I?'

'No, you leave that to me. It's only courtesy for me to tell him that I'm pinching one of his bright lads. But for now, I'm off to make a formal identification of Roy Old. I owe that much to Lottie. What am I talking about! I owe her more than I'll ever be able to say.'

'Steady on, boss. Think back to what you told Alison Higgins.'

Skinner took his right hand from the door handle. 'What I said to Ali about guilt and recrimination, I said to make her feel better. What I feel in here,' he tapped his chest, 'I can't change.'

17

To outward appearances, Death seemed to have dealt relatively gently with Roy Old. Skinner held his breath as he unzipped the body bag, but sighed loudly, with something which on another day would have been classed as relief when he saw that his colleague's features had survived the impact intact. Eyes closed, he looked almost serene.

'He could be asleep,' said Bob to Sarah, who was standing behind him. 'What would be the cause of death, d'you think?'

'The death certificate will say multiple fractures and shock. The soldiers who brought him in said that he had been thrown clear of his flight seat on impact, and landed face up on a rock. His spine and his pelvis were shattered, and the back of his head was smashed in.'

Skinner sighed. 'But he'll look all right for Lottie, and that's the main thing. I'll arrange for an undertaker to come for him as soon as I can.' He zipped up the bag and stood up.

'What are we going to do with the bodies once they're all recovered?' asked Sarah. 'We have to move them somewhere more, more . . .'

He laid his hands on her shoulders. 'That's taken care of. Charlie Radcliffe has commandeered the Aubigny Centre in Haddington. As soon as recovery is complete we'll move them down there for identification by relatives.'

She was barely listening to him. 'And undertakers,' she went on. 'What will we do about undertakers?' She sounded increasingly distressed. Bob put an arm around her shoulders.

'There are specialists,' he said quietly. 'People who are able to cope with something on this scale. They go from disaster to disaster, around the world. The airline is bringing them in. They're on their way here now, and they'll take care of the first part of it. All that the family undertakers have to do is make their local funeral arrangements. The specialists will ensure that the victims from London and the South, and the foreign nationals, are all ready to be shipped home, wherever that may be, as soon as they're identified.'

Her shoulders shivered under his touch. 'God, Bob,' she whispered, 'that someone could make a business out of that. It all sounds so cold and regimented.'

'It is – but it's necessary. You don't think the Co-op undertaker in

Tranent could handle this, do you? The families need to know that their people are being looked after properly and as quickly as possible.'

He led her out of the tent. It was almost full now, full of black bags in still rows. He squeezed her shoulder. 'Are you holding up all right?'

'Of course,' she snapped defensively. 'There's still work to be done. There are another eighteen bodies to be recovered.'

'Make that sixteen,' said Bob, nodding towards two laden stretchers, as their soldier bearers made their way carefully towards them.

'Right,' said Sarah, freeing herself of his encircling arm and disappearing back into the tent.

He watched her go, frowning with his concern for her.

18

'Bloody 'ell, Bob. Every time I see you it's in the midst of chaos.'

Skinner turned, his frown disappearing at the sound of a familiar voice. The newcomer had a friendly, inquisitive smile, and receding, gingery, close-cropped hair. He was dressed in a comfortable well-worn Harris tweed jacket, a check shirt, and navy slacks. His black shoes shone even in the watery light.

He stood only five feet four inches, not far from a foot shorter than Skinner, yet he was powerfully built, and even in his loose-fitting clothes, the width of his shoulders gave him a chunky, almost round appearance.

'It's the life we lead, Adam. It's good to see you again. I'm only sorry it's here.'

The two men shook hands. They made an odd and incongruous couple, stood there on the moorland. Mutt and Jeff, Little and Large, Bootsie and Snudge, likely to raise a laugh from any unknowing passer-by. Yet Bob Skinner and Adam Arrow were well-matched, and they had a bond between them that would have wiped such a smile away quickly. Occasionally, in dangerous places, dangerous people would laugh at the idea of Captain Arrow as a figure of menace. No one had ever laughed twice. No one at all had ever laughed at Bob Skinner.

Just over a year before, the policeman and the soldier had been together as Skinner had played out some of the most dangerous scenes of his life, leading to a climax in which Arrow had stopped a bullet. The nature of their jobs was such that they had not seen each other since the second day after that event, and now as they stood together, each knew that the other was thinking back to that night.

'So, my friend,' said Skinner at last. 'You're in MOD Security now, are you?'

'Another bloody contradiction in terms,' said the little round man, smiling.

'Had you finally run out of terrorists, then?'

'That'll be the day. I was past my sell-by date where I was, though. I knew that. The opposition knew that. Fortunately, so did my senior officers.'

'You were all right after . . .?' The question went unfinished.

Arrow shrugged his disproportionate shoulders. 'Sure. I had a cracked rib, but that were all. The jacket did its stuff all right. First time I'd ever been shot, that were; and it's my ambition never to get shot again, I'll tell you.'

Skinner smiled, remembering old pain. 'Mine too.' He paused. 'Still, we're both driving desks now, so it's one we've got a good chance of achieving.'

'Hope you're right,' said Arrow, sounding unconvinced. 'Trouble is, there are times when it's difficult to stay behind the desk. Know what I mean? From what I heard, it even follows you on to t' golf course!'

'Hah!' said Skinner sharply. 'That's another story. Some time I'll tell you all about it. But for now, we've got our hands full here.'

'Too right. What's the picture, then?'

Skinner pointed towards the mortuary tent. 'There are one hundred and eighty-eight bodies in there.'

'And our Secretary of State?'

'Not yet. Not as far as I know.' Skinner grimaced. 'I have a feeling we won't find him on this site . . . if we find him anywhere, that is.'

'What d'you mean?'

'I mean, my friend, that there was an explosion on the plane, and that from witness statements, from the seat plan and from the condition of the wreckage, your Secretary of State was right in the middle of it.'

'Shit!' Arrow whispered.

'Major Legge and his boys are up on their chopper right now, checking around the moor for other wreckage. So far there's been no word, but let's go back to the Command vehicle and check again.'

As they walked to the mobile headquarters, Skinner briefed his soldier friend on the disaster morning as it had developed. 'Your colleagues from Scottish HQ at Craigiehall have been a great help,' he said. 'If it hadn't been for them we'd still have bodies lying uncovered on open ground.'

They had reached the van. The policeman held the door open for Arrow to jump up inside.

'Hello, Sergeant Rose,' said the little man, showing the ability to put a name to a face instantly that is the mark of those in the security business.

'*Inspector* Rose now,' said the red-head. 'Captain . . . is it, still?'

''Fraid so. Our promotion system's slower than yours!'

Skinner looked at the lists on the pinboard. He counted fourteen names unmarked with a dot of either colour: eleven passengers from the two front rows, two from the rear, and one member of the flight crew.

'What have you recovered yet, apart from bodies?'

'Nothing,' said Rose. 'Victims first, effects second.' She paused, her eyebrows rising slightly. 'We think we've found the Black Box flight recorder, though. The divers have spotted an object that answers the description.'

'Bugger the Black Box, Maggie . . . Pardon the French. It's the Red one I need.'

'Eh?'

Skinner smiled. 'The Secretary of State's Red Box, Mags. All Ministerial papers are carried in steel boxes covered in red leather, and everywhere the Minister goes, so do they. They weigh a ton and they're fireproof.'

'Aye,' said Arrow, 'and now we're going to find out if they're bombproof.'

'Would they have been in the baggage hold, sir?' asked Rose.

'No, they'll have been in the cabin. The Minister's Private Secretaries don't let them out of their sight.'

Skinner slapped his thigh in a gesture of annoyance – a habit picked up unconsciously from someone he had met not long before. 'I'm sorry, Adam,' he said. 'I should have thought before about those bloody boxes. I'd imagine that you'll be desperate to recover Davey's as quickly as possible.'

'Aye. I've no idea what's in it, but God alone knows what might be. Weapons specifications, Intelligence reports, details of troop deployments where they ain't supposed to be deployed . . . There could be all sorts of secure stuff, and some of it could even be life-threatening in the wrong hands.'

'Right,' barked Skinner, suddenly and sharply. Arrow and Rose looked up at him, startled. 'My mind's been running in second gear all bloody day. I've been standing around just looking at things, not doing my job by *thinking* about them. I've been preoccupied by the scale of it all, but that doesn't change the basics. There was an explosion on that plane – an explosion that was too big to have been any sort of accident. This is a murder investigation, and it's going to be run like any other . . . flat out until we get a result! Christ,' he said, shaking his head, 'and I've just sent my Area Head of CID off to nursemaid her pal.

'Switch the priorities, Mags. *Now!* Leave a couple of soldiers to bring in the last few victims, but otherwise, call everyone in here for a briefing. I want every able body looking for wreckage, and in particular for anything that looks as if it could be debris from a bomb.'

He snapped out orders. 'Try to raise Major Legge on our communications, and find out how he's getting on with his helicopter search!

'Tell the divers to get their fingers out and bring up that flight recorder!

'Find out what's keeping the CAA investigation team!'

59

'We're going to need somewhere to examine the wreckage as it comes in. Ask the Army to give us another tent up here, at least as big as that one over there. And some tables this time. Generators too, to power lighting.

'We may be in the back of beyond, but this operation's going to be run according to the rules: *Skinner's rules!*'

19

The Deputy Chief Constable's briefing had just broken up. Seventy police officers and thirty soldiers were winding their way back towards the valley to begin the painstaking search that Skinner had ordered.

He and Arrow were standing just outside the Command vehicle, watching them disperse, when he heard the heavy sound of the Army helicopter once more, heading up from the south.

They watched as it lumbered over the horizon, swept over the crash-site, then swung round towards the area where the Head-quarters van was parked. As it headed towards them, close to the ground, Skinner caught sight of Major Legge, in the co-pilot's seat, waving and pointing, indicating that they were about to land.

No sooner had the big green aircraft settled on a flat stretch of heather than Legge jumped out and ran towards them, crouched over although the slowing rotors were well above his head height.

'We've found something, Bob. I thought you'd want to be with us when we went down to take a look at it.'

Skinner nodded. 'Aye, sure, Major – if I can borrow that flight gear again. The heather knocks hell out of the wool worsted!'

'Of course. It's still in the chopper.' The Major seemed to notice the policeman's companion for the first time. 'Hello,' he said, in recognition. 'It's Arrow, isn't it? SAS?'

'Arrow, yes, sir. SAS no; not any more. I'm on MOD attachment now. That's what brought me up here.'

Legge nodded. 'Of course. Bob did mention it, but I'd forgotten.

'So what have you spotted, Gammy?' asked Skinner.

'More debris. About a mile and a half to the south. It's all more or less together in a sort of gully, a ravine almost, in the moorland. We didn't go too low, for fear of blowing it around, but there are flight seats there, and quite a bit of other wreckage . . . some of it human, I'm afraid.'

'Let's go and take a look, then.'

20

The helicopter put down on a high knoll. It overlooked the heather-grown moor for at least a mile in all directions. Skinner stared all around him, at the acres of brownish heather. The landscape had been turned into a sort of patchwork by the watery autumn sun, as it picked out gold highlights on the tops of the bushes, and cast long shadows upon the rest. On another day, the countryman in Skinner would have thought it beautiful.

'Where is it, Major?' he asked as he, Arrow, and the four uniformed soldiers of the Bomb Unit stood alongside the silent bulk of the helicopter.

'Over here.' The Ulsterman pointed south. 'You can barely make it out from here, but if you look hard you'll see a solid, darker shadow across the ground. As I said, it's a sort of crevice, and from the air, it looked as if it goes down very sharply.'

Skinner strained his eyes until he picked it out, a sudden blackness amid the light and shade of the sun-washed moorland. He guessed that it was around half a mile away.

They made slow headway as they moved through the scrubs, spread out in a broad line. They walked with their eyes cast downwards in case there was debris tangled up among the undergrowth; but they found none, and in just under fifteen minutes they came to the edge of the ravine. It was around forty yards wide, bisecting the moor from east to west. No heather grew within it; instead its sides were grassy. They fell steeply towards a stream which ran through it, around a hundred feet below where the six men stood, looking downwards in horror.

Where the debris in the main crash-site had been spread around the shallow valley, here it was concentrated in a single area. Even looking down into the shadows they could see that little or nothing had survived the crash intact. Most of the plunging wreckage had smashed into the northern slope of the gully, more or less beneath their feet, but a few pieces had skidded down the opposite bank, tearing gashes in the grass. Others lay in the narrow stream, which was blocked in one place by a particularly large object.

Skinner waved and his five companions gathered around him. 'We have to go down there, lads. It'll be ugly, I'm sure, but nothing we haven't seen before. Apart from the bodies, we are looking to recover two red leather-bound steel boxes, one belonging to Colin Davey, the Defence Secretary, one belonging to my own Minister, Roland McGrath.

'They may not be here. There may be more wreckage further on, but let's get this lot searched right now.'

Arrow stopped him with a hand on his arm. 'Wait a minute, Bob. 'Ow many passengers are we short from the front rows?'

'Eleven.'

'Right. Let's count the flight seats. I can see quite a few down there.'

'Good idea,' said Skinner. He looked down again. Smashed and distorted against the slope at his feet, he could see clearly six seats still attached in rows of three. At other points in the ravine, lay other twisted pieces of metal which could have been seats. Most were blackened. Scorched stuffing protruded from one or two. Others seemed still to be occupied.

'I think there are twelve seats down there,' said the DCC. 'Let's hope so. I'd like to find everything before the Americans arrive.

'My FBI pal Joe Doherty was promoted out of the Embassy a month ago,' he muttered to Arrow, 'to a big job on the National Security Council. I've no idea who they'll send up here, or how many. But with Shaun Massey among the victims you can bet that whoever it is, they'll be gung-ho and looking for action!'

He turned to the pilot. 'Gerald, I'd like you to go back to the main site and bring up a recovery team with stretchers and body-bags.'

The young man nodded, saluted briefly and turned to jog back towards the helicopter.

'The rest of us . . .' said Skinner grimly '. . . well, let's get on with it!'

21

As Skinner had feared, the large object blocking the little stream was a body . . . or rather, part of a body. Dark red blood stained the water which flowed under and around it.

The remnants of what had once been a man lay on its back across the burn. The head, right arm, upper torso and right foot were missing. Most of the clothes had been blown off, but a few scraps of cloth still clung to the dismembered thing, and a brown belt still circled its waist.

As the DCC stared down at it, Adam Arrow glanced towards him and was struck by his eyes. They were slightly wide, and icy-cold, as if somehow his friend had learned to switch off his normal reactions, and to take in the detail of what he saw as if he were processing and filing any other piece of information. It was a rare skill, but one that Arrow recognised, since he possessed it himself.

'Look at the left thigh,' said Skinner softly.

Arrow leaned over the body and stared. The limb was mostly blackened meat, but in the midst of it all, he could see a cluster of small, round punctures. 'What the f—'

'Bullet-holes, Adam. I'd guess that this was one of the protection guys. You'll see the scraps of a holster in his belt. It looks as if all the bullets in his revolver discharged themselves in the blast, all at the same time.'

The soldier nodded. 'I've seen that 'appen,' he said. 'He must have been bloody close to the seat of the explosion, although not at the heart of it as there's some of 'im left. What did the seat plan show again?'

'Seat 1A was wee Mark, like I said. His dad, Roland, was next to him. Then the first protection man. 1D was Davey's Private Secretary, then Davey himself, then the Yank.

'Row 2 – A, B and C were MOD and Scottish Office civil servants. D, E and F were the second protection guy and two US Secret Service people.'

'Sir! Over here!' They were interrupted by a shout from one of Legge's Sergeants, thirty yards away up the steep slope.

They stood up from the truncated body and hurried towards him. The soldier was standing just beyond where one of the rows of three seats had slammed front first into the side of the gully. From yards away they could see that all three were still occupied, but all that showed of the three corpses was black, twisted and unrecognisable.

'D'you reckon two of them could be Davey and Massey?' asked Arrow.

'Who's going to give a stuff?' said Skinner tersely. 'It'll probably come down to guesswork at the end of the day. As long as the leaders can hold their martyrs' funerals, and pick up a few votes on the back of them, they won't care what's in the boxes.'

'Jesus, Bob,' Arrow muttered. 'And I thought you were an idealist.'

Skinner stopped in his tracks. 'I can remember a time when I was, pal. I saw the world as I wanted it to be; I assumed that people did things for noble motives. Somewhere along the line all that changed. I reckon it was having to do with the politicians that did it. I thought about some of the characters I work for, elected people, locally and nationally, and I came to see what most of them are really like.

'I reckon that men and women who seek office fall into three categories. Category one are the real idealists; folk with a mission to serve their country. Category two are those who want to help their fellow human beings. Category three are those who want the power and the glory. Mind you, they never own up to it; they pretend to belong to category one or two. But they're the ones who rise to the top. We are governed by the ambitious, Adam, by the category three men. By people whose decisions are designed to serve their own ends. The guy McGrath, wee Mark's father, was a prime example. He'd have shoved his granny off the ladder to get to the top himself.

'But he'll be useful in death, and Davey too. They'll have their fine solemn funerals, and in the cortège you'll find other ambitious people with eyes on the by-elections, waving their grief in public for the electors to see.

'I'm glad that I've got a simple job, Adam. I catch people who do wrong things, then I hand them over to be judged and punished. You soldiers are in much the same boat. Your country decides who it's enemies are, it tells you, and you kill them. It's easy for us, really. We don't need to please any voters. We just see what to do, and we fucking do it.'

Arrow looked at his friend. He saw his narrowed eyes, and the lines around them. He heard the hardness in his quiet voice. He listened to what he was saying, and he knew what he meant, and what he was feeling. For he had been there himself, in the dark bleak place that the world can become for those who have seen too much of other people's suffering.

Suddenly Skinner smiled, but savagely, without humour. 'Listen to me, Adam, on my bloody soapbox. I sound like a politician myself. Come on, let's see what this is.'

They walked across the last few sloping yards towards the Sergeant. He was crouched over what both men thought at first was a triangular object, until they saw that it was a box, impacted into the ground. It was blackened, as if scorched, and the mud had splashed up around it, but its red-leather covering still showed through in places.

Skinner bent over the box, and tried to pull it clear of the ground, but his hands slipped on the mud.

'Let me,' said Arrow. He squatted astride it and pressed his hands on either side, rocking it backwards and forwards, gently at first, then faster until at last it loosened and a handle came into view. The little soldier seized it, yanked, and the box came clear of the ground.

'Christ, it's heavy,' he said.

'Steel-lined, I told you. And, it seems, bombproof. Let's wash some of that crap off of it in the burn.'

The policeman jumped and trotted down the slope to the bank of the stream, with Arrow at his heels, carrying the heavy box effortlessly.

'Here, Adam, gimme it.' Taking the box, Skinner laid it on the ground and knelt down beside it. Looking closely at it, he saw a small patch of the red-leather binding, decorated with gold leaf, showing through the dirt and scorch-marks, running parallel with the edge. He tried to rub off some of the mud with the flat of his hand, but only succeeding in smearing it into the leather.

'Bugger it,' he said. 'Let's hope it's waterproof too!'

He picked up the box by its handle and lowered it into the burn; the air inside buoyed it up, making it feel suddenly lighter in his hand. He swung it to and fro in the clear water, watching as the mud washed off in its flow. After around half a minute's immersion he lifted it out, held it up and looked at its surface. One side was still almost black, but not with mud. 'Scorched by the blast, I'd guess,' said Arrow. Skinner turned the box around and laid it on the grass. One or two patches of dirt still stuck to the surface, but mostly the rich red leather shone up at him, glistening and damp; the rectangular line of gold-leaf decoration twinkled in places.

Suddenly he bent over the box, peering at it closely, then ran the fingertips of his right hand over the surface.

He beckoned Arrow. 'Look, Adam. D'you see what's embossed in the surface?'

The little man squatted down beside him, bending to follow his friend's pointing finger. He too felt the surface.

'It's a crest, isn't it?'

'That's right. The Scottish Office crest, to be exact. That means that this was Roland McGrath's Red Box. With luck Davey's should be around here too.'

'Aye,' said Arrow, 'and it looks as if t' buggers *are* bombproof at that.'

'Too bad their owners weren't. Come on, let's join in the search.'

They made their way back up the hillside, where Legge and the Sergeant who had found the box continued to pore through the flotsam of the disaster. The second NCO was at work on the other slope. Arrow broke off to the left, to widen the area of the search, while Skinner headed right. As he passed the Major, he called to him. 'Bob, here a second, please.'

The slope was at its steepest and Skinner had to dig his heels in to make progress upwards. When he reached Legge, he found him standing upright and grim-faced. On the ground, at his feet, the top part of a human body, with the head in right profile, was embedded in the bank of the gully, just as the Red Box had been. The policeman's stomach heaved, and he was glad that he had not eaten since break-fast. Even at that, for a few uncertain moments his record of never having thrown up at the crime scene hung by a thread.

He took a deep breath and gathered up his self-control once more.

'Look at it. If you can . . .' said the Major. Skinner nodded and crouched beside the thing. The arm was twisted and shrivelled, without a hand, and seemed to point up at them. The face was burned black, but the features were still obviously human, apart form the ear, which resembled nothing more than a piece of charcoal. The hair, rising from a high forehead, and the beard and moustache were frizzled and melted.

'Aahh!' he hissed. 'It's like some sort of demented sculpture, but still it's recognisable.'

'You know him?' said the Irishman, surprise in his voice.

'Yes. This was Roland McGrath, the Scottish Office Minister.'

'Well, if it's any consolation, the fellow never knew what hit him. The blast must have taken him out in an instant.' He dropped on both knees beside the head. 'Sorry, Bob, but this has to be done.' Care-fully, he dug his fingers into the mud beneath the remains and turned them over, freeing them from the ground. Skinner took a step sideways and watched. The left arm was gone, at the shoulder, and the torso ended just below that point in a tangle of bone and muddy organs. The policeman drew a quick breath and concentrated his gaze on the face. The left side looked more human, with unscorched flesh tones showing through the dirt. The left ear, although filled with mud and grass, was still there and reddish hair still clung to temple and jawline.

'Where was this fellow sitting?' Legge asked.

'Row I seat B.'

'Tells us something then. D'you know who was in Seat C?'

'A bodyguard. I think that's him down there in the burn, minus his top half.'

'Mmm. And the politicians were across the aisle?'

'Yes.'

'In that case, from the way the blast seems to have radiated, I'd say the bomb went off more or less in the lap of our late Secretary of State!' He lifted up the remains of McGrath, then placed them gently back on the ground. 'I doubt if we'll find even this much of *him*, or the souls on either side of him.'

He stood up. 'So how *did* the bloody thing get there? Interesting question, isn't it? How did the Secretary of State for Defence come to be sitting right on top of an explosive device powerful enough to tear an aircraft apart?'

Skinner looked at him, almost stunned by the idea. 'Any answers?'

Legge smiled, wickedly. 'Right at this moment, the only thing I can suggest is that you find out where he dined last night . . . and never ever eat their curry!'

The policeman winced. 'Bloody hell. Is that how you Bomb Squad guys manage to stay sane?'

'Absolutely,' said Legge. He was still grinning, but Skinner looked at him and acknowledged the effort behind his control and objectivity. 'You have to laugh your way through these things. Soon as my guys start to dwell on the effects and consequences of an explosion, then they're no good to me.

'Sure, man, you think that down there is something.' He pointed quickly at the remains on the ground, but without looking at them. 'I remember once in Ireland we were called out to a scene where this lad had his back to a steel chain-link fence when the bomb he was planting went off early. When we got there he was stretched out on the other side like a hundred long tubes of dog food.'

They were interrupted by a piercing whistle. They looked round and saw Arrow, fifty yards away, his fingers still tugging the corners of his mouth.

'Always wished I could do that,' said Legge. 'Let's see what the little bugger wants.'

They scrambled across the hillside towards him. Once, Skinner's foot settled on something soft and spongy. He froze in mid-stride, and discovered that he was quite unable to look down. With an effort he pushed himself off and hurried on.

'What's up, Adam?' he said as he reached him.

'This is. Remember you said those boxes were bombproof?'

He held up, very carefully by two of its corners, a buckled, angled sheet of metal. Skinner took it from him, and saw that originally, it had been two hinged pieces of metal, but that they had been melted and fused together into a wide L-shape. On the inside, the metal was bright and shining, almost mirror-like, as if all traces of dirt and contamination had been seared off. As he looked at it a distorted reflection of himself stared back.

He turned the strange object over so that the L pointed towards him. On this side the metal was lustreless. Instead it was covered in a black substance, which felt rubbery, yet crumbled away under his touch. Superimposed upon the black, there were other, strange marks. On the upper of the two pieces of fused metal, he saw, embossed upon it, two sets of four short parallel lines running from the edge on either side. They were black also, and pointed towards each other. On the lower part of the object there were two more black parallel abrasions, wider than the others and running from the bottom towards the centre.

As he looked at the marks, a cold certainty crept through him. But still, he held the thing up for Legge to see. 'What d'you think, Gammy?'

'You don't really need me to tell you, do you? I'd say that this is, or was, a Red Box.'

'If it is, since we've found McGrath's, this must have been Davey's. It must have been open when the bomb went off.' The DCC paused. 'And what would you say that these marks are?'

Legge took the object from him and held it out. 'I would say . . .' he began. Looking at him, Skinner was certain that for all of his training and experience, Legge gave a small shudder. 'I would say that these top abrasions, these two sets of four, are the fingers of whoever opened the box, fused into its surface. The others? Well, I would suppose that he had the box on his lap, and that those two wider marks are the tops of the poor fellow's thighs.' He gazed at Skinner and Arrow, this time without the faintest hint of a smile.

'But Bob, if I may correct your assumption, ever so slightly. You said that the box was open when the bomb went off. I'd put it another way. I'd say that *because* it was open, the bomb went off.

'I'd say that the bomb was *in* the bloody Red Box!'

22

'You are MOD Security, and you are sitting there telling me that there was a bomb in your Secretary for Defence's personal document case?'

Skinner had seen Adam Arrow under fire. He had seen him in a cold, killing rage. He had seen him in situations that would have thrown a scare into a rock. And he had never seen him rattled, not in the slightest . . . until now.

Special Agent Merle Gower stared at him across the table in the Command vehicle, fixing him with an unblinking gaze, letting her question hang in the air. Arrow stared down at his plastic coffee beaker, spinning it slowly in his fingers. Skinner could see the back of his neck turning pink.

Eventually he looked up at her. 'That's the way it looks at the moment.'

She whistled. 'Jesus! They told me that you guys were good. I recommended to my Ambassador that we should fly Secretary Massey up to Scotland on our own transport, but he laughed at me. Know what he said? He said, "Don't worry, Merle, it'll be fine. The Brits have those shuttle flights stitched up tighter than a fish's asshole."

'Now I'm going to have to tell him that Massey is dead because you let Secretary Davey board the plane with an exploding lunch-box. And I'm going to have to do it without the faintest hint of "I told you so". Incidentally, do any of you know who Shaun Massey was? Only the Ambassador's brother-in-law, that's all!'

Joe Doherty's successor in the FBI London Bureau was a short, fleshy, severely suited black woman in her late twenties, with gold-rimmed spectacles and close-cut curly hair. Looking at her, Skinner felt that he understood properly for the first time what a firecracker was.

She had arrived a few minutes earlier, driving a Vauxhall Vectra with the Hertz tag still hanging from the driving mirror, just as Skinner and Arrow had returned in the helicopter, with the two Red Boxes, and with three firearms recovered from shattered, dismembered bodies pinned in a row of three seats at the second crash point. One was a Smith and Wesson revolver, while the others were Colt Automatics. Now they lay on the centre of the table around which the trio were seated.

'Look . . .' Arrow began, but Agent Gower had a few shots left in her locker.

'Christ,' she said. 'If only he had listened to me. I mean, Scotland – Edinburgh. This is where you managed to let the President of Syria get shot a couple of years ago, isn't it?'

Involuntarily, Arrow gasped and flashed a quick glance at Skinner. Two deep frown-lines had appeared between the DCC's eyes.

'Come on, lass,' said the little soldier. 'These things happen, and your lot ain't perfect either. Reagan, the Kennedys, King, Waco, Oklahoma . . . That balls-up in Iran when your so-called Special Forces 'ad a go at rescuing those hostages. I could go on.'

Now it was the woman who was frowning. 'Don't "lass" me, Captain Arrow,' she said grimly.

Seated between them, Skinner threw up his hands. Beyond the table, at the far end of the cabin he could see Sir James Proud, who was standing beside Maggie Rose, glowering his disapproval of the exchange.

'Enough!' Skinner called, not a shout, but not far short of one. He gazed at the woman; then he smiled, and his frown disappeared. Gower, startled at first, then charmed, looked back at him in silence.

'We're in danger of getting off on the wrong foot here,' he said. 'Ms Gower, I think I'd better spell out the ground rules. I'm in charge of criminal investigation in this part of Scotland; and that's what we are dealing with . . . a crime, in Scotland. The bomb exploded over my territory: the aircraft came down on my territory: two hundred and four people died on my territory. This is where the crime was committed, and so it's my job to catch whoever did it. Understand?' She nodded.

'The fact is that you've got no status. You're sat here now because of your special interest, just as Adam is, but you are both simply observers. Any role you have to play, any opportunity to say your piece, is at my discretion. Now let me tell you, as gently as I can, that I don't tolerate hecklers in my team. If that's all you've come to do, then you'll be getting in my way, and with just one phone call I'll have you back in Grosvenor Square.'

He paused and put his hands flat on the table. 'That said, when Joe Doherty told me last month that he was leaving to become Deputy Chair of your National Security Council, he said that he'd found a first-class operator to fill his shoes. If that's what Joe thinks of you, that'll do for me, and so I would value any positive input you can give me.

'So. From now on, can we act as if we're playing on the same side?'

It was Agent Gower's turn to look flustered. She nodded. 'Yes, sir. I'm sorry.' She glanced across at Arrow, and saw his eyes twinkling back at her.

'Okay,' said Skinner. 'That's sorted out. Look, Agent, I sympath-ise. You've been in post for only a few weeks, yet here you are with the murder of a member of your Government on your hands. What you should remember is that he's just another dead guy now, one among many, and that we're not working here for countries or flags or anything like that. We're here to make sure that *all* the families of the victims see justice done at the end of the day.'

'I know that, sir,' she said. 'I'll keep it in mind. So, how can I help?'

Skinner reached across the table and pushed the two automatic pistols towards her. 'First off, take a look at these guns.'

She picked one up. 'These are Colt pistols. Secret Service standard issue. What's the other one?'

'That's the type of revolver our protection people usually carry.'

'Where did they come from?'

'From the occupants of Row 2 – seats D to F.'

Merle Gower sighed and put the Colt back on the table, quickly. 'I saw two of those guys just last night. They arrived at the Embassy with Secretary Massey.'

'Well, you wouldn't want to see them now,' said the DCC savagely. He went on quickly: 'Ms Gower, the first thing I'd like you to do to help is to contact Joe Doherty at NSC. I want a full dossier on recent threats made against your country in general and against members of your Government in particular. Adam, you do the same at this end.'

'That'll be under way already,' said Arrow.

'Good. Now, there's one more thing I want you to do, Captain. I want every member of Colin Davey's Private Office staff, and every-one else who even clapped eyes on that Red Box lined up for questioning by my officers. I'll send a couple of them down to London tomorrow.'

He stood up from the table. He had changed back out of the Army flight gear, but his woollen suit was creased, and muddy in places. 'Unless we get very lucky we are not going to solve this thing in an instant.

'What do we know so far? We know there was a bomb, and we're pretty certain we know how it was taken on board the plane. Once all the wreckage is pieced together, and once Major Legge has told us more about the device, we'll be able to prove all that to a jury. But that's the easy part.

'The hard questions are the who's, the why's and the how's. Who wanted to kill Davey, or Massey, or both of them? Why did they want to do it? And how, how in Christ's name, did they get access to the Secretary of State's Ministerial hand-luggage?'

He glanced at his watch, under the neon strip-lighting of the van. It showed 6.13 p.m. 'You two have your tasks for tonight. Tomorrow morning, I want a team meeting in my office at Fettes, at nine a.m.

72

sharp, but for now, with Jim Elder taking over the recovery and identification job, my priority is to find my wife and get her out of this hellish place, whether she wants to go or not!'

23

They sat in silence over supper.

They had driven down from the Lammermuirs, into and through Edinburgh in a two-vehicle convoy, with Sarah leading the way and Bob close behind. When he had ordered her finally from the dismal tent, lit in the evening by a few bare bulbs powered by a generator, she had looked more tired than he had ever seen her.

Even the birth of Master James Andrew Skinner six months before had taken less out of her than their dreadful day.

His first inclination had been to detail a Constable to take her car back to Edinburgh, but she had been adamant to the point of fury that she would drive herself. He had given in, but he had followed her watching all the way. Where normally she was a swift, assertive driver, instead she had been slow and deliberate and the thirty-five-mile journey to Fairyhouse Avenue had taken over an hour, even in minimal traffic.

Late in the afternoon, Bob had called his daughter in Glasgow, and had asked her to drive through to Edinburgh to relieve Tracey, the Nanny. He knew that he could have phoned the girl, and that she would have cancelled her night out, but his sensitivity to his wife's mood made him realise that it should be Alex who was there for them when they made it home, and not a relative stranger, however bright she was and eager to please.

There she had been, their daughter, hard at work in the kitchen, with a pasta sauce bubbling on the hob, and a bottle of Rioja ready to uncork. Alex was famous for her verbosity, but lately she had learned that there were times when nothing at all was the best thing to say. She had taken one look at her father's tired, drawn face when it appeared round the kitchen door, then, without a word, she had opened the fridge, taken out a bottle of Damm Estrella beer, uncapped it, and handed it to him. Next, she had mixed an outrageously large Bacardi and tonic, dropped in two ice cubes and a slice of lemon, and had taken it through to her step-mother in the sitting room, where she had collapsed on the sofa.

'Thanks, kid,' Sarah had said. 'Tough day at the University of Life, I'm afraid.' The tears had come then, floods of them, and great, wracking sobs which had shaken her body from top to toe. All the while, as her exhaustion worked itself out, Bob had stood in the doorway, watching Alex cradling her in her arms, woman to woman, knowing that there was nothing he could do to help her and feeling all the more desperate because of it.

Eventually, when Sarah had cried herself dry, they had settled down to supper. But still barely a word had been said. Bob had done his best, asking Alex the same question twice over about the difference between her final degree years and her diploma studies, but eventually he had abandoned the fruitless effort. The cork had stayed in the Rioja as he concentrated on his third, and then his fourth bottle of Estrella.

They sat in silence over supper.

Eventually Alex, having cleared away the last of the dishes, said: 'Look, you two, it's ten o'clock and baby brother Jazz looks settled for the night. I'm going to stay at Andy's. It's Friday night, so there's no need for me to rush back to Glasgow. Unless you'd rather I stayed here, of course, but somehow . . .'

'No, love,' said Bob. 'You've been magic, as ever, but I guess we're better left on our own from now on. So you just head on down to Haymarket. Andy should be home by now, I guess.'

She looked at him in surprise. 'But I didn't expect him back until tomorrow afternoon.'

'Change of plan. I'll leave it to him to tell you about it. It isn't something I want to go into now. You can save me a phone call, though. Tell Andy I want him in my office at eight-thirty tomorrow morning, for a briefing. And tell him to bring the bacon rolls!' His face cracked in a half-smile.

'Okay. I'll even grill the rashers myself! Now, good night, Pops. Good night Sarah.' She leaned over and kissed her step-mother on the cheek. Sarah looked up, wanly, and waved her fingers in a weak farewell.

Bob escorted Alex out to her car and waved her off on the short journey to Andy Martin's flat in Haymarket.

When he returned to their sitting room, he found Sarah sitting once more in tears, quietly, but it seemed to him, remorselessly. He went back into the kitchen and mixed her another drink, and took one more for himself, checking that there were still two or three bottles left in the drinks section of the fridge. The Estrella was as strong as it was golden, and normally three or four would have brought on a warm buzz, but on this dark night he could feel not the slightest effect.

He pressed the tall glass into Sarah's hands, sat down beside her and slipped an arm around her shoulders.

'Hey,' he whispered in her ear, 'I should have said this before. You were magnificent. I'm sorry I behaved so stupidly when you showed up. I don't know what got into me. Whatever it was, it wasn't rational. I've never been prouder of you than I was today.'

75

She shot him a sideways look, a strange furtive glance, from sharp mascara-smudged eyes that it seemed to him he had never seen before. 'Why?' she said, and took a long swallow from her Bacardi. 'What did I do? I just racked up the body-bags in a row, ready for collection.'

She picked up the TV remote-control unit and pressed the button. The big screen lit up, and suddenly Skinner saw himself, filmed from an illegally intruding helicopter, as he, Legge and Arrow and the rest had moved among the carnage in the gully. It occurred to him that the craft must have been close, yet he could not recall hearing it.

Then the scene switched to the main crash-site, showing soldiers carrying laden, covered stretchers toward the mortuary tent, in the late afternoon. As they watched, Sarah appeared in the doorway, waiting for the bearers with a clipboard in her hand.

'There I go,' she said grimly. 'I counted them in . . . and I laid them out!' She rested her head on his shoulder. 'Just bags, Bob. That's all. Lots and lots of bags, with things inside. I can't let myself think of them as people. I mustn't.'

He took the remote from her and switched off the TV. 'You can't avoid it,' he said. 'Because that's what they were, and you have to grant them that dignity. You're trained to deal with death, and you've seen things as bad as that and worse. Those killings in the Royal Mile, for example. The bomb at the Festival.'

Her head bowed. 'But so many, Bob. So many. That's what I can't get over. All those black bags!' Her shoulders shook again.

'The numbers don't matter. They're irrelevant. Within every mass killing, every death is a private truth for the individual. Everyone on that plane died the same solitary death. It is the most personal moment that any being will know, and the most lonely. There can be no other human experience like it. Birth is a team effort, or a partnership at least. Then the newly hatched person becomes a part of humanity, from that point on, and as such is never truly alone . . . until the very end. Living is a sharing experience, but dying can't be. We all go alone into that good night. Some of us go gentle, some raging.

'Sooner or later, you or some other doctor would have performed your final service for all of the people who went today, declaring them dead so that their passing can be recorded. You have to see this as having been a busy day at the office, because that is what it was. It may take strength of will to do that, but you have that strength. What you need now is sleep, so come on, my girl. Let's finish these nightcaps and head for bed.'

24

'Poor Mr Old! He was such a nice man, too.'

Alex shook her head sadly. 'I've known him for years. Long ago, when I was a kid, Dad would take me into the office sometimes, when Roy Old was his boss. He always made a fuss of me, and he always gave me things to do. Tidying up the paper clips, making tea and coffee, clearing up the dirty cups; things like that. He used to call me his wee policewoman.' She smiled at the memory. 'Ahh,' she sighed. 'It's such a shame.'

'Lightning strikes, love,' said Andy Martin, and knew, even before the shadow of a recent horror crossed her face, that he had said the wrong thing. 'Oh dammit,' he moaned. 'I'm sorry!'

She took him in her arms, touched by the anxiety in his vivid green eyes. 'It's all right, I'm used to your subtlety and tact by now.' She gathered a handful of his curly blond hair and tugged it, gently.

'Oh!' she said, a sudden recollection stirred. 'Pops wants you in his office at eighty-thirty tomorrow morning. He said something about bacon rolls.'

'Hah! Last time Bob and I discussed bacon rolls, he told me what to do with them . . . pretty graphically, too!'

'Take him black pudding instead, then.'

He smiled, but only for a moment. 'How is Bob? You said that Sarah's in a state, but how about him? I'd have hated to be at that place today. Is he okay?'

A candid look of concern crossed Alex's face as she looked at her fiancé. 'You know my Dad. He's such a rugged old sod, and well, we *both* know first-hand just how tough he can be. But tonight . . . I was worried for him. He was doing his best to shore up Sarah, and yet . . .

'I've always thought of him as carved out of rock, but this evening for the first time in my life, I thought I could see the cracks.'

25

They had called it a field, but in reality it was a mud-flat. The glue-like muck was ankle-deep. With each step it sucked at his heavy black shoes, and caught the hem of his blue uniform trousers.

Not long before, on television, he had seen a report on the aftermath of a hurricane. It had struck a Caribbean town on market day, cutting a swathe through the stalls and tents of the traders, smashing them to matchwood, tearing them to shreds, overturning vehicles, unwinding bolts of colourful fabric and tangling them together like a great patchwork quilt.

The picture came back to him as he looked around the muddy acres in which he stood. It was strewn with suitcases and rucksacks, all burst open, their contents spread around. Here and there his attention was caught by a sombrero, or a big black fan, bought for wall-mounting, but now broken on the ground, or a stuffed toy donkey with big, sad eyes, looking frighteningly realistic as if it were wondering what had happened to its owner.

When he saw the first victim, he thought at first that it was some more odd detritus from the baggage hold. He stared at it, and another picture came into his mind. The day before, driving to work, he had approached a road-kill lying in the kerbside. In spite of himself, he had looked at the bloody bundle of fur, trying in vain to determine what form of animal life it had been. Looking at the shapeless tangle on the ground, he felt the same sensation, hoping irrationally that the thing, with white bones protruding at odd angles from its blackened flesh, might be some large creature caught on the ground by the flaming aircraft, or another, outsize, stuffed memento, but knowing too that it was neither.

And then he saw the doll, lying in the mud, disjointed and unclothed. He saw it, he bent down towards the mud, and he picked it up . . .

Skinner sat bolt upright in bed. Cold sweat lashed his face. He thought, although he could not be certain, that he might have screamed. If he had, then the sound had not awakened Sarah; she lay beside him, tossing restlessly in her sleep. He wondered what dark dreams she was having.

He was breathing slightly heavily, and his chest was damp with sweat. He swung his legs out of bed and stood up in an effort to compose himself. Suddenly a snuffling cry sounded from the loudspeaker of the baby-minder. It was only Jazz, staging one of his occasional nocturnal interventions, but suddenly Bob was back in the depths of his nightmare. He sat back down on the bed, hard, and wondered if he had indeed screamed, and roused his son.

As he sat there, Sarah stirred and woke. Jazz cried again, approaching full volume this time.

'This is a first,' she murmured, seeing him. 'You normally sleep through that, or pretend to, till I've got up to see to him.'

He turned to look at her. Her earlier emotional exhaustion seemed to have been slept away; she appeared calm and settled.

He forced a smile. '"Build up for thyself treasures in Heaven",' he said. 'He probably wants changing. I'll see to it.'

'Good boy. Don't be long.'

'You go back to sleep. I'm awake for keeps, I think. It's five-thirty, and I've got an early start this morning.'

When the alarm woke Sarah at 7.20, Bob and Jazz were lying by her side, forehead to forehead, the father lost in thought, holding the sleeping child in his arms as if to shield him from anything the world could throw at him. She looked at them, and wondered.

26

'The Yanks worry me just a bit, Andy. They'll want a finger in this pie, and no mistake. That new girl from the Embassy, she's okay, once she stops talking and starts listening, but they'll want a heavy hitter on this one. The Gower woman was impressed by the fact that Massey was her Ambassador's brother-in-law: I'm more struck by the fact that he was the best pal of the man in the White House.

'I'm also struck by the fact that there's a Presidential election in three weeks, and that the incumbent will want to show a firm hand to the voters. It's a pound to a pinch of pigshit that he'll have sent over a top gun before this day is out, to show us Brits how to do it.'

Andy Martin picked up the last of the bacon rolls, which was still piping hot after having been revived in the Command Suite micro-wave. 'So how can I help you, boss?'

'You're helping just by being here, my friend,' Skinner said sin-cerely. Martin looked at him, and saw the dark marks of exhaustion under his eyes, and worry lines where none had been before. He sensed a tension in the man that he had never seen in all the years of their acquaintanceship, professional and personal.

'More practically, I would like you to handle the organisation of Roy Old's funeral. With Lottie's permission, I'd like to give him the full official send-off, like we did for the young lads who were killed in the last couple of years. Roy died on duty, just like them, hurrying to get back for a meeting. We'll call in on her later on today after the briefing, to pay our respects and talk things over.

'Another thing you can do, if it proves necessary, is keep the American out of my hair. Merle Gower has a part to play, but I won't have any spare wheels in the Command structure. So if they do send in a Shitehawk from Washington, I want you to nursemaid him. I've got you a new boy for your personal staff. He can drive him around.'

'I want McIlhenney!' said the new Head of CID emphatically.

'Fair enough, you can have him, but you're having this lad too. It's young Pye from Haddington.'

Martin's eyebrows rose. 'Young Sammy. Sure, I'll take him any time.'

'I thought you would. Right, here's the third thing you can do to help me. You can run CID like clockwork. You've got *carte blanche* to review the present structure and operating practice and make any changes you think fit. Your brief is to raise detection rates to a uniform level across the whole Force area, and then to keep the graph moving upwards. Continuous improvement is the name of the game, and in CID we have plenty of scope for that. Until our clear-up rates hit one hundred per cent we can never say, "We couldn't do any better." Your job is to make sure that I can go along to the Joint Police Board and say, with a clear conscience, "We're doing our best".

'As Head of CID, you won't be there to court popularity, but to earn respect. You acknowledge loyalty and reward achievement. You listen to your staff and you give weight to their views and their experience, but once the decisions are made, you make it clear that it has to be done your way. When somebody does that and gives of their best, you've succeeded. When someone doesn't, you've failed. And one of the reasons you're sitting there now is that you are incapable of living with your own failures. So when someone thinks that he or she knows better than the rest, or when someone is sloppy or careless, or obstructive or abusive, I know that you'll do something about it, and fast.

'In other words, I know that when necessary you'll do all the stuff that the late Roy, God rest him, was too nice and easy-going to handle.' He smiled sadly for a moment then continued.

'Before the shit hit the fan yesterday, I was on my way down to the Borders to do an unannounced bollocking job. I want you to take that over too. When you read the figures, you'll see why. I shouldn't have had to do that, but I knew that Roy couldn't. He was my failure, in a way. He wasn't sloppy or obstructive, and a less abusive man you'd never have met, but he didn't have the heart for the tough stuff. I made a mistake installing him as Head of CID, but *I* didn't have the heart to correct it. So, Chief Superintendent, you see what I want from you?'

'Yes, sir,' laughed Martin. 'You want a clear desk.'

'As far as day-to-day management is concerned, you're spot on. I want to be free to concentrate on crime strategy, and on the big issues, knowing that paper and problems aren't piling up in my in-tray when they could have been dealt with further down the line. But I've got an immediate need for that clear desk, and you know why, don't you?'

'Yes. Because the world and its brother-in-law will be watching you on this one, and you can't afford any distractions. Don't worry, you won't have any.'

Skinner sighed and leaned back in his chair. Martin thought that he had never seen him so tired. 'Thanks, Andy. You've no idea how much of a relief that is. You're right – the world, and his brother-in-law, *and* his best pal will be watching. But the fact is, I haven't a fucking clue where to start!

'Evidence and logic are my two guiding principles in detecting criminals. But so far, I've found only a scrap of the first, and not a sign of the other!'

27

Nine faces looked along at Skinner as he tapped the briefing-room table with his pen to call the meeting to order.

He was flanked by Adam Arrow and Merle Gower. Ranged around the table and facing him sat Andy Martin, the burly figure of Detective Sergeant Neil McIlhenney, young Sammy Pye, looking fresh-faced and eager, Maggie Rose, Brian Mackie, Mario McGuire, Alison Higgins, and her deputy, a young, sleek-haired, well-groomed Detective Chief Inspector named Dave Donaldson.

'Good morning, everyone,' said the DCC. 'Things were pretty chaotic yesterday, for all of us. What I'm going to say now will come as no surprise to those of you who were at the scene of the disaster, but to those who weren't, that's Ali, Dave, Brian and Mario, let me say that we're here to begin a murder investigation. A crime with two hundred and four victims.

'The press are clamouring for more information. I've asked Alan Royston to schedule a briefing for twelve-thirty: this is what I'll be telling them.

'We were able to establish at the scene of the crash, and it has since been confirmed by the Black Box flight recorder, that an explosion occurred on board the aircraft. We have been able to establish still further, to our complete satisfaction, that the explosion was caused by a bomb.'

He looked round the table, his eyes settling on Higgins and Donaldson. The Superintendent's eyes were wide with surprise, but her colleague sat impassively, waiting for Skinner to continue.

'You don't seem surprised, Dave.'

'I'm not, sir. I never doubted that's what it was.'

'Indeed?' said Skinner. He sounded interested, rather than irked. 'Most of us operate on the basis of evidence first, conclusions second. What makes you special?'

'I don't think I am, sir. I'm a believer in the laws of averages and possibilities, that's all.'

'What d'you mean?'

'Well, it's a matter of odds, isn't it? The odds against an aircraft coming down through mechanical or structural failure are pretty long, yet still it happens. The odds against the British and American

Defence Secretaries travelling on the same civilian plane are pretty long too, yet that happened yesterday.

'But when you take the two situations and put them together – the two guys travelling on the same plane and *that* plane coming down – well, to a statistician, the odds against an accident might have been exactly the same, but to a policeman, they have to be astronomical.'

The DCC smiled. 'Suspicious bugger, aren't you?'

Donaldson's expression took on a chorister's innocence. 'Who me, boss?'

'It's no fault in a copper, Dave. Just be sure you don't make one assumption too many, that's all.'

He turned his attention back to the rest of the gathering. 'Clever Dave here worked out that this was no accident; I dare say some of the rest of you did too. But what neither he nor anyone else could have guessed is how the bomb was taken on board. I know, and it's something I'm *not going to tell the press . . . and neither is any one of you!*

'The device was hidden inside the Defence Secretary's document case – his Red Box. It's made out of solid steel and bound in leather, and it's one of those rare items, like a protection officer's handgun, that is usually allowed to by-pass the airport security screening.

'There were two Red Boxes on that plane. One belonged to Roland McGrath, the Scottish Office Minister who was among the dead. That's been accounted for.'

He produced two colour photographs from a folder before him on the table. They showed front and back views of the fused piece of twisted, tangled metal which they had found on the moor. 'This was recovered in the area where the wreckage of the front two rows came down. We believe this was the second Red Box.

'The scientists and the bomb boys have been working on it all night. The lab confirms that most of the black coating on the outside was leather, although they can't tell us what the original colour was. They have confirmed also that other parts of the coating, those raised marks, are carbonised human tissue.

'The Bomb Squad have confirmed that there was an explosive device inside the box. Major Legge says that it was at least half-full of very powerful military high explosive, of the kind used in artillery shells, bombs and the like. There was no trace of the detonating mechanism, but he is guessing that there was a simple trigger device which completed a circuit as soon as the box was opened.

'Questions so far?'

Alison Higgins raised a hand. 'Have all of the bodies been recovered?'

Skinner nodded to Maggie Rose. 'All but two,' she said. 'We think we've matched a body to every seat except for Row 1, seats D and E. So far, the only trace we've found of Mr Davey or his Private Secretary was what was melted into the Red Box.'

On Skinner's left, Merle Gower leaned forward. 'Does that mean that you've found Secretary Massey's body?' she asked eagerly.

'We've found . . .' Rose hesitated. '. . . remains, which include a right hand with the second finger missing. That matches the description of Mr Massey which we were given by your Embassy. They said he lost the finger in Vietnam.'

'He got off lightly there,' said Skinner. 'Too bad his luck didn't hold.' He looked around the table once more. 'Ms Gower and Captain Arrow have reports for us. I can't stress strongly enough that what they say here is in deepest confidence, and must not go beyond this room. However, before they begin, there are a couple of things I'd like to deal with.

'As you all know by now, we lost Roy Old yesterday. We all knew Roy, and we all liked him, so be assured that the Force will pay him a proper tribute in due course. But he would have been the first to say that you cannot have a vacuum in a Police Force. Consequently, Andy Martin is here today as our new Head of CID and Roy's successor as my immediate deputy. Like Roy, and like the Heads of Divisions, he will have the title of Chief Superintendent.'

In a corner of his eye, he caught a glimpse of Alison Higgins. He thought that just for a second, her face betrayed a trace of disappointment.

He put the notion aside and went on. 'While I intend to devote myself full-time to this investigation until it is complete, if for any reason any of you is unable to report to me directly on anything which you feel to be important, you will report instead to Chief Superintendent Martin. Clear?'

Seven heads nodded around the table, that of Alison Higgins the most vigorously of all.

'Good. Now I want to clear up any doubts that anyone might have over jurisdiction. This is our investigation, be in no doubt about that. I don't say that out of territorial jealousy, but because the law has placed the burden on us. As I've said, I will take direct control over the operation. Normally I would look to the appropriate Divisional CID to supply the manpower; since the plane came down in your area, Alison, that would mean your people.

'However, you have your normal workload to handle, and that mustn't suffer. So I won't dump it all on you. What I'm proposing to do is to set up a dedicated team. The members will be DCI Mackie and acting DI McGuire from Special Branch, DI Rose from my office, DS Neil McIlhenney and DC Sammy Pye from Mr Martin's staff, and DCI Donaldson, whom I will second from other duties,' he glanced at Higgins, 'subject to your comments, Superintendent, for the duration of the enquiry.

'We will call in help from other Forces and Agencies as and when we need it, but we will co-ordinate everything and set the strategy. With that in mind, I want all the important interviews carried out by members of this team.'

He paused to sip from the coffee cup on the table before him, and to pick up a chocolate digestive biscuit.

'Okay, we've got a plane down as a result of an explosion; we know where the bomb was hidden. Where do we go from there? Thoughts, anyone?'

Around the table, people shifted in their chairs. There was an awkward silence for a few seconds.

'Don't all speak at once, will you,' said Skinner.

Dave Donaldson raised a hand. 'Shouldn't we begin by finding out all we can about Mr Davey's Private Secretary, sir, and everyone else in his office who might have been involved in filling that Red Box?'

The DCC nodded. 'You're right. That's exactly where we should begin. That's why you and DS McIlhenney are going straight to London with Captain Arrow after this briefing. You will interview all of Mr Davey's Private Office staff about the way in which his box was normally filled, and you will try to pin down a comprehensive eye-witness account of its movements from the moment it was brought into the office until the moment it left.'

Donaldson frowned. '*All* of them, sir? Are you sure we'll be able to see them all?'

'Bloody right,' Arrow interposed. 'They're all under orders to report to their office at two p.m. today, and they've all been under surveillance since yesterday. If anyone had tried to do a runner, he wouldn't have made it past the garden gate.'

'As well as quizzing them about the Red Box,' Skinner went on, 'you should also ask every person you interview what they thought of the late Private Secretary . . . his name was Maurice Noble . . . and you should ask them to give you a candid view of the Minister, too. Whatever gossip there is, make sure you bring it back.

'Finally, while you're there, I want you to speak to Sir Stewart Morelli, the Permanent Secretary. He'll be expecting you at four o'clock. Kid gloves for him, by the way. He'll have known Mr Noble pretty well. The senior Private Office appointments are usually made on his recommendation. So ask Sir Stewart for his comments on the man, and yes, ask him to tell you candidly what he thought of Colin Davey. You'd better make sure that Captain Arrow is with you when you see him. Adam's a familiar face, and that might encourage him, if he needs it, to be completely frank.

'You'll be supported by an officer from the Met Special Branch, but you two will be in charge, and you will lead the interviews. You'll find the Met guy waiting for you in Whitehall.

'Questions?'

Donaldson and McIlhenney shook their heads.

'Okay. Adam, would you like to give us your input.'

The little soldier leaned forward. 'Thanks, Bob. The first thing I should say is that every person on the Minister's staff has been given a full security check by my unit. I hold the vetting reports, and I'll let you see them.'

'Did you vet the Secretary of State, too?'

Arrow shook his head. 'No. We're not allowed to snoop on our own Ministers. If that's done, and I don't know whether it is or not, it'd be by the Security Services.

'I did Maurice Noble, though, and I can tell you about him. Age thirty-four, an Oxford economics graduate, he'd been in post since May. Didn't drink alcohol, and stopped smoking ten years ago. Liked a punt on the greyhounds, though. He had a mathematical system, and he bet a fixed amount each month. On the whole, he was a winner.

'He was married three years ago, to a barrister called Ariadne Tucker, same age as him. They lived in a brick terrace house in Putney with a mortgage well within their means. There are no kids, they drive a three-year-old Mazda MX5, they eat out a lot and they have a cat called Tigger.

'Maurice had a medical problem at one point, about five years ago. He contracted hepatitis on holiday in India, and it left him prone to bouts of depression. But it was controlled by medication, and the MOD doctors passed him fully fit for the Private Secretary job.'

'When did you do his vetting?' asked Brian Mackie.

'April. Before 'e was offered the job with Davey.'

'I suppose it won't have been topped up since then?'

Arrow shrugged his shoulders. 'We keep an eye on bank accounts, and we tap telephones at random, but there's been nothing other than that since he's been in post. Normally, we'd have taken another look at him after a year.'

'Fair enough.'

'Now for some other stuff, which will probably be more relevant than Maurice. I'm sure you can guess that we're always on the look-out for threats to Ministers. Just recently, they've been on the increase. We take them all seriously, till we're satisfied that there's nowt in 'em, but most of them turn out to be cranks.

'Currently, there are three that we're worried about. The first is an Irish outfit, a Republican splinter group that doesn't like the way things 'ave gone over there. They've 'ad one go already, a year or so back, when they tried to smuggle a bloody huge car bomb across the border. They lost half their strength then, but there are still a few of them on the loose. We believe that they're out to pull off a big score, and the word was that Davey was a target.

'Then there's the Enviro-terrorists.'

'Who?' said Maggie Rose.

'A group of Australasian radicals who are still carrying a grudge over French nuclear testing in the Pacific, and our support for them. They made some public threats when the first tests were carried out, but after that they went quiet. Then, a couple of weeks ago, the New Zealand Special Branch dropped us a tip that they'd been funded by the Iranians to make some mischief, and that they had it in mind to stage a big stunt in Europe, probably an assassination. They wouldn't get near Chirac, or our PM, but the French and British Defence Ministers, and Army Chiefs of Staff are seen as likely targets.

'Finally, there's General Yahic.'

'Who's he?' asked Donaldson.

'Miroslav Yahic. He's the most fanatical Serb commander of them all, and he's still holed up in a little enclave in Bosnia. The leadership try to keep him quiet, but his men seem to be loyal to him rather than them, so short of shooting him they can't do a thing about him. He's declared a personal war on all the NATO countries, and he means it.

'You may have read or seen telly reports a week or two back about the assassination of a Dutch General in his car in The Hague. Then, a few days later, an American fighter was blown up on the ground at a base in Germany. The Intelligence community is dead certain that Yahic was behind both of those attacks, and they've put the word out to expect more.'

He looked around the table. 'Those are the likeliest leads I can give you, but there may be others.'

'Which one do you fancy most?' asked Skinner.

Arrow considered the question for a few moments. 'Personally, I'd rule out the Irish. We think we know who they are, and they're under pretty constant surveillance. I reckon that if they were planning something like this we'd 'ave found out about it, and neutralised 'em.

'The Australasians? I'm not sure. They can't be ruled out, and we should check for links to them among the people we interview, but I don't see them 'aving the bottle for something like this. Even if they had, I don't see them, or the Paddies for that matter, taking out a planeload of people just to get Davey.

'No. Out of all that lot, I'd bet on Yahic. He's a fanatic and he certainly wouldn't draw back from the thought of killing a couple of 'undred people. This guy's wiped out whole towns. Yesterday's casualty list would be just a village by his standards.'

'Excuse me, Captain.' Every head turned to stare at Sammy Pye. The young Constable, the only man at the table wearing a suit, looked little more than a schoolboy as he stared eagerly at Arrow. 'I was wondering. Could Mr Massey have been a target as well? If this guy Yahic was behind it, wouldn't it have been a real coup for him to get both Davey and the American Defense Secretary at the same time?'

'That's a reasonable question, Sam,' said Skinner. 'And it's one that I've asked myself. But I think the answer is no, Secretary Massey wasn't a target. Adam?'

'That's right, Bob. Yahic's Intelligence isn't that good . . . I hope! On the British side, only half a dozen of us knew that Massey would be on the plane: Davey himself, Maurice Noble, his assistants, Sir Stewart Morelli and me. And we didn't find out until Thursday evening, when the Ambassador called Morelli. The airline people were only told to block off the two front rows. I heard Maurice Noble make that call myself, and he didn't say who'd be in them.'

Merle Gower, on Skinner's left, leaned across him. 'On our side, we only found out when Secretary Massey arrived on Thursday afternoon that he intended to fly up with Mr Davey. We had a seat for him on a military jet but he said that he wanted a chance to talk to Davey away from the Generals.'

'Who knew?' asked Skinner.

'The Ambassador told me,' she said, 'but as far as I know, no one else. I called the airline to book three tickets on the Embassy account. My name was on all three reservations.'

'So how, I wonder, did McGrath and wee Mark get into the front row?' Skinner mused. 'Two of Secretary Massey's staff should have been in those seats, and another in the seat that Miss Cunningham occupied. I think we have to assume that he told them to swap when Minister McGrath and his party turned up.'

'I guess so. Anyway, that answers your question, Sammy. If it was Yahic, then Massey being on board the plane was a bonus for him.' He turned to the American once more. 'Now, Merle, do you have any other information for us?'

The woman nodded her dark head. 'First off, I can corroborate Captain Arrow's Intelligence about the Yahic group. The CIA had an infiltrator on his personal staff – until recently, that is.'

'What happened to him?' asked Andy Martin.

'His name appeared in a list of fatalities a month ago, after the group was involved in a shoot-out with the International Force. Generals' aides don't normally come under fire, so the Company thinking is that he was compromised and executed.

'We know about the Australasian group also, but I can update your Intelligence on that, Captain. There was an Iranian connection, it's true, but it has now been terminated.'

'What,' said Arrow, 'like *With Extreme Prejudice?*'

Merle Gower smiled. 'Not that extreme! No, let's just say that certain economic pressure was brought to bear by our client states

89

within the Islamic community. As a result, the funds on offer to the group have now been withdrawn.

'I agree with Captain Arrow's assessment of the threat posed by General Yahic. However, I have another contender to throw into the discussion. You will not be surprised to learn that the Iraqis are our Number One Intelligence target these days. A couple of weeks ago, one of our sources in Baghdad came up with a dossier on deep-cover agents whom the regime has in position in various Western countries, including Britain, France and the US.

'We don't have names or faces to put to them, but we do know their code names and their occupations. For example, the sleeper in the US was known as Eagle, and he was a freelance computer software engineer. We nailed him yesterday, and we believe that we can tie him into the Oklahoma bombing.

'The French plant is called Mouse. She is a bank clerk.

'The London agent is code-named Robin, and he or she is a civil servant.'

Skinner whistled, and threw a glance at Arrow. 'Do we know which Department?'

Gower shook her head.

'What's the purpose of these people? Are they spies?'

'Some of them are. Others are assassins. The Iraqis are lousy when it comes to Intelligence gathering. That's why they got it so badly wrong over Kuwait; they miscalculated completely the extent to which Bush was prepared to go to protect the Saudis. But they keep on trying. Eagle, Mouse, Robin and all the rest are trained in either sabotage, espionage or assassination. They're in place to do damage or to gather information, whatever their specialty. But they're not used indiscriminately, and they're not all currently active. We believe that Mouse was involved in the Paris bombings last year, but that she's been put back to sleep. Robin, we are told, has just been activated.'

Skinner, upright in his seat, looked down at her. 'Who else in the UK has this information?'

'No one as yet, to my knowledge. Langley has only just finished evaluating it. However, a full report is on its way over, by courier. And that's the last thing I have to tell you. Washington has decided that I'm too raw to be representing the US in the investigation of the murder of the President's best buddy. So they're sending someone else. He's bringing the report.'

Skinner grinned at Martin, across the table. 'So who's the seagull going to be?'

She looked at him, puzzled, until she guessed his meaning. 'It's the Deputy Chair of the National Security Council, no less. My predecessor, Mr Doherty.'

'Joe! Well, thank You, God, for that. They're sending us a professional. Let me know when he's due to arrive, and I'll arrange to meet him.'

Skinner picked up his folder from the table and glanced at his watch. It was 9.40 a.m. 'Right, ladies and gentlemen, class dismissed. Dave, Neil, go home and pick up enough gear for a few days, then get yourselves out to the airport, with Adam, as quick as you can. Maggie's booked you on the eleven o'clock plane. Your tickets will be waiting at check-in, and the flight won't leave without you.'

As the meeting broke up, Skinner signalled to Superintendent Higgins to stay behind. 'Alison,' he said, once they were alone, 'you're not too disappointed, I hope, that I chose Andy to succeed Roy.'

She shook her blonde head, and her ruddy complexion seemed just a shade more red. 'No, sir. Andy's the right man for the job. I expected it, really.'

'How would you feel about taking his place in charge of Drugs and Vice?'

Higgins stared at him in surprise. 'Honestly, sir? I wouldn't want it. I'd prefer to stay where I am for a bit longer, then perhaps to be considered . . .' She faltered, and Skinner could see that she was wondering whether she had gone too far.

He grinned at her. 'For a job back in uniform, were you about to say?' She nodded.

'Then keep this to yourself for now. Charlie Radcliffe told me last night that he's planning to retire in six months. The Chief Constable will appoint his successor personally, but I'll recommend to him that he chooses you.'

The Superintendent flushed bright red. 'Thank you very much, sir.'

'Don't thank me till you've thought it through. I know that I wouldn't fancy putting on a uniform for what could be the rest of my career.'

Higgins looked at her feet, diffidently. 'Actually, I have some long-term career ambitions, sir, and that move fits in very well with them. Chief Super at age thirty-nine would keep me on course. I come from Dundee, you see, and my secret wish is that I might go back there one day as an ACC.'

'Don't sell yourself short now, Ali,' said Skinner, smiling. 'There's no point in aiming for the second top rung on any ladder.'

'I'll bear that in mind, boss. Meantime, can I make a suggestion? How about Dave Donaldson as Andy's replacement?'

'A good thought, and one that's crossed my mind, too. I'll discuss it with Andy. But let's get this crisis over with before we get round to making that decision.' He paused. 'How were things yesterday, with your friend?'

Higgins winced. 'As you would expect, really. Poor Leona! She was numb at first. But it helped when Mark came home. Honest to God, sir, what a miracle that was, that he should survive, out of them all.'

'Did his mother tell him? About his dad, I mean.' Suddenly, a picture of Roland McGrath, as Skinner had seen him last, burst into his mind extinguishing for a few seconds all other sights and thoughts. The Superintendent, looking at him, thought she saw him shudder, but she knew better than to comment.

Instead she shook her head. 'No, boss, Leona didn't tell him. I volunteered for that. I reckoned that it went with the job of godmother.'

'So how did the wee chap take it?'

'Just as you'd expect from Mark, with a stiff upper lip. I told him that his Daddy had been taken away by God, which was probably a mistake. Although I did my best to make it clear that he was gone for good, I'm sure that somewhere in here . . .' she tapped her forehead '. . . he's clinging to the idea that it's a return ticket.'

'He's bound to. Kids that small can't really deal with the concept of death. I remember when Myra, my first wife, was killed. Alex was only four at the time. I didn't let her go to the funeral, and afterwards I wished I had. She never called me a liar or anything, but I could see that she didn't believe me when I said that her mum wouldn't be back.

'It didn't hit home until she she was nearly eight. One evening she sat around without saying a word, which was unprecedented for her, till it was time to go to bed. Not long afterwards, I heard her crying her eyes out.

'I went in to see her, and she said "Daddy, what does 'dead' really mean?" So I told her again, and this time she understood. I thought that some kid had said something to her, but that wasn't it. I found out that her pal's cat had been killed on the road, and that Alex had seen it. That reality was what brought it home to her.

'So a word of advice, Fairy Godmother. Think seriously about persuading your friend to let Mark go to his father's funeral. It could be the right thing to do. And something else. Make sure that he's given the best counselling available, now and for a long time to come. Sooner or later he'll start to think about his own experience. Long term, that could be harder to handle than his father's death, so you have to make sure that he's as well prepared for it as can be.'

Higgins stood in silence for a while. 'I hadn't even begun to think of all that,' she said at last. 'But you're right. I'll talk to Leona about the funeral. And the other thing – do you have any idea who could help us?'

'I know a psychiatrist, Kevin O'Malley. I'll ask him to recommend someone. And Sarah will make some enquiries up at the University. There are people who specialise in handling traumatised children.

Okay, so this one doesn't even know yet that he's been traumatised: that'll just be an extra challenge.'

'Thank you, boss. As I said, I'll discuss it with Leona.' She paused. 'I don't suppose you'd like to call on her with me? I know that she'd like to thank you personally for rescuing Mark from the plane. And he'd like to see you again, too. Can you spare the time?'

'Of course. I want to speak to Brian Mackie, but if you wait in my office, I'll be with you in a few minutes.'

28

The Special Branch suite was on the same level as the Fettes Command Suite, in another section of the unattractive building.

Detective Chief Inspector Brian Mackie was in the midst of briefing Mario McGuire, his new recruit, on current activity when Skinner swept into his office.

'Good,' he said. 'You're still here. I've got a task for you guys.'

McGuire smiled. 'That's good, boss. I hate quiet Saturdays, and the DCI here's a Hearts supporter, so we both need something to occupy us!'

'You'll like this, then.' He jerked a thumb casually over his shoulder. 'What you heard back there from Adam and the American woman was classic MI6/CIA stuff. International intrigue, terrorist plots and all that. Sure, it happens—'

'I know,' McGuire interrupted. 'I've got a bullet-hole in me to prove it!'

'You and—' Skinner began, cutting himself off short when he remembered that neither Mackie nor McGuire knew the story of his own wounding. They had been told at the time that his leg injury had been sustained in a domestic accident . . . a story neither man had believed for one second.

'As I was about to say,' he went on, glowering at McGuire, 'international intrigue is one thing, but it shouldn't blind us to other possibilities, or deflect us from doing our job in the normal way, identifying all the options and investigating them all. Special Branch can leave Arrow, the Americans and me to make the running in investigating the external candidates. I've got another job for you guys.

'I want you to run an entirely separate investigation into the late Colin Davey MP. I want you to find out everything there is to know about him. Who were his friends, who were his school-chums, was he popular or unpopular, did he drink, did he smoke, did he go with tarts? I want a complete background report on the man, not on the Minister. Most of all I want to know whether there is anyone in his private life who might have thought that the world would be a better place without him.'

'Don't you buy the General Yahic theory, sir?' asked Brian Mackie. 'Or the idea of an Iraqi agent in Whitehall?'

'Oh no, Brian, I wouldn't rule them out. Yahic sounds like a prime suspect, and as for the Iraqis, they're complete effing nutters.'

McGuire smiled at the modification in the DCC's customary squad-room language, and Skinner caught his meaning.

'Sarah's warned me about swearing in front of the baby,' he muttered diffidently, 'but I can't change a career habit overnight.'

He went on: 'As I said earlier, investigating Yahic and Agent Robin is down to the Intelligence people. It'll be taken seriously, for sure. Apart from our own interest, the Americans will not allow Massey's death to go unpunished, whether or not he was a target. They'll want someone's head on a pole, and they'll give us all the help we need. My problem may be holding them back.

'But digging up the dirt on a member of our own Government is another matter entirely. I won't be sharing information with Joe Doherty on that side of things. If there is a home-grown candidate, we have to investigate him discreetly and keep the knowledge away from the Yanks. I want a trial at the end of this investigation, not someone dead in a ditch with a bullet in his ear.'

Mackie's eyebrows seemed to rise halfway up his domed head. 'That's not Mr Doherty's style, sir, surely?'

'Not personally, but Joe will be reporting back on this one, and some of his zealot colleagues don't play by the same moral code as the rest of us! So, you two. Get yourselves off down to London.' He handed Mackie a sheet of paper bearing two handwritten telephone numbers, and a sealed envelope.

'Those are the home and mobile numbers of Cyril Kercheval, your contact in MI5, and a letter of introduction and authorisation from me. Cyril is an Assistant Director with unspecified responsibilities. He may or may not choose to admit it to you, but these include keeping tabs on senior politicians and the like. He may give you direct help or he may send you to see other people, for example his contacts in Special Branch. You probably know some of them already, Brian.'

'Okay, sir,' said the tall, slim DCI. 'Do we fly down this afternoon?'

'That depends,' said Skinner. 'Set up your meeting with Cyril, then book your travel accordingly. Stay down there as long as necessary, but report to me on a daily basis.

'Good luck, and remember – be discreet. Anything you turn up, keep it to yourself. Since all this public accountability crap came in, MI5 leaks like a sieve!'

29

'Hello there, wee Mark. And how are you today? A bit drier than you were when we first met, I notice!'

Skinner picked up the child in both hands and held him high above his head. Mark shrieked with laughter, the sound echoing strangely around the silent Victorian house.

'Mr Skinner's brought you a present,' said Alison Higgins, holding out a brown paper bag as the DCC put the boy down in front of her.

'Thank you very much!' he said, grabbing the bag from his godmother and tearing it open eagerly. 'Wow!' he said as he uncovered the contents – a child-size uniform cap, crested and with the legend *Police Cadet* embroidered on its blue band. He put it on and the brim fell over his eyes.

'He's a remarkable wee chap,' said Higgins quietly to the DCC. 'When he went to school they gave him an IQ test designed for his age group. He's away up there in the Mensa class, and he has a memory that's virtually photographic.'

'Indeed?' said Skinner. He knelt beside the five-year-old, tipping the cap back from his forehead. 'Our Sergeants and Constables give these to boys and girls when they go to speak in schools,' he said. 'We don't have any that are quite your size. Still, that should last you for a few years; then, when you're big, you might decide that you want to wear a real one.'

'I think he might, at that,' said Leona McGrath, rising from her armchair as Skinner stood up. 'I can't begin to thank you for what you did yesterday.'

The DCC shrugged, embarrassed. 'I just happened to be there first.'

She shook her head. 'Andrew Hardy told me all about it. One of the soldiers had described it to him. He said that you simply smashed your way into that cabin. And the water was so deep. Mark isn't a natural swimmer like most youngsters; he just sinks like a stone. He couldn't have clung on above the surface for much longer, and if he had fallen in—' She stopped herself, just as her voice began to rise. 'If he had survived the crash, only to—'

'But he didn't, Leona,' said Alison Higgins. 'Just keep that good thought in your head, and don't let yourself indulge in might-have-beens.'

The widow McGrath straightened her back. She had a remarkable bearing, Skinner thought, and great dignity. She was a small woman, not much over five feet tall, but she seemed to exude vigour. She nodded her grey-flecked brown curls. 'Yes, Ali. You're quite right, as usual. I don't do that. I have to look forward, for him, and for Roly.'

'That's the spirit, girl.' The voice came from the doorway. Skinner turned and saw, framed there, a tall man. He looked to be around forty, and was dressed in a formal dark suit and white shirt, with a black tie. *Dressed for the occasion*, the policeman thought.

Leona McGrath turned at the sound of his voice. 'Marsh. How good of you to look in again.'

'Don't be silly. It's the least one could do.' As he stepped into the room, she went to greet him, hands outstretched, rose on her toes as he bent his head forward, and kissed him lightly on the cheek.

'You probably haven't met,' she said, turning, drawing him with her. 'Alison Higgins, Deputy Chief Constable Skinner: this is Marshall Elliot, Roland's constituency agent.'

Skinner shook the proffered hand. 'No, we haven't met,' said Elliot, 'but I know who you are – Edinburgh's most celebrated policeman. In my job, I meet your Special Branch people from time to time, when we have a VIP visitor. Your name is mentioned frequently.

'Miss Higgins,' he said, with a courtly nod that was almost a bow. 'I've heard a great deal about you also, from Leona. You're a Police Officer too, aren't you?'

'That's right – Detective Superintendent. We have met, though. Very briefly, a few years ago at one of Roly's constituency evenings. But you were terribly busy. I wouldn't expect you to remember.'

'Nonetheless, I stand rebuked. Ungallant of me to forget a lady's face. Unprofessional too, if you're a constituent! Against all my training.' He turned towards Leona McGrath. 'Look, my dear, I'm not interrupting, am I?'

She shook her head. 'Of course not. I wanted to talk to you anyway, about the funeral.'

He sighed, involuntarily. 'Ahh. In fact, that's why I'm here. To offer my services in making the arrangements. We can expect quite a turn-out, you know.' He hesitated. 'I can say this in the company of the police, I'm sure. I had a call from Downing Street. The Prime Minister wishes to attend. And I've been told to expect a representative of the Monarch.'

Leona McGrath's eyebrows rose. 'All the more reason for me to accept your offer, Marsh. I was going to ask you anyway. It's quite beyond Roland's dad, and I . . . Well, I want to give Mark all my time for the next few days.'

'Yes,' said Alison Higgins. 'That's really good of you, Mr Elliot. If there's any help I can give, privately or professionally, just let me know.'

'We-ell,' said Elliot. 'There *is* something professional that we might talk about later.'

Skinner put a hand on the man's shoulder. 'Perhaps you and I could deal with it now, Mr Elliot.'

'Fine. Let's step in here.' He moved through the double doors which led from the McGrath sitting room out into a long conservatory; not a modern PVC and glass pagoda, but a solid structure which, the DCC thought, might have been built with the house a century and more before. The extensive garden was immaculately kept, with touches of colour even in late October.

'There are some lovely old houses down here in Trinity,' said Elliot. 'I used to gibe at Roly, that he didn't actually live in the contituency, but it's easy to see why he didn't want to move from here . . . Mind you, it might have been forced on him soon.'

'What d'you mean?'

The man lowered his voice. 'Well, though one shouldn't breathe such heresy, there was a real chance that Roly would have lost the seat at the next election. Not that people thought that he was a bad MP, you understand. Above average, most would have said. The Association liked him, even the whingers . . . and we have the usual ration of them . . . but the majority was under three thousand, and would have been under serious attack from Labour and the Scot Nats at the General Election.'

Skinner glanced at him. 'What about the by-election?'

'My dear chap, one doesn't discuss the by-election until after the funeral.' He smiled. 'In public, that is. Privately, if Central Office decides on a quick poll, which they will, and we choose the right chap, which I'm sure we will, then the wave of sympathy over Roly's death will sweep us back in. Increased majority, I should think.'

Elliot sounded contemplative for a moment, but his tone changed abruptly, almost guiltily. 'Anyway, to business. What I wanted to ask was, have you recovered Roly's body?'

Skinner looked grim as he nodded. 'Yes, we're satisfied that we have it.' He almost added, 'Or as much as we're going to find.' He stopped himself just in time, but Elliot had been thinking along the same lines.

'How about identification?'

'We'll use dental records for confirmation. We won't need to ask Mrs McGrath to look at the remains. Don't you worry about any of that. We'll give you a body in a closed coffin. Just you make sure that it stays closed!'

'Understood. When do you expect to release it? That's the professional matter I wanted to raise,' he added.

'Monday, at the latest. When were you thinking of having the funeral?'

'Next Friday,' said Elliot. 'Provided that doesn't clash with Davey's service. Have you found . . . him, yet?'

'Pass,' said Skinner.

'Ahh, I see. Nothing identifiable. So what will they do about a funeral, do you think?'

'Stuffed if I know. We can give them a boxful of something. The trouble is, at the moment it would be a sheep.'

'Ugh.' The agent screwed up his face. 'Have you established the cause of the accident yet?'

Skinner took him by the elbow. 'Let's go back inside. That's something I still have to break to Leona. It might be helpful if you were there when I tell her. She'll need friends around her.'

30

The Press Briefing Room was as full as Skinner had ever seen it, even in the times of major crises which had marked his career. Six television cameras, including the Force Video Unit, pointed at him, from behind ranks of reporters.

'I have a very short statement to make, ladies and gentlemen, after which I do not intend to take any questions.

'It has now been established that yesterday morning's disaster on the Lammermuirs was caused by an explosion in the cabin of the plane. We are satisfied that a device was smuggled on board the aircraft, although we do not know whether it was intended that it should detonate in flight.

'This Force has now begun a murder investigation. I am in direct control of enquiries, assisted by Chief Superintendent Andrew Martin. He has been appointed Head of CID, in succession to Roy Old who, as you will know, died in yesterday's tragedy. Mr Martin and I will call on other Forces for co-operation and assistance as necessary.

'I have nothing more to say today, but further briefings will be held as appropriate.'

He stood up amid a clamour of shouted questions, and a forest of waving tape recorders, and walked from the room.

As he passed the back row of journalists, Noel Salmon, an untidy, black-stubbled man who worked for Skinner's least favourite tabloid, chuckled to his neighbour, 'D'you reckon Andy Martin planted the bomb so he could get Roy Old's job?'

As a collective moan escaped the lips of all those journalists who were near enough to hear the remark, the DCC froze in mid-stride. He reached down, grabbed the podgy reporter by his leather belt, hauled him from his seat and propelled him bodily from the room. Sammy Pye, on duty by the double doors, held them open for him, unquestioningly, then had the innate good sense not to follow.

The corridor wound to the right towards a stairway, fifteen feet from the doors. Skinner turned into it out of sight, and threw the man against the opposite wall, face first, and very hard.

Salmon squealed: 'That's assault!'

'No, it's not, it's carelessness. I just dropped you, that's all. I wouldn't dirty my knuckles on a little shite like you, son. But if I ever hear of you saying something as crass as that again, then for the rest of your life you will never know a day when you don't regret it. Now you get on your way, and don't ever present yourself in this office again, or in any other run by this Force.'

Salmon lived up to his name. His face was a deep pink colour. 'You can't take on the Press, Skinner! I'll get you!'

The policeman's face twisted with scorn. '*You?* You graceless wanker, you could barely get your own tea. Now shift out of here before I charge you with imitating a human being.'

He pushed the man towards the door, and trotted up the stairway. He was still shaking with anger as he sat down behind his desk. When Maggie Rose came into the room the phone was in his hand and he was dialling a London number.

'Reggie,' he barked, when the call was answered. 'Bob Skinner. Remember you told me that a couple of years ago you sorted out a problem for that newspaper proprietor fellow, the one that owns those nasty tabloids, and that he owes our side a few favours as a result? You do? Good! Well, now *I've* got a wee problem, and I'd like *him* to sort it out. In fact, I'd like him to make sure that my wee problem never gets a job in journalism in Britain again . . . *ever*.'

31

Neil McIlhenney was never at his best with lachrymose women. In fact, he was rarely at his best with women in any situation. In their occasional matrimonial jousts, Olive McIlhenney could best her husband in many ways, from simple tears to extended silence, and others which she still kept hidden in her armoury, just in case.

The moments in his career which he had enjoyed least had been those on the Drugs and Vice Squad when Andy Martin, its Commander, had decreed a crack-down on Edinburgh's burgeoning massage parlours – establishments in which the massage, on offer only to men, was of a localised and specialist nature.

Although he had given of his best, his diffidence had been noticed, prompting Martin to comment to Bob Skinner, 'See that McIlhenney! If I sent him in to sort out a male brothel, he'd tear the place, and the characters in it, apart with his bare fists. But take him on a raid on a sauna and he goes in with his cap in his hand. The fact is, the big fella's just scared of women!'

'At times, who can blame him?' the DCC, fresh from a roasting by his exam-stressed daughter, had muttered.

No, McIlhenney was an old-fashioned man's copper, and so, faced across the cream-topped table by the sobbing Shana Mirzana, he was happy to play the part of junior officer, leaving all the questioning to DCI Dave Donaldson.

Ms Mirzana had been Assistant Private Secretary to the Secretary of State for Defence. She was the third member of the Private Office staff whom Donaldson, McIlhenney and Adam Arrow had interviewed. Their Metropolitan Police colleague, Detective Sergeant Garen Price, was there simply to throw the cloak of his jurisdiction over the proceedings. He sat in the corner and sipped coffee.

'I know this is difficult for you, ma'am,' said the DCI, 'but you will understand that an investigation as serious as this must go ahead with all speed. So if you'll compose yourself, please.'

Listening, McIlhenney was struck by the way in which Donaldson kept a sympathetic tone in his voice, but did not disguise the fact that the woman was there to be questioned, aggressively if necessary. *You're a cold-hearted bastard under that smooth surface, Dave*, he thought.

She nodded, dabbing her eyes with a white handkerchief. 'Of course,' she said. 'I'm sorry. I will try to help you.'

'We know you will, Shana,' said Adam Arrow, offering a familiar face as a reassurance. 'Just keep calm.'

He had shown them her Personnel file and her vetting report. She was twenty-seven, the granddaughter of an immigrant from India just as it gained nationhood, his departure sped, no doubt, by the fact that he was a Muslim. The family religion had been retained in Britain, but half a century on, as she sat before them, Shana wore an outfit which was distinctly Western in its style and cut. She had indeed liberated herself considerably, as her LSE degree bore out. She was the daughter of an orthopaedic surgeon, and, while not on as fast a track as Maurice Noble, she was expected to carve out a good civil-service career.

The vetting process had thrown up no skeletons, other than a student membership of the Young Conservatives, and a speeding conviction at the age of twenty-two.

'When was the trip to Scotland first put on Mr Davey's diary, Ms Mirzana?' asked Donaldson.

'It was talked about perhaps three weeks ago, when the Chief of the General Staff first invited the Secretary of State to visit the exercise.' She spoke with the few faint traces of a Midlands accent to have survived a good education.

'However, Mr Davey did not wish to commit himself at first. He said that he would think it over. I think he didn't really want to go. It was only after we heard from Washington that Mr Massey would be coming that he felt he should put in an appearance. The Secretary of State doesn't like exercises,' she explained. 'His predecessors have worn battledress and driven tanks, but he won't – sorry, wouldn't have done – that sort of thing.'

'So it was only because Massey was going that he went?' said Donaldson.

Shana Mirzana surprised them by smiling, for the first time. 'Well, not quite. You see, Mr Massey had insisted that he be accompanied by television crews from America, to help the President in the election. When Mr Davey heard that, he said that he had an election coming up too, and that if our cousins were going to do that sort of thing – well, so would he.'

'I see. So when did he decide to go?'

'Tuesday afternoon. Maurice told me just after the Secretary of State had gone off to the House. The Permanent Secretary had been going in his place, and could still have gone, but when Mr Davey changed his mind, Sir Stewart decided to withdraw.'

'Did Mr Noble always go with Davey on these trips?'

She shook her head. 'Most of the time. Occasionally, I would go.

103

Once or twice at weekends. Maurice didn't like being away from Ariadne, but usually Mr Davey would insist.'

'And did he insist this time?'

'Yes, he did. Because of the Americans being here.'

'How did Mr Noble feel about that?'

'He didn't say anything in particular, but I had the feeling that he wasn't very pleased.' She hesitated. 'I can't be sure, but . . .'

'Go on, please,' said Donaldson. The woman looked questioningly at Adam Arrow, who nodded.

'Well, Maurice didn't discuss his private life with me as a rule, but there was an inflection in some of the things he did say that made me think . . . that things weren't all right at home.'

'Had his behaviour changed at all recently?'

She considered the question for a few moments. 'When he came into the job at first, he was very enthusiastic, very positive, very outgoing. But that soon changed: just lately he had been very quiet. That happens to people in Private Office, though; I know from experience. The job is very stressful, and when your Minister is very demanding, as Mr Davey was, it can take over your life. You have to walk a tightrope at times.'

'What do you mean?' asked Neil McIlhenney, interested enough to involve himself in the interview for the first time.

'I mean that the people who do jobs like ours are the Minister's voice when we speak to Department. If the Minister says something critical, or rude, then we have to pass it on, in the terms in which he commented. That can create potential difficulties for us, since we're mainstream civil servants on secondment, and since the people we're bawling out on Our Master's behalf will be very often in a position to have a considerable influence on our future careers. We have to convey meaning directly without ruffling feathers, and that is very difficult. More than one Private Secretary has found that some very high-level knives were out for him after he'd finished his stint and gone back into Divisional work.'

'How would you say Mr Noble was coping?'

'He was having difficulties. I sat in on a meeting last week, and when it was over the Secretary of State asked Maurice to wait behind. Even before the door was closed, I heard Mr Davey begin to tear into him for being too soft in a memo to one of the Procurement Divisions. He came out looking very white, and didn't say anything for a while. I felt sorry for him.' She paused again, then burst out angrily, 'Actually, the Secretary of State could be a real shit!'

Immediately, as if a second thought had hit her, she looked at Arrow and said, 'Please don't repeat that, will you? We're trained to be loyal to our Ministers above everything.'

The soldier smiled. 'That's all right, Shana. This one's dead, so it doesn't count. As it 'appens, I think you're being too kind to him.'

'Was that the general view of Mr Davey?' asked Donaldson, trying to regain control of the interview.

'No,' said Ms Mirzana, freed by Arrow's reaction. 'I'd say it was the universal view.'

'Why?'

'Have we all day? Let me see.' She thought the question over. 'Quite apart from Mr Davey being a school bully who graduated somehow to the Cabinet table, quite apart from him being an opportunist, a misogynist, cruelly sarcastic, and taking a delight in the misfortunes of others, quite apart from all that, there was a special sort of nastiness about him, the sort that in a roomful of shits, has a smell all of its own.'

'That just about sums the man up,' said Arrow, laughing out loud. McIlhenney joined in; he had warmed to this woman. In fact, he was studying her technique in vituperation, one of the longer words of which he was proud, for a future debate with an unprepared Olive.

Donaldson allowed their mirth to subside. 'What about Mr Noble? What did people think of him?' he asked quietly.

'A nice man, probably out of his depth in any event, but completely unsuited to be Principal Private Secretary to a man like Davey. I don't know what Sir Stewart could have been thinking of when he made the recommendation.'

'Don't worry,' said the DCI. 'I'll ask him.' He forestalled her frown. 'But I won't drop you in it, be sure of that. Earlier, you said that you thought Mr Noble could have had problems at home. Have you ever met his wife?'

'A couple of times. She dropped in at the office once to pick up some theatre tickets. Maurice was busy so I took them down. The other time was at their house.'

'You've been there?'

'Yes, I've called in a few times. Once, Ariadne was there.'

'How did Mrs Noble strike you?'

'Formidable. And no one refers to her as Mrs Noble. It's always Ms Tucker. She's one of the youngest Queen's Counsel in England, you know, and one can see why. She has a very quick tongue, and an even quicker mind. She's statuesque, too; long legs, wide shoulders and very blonde hair, beautifully cut – to accommodate the wig, I imagine. All in all, she's quite a package.'

'How did she strike you as a partner for Maurice?'

The woman smiled guiltily. 'Do you remember your A. A. Milne?'

Arrow and McIlhenney turned their eyes from Ms Mirzana to DCI Donaldson. 'Yes,' he said, flushing perceptibly.

'Well, Maurice once told me that they have a cat called Tigger. When he said that, I had an instant picture of Ariadne as Kanga and him as Baby Roo!'

This time, Donaldson joined in the laughter. When it had subsided, Arrow drew his chair an inch or two closer to the table.

'One final thing, Shana,' he said. 'We'd like to talk about the preparations for the trip.'

She shrugged her shoulders. 'They were just like any others. Joseph, our Executive Officer, made all the travel bookings and hotel reservations. And as usual, you handled liaison with the Police at the ultimate destination in Scotland.'

'That's right. Did you *hear* Joseph make all the bookings?'

'Yes, I did. You know the office, Adam. It's open plan.'

'Sure, but were you there all the time he was doing it?'

'Yes.'

'And were you listening to everything he said?'

She hesitated. 'I wasn't hanging on his every word, but I do know that if he'd broken Security, I'd have picked it up. The flight bookings were made for an unnamed group and the hotel rooms were booked in the name of Mr Noble's party.'

'What about the Red Boxes? Who packed them?'

'There was only one, and I did it.'

Adam paused and looked at her. Without changing tone, he asked, 'What was in it?'

She made a palms-out gesture. 'The usual stuff. Correspondence folders, submissions and Intelligence reports. Joseph gathered all of them together and I packed the box. I locked it, and I gave it to Maurice.'

'When did this happen?'

'Thursday evening. I think I packed the box at about ten past nine. It was another late night.'

'Did Joseph see you pack the box?'

'Yes.'

'After you locked it and before you gave it to Maurice, was it ever out of your sight?'

'No. Not for a moment.'

'And what did Maurice do after he took it from you?'

'He went home, and so did I, in a Government pool car. That was it. Even we finish work sometimes.'

'And the box went with you?'

'Yes. On the seat between us.'

'Was there anything in it that he would have had to work on?'

She shook her head. 'No. We'd been through it all.'

Arrow leaned back in his chair, nodding his satisfaction. Donaldson, on cue, stood up. 'Thank you, Ms Mirzana. That'll be all for now.' He made to show her to the door but Arrow beat him to it. As he ushered her out, his hand brushed her hip, close enough for him to drop a note, unseen by the others into the pocket of her jacket, close enough to whisper, unheard by the others in her ear.

106

32

As always, there was a pile of paper in the in-tray. Skinner attacked it, working mechanically, initialling document after document and passing it across the desk to Maggie Rose. She sat opposite him, taking each item and sorting it by subject.

Abruptly, the DCC tossed his pen on the desk, picked up the phone and dialled a number. 'ACC Elder, please. Mr Skinner here,' he said to the officer who answered the telephone. He heard her call across the command vehicle; a few seconds later Elder came on line.

'Hi, Jim. Just thought I'd give you a call to see how it's going up there on the moors.'

'"Painstaking" just about sums it up. All the bodies have been moved down to Haddington now. Charlie Radcliffe's there now, dealing with the relatives as they turn up. We've got a name to nearly all the remains now: one or two of the foreign nationals are unaccounted for, that's all. We're waiting for photos and dental records from Japan and the Czech Republic.'

'So what's happening on the moor?'

'We're gathering in the cabin baggage. I've had quite a few calls this morning from businesses, trying to recover papers and the like. There was one bloke from a Japanese electronics firm. He went on for ten minutes about this bloody briefcase and what was in it, about how many million dollars it was worth, until eventually I told him that if he'd get his arse down here and help us identify the poor bastard who'd been carrying it, *then* I'd start to worry about his bloody case.

'The Air Accident Investigators have started work in earnest, too. They're gathering in all the pieces of wreckage. The woman in charge said they'd take it down South to their HQ and try to put it all back together as best they can. When something like this happens, they look at the way the aircraft reacts to the stress, to see if there's any way they can build them stronger.'

'That's good,' said Skinner, 'but remind her as tactfully as you can that we have our own investigation under way, and that anything she takes away, we could want back at some stage. Ask her, too, if she'd give us a full report on the location and nature of the explosion, to back up Major Legge's findings. From the sound of things, Jim, you're going to be up there for quite a while. Any problems?'

Elder gave a long, deep sigh. 'Yes. Human nature. The place is crawling with ghouls. The Longformacus Road is still closed off to private traffic, but that hasn't stopped them. It's a grey, misty, miserable day up here, yet they're hiking across the moor in their droves just to see what they can see. My people and the soldiers are turning them back as soon as they arrive, but there are so many that they're interfering with the recovery process. I'm thinking of telling the Press Office to put out a statement from me saying that anyone else who turns up here without a valid reason will be charged with obstructing the police. What d'you think?'

'I'd do that like a shot. Look, Royston's still here. I'll put Maggie on the line. You tell her exactly what you want to say and she'll make it happen within ten minutes. I've just told the world that we have a murder investigation under way, so we'll have quite a few media people still on the premises.'

He handed the phone across the desk to Maggie Rose. She listened attentively to Elder, making notes on a pad. When he had finished his dictation, she offered the phone back to Skinner, but he shook his head, and she rang off.

'Okay, Mags, go and grab Royston. Once you've done that, we'll . . .' His voice tailed off, and he slumped back into his chair.

She stared at him, concern showing in her face. This was a Bob Skinner she had never seen before.

'Boss, there's nothing else you can do,' she said gently. 'Mr Elder's in charge and coping out there. You've got interviews proceeding in London, and Brian Mackie and Mario off on another line of investigation.'

'Don't tell me how to do my job, lady!' he barked at her suddenly, and in spite of herself, she flinched. 'You just go and do yours!'

'Very good, sir,' she said, in little more than a whisper, and left the room.

Skinner swung round in his swivel seat and stared out of the window at the grey afternoon, raging inwardly against his feeling of being becalmed, and against the indefinable sensation which had gripped him since the previous morning that somehow, he was not completely in control.

A loud stage cough behind him brought him back to the present. He turned to see Sir James Proud standing in front of his desk. As the most junior Constable would have done, he stood to acknowledge his Chief Constable, noticing as he did so that Proud Jimmy had closed his door behind him.

'Bob, son,' said the Chief. 'Are you all right?'

Skinner felt himself flare up again, but checked it. 'Of course I am, Jimmy. What makes you ask that?'

'It's bloody obvious what makes me ask it. I was across the corridor with my door shut, yet I still heard you shout at Maggie Rose. When I went to see what was up, the lass brushed past me, nearly in tears. And that's not like Maggie. I've never heard you rip into someone like that, man. You're a hard bugger, but bullying junior officers isn't your style. Come to think of it, I thought for a moment, yesterday on the Lammermuirs, that you were going to take a pop at *me*. Or was I wrong?'

Skinner smiled wryly and looked at the carpet. 'No, Jimmy, you weren't. I admit it, I was steaming mad that you had called Sarah out to that thing, and I was ready to tackle you about it. I'm sorry.'

'Ahh,' said Sir James knowingly, 'I wondered if that was it. Look, Bob, I'm sorry, but when I got the message yesterday I never had another thought but to call Sarah. She's far and away the best we've got.'

'I know. You did the right thing.'

'I still felt guilty about it for most of yesterday. It must have been a dreadful job for her. How did she react?'

'She had a bad night last night, but I think she cried it out. She seemed okay this morning, anyway.'

'That's good,' said Proud Jimmy kindly. 'But you, my friend – can I worry about you now? That was a hellish job you had too, especially, from what I hear, out at that second crash-site. I spoke to Legge afterwards. He told me all about it – said it turned his stomach, and he's seen plenty.

'You're not Superman, Bob Skinner. You're as entitled to be affected as anyone else, if only you'll admit it. Go easy on yourself, and on the people around you, eh? Look, it's Saturday afternoon. Get yourself home to your family and try to enjoy what's left of the day.'

Skinner sighed, and shrugged his shoulders. Suddenly he felt horribly tired. 'Aye okay, Jimmy. The girl Gower said that Joe Doherty'll be up on the nine o'clock plane tomorrow. Until then, I'll do what you say. We're dining out with Andy and Alex tonight, so I'll have to try to be decent company for them. But I've something to do before anything else.'

'What's that?'

'I've got to get down on my knees and offer Maggie Rose a heartfelt apology!'

33

'I noticed you were on first-name terms, Captain,' said Donaldson.

'And why not?' the little soldier asked. His tone was light, but something in it warned the policeman that Arrow's sense of humour did not extend to his own affairs.

'I'm in Private Office a lot, so Shana and I see quite a bit of each other. I was on first-name terms with Maurice Noble, too. And I was on first-name terms with all the lads in my SAS squad. So what?'

Donaldson knew nothing of Arrow's military background. 'No matter,' he said, and moved quickly on. 'Let's get the next guy in. Joseph Webber, Executive Assistant.'

'Aye, that's right,' said Arrow. 'I'm on first-name terms with him, too.'

Joseph Webber was a year short of forty, older than either Maurice Noble or Shana Mirzana. He had been a civil servant for twenty-one years, the last eight of them spent in Private Office. This was far beyond the normal posting even for a junior grade, but the Annual Reports in his Personnel file revealed that he was trapped there by his own faultless efficiency.

His vetting report revealed him as a contradictory character. He was single and lived in a small flat in Pimlico. His life was dominated by his work, and his only hobby seemed to be the consumption of large quantities of beer in the Red Lion pub, around 200 yards from the great grey Whitehall headquarters of the Ministry of Defence.

The effect of the previous evening's consumption was showing around Webber's eyes as he took his place at the table opposite his three interrogators. The black circles stood out in his otherwise pasty face.

'Must have been a hell of a shock,' said Donaldson abruptly. Webber looked at him blankly.

'The accident, I mean.'

'That? Yeah, I suppose so,' said the man, in an accent which reminded Neil McIlhenney of a market-stall trader in a television soap.

'You don't seem overwhelmed by grief.'

'What do you want me to do? Gnash my teeth? Weep uncontrollably? I'm afraid that's not me. These things happen, that's all I can say.'

Donaldson gazed at him. 'Don't you feel touched by it at all?'

Webber shrugged his shoulders. 'I feel sorry for Maurice. He was a harmless enough geezer. But people come and people go. I've seen enough of them go in my time in here, and he's just one more.'

'Don't you feel sorry for Colin Davey too?'

The civil servant stared unblinking across the table. 'Not a bit. The world's a better place without him. The man was a complete arsehole.'

'What did he do to you?'

'He threatened to have me moved on from here, for a start.'

'But you've been here for eight years, man. Haven't you had enough of it?'

Joseph Webber laughed softly, revealing years of dental neglect. 'I told Sir Stewart: the day I move out of here, I go straight through the big front door, out into Whitehall and I don't come back. This place is like a fuckin' beehive, mate. I spent thirteen anonymous years as a mainstream drone and the thought of putting in another twenty of 'em makes my blood run cold. I like Private Office because it's the centre of the hive. I know how it works, I know how to make it run smoothly, and I know how to spot banana skins before someone steps on 'em.'

'So why did Davey want you out?' asked Arrow.

'Because I knew about him, and he knew it, that's why. I know everything.'

'What d'you mean by that?'

'You're Ministry Security, Adam, you find out.' Webber and Arrow stared across the table at each other for several seconds, neither man blinking.

'We'll maybe come back to that later,' said Donaldson, breaking the stalemate. 'If you know everything, Mr Webber, what can you tell us about Maurice Noble?'

The man looked up at the ornate plastered ceiling for a few seconds, then out of the net-draped window at the Saturday afternoon traffic as it moved smoothly along Whitehall.

Finally, the black-ringed eyes swung back across the table. 'Maurice was a poor sad little bugger, who was out of his depth in just about every way. Over the last few weeks I watched him come apart.'

'Hold on a minute, Joseph,' said Arrow. 'He was put forward for the job by Sir Stewart. He's not a guy to make mistakes.'

'He made one this time.' Webber paused. 'Maurice coped okay at first, but Davey's behaviour and his attitude began to get to him after a while. Then outside factors began to have an effect.'

'Such as?' asked McIlhenney, intrigued.

'Such as he reckoned that someone was 'aving it off with his wife.'

'Did he tell you that?' asked Donaldson quickly.

Webber nodded. 'One night we were working late, as usual. Shana 'ad gone off to meet her mystery bloke . . .'

The DCI's eyes narrowed. 'Who's he?'

'Like I said, that's a mystery.'

'Now look, Mr Webber, withholding information—'

'Leave it,' said Arrow quietly. Donaldson turned and stared at him.

'Go on Joseph,' said the soldier. 'You were working late, you said.'

'Right. It was gone half-nine when we left, so I headed straight for the Red Lion. I asked Maurice if he wanted to come along and 'e did. I'd never seen him drink before, but Christ, 'e made up for it that night. I was banging the pints away to make up for the two hours or so I'd lost, and 'e kept pace with me. Not on beer, but on large gin and tonics.

'Eventually we slowed up, and he began to talk. He told me that the job was getting him down, not because Davey was such a bastard – he said that he could 'andle that all right – but because it was keeping him away from home for too long. He said that no Secretary of State 'e'd ever heard of worked his staff so 'ard, and he was right.

'He was half-pissed by this time, so he told me that he'd always had trouble keeping Ariadne happy. Now the hours he was working were making it bloody near impossible, and he blamed Davey for it personally.

'He said that he was sure she'd got bored wiv 'im, and that someone else was in there doing the business. I said to him, "What are you doing sitting 'ere getting pissed with me then? Get on home and fight for her." But he said that he was past all that: he said that he loved her but that she was too much woman for him, and she knew it. Poor little bugger. He was so sad he put me off my beer, so I slung him into a taxi and headed off home.'

'When did all this happen?' asked Donaldson.

'About three weeks ago.'

'Didn't you think to suggest that he get medical help?' said Arrow, frowning.

'As a matter of fact I did tell 'im that, but short of twisting his arm up his back I couldn't force him, could I?'

'Didn't you think to talk to me?'

'Yeah. I thought about it, and I decided against it. I reckoned that you might have decided he was a security risk and had him removed from the job. The guy was near enough suicidal as it was, without that. And anyway, where I come from, you don't grass. *Omerta*, the Sicilians call it – the vow of silence. Down the East End we don't need vows; it's in the blood.'

'D'you realise that makes *you* a security risk, Joseph?' said the soldier.

Webber smiled, widely enough to reveal the full extent of his dental catastrophe. 'Frankly, my dear Adam, I don't *give* a damn! I made a decision this morning. I hauled my ragged arse out of bed, I stared in the mirror at the wreck of my face, and I said to myself, "Joseph Webber, you've given the beehive twenty years of your life. It ain't getting any more." So I sat down, and with a shaky 'and, I wrote out my resignation. On the way in here, I posted it. I'm going to get a life, mate, before it's too late.'

Arrow leaned back in his chair and smiled. 'Well, good for you, Joseph. There's hope for you yet.'

'Before you go, Mr Webber,' said Donaldson heavily, 'will you tell us about Thursday evening, and about the preparations for the trip to Scotland. Who packed the Red Box?'

'Shana did, as usual. I got the material together . . . there wasn't much, Adam, mostly correspondence, one procurement decision and one Intelligence paper on the Middle East . . . and she boxed it.'

'Did you see her do that?'

Webber looked at the policeman sharply and shrewdly, but made no comment on his question. Instead he nodded, emphatically.

'After that, what happened to the Box?'

'Shana gave it to Maurice and we all went 'ome. Well, the other two did. I went to the Red Lion.'

'Right,' said Donaldson. He pointed at the black tape recorder on the table. 'When this is transcribed, I'll ask you to look at it, and if you're happy that that's all you can tell us, you can sign it as such. For now, thank you for coming in.'

Webber was almost at the door when Arrow called out to him. 'What are you going to do, Joseph, outside the beehive?'

'My old man wants to retire, so I'm going to run his business.'

'What's that?'

'A pub.'

34

'Hello. Is that Cyril Kercheval?'

'Who's calling?' There was a slight distortion on the line, but it could not disguise the suspicious tone in the voice.

'This is Detective Chief Inspector Brian Mackie. I'm calling from Edinburgh.'

'Who gave you my mobile number?'

'So that *is* Mr Kercheval?'

'Yes, yes. But I repeat, who gave you this number?'

'My boss, Bob Skinner.'

'Ah! Our resident in the North. In that case I'd better speak to you; his star burns brightly in our heavens these days. What can I do for you?' The distortion had cleared, and Kercheval's tone with it. Now he sounded bright and breezy.

'My colleague and I would like to meet with you, Mr Skinner has asked us to undertake an investigation, and he's given us your name as someone who might help.'

'How urgent is this?'

'Extremely.'

'D'you mean over the weekend? I've got a winter foursomes tie tomorrow morning at Sandwich, but I could come up to Town after that, at around three. I have to say, though, I'd prefer Monday.'

Mackie thought back to Skinner's orders, to the stress he had laid on discretion and to his comment about the porosity of MI5. He guessed that if a senior man was summoned for an emergency meeting with two policemen from the North, that might attract the sort of attention that the DCC was keen to avoid.

'Okay, sir,' he said. 'Monday it is, unless Mr Skinner feels particularly strongly that it should be earlier. If he does, I'll call you back on this number.'

'Fine.' Kercheval paused. 'You'll be flying down, so let's meet at eleven a.m. My office – or would you prefer neutral territory?'

'In the circumstances, I think we would.'

'Right, in that case let's make it a working lunch. You like Chinese? There's a place called Mr Kong in one of the streets up behind Leicester Square. Lisle Street, or Gerrard Street, I can never remember which. I'll see you there at twelve-thirty.'

'Very good, sir, we'll be there on time.'

The MI5 man grunted. 'I'm sure you will. Between now and Monday I'll try to imagine what you want to talk about. Mind you, even now I have a suspicion!'

35

Sir Stewart Morelli preferred neutral territory also. He had left a message for Arrow that he would receive the Scottish gentlemen at his club, at 4 p.m.

They arrived promptly at St Stephens, which was tucked away behind Birdcage Walk, not far from Parliament Square and the Palace and Abbey of Westminster. Arrow announced their appointment to a soberly-dressed attendant, who nodded and said, 'Yes, gentlemen, you are expected. Please follow me.'

He led the three men – DS Price having been stood down – through to a smoking room, the walls of which were hung with portraits of former members, with a few Prime Ministers, one of recent memory, among them. McIlhenney, scanning them with the expert eye which few of his colleagues knew he possessed, nodded his appreciation of the better works.

As they entered, the Permanent Secretary at the Ministry of Defence rose from a high-winged leather chair beside a window which looked out to the rear of the club. He was a strikingly handsome man of medium height and build, with a square jaw and a full head of greying hair, immaculately groomed and swept back from a wide forehead. Even on a Saturday afternoon, he was dressed in a formal dark three-piece suit, and wore highly polished black shoes.

Had Arrow not told them that he was in his early fifties, both Donaldson and McIlhenney would have placed him at around forty-five.

'Captain,' he said heartily. 'Bang on time as always.'

As the soldier introduced his companions, a faint shadow of petulance crossed the Permanent Secretary's face. It was lost on the brash young DCI, but McIlhenney knew at once that Morelli had expected to be meeting with an Assistant Chief Constable, at the very least.

'Thank you for seeing us, Sir Stewart,' said the soldier.

'Not at all, man. Least I could do in the circs. Have you finished your interviews with the Private Office people?' He looked at Donaldson, ignoring McIlhenney completely.

'Yes, sir,' said the DCI. 'Thank you for your co-operation in arranging them so quickly.'

Morelli flicked the fingers of his right hand in a deprecating manner. 'Were they of any value?'

'Certainly, sir. Exactly how valuable remains to be seen, but they were interesting.'

'Mmm.' He turned his gaze to Arrow. 'I'd have appreciated it if you'd come clean with me about the cause of Davey's death, Captain. If someone blows up my Secretary of State, I expect to be told about it, rather than to hear the news from a police statement on lunchtime television.'

'My apologies, Sir Stewart, but it was only this morning that we got confirmation from the Bomb Squad. I did try to contact you before we left Edinburgh, but you were unavailable.'

'Very well. You can update me now, though.'

Donaldson felt a sudden need to assert himself. 'In confidence, sir, I can tell you that the bomb was concealed in the Minister's hand-baggage. That's how it got on board.'

'Good heavens!' said the Permanent Secretary. 'You mean in the Red Box?'

'Exactly, sir.'

'No wonder you wanted to interview his staff. What did you get out of them?'

'We found out that the Assistant Private Secretary packed the Box, then gave it to Mr Noble, and he took it home with him. All this was seen by Mr Joseph Webber.'

The Permanent Secretary gave Arrow a strange angled nod. 'If Webber confirmed it, you can accept that as gospel. Don't know how he does it with his lifestyle, but I have no more reliable man in the Ministry. So . . . if Mirzana gave it to Noble, and it blew up on the plane, then someone must have had access to it at the airport.'

'Not necessarily,' said Donaldson.

'But surely . . .'

'The bomb could have been placed in the box while it was at Mr Noble's house, sir.'

Morelli sat bolt upright in his chair. 'Are you suggesting that Mr Noble planted it himself, or his wife? Are you mad?' He hissed the words quietly, lest he wake the sleepers around them. Red-faced, he glared from Donaldson to Arrow and back again. McIlhenney, glad that he was only a humble Detective Sergeant and, therefore, of no consequence to Morelli, sank back in his leather armchair.

Donaldson stood, or at least sat, his ground. He returned the man's gaze and shook his head. 'No, sir. I'm not making suggestions. I'm looking at possibilities.'

'That isn't one!' the Permanent Secretary snapped.

'Yes, it is, sir, but not one I'll dwell on. I'd rather look at Mr Noble himself. The picture which we're getting is one of a man with an episode of depressive illness behind him, showing clear signs that the problem was recurring. Noble confided in Webber that the excessive hours involved in his job were getting him down, that he felt inadequate to his wife's demands, and that he was sure she was seeking consolation somewhere else. He also said that he blamed Mr Davey directly for the situation.

'Sticking strictly to possibilities, we must consider whether Noble might have been unbalanced sufficiently to smuggle the bomb on board the plane, where he knew he would take Mr Davey with him.'

Morelli's face had gone from red to white. He stood up, shaking his head violently, and stared out of the window. 'No! Absolutely not,' he blustered. 'I knew Maurice. I put him in post. He was a bloody good chap, with the potential to sit in my chair one day. The idea of him doing something like that, why – it's preposterous.'

He looked round. 'Captain, you knew him too. Tell Mr Donaldson, will you?'

Arrow frowned. 'Tell him what, sir? I heard Webber's story, and I believed it. You're just after saying how reliable he is. He told us that Maurice got drunk with him the night all this came out. Hepatitis, alcohol and depression are all directly related. No, sir, I won't rule out the possibility of suicide.'

The Permanent Secretary shook his head as firmly as before. 'But not in that way, surely. Not taking all those lives along with his own.'

'Maybe he meant to trigger the bomb later, when he and Davey were alone. Maybe the Minister opened the box himself and set it off. Who knows? But on the basis of what we've heard today, it's the most solid lead we have.

'The next thing we have to find out is whether Maurice had the ability to construct a device, or whether he'd been shooting his mouth off in the wrong company, to someone who might have supplied one.'

'So what's your next step?'

'We have to speak to Maurice's wife.'

Sir Stewart shook his head violently. 'Oh no. You can't land on the poor woman at a time like this. I forbid it, d'you hear?'

'You can forbid Captain Arrow, sir,' boomed Neil McIlhenney, from the depths of his chair. Suddenly, he was very visible indeed. 'But you can't forbid us. We're Scottish Police Officers investigating a serious crime, and we will not allow *anyone* to impede our enquiries. So unless we're told otherwise by our Commanders . . . they are Chief Constable Proud, DCC Skinner or Chief Superintendent Martin, if you want to ring any of them . . . we will be calling on Mrs Noble tomorrow morning.'

He glanced sideways at Donaldson. 'That right, sir?'

The DCI nodded gratefully. 'It is indeed, Sergeant. If the lady spent the night under the same roof as that Red Box, we have to interview her.'

Morelli stared down at Arrow, who sat in his chair, his feet not touching the ground. 'Go ahead then. Do what you must. But for Christ's sake, Adam, make sure that these people are discreet!'

36

Andy and Alex were at the restaurant before them, befitting their situation as hosts for the evening. There are several Pierre Victoire restaurants in Edinburgh, but Alex had voted for the version in Dock Place, which she claimed was the biggest, best and noisiest of them all.

'Sorry we're late. Blame the taxi this time, not the baby,' said Bob, hanging Sarah's overcoat, and his own, on a peg on one of the restaurant's many pillars. It was 8.30 p.m. and in every corner, dinner parties were in full swing.

'You're not,' said Andy. 'They've only just brought the drinks. Here, get outside these.'

He filled Sarah's glass, then Bob's, with the house champagne. 'Cheers,' he said, clinking glasses around the table. 'Look, everybody. This evening was planned as a celebration, and despite everything that's happened over the last thirty-six hours or so, let's try to keep that in mind.'

'For tonight, Chief Superintendent, you're the boss,' said Bob, taking a long sip of the champagne. 'In that case, I warn you, I may just get pissed.'

Alex was staring across the table at Andy. '*Chief* Superintendent?'

He smiled. 'Sorry – didn't I mention it? It's only a courtesy title these days, you know, just like your dad's. The review abolished the Deputy Chief and Chief Super ranks, but most Forces kept the titles because in practice officers need to know which Superintendent is the boss, and which ACC is the Chief's Deputy. Anyway, enough of the shop talk; that's not what we're here to celebrate.' He turned to Sarah, sitting beside him. 'How're you doing?'

'I'm fine,' she said quietly. 'I got it all out of my system last night. But I tell you something – I couldn't take another day like it. No one should have to experience that twice in a lifetime.'

'And how's wee Jazz?'

'He's fine too. We left him holding the floor with his Aussie nanny. She's staying over tonight.'

'That's a great arrangement you have: the girl being a qualified children's nurse, but having her own place, and living in only when you need her.'

Sarah nodded. 'It's ideal. Jazz is looked after, she keeps the place tidy, and does the prep work on our meals, and on top of that, most evenings we have the house to ourselves. Susan Kinture was very good about it when I told her I'd like to lure Tracey away from her. She said, "Fine. Bracklands is so bloody big, I can never find all the staff I have in here anyway!" She's a great lady, the Marchioness.'

Abruptly she sat up straight in her chair. 'But enough of our shop talk, too! Celebration, you said. A celebration of what?'

As if on cue, Alex brought up her left hand, which had been hanging just below the level of the table. The diamonds caught the candle-flame, and sparkled, yellowish, in the gloom. The sapphires, at the heart of the design, shone midnight blue.

'Hey,' said Bob. 'Another surprise.'

'One you can live with, I hope,' said Andy.

'Hell, man, we've been through all that. I couldn't be more pleased.' Alex's eyes were shining as he kissed her, reaching out to shake Andy's hand at the same time. Sarah beamed and hugged them both, then grabbed Alex's left wrist.

'Let's have a look at it, kid.' She held Alex's hand under the candle, peering at the ring. 'Why, it's beautiful. It looks unique.'

'It should be. Hand-crafted by Laing the Jeweller. Designed by Michael himself.'

Bob whistled. 'Jesus. Whose idea was that?'

His daughter jerked a thumb at her fiancé. 'His, believe it or not. I'd have settled for H. Samuel.'

'Hah,' Bob grunted. 'Why change the habits of a lifetime?' He refilled all four glasses. 'Time for a toast. Let's be traditional for once. The happy couple!' His wife echoed his words, and together they drained their glasses.

'Good stuff that,' said Sarah. She poured two more refills, adding, 'Let's have another toast. One we can all drink this time. To Michael Laing!'

Another bottle of champagne later, they were ready to do justice to Pierre Victoire's menu, with starters which included warm brioche with mushroom sauce, creamed scallops with smoked salmon, and melon with crispy bacon, and main courses which ranged from baked monkfish to venison casserole. The clamour of the evening roared around them but they did not notice, because they were part of it.

The men chose cold beers as dessert, leaving their ladies to tackle the sticky toffee pudding.

'Here, friend,' said Bob, taking a swig of his Budweiser straight from the bottle. 'D'you realise wee Jazz is going to be your brother-in-law?' Andy choked on his beer, and Alex spluttered on her sticky toffee.

As the laughter subsided, Sarah looked across at her step-daughter. 'My God, I forgot to ask. Have you set a date yet?'

121

'Give us notice of that one, for Christ's sake,' said Bob sincerely.

'Relax, Pops. We're in no hurry, are we Andy?' He smiled and shook his head in agreement, perhaps not entirely sincerely. 'We just thought we should put a label on it; mark out the territory, so to speak. I want to get my studying over with before getting married. I've still got to finish my diploma year at University, then put in my two years in a solicitor's office, before I can think about going to the Bar.'

'That's all up to you, Babe, but do one thing for me.'

'Name it, Father.'

'Don't make any formal announcement for a few weeks, and keep the ring out of sight.'

'Why?' Her face clouded over.

'Because if Andy's appointment as Head of CID, and his engagement to my daughter were announced in virtually the same breath, the comedians in the Press would have a field day. I've already filled in one bloke today for taking your man's name in vain, and I don't want it to become routine procedure.'

She gulped. 'Sorry, Pops. I never thought. Our timing's lousy.'

'Not your timing, love – God's. Or rather, someone else's!'

37

Arrow waited until the stairway light, on a push-button time-switch, flicked out before turning the brass handle.

As he had suspected, the door was unlocked. He pushed at it very gently, until a little light spilled out, not from any source in the narrow hallway but from deeper within the apartment. Opening it to the minimum to avoid the creaking of the hinge which he knew would have come at a certain point, he slipped soundlessly inside.

Three doors opened off the hall, all panelled with frosted glass. The one on his left shone with a soft pink light, against which he could make out the shape of a dressing gown hanging on a hook. Holding his breath and moving with ghost-like silence on the balls of his feet, he crept past it to the door facing him, opened it and slipped inside.

The room was warm. The imitation coals in the gas fire still glowed, telling him that it had been switched off for only a few minutes, and the television screen still shone with a blue-grey luminescence. As his eyes became accustomed to the darker surroundings he could make out the shape of the furniture – a two-seater settee, an armchair, a sideboard, and in the heavily curtained bay window, a small round table.

He dropped into a crouch behind the sofa and waited, ready to spring into action at any moment.

The minutes dragged out. He shifted his position occasionally to ease the weight on his joints. *The side-effects of an office job*, he mused. *I never used to feel stiff, lying in ambush for people in the dark.*

At last he heard the sound of someone moving. The pink-lit door off the hallway swung open, and suddenly, the rest of the apartment was brighter. Instinctively, he dropped deeper into his place of concealment, ready to react at any moment to discovery, but instead, he heard the sound of the third door opening, then closing quickly, and saw the effect of a second light being switched on.

Seizing his chance, he sprang to his feet and, like a nervous cat, moved back out into the hallway. He saw at once that the dressing gown was still hanging behind the door.

When she returned, he was already in bed. She jumped when she saw him, with a small involuntary gasp, her pert breasts bouncing in a particularly intriguing fashion.

'Adam, you swine! You're always playing games! How long have you been here?'

'About ten minutes. And I'm always telling you about leaving that bloody door on the chain. One night it might not be me who comes through it.' He took a corner of the quilt, lifted it up, and Shana Mirzana slipped into bed beside him.

'You're warm,' she said, rubbing herself against his body, feeling his arousal. She touched the light stubble around his chin, and kissed him, sniffing quickly at his breath as she did so. 'Been drinking?'

'Watch it. Even breathing it in is against your religion, ain't it? I had a quick meal and a beer with the Scots lads in the Sherlock Holmes, that's all,' he said. 'I made my excuses as soon as I could. They're staying in the Strand Palace, but they were off in search of t' nightlife when I left.'

'They'll be lucky.'

'Ah, but they'll have help. They were meeting up with that lad from the Met in some pub up Wardour Street.'

'Did you tell them where you were going?'

'Bloody 'ell no. What's the use of being a spook if you can't keep secrets?'

'Does *anyone* know about you and me, Adam?'

'Not as far as I know, but it's an interesting question. Who spies on the spies? I'm in the business and I don't know. Imagine though, if there's no one checking up on me, the power I'd 'ave. There was no one checking up on George Blake, and look what he did.'

She propped herself on an elbow and looked down at him. 'But you must have a boss.'

'Sure, I have. John Swift, my sidekick, and I report to the Permanent Secretary. We're on secondment from the Army.'

She laughed. 'Swift and Arrow! Quite a combination!'

He forebore to tell her that those were not the names on their birth certificates, a security measure designed to protect their families rather than them. Instead he chortled, 'We get straight to the point, though,' and dived beneath the quilt.

Her gasps turned into squeals as his searching tongue sought her out, until at last she took him, urgently, under the arms and drew him up, on top of her, plunging him into her . . . not like an arrow, she thought idly, but like a lance – writhing and moaning, bucking urgently against him as he thrust, and thrust, and . . .

They came together in a great roaring climax, their muscles tensed almost to the point of cramp, until at last they relaxed and slumped, replete, into each other's arms.

'To the point you do indeed get,' she murmured ungrammatically, sliding out from beneath him. She pulled herself up into a sitting position and gazed at him as he lay there, face down and smiling. She ran her hand over his skin. It was almost as brown as hers. She tugged his hair.

'Hey,' she said. 'Do you realise how vulnerable you men are? However tough, however strong, however highly trained, there are always moments when man is completely at the mercy of woman.'

He rolled over and smiled up at her. 'The thought does occur to me from time to time, but always too late. Fortunately there are damn few women in my line of work.' A small cloud seemed to cross his smile. 'Mind you, I've got a mate who took up with a wrong 'un once.'

'What happened when he found out?'

The cloud thickened. 'Let's just say it put an end to their relationship.'

'What a shame.'

'Aye, it were indeed. Still, it all worked out in the end; for him at any rate.'

She leaned down and kissed him again. 'Would you like another drink? I may not take it, but I do keep it. There's some white wine. I'll have a Pepsi.'

'Aye, that'd be nice. I'll get it. In t' fridge, is it?'

When he returned a few minutes later with the bottle, in a cooler, a Pepsi and two glasses, she was leaning against the headboard smoking a cigarette. 'Want one?'

'You know I don't, apart from the odd cigar. What the 'ell are those things anyway? They smell pretty strong.'

'They are. They're Turkish. I buy them from time to time. I got to like them when I was a student. I don't smoke for effect, boy. I smoke for . . . nicotine!' She laughed at his frown.

He poured his wine and her Pepsi, then slipped back into bed beside her. She offered him the cigarette. He took an experimental puff, and felt his head swim as he inhaled. Quickly, he handed it back to her. 'Bloody hell! I'll stick to cigars.'

She sipped her Cola. 'So how are your interviews going?'

'Well enough, but we're not finished yet. We're going to see Ariadne Noble tomorrow.'

'Ariadne Tucker QC, you mean,' said Shana. 'Remember; she's particular about that.'

'Do you know anything else about her, other than what you told us?'

'Like what?'

'Like whether she 'as a bit on the side.'

She shrugged her shoulders, doing fetching things with her breasts once more. Adam leaned over and nuzzled them with his forehead. She laughed. 'Down boy. Time enough. You are staying, aren't you?'

'Yeah, why not. I've got nowt better to do.'

'Bugger.' She dug him in the ribs with an elbow.

125

Sipping more Pepsi, she leaned against him again. 'It was a bomb that caused the crash, then,' she said, suddenly serious. 'I saw that Scottish policeman on the news. What was his name again?'

'Bob Skinner.'

She grinned again, briefly. 'He looks quite dishy.'

'His wife thinks so.'

She took a curl of his chest hair and wrapped it round her index finger, tugging gently. 'Adam?'

'Mmm.'

'You made a big deal of asking about the Red Box. That doesn't mean that you think the bomb might have been hidden in it, does it?'

'No. It means we *know* that it was hidden there.' Her wrist lay against him, and he felt the pulse at the base of her thumb quicken.

'Joseph did confirm what I told you, about how the box was packed, didn't he?'

He smiled. 'Of course he did. You can relax on that score.'

She sighed with relief. 'Thank you, Allah, for that. What a nightmare.'

'Of course,' said Arrow, 'we can't account precisely for the box *before* it was packed. Suppose the device was already in there? Suppose you'd put it in earlier? Would Webber have known that?'

She sat up straight. 'He was standing beside me when I packed it. He'd have seen it!'

She glared at him, not smiling now, not teasing. 'Are you serious?'

He stared back at her, poker-faced. They sat there for several silent seconds, like naked brown statues.

'No,' he said at last, a huge smile creasing his broad features.

'Adam, you little bastard!' she said, grinning in spite of herself. She grabbed a handful of chest hair and tugged as hard as she could.

126

38

Skinner dozed, and dreamed of mud.

They had returned from the restaurant just after midnight, their taxi having first dropped Andy and Alex at the West End. Having checked that Jazz was sound asleep, Sarah had gone straight to bed, but Skinner had remained downstairs, padding around barefoot, sucking idly on yet another bottle of beer.

Finally he settled down on the settee to replay a video tape of the evening's televised football. Motherwell had been his boyhood team, and thus had retained his lifelong adherence, yet he watched their resounding victory over Rangers with a strange apathy.

He had lived up to his earlier announcement by consuming a substantial quantity of alcohol, yet he could feel no effect, not the slightest trace of exhilaration, not the slightest fuzzing of his thought process. What he felt instead was restlessness, an almost over-whelming urge towards physical activity, and driving wakefulness.

The tape had run out, to be replaced by yet another screening of *The Devil Rides Out*, when Sarah appeared in the doorway, wrapped in her white towelling robe.

'Bob, it's gone one-thirty. I'd like to sleep, but I can't knowing that as soon as I've dropped off you're liable to come up and plant your big feet in my back! Come to bed, please.'

He sighed, deeply. 'I just don't feel sleepy, but to please you, okay.'

He had lain there beside her in the dark, listening as her breathing slowed and smiling at her occasional soft snores, but resolutely awake himself. Finally he had switched on his reading light and picked up his bedside novel, a piece of Terry Pratchett fantasy which he was reading for the second time.

He had enjoyed perfect sight all his life, but he was reaching that point in early middle age where tiredness at the end of a long day was beginning to take its toll of his eyes. Gradually, the script became fuzzy; gradually he had held the pages further away, to try to retain focus; eventually the book had slipped from his fingers.

Skinner dozed, and dreamed of mud.

He was back in the field, staring across its flat grey acres, standing in his muddy-trousered uniform amid the jetsam of the crash. The unclothed, disjointed doll was at his feet. Unthinking, he bent and seized it by an arm, to pick it up. It hung awkwardly in his grasp, the limbs flopping unnaturally, the head lolling backwards.

It was quite a large doll, and strange in the way it was put together. Probably very expensive, he thought, remembering the model which he had bought for a friend's new-born daughter. The ball-sockets joining limbs and head to the trunk were remarkably lifelike, with no sign of the rubber bands which showed when most of the cheaper types were twisted to this extent. The touch of it, too. In his hand it didn't feel like plastic, as had his purchase. This one felt almost . . .

He dropped it, with a shriek of horror . . .

. . . and woke in the same instant, his lips still drawn back in the shape of his dream-scream.

This time Sarah woke with him. 'Bob, honey! What is it?' She took him in her arms.

'It's okay,' he mumbled. 'I'm sorry.'

'What was it? What were you dreaming about?'

He shook his head. 'Nothing. It was nothing.'

'It was hardly nothing, man. You're in a lather.' It was true, he realised, conscious of the cold sweat on his body.

'It was just a bad dream love. You remember, I had them for a while after that business a couple of years back, when I got shot.'

'Sure I remember. But you didn't wake up screaming then.'

'No? Well, maybe it's only now that the full impact's coming home to me. Don't worry about it, it's just a one-off. The cold sweat's probably just the booze working its way out. Now go on, get back to sleep. I'm fine now.'

To convince her, he switched off his reading lamp. In the dim green light of the radio-alarm's LCD clock, he saw her looking up at him doubtfully, but he forced a smile and pulled her to him.

It look longer than before but gradually she settled to sleep in the crook of his arm. He kissed her hair, and pulled the quilt up over her bare shoulder. He stared up at the ceiling, half-afraid of what he would see; but all that was there was magnolia emulsion, reflecting a faint green tinge from the alarm.

As he lay there wide awake, a part of his mind knew that it was not so much that he was unable to sleep, but that he dared not.

39

The home which Maurice Noble had made with Ariadne Tucker was part of a brick terrace in a narrow street which could boast by about 200 yards to be part of Putney rather than Wandsworth.

'What's the difference?' growled McIlhenney, his head throbbing as a result of the disastrous liking which he had taken to Young's Black Horse ale, after he and Donaldson had taken their leave of Adam Arrow.

'About fifty grand, in a good market,' their soldier companion informed him. He was walking between them, amiable and bright-eyed, as they covered the short distance from their Government pool vehicle to the Noble front door. He had to reach up to ring the bell.

The woman who opened the door was statuesque, with wide shoulders and long legs – a perfect match to Shana Mirzana's description. Her dyed blonde hair was neatly cut; McIlhenney could imagine it crowned by a barrister's wig. There was only one thing wrong: she was at least fifty-five years old.

'Ms Tucker?' Arrow ventured tentatively.

The Amazon fixed him with a glare borrowed from Edith Evans's Lady Bracknell. 'Mrs Tucker, actually, young man,' she boomed. 'I assume that you are the gentlemen who wish to see my daughter. You may come in.'

She led them through a tiled porch into a narrow hall, with rug-strewn, sanded floors. On the left rose a staircase with natural pine balustrades which matched the four doors leading to various rooms. Mrs Tucker opened the first and marched through, with the three callers trailing in her wake like a line of cygnets.

'Ariadne, my dear,' she announced. 'These are the people you were expecting. Gentlemen, you are . . .?'

Arrow stepped up as she waved him forward and introduced himself, and the two policemen. Maurice Noble's widow rose from her chair and shook each man formally by the hand. She was a younger, even more imposing version of the older woman. Where Tucker Mère's jowls and turkey neck betrayed her age, the daughter's skin was sleek, taut and unwrinkled. Her hazel eyes were even more commanding than her mother's, set off by long lashes and heavy blonde brows. Perhaps, McIlhenney surmised, as a concession to widowhood she was dressed in a simple black T-shirt and leggings. Barefoot, she still towered over Arrow, and looked up only slightly at Donaldson and his Sergeant.

'Sit down, please, gentlemen,' she said, pointing to a three-seater Chesterfield and a captain's chair, both in unusual blue leather. 'Mother, make yourself scarce and do the coffee thing, there's a dear.' Donaldson tried to imagine the response if Mr Tucker, were one still in residence, had issued such a peremptory command to the matriarch, yet she simply nodded and left the long drawing-cum-dining room by a door in its furthest wall.

As soon as she had gone, her bereaved daughter looked across at the soldier, who had chosen, appropriately, the captain's chair. 'So you're Adam Arrow,' she said. 'My husband talked about you. "Chilling efficiency, masked by a veneer of gauche Derbyshire charm." That was his description. Was it fair, do you think?'

Arrow smiled at her, deliberately giving her full voltage. 'Time will tell, Ms Tucker.'

'Maurice did say that you had been something frightful in the Army before you moved to Security. Is that why you're on this investigation? Have they set one to catch one?'

'This isn't my investigation. It's a police matter; my role here is liaison.'

'Ho hum,' said Ariadne, unconvinced.

Arrow ignored her scepticism. 'Look, Ms Tucker, you have our deepest sympathy, and we are really sorry to have to impose upon you so soon after the tragedy, but you will appreciate, I hope, that it is necessary.'

She waved a hand. 'That's okay. I understand.'

'You'll be aware by now that the crash in which your husband was killed was the result of an explosion.'

She nodded, grim-faced. 'Someone got that swine Davey at last. What a pity he had to take poor Maurice with him, and all those other people.'

'That sounds as if you disapproved pretty strongly of our late Secretary of State.'

'The man was an absolute shit. Don't you agree with me, Captain?'

Arrow shrugged. 'I don't have a view. My reporting chain leads to the Permanent Secretary's door, not to his. All I'd say is that Ministers are like soldiers, in that they don't have to be nice, just effective.'

'And are *you* nice, Adam?' she said, in a voice not entirely becoming in a widow.

'Who knows?' he retorted, his eyes suddenly hard behind the smile. 'But I'm bloody effective.'

I'll bet, thought Dave Donaldson, a spectator at the sparring match. He decided that it was time for him to assert his presence.

'How did your husband seem when he left on Friday morning, Mrs Noble?' he asked.

She flashed him a look when he used her marital title, but let it pass. 'I couldn't tell you. I didn't see him. He had an early start. He called "Goodbye," then I heard the taxi leave. My door was closed so I couldn't describe his tone of voice.'

'You mean you were still asleep when he got up?'

'No, Superintendent, I mean we have, sorry *had*, separate rooms.' Suddenly a large marmalade cat sprang up and over the back of her chair, to land in her lap. 'Not now, Tigger,' she said without annoyance, tossing the animal gently down on to the pale blue carpet. Simultaneously, Shana Mirzana's A. A. Milne analogy sprang into the mind of each of the three men, but none felt the slightest like smiling.

'Separate rooms,' said Donaldson. 'Forgive me, but does that mean that you and your husband were having problems with your marriage?'

'And did I pop a couple of dynamite sandwiches into his little lunchbox, were you about to ask?' Her voice was heavy with sarcasm. 'No, Chief Inspector, you may not draw either of those conclusions.'

'Maurice worked silly hours in Private Office, thanks to the appalling Davey. Sometimes, in my profession, I burn midnight oil too, preparing for consultations, and for court. For example on Thursday evening, I was preparing my closing speech to the jury in a major fraud trial in which I am appearing for the defence.

'Each of us needed our sleep. So if one of us was working late, rather than disturb the other, we did the sensible thing.'

'How many nights a week were you that sensible?'

'Most of them,' she said curtly. She turned to Arrow. 'If we were in court, and I was in the witness box, my Counsel would be objecting to this chap's line of questioning . . . Your Honour.'

'I think,' said the soldier, 'that my colleague is doing his best to establish Maurice's state of mind, and being as delicate about it as he can. Me, I'm just a gauche Derbyshire lad, so I'll come straight out with it. Were you playing all your games at home, Ms Tucker, or were some of them away fixtures?'

The woman sat bolt upright in her chair, a flush springing to her cheeks. Her mouth formed a reply, but just at that moment the door at the far end of the room creaked open, as Mère Tucker reappeared with a large tray laden with cafétière and cups.

Her daughter jumped to her feet and went to meet her. 'Thank you, Mother, I'll take these. Leave us, please.'

The older woman looked doubtful, but Ariadne grabbed the tray and shoo-ed her back through the door from which she had emerged. As it closed, she laid the tray on the reproduction mahogany dining table and stormed back to confront Arrow.

'What the hell right have you got to ask such a question?'

'All the right I need. I'll ask you again. Were you being unfaithful to Maurice?'

'You can't jump to that conclusion simply because of our civilised sleeping arrangements.'

'It's not *our* conclusion, and that isn't the only reason for the question. We have information that Maurice thought you were seeing someone else.'

She stood glaring down at Arrow, her hands on her hips. 'Where did you get that from? Not the Mirzana girl. Maurice was basically frightened of women; he'd never have confided in her. It could only have come from Joseph Webber, the office sponge. You accuse me on the basis of his gossip?'

'No one's accusing, Ms Tucker,' said Neil McIlhenney, his head pounding with the tension and the fading effects of the ale. 'We're simply asking.'

The big bluff Scot seemed to mollify her. 'Look,' she said. 'Maurice had a history of clinical depression. The job put pressures on him that he didn't anticipate when he took it, and that so-and-so Davey was responsible for them. He didn't care a scrap about his staff; he didn't allow for one second that they might have demands on their time other than his. He was a thoroughly selfish bastard and he was doing Maurice's head in.

'The trouble was that my poor husband wouldn't admit it, and the result was that his depression was coming back, with a touch of paranoia thrown in. I tried to put my foot down and make him ask for a transfer back to Division, but he wouldn't have it. That's the full story about Maurice.'

She slumped back into her chair. The cat jumped up in her lap again. This time she allowed it to remain.

'So when did you see your husband last?' asked Donaldson.

'Very briefly, late on Thursday evening. I was working in my study, when I heard him come in just after ten. He pottered about for a while downstairs. I'd left him some supper and some orange juice.'

'He didn't drink alcohol?'

'Never.'

'Not at all?'

'Emphatically not! Anyway, once he had finished his supper and whatever else he was doing, he came upstairs. He looked in to say that he was off to Scotland next morning and that he was going to turn in. I said okay, I kissed him good night, he went off, and that was the last time I ever saw him.' She steepled her hands and stared glumly at her thumbs. Arrow thought he might have detected the faintest trembling in her chin.

'You mentioned earlier that he left by taxi,' he said. 'Where was he heading? Not to the airport, surely.'

'No, he was going to Dolphin Square, where the Secretary of State has a flat. A pool car was collecting them from there.'

'I see.'

He looked across at Donaldson, and gave the faintest nod toward the door. The policeman took his cue. 'Fine, er, Ms Tucker. We won't put you through any more. Come on, gentlemen.' The three men stood up. She made to follow them but Arrow motioned her to stay seated. 'It's okay. Don't disturb the cat, we'll see ourselves out. We'll let you know when there's something to report.'

'Thank you,' she murmured. 'But don't hurry back.'

The policemen and the soldier filed back out into the street. No one spoke until they had almost reached their pool car, where the grey-uniformed driver sat waiting patiently.

'What did you think of her then?' asked Neil McIlhenney finally.

'A big Momma for Baby Roo,' said Donaldson. 'Too big for most guys, I'd say.'

'That was some line about dynamite and lunch boxes,' said McIlhenney. 'She can't know about the Red Box, can she?'

'Not unless she booby-trapped it,' muttered Adam Arrow grimly. 'But if she had, I doubt she'd have come out with a line like that. Still, we should close our minds to nothing.

'There was one thing that really stood out, though,' he said. 'She's a Queen's Counsel, and Queen's Counsel aren't supposed to lie, or so they say. But that lady never did give us a straight answer to the key question: Did she have someone on the side?

'I think we should take a longer look at Ms Ariadne Tucker.'

40

Fortified by the unforgettable experience of one of Sarah's American-style Sunday breakfasts, Skinner felt more or less human when he strode into the almost empty headquarters building at twenty-five minutes past noon.

He had welcomed the message that a delay on the trans-Atlantic flight meant that his American guest would not be catching the 11 a.m. shuttle. Still, he knew that his condition was fragile, and so, even before taking off his jacket he filled his coffee filter with the stronger of the two blends which he kept in his cupboard, topped up the water reservoir and set the machine to work.

The jug had only just filled when Merle Gower appeared in the doorway, her dark business suit contrasting with Skinner's denims and sweatshirt.

'Sir?' she said. 'The officer at the desk said we should come up. Mr Doherty is here.'

Skinner laughed. 'Jesus Christ, Joe,' he shouted. 'Are you so bloody important now that you have to be announced? Come on in.'

The Deputy Chair of the American National Security Council was still very new in post. While Doherty's sudden leap to stardom had surprised Skinner, and by reports, most of Washington, it had not astounded him. The policeman had held him in high regard during his spell as the FBI representative in the London Embassy, the Bureau's senior overseas posting, and had admired the powers of intellect, analysis and tenacity which had led his Director to nominate him for the crucial NSC post.

He strode into Skinner's office with hand outstretched in greeting. 'Hi there, Big Bob. I didn't expect that we'd meet again so soon. But trouble seems to attach itself to you like filings to a magnet, don't it.' He spoke with a soft mid-Western drawl which, added to his lack of height and slimness of build, made him a very unstereotypical law enforcer.

'Stop it, mate. The same thought's been occurring to me.' He poured three mugs of the strong coffee, added milk to his own, and stood back to allow Doherty and Gower to adjust theirs to their taste. As always Doherty took his black with half a spoon of sugar, barely stirred.

'So, wee man,' said Skinner, as they settled into the low chairs around his coffee table, 'how's the new job, then? I'm sorry I didn't have a chance to wish you luck before you went.'

The thin sallow face relaxed in a grin. 'No one did. One day I was in my hutch in the Square, and the next I was in DC. The job is daunting. I should think there's some comparison with your own role as Security Adviser in Scotland, but . . .'

The DCC nodded, and took a swig from his mug. 'Sure, multiplied by a factor of around two hundred, I should think. What ground do you cover?'

'Shit, you name it, the President's liable to throw it at us. Anything that can loosely be called a threat to America's security lands on our desks.'

'So how come you're involved in this thing? I can tell you now that your national security is not an issue here.'

Doherty grinned mischievously. 'Don't you believe it. Our Chief Executive takes the view that his re-election is a matter of national security. So he's ordered the NSC to conduct a high-profile international investigation of the murder of Secretary Massey. He's been on the hot line to your Prime Minister asking for his co-operation. So here I am.'

'Have you got a note from Teacher?'

'Believe it or not, I have.' Doherty delved into his briefcase and produced a white envelope, of about A4 size. He handed it across to Skinner, who opened it, full of curiosity, and drew out its contents. As he looked at it, Doherty and Gower saw his eyes widen.

The White House crest caught his attention at once. His eyes swept to the foot of the page and saw the clear signature of the President of the United States. Only then did he read the letter. It was short and succinct, advising the reader that Mr Doherty was on a personal mission from the White House, and *requiring*, not seeking co-operation with him.

The policeman handed it back, with a smile. 'Can I have a photocopy?' he asked. 'For my memoirs.'

The American smiled. 'Sure you can. Is that gorgeous, leggy secretary of yours about?'

'It's Sunday, Joe – remember? I can work a photocopier, though. Have you got anything else in that bag of any relevance to the investigation?'

Doherty nodded. 'Merle told you, I think, about the Iraqi network which the CIA tapped into. I have a report on it, and on the UK end.'

'Does it give any clue as to who Agent Robin is?'

'Nope, not even what gender. The file copy which came to us says only that he or she is a civil servant, and was recruited on campus as a student, by an Iraqi Intelligence Agent.'

'How old is the information?'

'Pretty fresh.'

'Merle said that Robin had been activated just recently.'

Doherty nodded. 'That's true. But there seems to be a pattern. They never have two agents running at once. The man we caught, Eagle, was active a couple of years back, Mouse in France last year, Hawk, in Germany four years ago. Robin was the last of the sleepers and the pattern indicates that he will have been activated by now; our analysts believe that the Iraqis will have been keeping him until he had reached the right level in your civil service before switching him on. Unless of course your people have stumbled upon the Robin's nest and eliminated him without telling anyone.'

'Come on, Joe, we wouldn't do that.'

The little American laughed. 'Bob. You can put your hand on your heart and tell me that? And I took you for an honest man.'

Skinner changed the subject. The banter was coming too close to home. 'What are you going to do with that file?'

'I'm going to feed it into the investigation. You're in charge, so that means it's all yours, for what it's worth.' He paused. 'So, what have you got? Merle filled me in on your briefing yesterday. Any developments since then?'

Quickly, Skinner described the bomb team's findings, and explained the direction in which his investigation was heading. 'These Red Boxes are pretty secure items. Yet somewhere along the line this one was booby-trapped. So the obvious conclusion is that this was an inside job, but possibly linked to an outside agency. This rogue Serbian General and Agent Robin both sound like likely candidates.

'I'm expecting a preliminary report from Chief Inspector Donaldson some time this afternoon. Maybe after that we'll be able to wrap it up quick, and your President can grab some credit in time for his election.

'Don't hold your breath, though. In my experience, the obvious conclusion is usually wide of the mark!'

41

Alison Higgins smiled down at her godson as he sat at the desk in his bedroom, staring intently at the monitor of his computer.

Mark was a highly intelligent little boy, and with his gifts came a tendency to be more serious than his contemporaries. Where they would have been playing with the latest blood and thunder video game, he was exploring the marvellous world of Leonardo da Vinci on an interactive CD-ROM package which Alison had given him as a sixth birthday present.

She noted with some concern that he had selected the section which described the great inventor's designs for flying machines, but he seemed unconcerned as he appraised an animation of a pedal-powered wing. 'It's like a hang-glider, Auntie Alison, isn't it?' he said.

'That's right, Mark, it is, and Leonardo designed it five hundred years ago.'

'What happened to it? Did it crash?'

A tremor flicked at her stomach. She framed her reply carefully. 'It's only a design, Mark. There's no record of it ever being built, or ever flying. But if Leonardo *had* built it, I'm sure that it would have worked. He was a genius.'

'What's that? A genie, like in *Aladdin*?'

She laughed. 'No, not quite. A genius is someone who's very, very clever.'

'Like my dad is?'

She winced inwardly at his use of the present tense, and at the awkwardness of his question. The late Roland McGrath had been called many things in his abbreviated lifetime, but genius was a description that had never been applied to him. 'Your daddy was a very clever man, Mark, that's right, but in a different way from Leonardo. Your dad was very good at looking after people, the people who voted for him, and very good as a Minister.'

'The Ministry comes in Red Boxes, doesn't it?'

Alison shook her head. 'No, not quite. The Ministry is a big organization, like the police. It's run by people like Mr Hardy and your dad: all the papers that the different parts of the Ministry send to them are delivered in Red Boxes.'

Mark looked up at her, with a faint pathetic light of hope shining in his eyes. 'Is my daddy at the Ministry just now?'

She knelt beside him and took his hand. On the monitor screen the pilot of da Vinci's powered wing was pedalling rhythmically.

'No, love,' she said. 'Like I told you, your daddy's gone to be with Jesus.'

'But why did he go?'

'He didn't have any choice in the matter. None of us do, when it's our time.'

The child's chin trembled. 'But I want him. I want my daddy!' He gulped in a great breath of air. It emerged in a long, rending wail, which exploded into violent heaving sobs. Alison gathered him to her and hugged him, rocking him in her arms.

'I know you do, my love, but it just can't be any more. You've just got to be the best boy you can be for your mummy. She needs you to be strong for her. You can do that.' She felt his head nod against her chest.

'Here's something you can do. I did it when my dad went to be with Jesus. At night, when you go to bed and Mummy puts out the light, close your eyes tight and think of your daddy. Make a picture of him in your mind.' She rubbed his head. 'He'll be real in there. You try it and see if he isn't. Will you do that?'

'Yes,' said Mark softly.

She kissed the top of his head, and ruffled his hair. 'There's my good boy. Now let's dry those eyes before Mummy sees you. That would upset her and we don't want that.'

She released him from her hug. Picking a paper handkerchief from a box on the desk she wiped his face and nose. 'There you are. Good as new.' She stood up. 'Go on back to Leonardo. See if you can do the puzzle.'

He looked at her, reproachfully. 'Auntie Alison! I did the puzzle weeks ago!'

She laughed. 'Well, see if you can do it again, then. Maybe the gremlins have been in and changed it.'

He looked at her with that special pity which bright children reserve for ignorance in adults. 'Auntie Alison, there are no gremlins. And once I've done something I always remember it.'

It was true. Since the age of two, Mark's remarkable memory had been in evidence, and had been a talking point for all of his parents' friends.

Leaving him to his educational play, she went downstairs to the living room where Leona McGrath was watching a political magazine programme on television. 'Come and see this,' she said. 'They're discussing the accident, and what it means for the Government. They're saying that if they lose Roly's seat, and Colin Davey's it could be all up for them.'

'Is that likely?' asked Higgins.

Her friend looked at her and hunched her shoulders in a 'Who knows?' gesture. 'Davey had a rural seat, with a majority of twenty-three thousand. Even we should hold that. But our seat's a different matter, with such a small majority. I know that Roly and Marsh were pessimistic about our prospects at the General Election.'

'Ah, but Mr Elliot told Bob Skinner that he thought that in the circumstances of the By-election, the right candidate would hold it.'

'Did he indeed,' said the little widow, intrigued. 'I wonder who he had in mind.'

42

Skinner had just refilled the coffee mugs when his scrambled direct line rang. He stepped across to the desk and picked it up.

'Yes?'

'DCI Donaldson, sir. I'm calling from Captain Arrow's office in Whitehall.'

'Hello, Dave. I've been expecting your report. Look, I've got company here, Mr Doherty and Ms Gower, so I'm going to switch to hands free.' He pushed a button on the receiver and replaced the handset. 'Right, how's it going down there?'

Donaldson's voice boomed tinnily around the room. 'Interesting, sir. We've satisfied ourselves that the Red Box was clean when Maurice Noble took it home with him.'

'That doesn't really surprise me. Go on to the interesting bits.'

'Right. For a start, Maurice Noble's colleagues say that he was showing signs of depression. This was related to the excessive hours that Mr Davey made his staff work, and to his belief that his wife was having an affair.'

'Have you spoken to the wife?'

'Just left her, sir.'

'What did she have to say? You did put it to her, didn't you?'

'Of course, boss. We asked her directly. She didn't admit anything.'

'But you have room for doubt?'

'Substantial.'

'Okay. Is Adam there?'

'Yes, sir. I'll put him on.'

Skinner picked up the receiver, cutting out the loudspeaker. 'Adam, I think maybe we should put a tail on Mrs Noble. Do you agree?'

'Too right. I've put a tap on her phone already.'

'Is that authorised?'

'I've fookin' authorised it.'

'Fine, if you can do that. Now I want you to use Donaldson and McIlhenney for the tail. They're both good guys, and I trust them. While they're keeping the lady in their sights, I'd like you to do something else for me. It sounds as if we have to consider suicide by

Noble as a possibility here. I want you to go back into his past and find out whether he had the skill to make an explosive device.'

'Okay,' said Arrow. 'From memory, there was nothing to indicate that, but I'll take a look. Maybe he 'ad a *Boys' Own* Chemistry set when he was a lad. Anything else?'

'Yeah. Let's cover all the angles. If the Red Box spent the night at Chez Noble, I'd like to have the place checked for any sign of an illicit entry while they were asleep. Ask Dave Donaldson to arrange to borrow a Scene of Crime Squad from the Met.'

'Right, I'll do that.'

'Good,' said Skinner. 'Now, Joe Doherty has with him the American file on Agent Robin. I've got Brian Mackie flying down there tomorrow. I'll ask him to give it to you.'

'You can if you like,' said Arrow, 'but it ain't news to me. MI6 found out about Robin before the Yanks did. The CIA obviously didn't tell the NSC, but it were our lot that tipped them off! Don't worry about Agent Robin, Bob. We've got an operation in place in that respect, and I'm pretty certain that Robin isn't the person we're after! The best thing we can do is follow the leads we 'ave, and keep an eye out for traces of General Yahic.'

'Very well,' Skinner said cautiously. 'I'll go with your judgement on that. Good luck.'

'Cheers, mate. I'll keep in touch.' Arrow hesitated. 'One thing though, Bob. Are you all right?'

'Me! Of course. Why?'

'Cause from where I'm listening, you sound absolutely knackered!'

43

Bob Skinner lay in the dark. It was 2.3o a.m., and he was afraid.

He lay alert, listening to his wife's soft breathing, because he was afraid to fall asleep, afraid of another dream visit to those muddy acres, afraid of the horror but also of the reality of his vision of the night before.

He knew with a great certainty that the nightmare was not over, only interrupted. He could remember none of the detail, only the horror, but he was certain that if he yielded to his sandy, heavy eyes, he would be back in its midst, not screaming awake this time, but moving on towards something in the darkness, something that he knew was there, something frightful, something awful. He was afraid too that even his wakeful state would not be a defence for ever, and that soon the final recollection would break through the wall in his consciousness which he had built against it, and kept cemented firm.

He slipped out of bed, moved noiselessly over to his wardrobe and found running shorts, a sweat-shirt and trainers. Rather than stumble about in the bedroom and risk waking Sarah, he stepped out to the landing and clothed himself, then tiptoed downstairs and let himself out into the street. He locked the door behind him, zipped his keys into a pocket in his shirt, and trotted towards the road, running across the lawn and leaping over the corner of the gravel to maintain his silent escape.

Had he looked back, he would have seen Sarah at the bedroom window watching him anxiously as he loped into the night, down Fairyhouse Avenue.

He ran with long easy strides, not pushing himself as he climbed the hill and took the turn which led on to Queensferry Street. He crossed the wide road almost at once, picking up his pace as he ran past Stewarts Melville College then turned right, heading down the hill towards Dean Village.

As he ran in the light, cold drizzle which was falling on the centre of Edinburgh, the waking nightmare faded. He settled into a steady, metronomic pace, and he began to think through his investigation. He replayed all the decisions he had taken, and all the orders he had given.

He thought back to Donaldson's report, and to his description of

Maurice Noble's depression, and to his fears over his wife. *Could Noble have been a perverted suicide?* he asked himself. The very question made him feel frustrated.

One of the things which he disliked most about his senior command role was the extent to which it took him away from day-to-day contact with criminal investigation. Throughout his career as a detective, one of his great strengths had been his ability to get to know the people he was confronting, by studying their actions, by speaking to those who knew them and finally, in many cases, by staring into their eyes across the table in an interview room.

The essential delegation which his rise through the ranks had forced upon him had robbed him of much . . . too much, he thought . . . of that closeness with the crime-fighting process. It was not that he distrusted his staff or doubted their ability to form their own judgements. On the contrary, Skinner believed that his handpicked team was the finest in the country.

His problem was that as the commanding General and Field-Marshal-in-waiting, for all the power and glory, he derived less satisfaction from the job than he had as a member of the frontline team.

Of course, since moving into the command suite he had enjoyed one or two personal successes. But they had been accidents of fate, rather than part of the due process. Now he had chosen to place himself publicly at the head of the most demanding enquiry his Force had ever faced, and he was troubled.

The carnage on the Lammermuirs had thrust torments into his dreams, and he knew that they were taking a physical toll. Yet, apart from that, since the early hours of the investigation when he had stood frustrated in the Command Vehicle, trying to think of all the things he should be doing yet having difficulty in stringing them into a logical sequence, he had had the strangest feeling that somehow he was floating above events, unable to reach down and influence them.

On other investigations he had felt sometimes that all was not as it seemed, and that somewhere in the pattern of events there was an obvious link which he was missing. In the past, he had worried away tenaciously at the scenario; he had adjusted the living jigsaw until the last piece was in place.

But this was different. This time he had set an investigation under way without any clear idea of the direction in which it was heading. And this time, there were the nightmares. For the first time in his life, professional and personal, he knew that he was not in control.

Bob Skinner ran on through the sodium-lit darkness. It was 3.10 a.m., and he was afraid.

They took him completely by surprise, as they jumped from the doorway to confront him. They were big fellows, three of them, heavily built, and he knew at once that they were not about to ask him for a light. He broke his stride and tried to dodge around them, but they spread out to block his path.

His mind had been so preoccupied with his troubles that he had lost track of where he was heading. He looked around him and saw that he was in Dalry Road, a main thoroughfare, but one where no traffic ran other than the occasional police car at that time in the morning.

He was breathing heavily. The three men circled around him, forcing him to take a defensive position with his back to a shop window. Skinner was afraid no longer. These were flesh and blood things. He felt an old familiar sensation creep over him, a coldness inside, an anticipation of danger. Something else invaded him too, or rather someone, another personality, one who was looking forward to what was about to happen, who knew what power he possessed, and who would take pleasure in using it.

He scanned the trio, trying to make out faces, but they were all dressed in what could have been a gang uniform – tracksuits with heavy hooded tops. 'You guys really don't want to do this,' he said. 'For a start, I'm a Police Officer. For another thing, there aren't enough of you. Away home to your mothers before your tea gets cold.' There was a wicked gleam in his eye.

If all three had charged at once, even he would have stood no chance, but as two came forward, one of the men, the thug on his left, hesitated.

Skinner sent the first attacker spinning backwards in less than a second, disabled by a short, brutal right-handed chop across the Adam's apple. Almost simultaneously, the man in the middle, the biggest of the three, was folded in half by a lightning-fast kick to the groin. Before he could hit the ground, Skinner grabbed him and using his momentum, swung him round and slammed him head-first through the plate-glass window behind him. As the shop alarm began to ring out, the third man, who had plucked up enough courage to move in to attack, froze in mid-stride. The policeman seized him by the shirt, pulled him towards him and head-butted him as hard as he could on the bridge of the nose.

Skinner was still holding the man, smiling savagely as the blood erupted from his smashed nose, when he felt the thump on his back. He threw down his attacker and turned in surprise, to face a tall, slightly built girl, as she lunged at him for a second time with a long-bladed knife. He had no time to wonder from where she had come. Instinctively he side-stepped, and grabbed her wrist, twisting it sharply upwards, and hearing a crack. She screamed and dropped the weapon. Still holding her, Skinner bent to pick it up with his left hand.

All of a sudden he felt the pain. It began just below his right shoulderblade and swept through him. He gasped in a breath, and it erupted into agony. His eyes swam, and he slumped to his knees, loosening his grip on the girl. As he fell forward, face down on the wet pavement, he heard her footsteps as she raced off down Dalry Road.

Above him, the shop's alarm bell continued to ring out shrilly, but to Bob Skinner, the sound grew fainter and more distant. He clung on to it for as long as he could, but eventually it faded altogether as a darkness swept over him, one in which there were no dreams.

44

The doorbell rang, but Sarah was halfway downstairs, pulling her robe around her. It was just after 4.30 a.m., and she had been lying awake, waiting anxiously for Bob to return, when she had heard the car pull up outside.

She threw the door open. Andy and Alex stood on the threshold, unkempt and speedily dressed.

'What is it?' she snapped urgently. Andy stepped into the hall and put his hands on her trembling shoulders.

'It's Bob,' he said. 'He's in the Royal.'

Sarah gasped and looked at Alex, noticing, for the first time, that she had been crying.

'A patrol car found him in Dalry Road. It was answering a call-out to investigate a shop alarm that had been reported ringing. The officers recognised him and had the presence of mind to get a message to me. They said that it looked as if he was attacked when he was out running. He's been stabbed.'

Sarah's hands flew to her face. 'Oh my God! How bad is it?'

'They don't know. I called the hospital. They told me that he was alive, but unconscious, when the ambulance got there. They rushed him straight into surgery. Apparently he has a single wound in the back, penetrating the chest cavity.'

'Do you know who did it?' she gasped.

Martin nodded. 'I think so. The patrol car stopped a girl in Dalry Road, running away from the scene. She had a broken wrist. There were three blokes at the scene, all of them hospital cases. The ambulance crew had to give one of them an emergency tracheotomy. The Big Man went down fighting and no mistake.'

Upstairs, Jazz began to cry. 'I'll see to the baby,' said Alex. 'Sarah, you get dressed and Andy'll take you to the Royal.'

She nodded, and headed for the stairs.

'That's right,' said Martin, a meaningful look in his eye. 'And when we get there, I'm going to talk to those three guys, and the girl. I have friends in that hospital – and none of those characters will be having anything but the minimum treatment until they've told me the whole story!'

45

Edinburgh Royal Infirmary has seen many advances in medicine. Unfortunately the same philosophy of constant improvement has not driven hospital building in Scotland's capital, where some medical staff still work in accommodation which has served six generations and more.

The room to which Sarah was shown to await Bob's emergence from theatre was in the heart of the oldest part of the Infirmary. It was a small lounge serving the doctors attached to the main surgical wards.

She sat there, white-faced, sipping hot sweet tea from a white mug. Alan Royston was at her side, but the Police Media Relations Manager kept a sympathetic silence, knowing instinctively to leave her to her thoughts.

Eventually, Sarah felt sorry for him, felt she should break the silence. After all, he was a member of the Skinner team, and would be suffering himself during the helpless time of waiting. However, well-meaning though she was, what she said brought him little reassurance.

'It's at times like this, Alan,' she said, 'that it's awful being a doctor. There are no mysteries for me. I know what's happening in theatre right now, and I know what the worst case is. The Senior House Officer who received him in Accident and Emergency showed me where the wound is. Depending on the angle of entry it could have punctured a lung, or it could have penetrated the heart.'

Royston paled. 'His heart? But surely, that couldn't have happened or he'd be . . .' The words faded on his lips.

'Dead already? Not necessarily; a healthy heart is a powerful organ. But Andy said that the police got there within two minutes of the stabbing and he was unconscious by then. That isn't a good sign. Against that, there was a heartbeat when he was brought in. Erratic but still strong, the SHO said.'

'How long should he be in surgery?'

She glanced at her watch. 'He's been in theatre for going on three hours now, but there's nothing unusual in that. I expect they'll be a while yet.' She squeezed his hand. 'You have no idea how strong Bob is. He'll be fine.'

Royston looked at her, and was perceptive enough to realise, as perhaps she did not fully, that she was talking to herself, rather than to him. He admired her strength, and her control. For himself, he was held together by the simple fact that he could not imagine Skinner not surviving.

The door opened. Sarah looked up, with a tiny involuntary jump, as Andy Martin came into the room.

'Nothing yet?' he asked.

She shook her head. 'What have you been doing?'

'Getting to the bottom of what happened.' He looked at her with a strange, grim smile. 'I called Maggie Rose in, and Mario came with her. We talked to the coppers who found him. They said it was like a charnel-house down there. What a state those three guys are in! The bloke with the swollen Adam's apple and the tube in his throat got off lightest. One of them has a suspected fractured skull from going through a shop window, and as well as that he's unlikely to father a child again. The third one has a smashed nose and cheekbone.'

'What happened?' Sarah asked.

'The guy needing the new nose told us all about it. The three of them are druggies. They were buying gear, and they were a bit light on readies. When Bob came along, they decided to mug him.'

Sarah let out an impromptu, incongruous laugh; its tone was slightly hysterical, Alan Royston thought.

'What? Only three of them?' she said.

'According to the guy, that's what Bob said to them too. They should have believed him.'

'What about the girl? What was she doing there?'

'She was the dealer, believe it or not. I know her – Fay Knight, her name is. Big Neil and I nicked her earlier on this year. She didn't have any stuff on her, and our witnesses were frightened off by her minders, so the case collapsed. We've got her now, though. It was a typical street operation. She was taking the money, and handing out chitties to the buyers. The man holding the drugs was in a stairway across the street; he doled them out when the buyers gave him the note from the girl saying how much. He seems to have legged it at the first sign of bother.'

'That's a complicated buying process, isn't it?'

'Maybe, but it builds in added security for the suppliers who control the network. It means that no street dealer ever handles both drugs *and* money.'

Sarah raised her eyebrows. 'Yeah, it's careful okay. So why are you so sure you'll be able to convict the girl for dealing this time?'

Martin looked at her, his smile gone. 'Because those three guys downstairs will all give evidence against her. It was the girl who stabbed Bob. She was back in the doorway and he didn't see her until it was too late. The man with no nose said that she tried to stab him again. He got the knife off her, and broke her wrist in the process, but then he collapsed. The girl took off down the street, but ran right into our people in the patrol car. They arrested her. I've charged all four of them with attempted murder, but I expect the Three Stooges to give evidence against Fay and to plead guilty to a reduced charge of assault themselves. That's the deal the Fiscal will do.'

Sarah stood up, and leaned against him, pressing her face against his chest. 'Attempted murder,' she whispered. 'Pray God it stays that way.' He felt her tremble, and held her tight.

'Andy?' Even muffled against him, her voice was suddenly cold, and harder than he had ever heard. 'D'you think they'd let me set that bitch's broken wrist? I'd love to make a really bad job of it!'

46

When Brian Mackie and Mario McGuire arrived at Mr Kong's, on the fringe of colourful Chinatown, Cyril Kercheval was waiting outside.

'Wouldn't you know it,' he said, as soon as the introductions were over. 'This place is closed today. But no worry, I've booked us a table next door.' The two Scots looked askance at his choice, a narrow establishment whose customers were jammed together around a range of tables of varying sizes. The place seemed more like a greasy chopsticks café than a restaurant.

'Don't let appearances fool you,' said Kercheval. 'It has a huge menu, and the food's all terrific.'

'Fine,' said Mackie, 'but is it secure?'

The MI5 man roared with laughter at the question. *This fellow is archetypal,* thought the DCI. Around fifty, with a significant beer-gut, he wore a trenchcoat over a crumpled suit, and a stained MCC tie.

'Could hardly be more secure, dear boy. The Yuppies only come here at night. Lunchtimes, it's full of Chinese, and for most of them English is very much a second language. This is one of the most discreet meeting places in London, but to make you happier, I've booked a table away in the far corner.'

As he opened the door and held it for the two policemen, the sound boomed out to meet them, a sing-song blend of unrecognisable speech. They eased their way to their table through a central aisle which was barely wide enough to allow them to pass. They hung their overcoats on pegs on a side wall and took their seats. Three thick menus awaited them, one at each place.

As they sat down, Kercheval's mood and manner changed. 'Listen, chaps, I was appalled to hear about our friend Skinner. What's the latest on his condition?'

McGuire looked across at him, grim-faced. 'Touch and go,' he said. 'My wife's his PA, so I went to the hospital with her. He was in surgery for four hours while they stabilised him, and repaired the damage. He was stabbed through the base of the right lung. The surgeon said that wouldn't have been life-threatening on its own, but the knife nicked an artery as well. There was massive bleeding in the chest cavity: they had to give him six pints of blood, apparently. He was in Intensive Care when I left the Royal, sedated and hooked up to a ventilator. They say that it'll be dodgy for the next forty-eight hours.'

Kercheval shook his head sadly. 'The telly said it was a random assault. Is that true?'

'More or less. The boss likes to run when he has thinking to do. Last night he just ran into the wrong place.'

'Tch! Terrible. We're used to that sort of thing in London, but I didn't think Edinburgh was like that.'

'It isn't, as a rule. Nor will it get that way. The attack was drug-related; we'll make the best we can of it. We've got the people who attacked Mr Skinner, but there was another guy who ran off. He was the dealer. We're after him, and his supplier. I'm willing to bet that Andy Martin – he's the boss's Deputy – will have their heads on poles in Princes Street before the day's out.'

'Let's hope so,' said Kercheval. 'I haven't had too many dealings with Bob Skinner through MI5, but I do know that he's very highly regarded by the people at the top.' He paused as a waiter made his way to their table. 'Want me to order?' he asked. The Scots nodded. 'Fine. One chicken oyster sauce, one beef black bean, one duck yellow bean, one prawn chow mein, plenty of boiled rice and two large bottles of sparkling mineral, thank you very much.' The waiter's fingers flashed over his pad. He bowed and withdrew, dancing expertly through the tight-packed tables.

'The people at the top, you said.' Brian Mackie leaned across the table, looking quickly around him for prying eyes, but spotting none. 'Who are they, exactly?'

Kercheval beamed at him indulgently. 'My dear chap, we live in the age of openness. You're Special Branch, you should know that we're all in the phone book now, more or less.'

The DCI shook his head. He paused as the waiter uncapped a litre bottle of Ashbourne sparkling mineral and poured three glasses. 'No, Cyril,' he said as the young man left, 'I meant higher up the tree than that. In Special Branch, I report to Bob Skinner, period. To whom does your Director General report?'

The MI5 officer took a sip from his glass. 'Interesting question. I suppose it depends upon the issue. In theory, it's the Prime Minister, as Head of the Security Services, but in practice we're monitored by a committee of Permanent Secretaries; Home, Foreign Office, Defence and Cabinet Office.'

'And how about them? Who oversees the committee? Is it the Prime Minister alone?'

'In theory, again, yes it is. But in practice, he'll normally listen to the views of his most senior colleagues.'

Mackie nodded. 'That's more or less what I assumed. So, when it comes to that final group, the core team of Ministers, who scrutinises them? By definition, they're in possession of the most sensitive information in the country, so whose task is it to ensure that none of them are security risks?'

Kercheval looked at him long and hard. 'Skinner did brief you well, didn't he. The answer is that the task devolves back upon the Security Service. Upon me, actually.'

Mackie was about to react to the admission when their waiter, and another wound through the throng, bearing their lunch order, plus the obligatory pot of Chinese tea. 'Let's enjoy lunch,' said the Londoner as the dishes were laid out on a warming tray. 'It rather deserves it.'

Mario McGuire looked at him gratefully. He had missed most of a night's sleep, and breakfast. He attacked the selection of dishes methodically, showing that his Italian descent was no constraint on his aptitude with chopsticks. Cyril Kercheval's confidence in the quality of the kitchen was well founded. They ate in virtual silence for almost fifteen minutes, until all the plates before them were cleared.

'Right,' said Kercheval at last. 'Back to business, and no more sparring. What do you want?'

Mackie leaned back in his chair, until his head touched the wall behind him. 'Do you have a file on Colin Davey?'

'I *might* have. Was he the target?'

'He *might* have been. *Might* we see your file?'

'I'll have to ask. I'll have to go to the DG, and I'm certain that the DG will have to consult the PM.'

'We understand. When he does that, could you make sure that he tells the Prime Minister that the request comes directly from Bob Skinner?'

'That'll help, will it?' There was a very slight edge of sarcasm in the question.

'It should do,' snapped Mackie testily. 'Big Bob saved his life once.'

Kercheval blinked hard. 'Indeed. Then I'll make sure he knows who's asking.'

'How long will you need?'

'Give me till tomorrow. In which case, when shall we three meet again?'

'You name it.'

'If you say so. In that case, there's a splendid Italian place in Wardour Street . . .'

47

Arrow slipped into the Intensive Care Unit, and closed the door quietly behind him.

'Sarah,' he whispered.

She looked over her shoulder. Seeing him, she beckoned him towards her with her left hand. The other lay on the bed cover, grasping tight to her husband, as if she were holding him with her. He lay on his back, with his eyes closed. A thick tube led from his mouth into a ventilator; its steady rhythmic pumping was the only sound to be heard.

There was an empty chair alongside Sarah. As Adam sat down, he looked around. There were three other beds in the Unit, each of them occupied by a single male patient, wired to a green-screened monitor, and everything and everyone was under the observation of a central nurses' station.

'I didn't expect to see you,' she said in a dull, flat, exhausted voice.

'I 'ad to come,' said Arrow. 'To see Andy, to brief him on what's been happening in London.'

'Aren't DCI Donaldson and Neil down there? Couldn't they have done that?'

He smiled at her gently. 'Course they could, but I wanted to come anyway, didn't I. How's he doing?'

She glanced up at the monitor. 'He's still in shock, but his pulse is beginning to stabilise. It was weak and reedy when they brought him out of surgery, after they'd done all they could in there. Lung and brain functions aren't a problem – so far, at least. It's the arterial damage that's the danger. If they've been able to repair it properly, and stop the bleeding, then his body will recover from the shock, his heart-rate will slow down and his condition will stabilise.

'If they haven't, then . . . then he'll . . .'

Arrow took her free hand and gave it a squeeze. 'Don't say that. This is the big fella, remember. The toughest guy I've ever met. He'll pull through.'

She looked at him, then leaned down, touching her forehead to his shoulder. 'The surgeon wasn't prepared to say that. Adam, you're SAS, you know the score as well as I do. With that wound most people would have died in the ambulance. Even the strongest can be brought down.'

'Yes,' he said. 'But some people just have that bit extra. 'Like 'im. And that bit don't show. Surgeons can't spot it just by looking at your insides.' He glanced up at the screens. 'How long till he does stabilise?'

'It'll be about forty-eight hours until we can start to relax. They'll keep him under for that long, and on the ventilator. After that, if everything's okay they can let him start to come round and allow his system to take over. But until then, that pulse-line up there is a single, weak thread, and he's hanging by it.'

He squeezed her hand again. 'He will hang on, though. And, hard as it is to find anything positive in all this, once he's over the worst, at least he'll be forced to take a rest. I might as well tell you, I was worried about him. When I saw him after the accident, then when I spoke to him yesterday, there was something about him. He seemed strained.'

Sarah looked at the little man. 'He's barely slept since the accident, you know. When he has dropped off, he's been having nightmares.'

Arrow nodded. 'That fits. I've seen those signs before. You find them in someone running on an empty tank. There's a name for it in the Army. We call it combat fatigue.' He paused. 'And talking about fatigue, shouldn't you get some rest?'

She shook her head. 'How would I do that, Adam? I'm here for the duration, for as long as it takes. Alex, and Tracey, the nanny, will look after Jazz. When this big hoss comes round, the first thing he sees is going to be me, sat right here! And if I ain't wearing any make-up, and if I do have bags under my eyes, well that'll be just too damn bad!'

48

'Is Mr Bob coming today?'

Mark was wearing his Police Cadet cap, tilted back on his head at a rakish angle, balanced carefully but still precariously.

Alison Higgins shook her head. 'Not today, Mark, I'm afraid. Not for a wee while. Off you go and play now.' The child turned and began to climb the stairs slowly, one hand on his hat.

'It's awful, isn't it?' said Leona McGrath, as Higgins slung her coat on the antique mirrored stand in the hall, fluffing her hair back into place. 'Will he be okay?'

The Superintendent looked at her and shrugged, as they walked into the living room where Marshall Elliot stood, with his back to the fire. She nodded him a quick 'Hello.'

'His poor wife,' said Leona. 'I feel so sorry for her. When they told me about Roly, it was a huge shock, certainly, but that was it. In that instant, my life had changed but at least I knew it. But there she is, poor Mrs Skinner, not knowing whether he'll live or not. I couldn't stand being in that sort of limbo.'

'It's not Mrs: it's Dr Skinner.'

'God. That makes it worse. Means they won't be able to tell her anything but the plain truth.'

'Doctor or not, Sarah would raise hell if they tried to kid her on,' said Higgins. 'She's a tough lady. She'll survive even if he doesn't. She's good for the boss, you know. He used to be a very private guy, until she came along. She brought him out of himself, made him more demonstrative. He laughs more than he used to, and he just dotes on the new baby.

'If he dies, Sarah won't just fade away. She'll see it as her duty to make sure that no one ever forgets him.'

Leona McGrath stood by the doorway to the conservatory, and stared out at the greenery arranged around the cane furniture.

'Yes,' she said at last. 'That's very well put. That's what I've been coming to realise too.'

49

'Thank you for the data on Agent Robin, sir,' Arrow said respectfully to Joe Doherty. 'I've passed it on to the appropriate people.'

There was no humour in the room, only concern, but Arrow, Doherty, Andy Martin and Merle Gower all knew that it had to be business as usual.

'What did you think of it?'

'It had a familiar ring to it.'

A thin smile flicked Doherty's lips. 'That means you had it before the Agency, doesn't it? Did you give it to them?' Arrow nodded.

The sallow-faced American glowered at his countrywoman. 'Those devious bastards at Langley! The SIS gave them information and they fed it into the NSC as their own work, all to show how clever they are and protect their funding. I tell you Merle, that organisation of yours is in deep shit when I get back to the States.'

Arrow's face betrayed nothing, but he was surprised. He had assumed that Gower was FBI. He wondered if the Foreign Office knew that the Americans had slipped a Company representative into the UK.

'Adam,' said Doherty, 'I am embarrassed. They will pay for that also. Do you have a lead on Robin, as yet?'

The soldier was impassive. 'You know how big an organisation our civil service is. And that's all we were given to go on; Robin is a civil servant. No department, grade, age, gender, or anything else. But there *is* an operation in place. The appropriate people are looking into it now.'

'And the "appropriate" people would be?' snapped Gower, so testily that Doherty flashed her a warning glance.

Arrow was unruffled. 'The SIS uncovered the existence of Robin and the Iraqi network by means which they are not prepared to discuss with anyone, even with you, Agent Gower. They're our foreign Intelligence gatherers. Internal security, as you should know, is usually the job of MI5. I believe that the investigating team may have a line to Robin, but I can't say more than that.'

'Why not?' Gower snapped again, unintimidated by Doherty.

At last, Arrow's grip on his temper slipped. 'Because it's a secure operation and we don't want it bloody well compromised, okay?' he shouted.

The woman opened her mouth to reply, but Doherty overrode her. 'Is there a possibility that Robin is our man?'

'It's too early to say with certainty,' said Arrow, recovering his composure, 'but I'm told that's unlikely, unless he's part of a team. Even then, it's doubtful.'

'The main thing is, Adam,' said Andy Martin, 'that you have Robin in hand.' Unusually, he was wearing spectacles. Without the extra green tint of his contact lenses, his eyes looked bloodshot and lustreless.

'Aye, that's right.'

'So of our fancied outside candidates,' said Doherty, 'that just leaves General Yahic. What should we do about him, do we think, colleagues? What's the CIA view, Merle?'

Her eyes burned in her dusky face. 'As I understand it, sir, the prevailing view in the Agency is that we should take him out.'

'Bloody clever that would be,' said Arrow, his voice heavy with irony. 'We'd learn a lot if we did that.'

'Yeah,' said Doherty. 'That is not the NSC's preferred option, Merle. No, people, we have a great deal of devolved authority in this room. I propose that we should each take time to consider what practical steps we can take to determine whether or not Yahic was involved in the bombing.'

'In my experience,' said Arrow, 'the best way would be to invite him for a chat and to ask 'im!'

50

'All rise.'

The Court Officer's stentorian voice boomed out, as the red-robed Judge pushed himself out of his chair. As one, accused, counsel, clerks and the few spectators in the public gallery obeyed his command. Among the last group was Neil McIlhenney, seated in the back row and out of sight of the defence benches to all but a very tall barrister on tiptoe.

He and Donaldson had shared the duty during the day, one in the gallery, one in the unmarked car which they had borrowed from the Ministry of Defence pool. Periodically, they had called Edinburgh to check on Skinner's condition.

McIlhenney had sat through the opening stages of Ariadne Tucker's final speech to the jury . . . the one which she had been preparing on her husband's last night alive . . . and had been professionally impressed. Without, admittedly, having had the benefit of any of the evidence, he would have been prepared to acquit her client, an Anglo–Greek businessman accused of twenty-seven different swindles involving commercial and residential property and high value motor cars.

She had still been going strong at three-thirty, at which point the thoughtful Judge, who had begun the day with kind words to the recently bereaved senior for the defence, had decided, again in deference to the strain under which he imagined her to be suffering, that he would call a halt and send everyone home early; everyone, that was, save the accused.

'Thank Christ for that!' McIlhenney had muttered under his breath. As a young white-gloved Constable flanking a prisoner in the dock in the High Court in Edinburgh, he had once fallen asleep halfway through a prosecution summing-up. The incident had come close to ending his career and the memory of it would live with him for ever.

As the jury filed out, the heavily built Sergeant glanced idly around the public gallery. There were four people in the front row, three middle-aged women and a younger man, all peering down into the well of the court. As the policeman looked on, one of the women, fat, swarthy and fifty-something with hair dyed black, waved down at the accused and blew him a kiss.

In the row behind, a Japanese couple stood to attention, holding on to Harrods carriers; sightseeing in the *Old Bairrey*, McIlhenney guessed. Suddenly, to his astonishment, the man plunged into his bag, took out a small video camcorder and began to film the court, unobserved by any of the attendants.

He looked around the rest of the gallery as he turned to leave. Three people were filing out – court groupies, he assumed – but in the back row a tall man stood in a brown Army uniform, gazing down into the court as if making eye contact with someone. McIlhenney thought back. He was fairly certain that the man had not been in court when he and Donaldson had last changed shift, and equally sure that he had not seen him enter. A good copper to the last, he took, as routine, a mental snapshot of the man's face and filed it away. He had barely done so when the officer turned on his heel, stepped into the aisle, and sprinted up the stairway and out of the court.

Their Cavalier was parked in the street outside. It was a touch conspicuous, even for a Vauxhall, McIlhenney thought, but necessary, he knew, if they were to tail Ariadne Tucker Noble as closely as they had been instructed.

'Is that it?' DCI Donaldson asked as the Sergeant climbed in behind him.

'For today, aye, but our girl looked like she was getting warmed up for a long address, and the jury'll have a lot to consider. I'd say that Ms Tucker'll be here till Thursday at the least, maybe Friday.'

They sat in their car, which was pulled over into a lay-by. They had spent a good part of the day keeping wardens at bay with their warrant cards, and in the case of one zealot, with some heavy threats.

McIlhenney had been back in the car for almost twenty minutes before Ariadne Tucker appeared in the doorway of the court, carrying a huge briefcase. She stood there, on the pavement, looking up into the flow of traffic. The two policemen hunched down in their seats, in case she looked in their direction, but she was intent. Within a minute, a taxi appeared and she climbed in.

'Okay, sir,' said the Sergeant. 'Follow that cab.' He paused. 'Ah've always wanted to say that.'

As the black taxi drew away from the Criminal Courts, Donaldson slipped neatly on to its tail. The driver headed up Giltspur Street, then, signalling at the last minute, swung left towards Farringdon Street. The DCI made the turn without indicating. He drew a horn blast from the car behind, and swore, fearful that their target would turn at the noise and spot them, but through the rear window of the cab they could see Ariadne with head bowed, as if reading.

They followed her in thickening traffic towards the Thames, and Blackfriars Bridge. 'I wonder if she's going across the river?' mused McIlhenney. His question was answered almost at once as their quarry peeled off the road to the bridge and veered round, to head westwards along the Victoria Embankment.

Donaldson kept position close behind the taxi; normally he would have preferred to keep more space between them, but amid the heavy flow of vehicles, he had little option. They carried on in formation along the length of the Embankment, until as they closed on West-minster Bridge the cabby, giving more warning this time, signalled a right turn, towards Parliament Square. The policemen were almost trapped by a red light, but made it through safely, then picked up pace to match the taxi as it accelerated to catch the next set on green. 'This is magic,' said McIlhenney, as they swung round the green with St Margaret's on their left.

'She can't be going home,' said Donaldson. 'If she had been she'd have headed along Millbank.'

'Chances are she's going to the bloody hairdresser,' laughed the Sergeant, as Donaldson allowed the cab to pull ahead in the lighter traffic of Victoria Street.

Almost at once, his supposition was proved wide of the mark. Indicator and brake lights came on in the same second as the cab drew to a sudden halt. 'Take a left, quick,' said McIlhenney. Donaldson had already seen the turning and swung the Cavalier into the side street. As they took the corner, the Sergeant stared back along the pavement. He caught a glimpse of Ariadne stepping from the taxi, and as she did so, of a man moving forward from a doorway to greet her. There was enough daylight left for him to see that he was wearing a brown Army uniform.

Donaldson braked as soon as the Vauxhall was out of sight, and McIlhenney jumped out. He was headed at a half-trot up the slight slope, and turned into Victoria Street, just in time to see the soldier kiss Ariadne, and hug her to him. 'Oh aye,' the Sergeant muttered. He was about to step back into Abbey Orchard Street, for fear of being spotted, when the pair turned away from him, the soldier's arm around the woman's shoulders, and stepped into the doorway from which he had emerged.

Donaldson appeared at his shoulder. 'Where'd they go?'

'In there, sir. The guy was in the court. They must have arranged to meet here. Let's see what this place is.' They advanced towards the spot, just as the taxi drew away. Through the glass, the DCI thought he saw the driver wave goodbye.

'It's a wine bar, sir. What's it called?' McIlhenney peered at the sign. 'Methuselah's. Very twee. Do we go in?'

Donaldson shook his head. 'No, no way. She'd spot us. We're in luck, though. New Scotland Yard's just across the street. I'll phone Garen Price, and tell him we need a hand.'

'You might ask him to bring us a camera, too. We'll want to identify that soldier. I'm not brilliant on Army uniforms, but I've got a feeling that his was the same as Major Legge's – the RAOC.'

'What, you mean . . .'

'Aye, sir, I do: the explosives experts!'

51

'Jesus, Neil, are they ever coming out of there?' It was almost seven-thirty; Ariadne and the soldier had been in Methuselah's for almost three hours. The two Scots policemen sat in their borrowed Cavalier, parked on Victoria Street a hundred yards away from the bar.

'I don't know, but I'll tell you one thing. Whatever they're drinking, they've had more than one bottle. I hope our Welsh pal isn't keeping pace with them.'

Just at that moment, as if McIlhenney had summoned him, white light spilled out into the street as Methuselah's door opened and Detective Sergeant Garen Price stepped out. He looked around for the car and then ran towards it. 'All these Welsh boys play rugby,' said Donaldson. 'From the way that one moves I'd say he was a hooker.'

'What, like Lily Savage?' said McIlhenney, but the line was lost on the DCI. He reached back to open the rear nearside door for his Metropolitan colleague.

'They're just about to leave,' Price gasped, as he climbed in. 'He's calling a cab and she's paying the bill.'

'What were they doing in there?' Donaldson asked.

'Eating,' said the Welshman, smiling.

'Not eating each other?'

'They were affectionate, guv, but they were more interested in the lentil soup and the creamed smoked haddock. Very tasty they were too,' he added, with a smile.

McIlhenney's eyebrows rose in indignation. 'Christ, listen to him! We've been out here freezing our gonads off and he's been at the scran!'

The bullet-headed Welshman grinned even wider. 'Had to keep up appearances, mate. I'd have looked a right dildo sat there for three hours munching the free peanuts and gherkins.'

'How did they seem?' asked Donaldson.

'She looked relaxed enough. The guy seemed a bit tense, though. She was always stroking his hand and the like, as if she was soothing him.'

'Maybe the bugger has reason to feel tense.'

'Hoi, here they come.' Price pointed back down Victoria Street, towards another black cab which was waiting outside the bistro. A few seconds later Ariadne Tucker and her escort appeared.

He opened the taxi door and held it for her. She was slightly taller than him, and had to bend to kiss him. She hugged him, quickly, and stepped inside the taxi. To the watchers' surprise, the soldier closed the door after her.

'Dammit!' snapped Donaldson. 'They're splitting up.'

'What'll we do?' asked McIlhenney.

'You two bale out and follow the soldier, wherever he goes. I'll tail Ariadne home . . . if that's where she's headed!'

52

Andy Martin looked at the bed and saw his father, on the day he died.

Phil Martin had been in his early fifties when the cerebral haemorrhage had struck him down, without warning, in his stand seat at Parkhead, ten minutes from the end of an early season Celtic vs. Aberdeen league match.

He had been rushed to the Southern General Hospital, but not even the skills of Scotland's fineset neurosurgeons could save him.

His son had arrived at the hospital late in the evening, having been flagged down on his way back from a day on the beach by a police colleague warned to look out for him.

He had been shown into a small room, not unlike this one. He had seen a still figure lying beneath a single sheet. He had been told the prognosis by the consultant neurologist. Finally, after a heart-rending discussion with his mother, he had given his permission for his father's ventilator to be switched off, and with it, his life.

He had been to neither church nor confession since the day of the funeral, but now, looking at his friend, he remembered his own decision and offered up a prayer that Sarah would not be forced to do the same thing.

'How's he doing?' he whispered, taking the seat beside her.

'His pulse is still firm and stable, but it isn't coming down fast enough for my liking.'

'What does the surgeon say?'

'Oh,' she sighed, 'he says I shouldn't worry about it. He says the shock was pretty severe, and that it's still only twelve hours or so since he came out of surgery. He's right, of course, but still . . .' She glanced up at the bank of monitors, her young face pale and drawn. 'I just don't like it, that's all.'

Andy took her hand. 'Sarah, my dear. You need a break from here.'

'No!' Her mouth drew into a tight line. 'I'm staying with him.'

He nodded. 'Fine, I understand that. All I'm saying is that you should go home for a couple of hours. Have a bath, see the baby, and have something to eat, then come back. Alex has a meal ready for you. I'll sit with him while you're away.'

She looked at him, wavering. There were dark circles under her eyes.

'Go on,' he said. 'There's a traffic car waiting for you downstairs. It'll take you home, and have you back here before midnight.'

She shook her head, still reluctant. 'No. What if something . . . happens?'

'Sarah, I promise you that if his condition changes, either way, that police car will have you back here in ten minutes.' He took her arm, and standing, drew her to her feet with him. 'Now on you go. There's another fellow back home needs you as well.'

Finally, she nodded. 'Okay, but you will call if anything changes!'

'I promise. But everything'll be okay, you wait and see.'

Her mind made up, she kissed him on the cheek, and left the Unit – hurrying, almost, lest her resolve should crack.

The door had barely closed behind her when Bob's arm moved on the cover, trembling perceptibly. His fingers twitched as if he was reaching, in a dream, for something familiar which had disappeared.

Instinctively, Andy took his hand, and grasped it tight. The tremor stilled at once.

'There, there, Big Man,' he whispered. 'It's all right, she'll be back. The reserve team's on for a few hours, that's all.' He gazed at his unconscious friend, and saw the slightest flicker of his right eyelid.

'Christ,' he said. 'I wonder what's going on in there? Knowing you, though, it'll be about police work!'

53

'You two took your time. Where the hell have you been?' Dave Donaldson pushed himself out of his armchair as McIlhenney and Price appeared in the doorway of the Strand Palace bar.

'Bloody Aldershot,' growled McIlhenney. 'The fucker led us all the way to bloody Aldershot.' He glared at the DCI. 'Rank has its privileges, so get them in. Mine's a pint, and Garen'll have the same.'

'Okay, I'll swing for that. You sound as if you've earned it.' He stepped across to the bar, a few feet away, and ordered the drinks.

'How about you?' asked his Sergeant. 'Did you have any more excitement?'

'Nah. She went straight home from the wine bar. Her mother was still there. She seems to be in residence, so I don't imagine that Ariadne'll have a gentleman caller through the night.' He nodded to Price. 'I left one of your night-shift colleagues there just in case, though.'

He handed a precisely metered pint of ale across to McIlhenney, who looked at it sceptically.

'When I got back here,' said Donaldson, returning to their table with the other beers, 'there was a SOCO report waiting for me, about the Noble house. The Scene of Crime people went over the place today. Their report was interesting. They found definite signs of an attempted break-in, via a small, unalarmed mezzanine window.'

'Oh aye?' said the Sergeant, his level of interest and his eyebrows rising simultaneously.

'That was all, mind you. There was no concrete evidence that anyone had been inside, but the window had been attacked, and although, as I said, it would have been a tight fit, it was big enough to admit a slim-built person – a youth, maybe, or a woman.'

'Could they say how recent this was?' asked Price.

Donaldson shook his head. 'No, not for sure. They reckoned the marks were pretty fresh but they couldn't put an exact date on them. They lifted a print, though, off the window frame, and some strands of wool, like from a glove.'

'Wearing gloves, yet leaving prints?' queried McIlhenney.

'That's what I said to myself too, but the report reckoned that the housebreaker would have had to take a glove off to get any purchase on the window.'

'Did you check whether an attempted break-in had been reported by either of the Nobles?'

'SOCO were up to that one, Neil. That was included in their report. There's been nothing notified to the police at that address, ever, apart from an incident a year ago, when Ariadne complained that she had been receiving anonymous letters.'

'Eh?' said the big Sergeant, choking in mid-swallow. 'What happened?'

'The local CID dealt with it. Apparently there had been three letters addressed to her husband, accusing her of having a bit on the side. Their investigation was fruitless, but the letters stopped anyway, according to the Nobles.'

'Do any of them still exist, sir?'

Donaldson laughed. 'Apparently wee Maurice was so outraged that he burned the first two. His wife hung on to the third, and gave it to the police. They couldn't get a thing from it, other than the fact that it was done on word-processing software, printed on a high-quality laser and posted in Tottenham. Once the investigation had been abandoned, Ariadne asked for the letter back, so that it could be destroyed as well.'

McIlhenney looked at him in astonishment. 'And they gave it to her?'

'Apparently so. Who knows, maybe strings were pulled.'

'Some strings, sir. Are we going to do anything about it?'

Donaldson shrugged. 'I don't know. I'll speak to Arrow and to Andy Martin in the morning.'

McIlhenney's expression grew grim. 'When were you in touch with Edinburgh last?'

'About an hour ago. There's no change; he's still unconscious.' They sat in silence for a while, until eventually McIlhenney went back to the bar for three more pints.

'So tell us about the soldier,' said Donaldson as he resumed his seat.

'McIlhenney glowered at him again. 'Bloody Aldershot, like I said. He caught a train at Victoria, so like good coppers we got on too. When we get to the other end, does he order a taxi? Does he hell! He's a fit lad so he walked the two miles instead. Eventually he arrives at a bloody Army camp.

'There was a security post there, and he showed a pass. That stuffed us. I mean, we could hardly walk up to the Redcaps and say, "Excuse me, but who was that soldier boy who just walked in here?" We couldn't do anything but turn around and come back. A waste of bloody time,' he growled.

'Not altogether. At least we know where he's based now; there can't be an infinite number of RAOC Lieutenants there.'

McIlhenney shook his head. 'We could have worked out where he was stationed, and as for identification, we managed to get some decent pictures at Victoria. We dropped them off at the Yard on the way back here.'

Donaldson nodded approvingly. 'Well done. We'll show them to Arrow first thing in the morning. While we're at it, we can discuss what to do about Ms Tucker's possible midnight caller . . and about those anonymous letters!'

54

Sarah woke with a start, disoriented. She gazed at Bob on the bed, bathed in the pale green light of the monitor screens, and wondered what could have disturbed her.

He looked so peaceful, lying there. She thought of a hundred other times in their short life together when she had watched him sleep, and could not recall having seen him look so restful. She pressed his hand gently, lovingly.

All at once she realised what had roused her. She realised too how closely she was in tune with the working of his body. The touch of his hand was noticeably warmer than it had been an hour earlier. She looked at the heart-rate monitor. The blips of his pulse, while still regular, were moving across the screen at a significantly faster rate than before.

She grabbed the panic button, which hung on the end of a long cable at the head of the bed and pressed it, once, twice, three times. Within seconds the Night Sister came bustling in from her station. 'What is it, Dr Grace?' she whispered.

'His temperature's taken a hike. And look at the pulse! Something's wrong.'

Distrustful of monitors, the white-haired sister lifted Bob's right wrist from the bed, and held it for around twenty seconds. 'Don't get yourself in a panic, my dear, but I think I'll ask someone to come up here.'

'Who's going to be around at this time of night?' asked Sarah anxiously.

'Mr Braeburn, the consultant. He's staying on the premises tonight.'

'What? Because of—'

Sister looked at her reassuringly. 'Of course not. He has an early start in surgery tomorrow, that's the only reason,' she said, lying in her teeth, but knowing that Sarah would believe her because she wanted to. She hurried back to her station.

In less than five minutes, the door opened and Mr Braeburn slipped into the Unit. He was a tall, thin man with fine surgeon's hands. His hair was so unruly that for a moment or two Sarah had difficulty recognising him as the same person who, still in his theatre clothes, had briefed her that morning on Bob's surgery and on his prospects.

'Hello again, Doctor,' he said. 'Let's have a look at the prize patient, shall we?'

He went quickly and expertly through a string of procedures, checking pulse, heart, breathing, temperature and blood pressure, lifting one of Bob's eyelids and testing his pupil reaction with a pencil torch.

When he was finished, he withdrew to the head of the bed, motioning Sarah to join him. 'It's damn funny. Blood pressure is as it should be, so I'm quite certain that the arterial sutures are holding, and that there's no internal bleeding. He's not in the clear yet, by a long way, but physically he's in good shape for someone who should have been dead when he was brought in here. He's heavily sedated, yet he seems agitated.'

He clutched his chin between thumb and first finger. 'I think I'm going to ask Sister to give him some more sedative, just to slow that heart-rate down a bit. He looks like a man who could handle some extra jungle juice.'

She looked up at him. 'But what's causing it? What's raising his pulse?'

Mr Braeburn shrugged. 'Who knows? I wish I knew what's going on inside his head, because the best answer I can give you is that something in there is making him fight the sedative!'

55

'He looks like a real fookin' bandbox, doesn't he? If I'd kept my uniform as neat as that, when I wore one, I'd 'ave been a Colonel by now.'

'You don't know him, then?'

Arrow looked at Donaldson with the disdain normally shown only by Glaswegians when they are asked by Southerners whether they know someone from Edinburgh.

'Neil,' he said slowly. 'I know the Army isn't what it was. I know we've shrunk a bit. But if I knew every one-pipper in every Regiment, we'd really be in trouble!' He handed the photograph to the DCI. 'How old would you say the lad was?'

The DCI made a shrugging gesture, then handed it back. 'Dunno. I didn't get a close enough look at him. What do you think, Sergeant?'

'Mid-twenties, I'd guess.'

Arrow sank back in his chair, making himself look even smaller. 'A bit young, maybe, to be having it off with an 'igh-powered lady in her thirties?'

'Who can say for sure?' countered Donaldson. 'Maybe Ariadne has a thing about men in uniform.'

'Could be,' said the soldier, 'though wearing one never did *me* any good in that regard. But then,' he added with a twinkle, 'I'm only little!'

He rose from his chair and walked over to the window of his top-floor office. It faced south, out across the autumnal Embankment, and over the cold grey waters of the Thames. He stood there, watching a barge as it made its steady way downriver, flapping the photograph idly in his left hand, and tapping the glass with the knuckles of the other.

Eventually, he turned back to face Donaldson and McIlhenney, holding up the snapshot. 'Right, lads. Leave this with me. I'll have someone check the records downstairs. We've got, or should 'ave, a photograph of every serving officer in this building, so it shouldn't take us long to trace this guy. Meantime, what about these anonymous letters that you mentioned? What does Andy Martin say you should do about them?'

'He agreed that we should follow them up,' said the DCI. 'We want

171

a complete picture of this couple. I'm intending to call on Ariadne again this evening. Want to come with us?'

Arrow shook his head. 'No, I don't think so. I've got other plans for this evening. Anyway, this is a purely civil matter. If I was there she might want to know why.'

'Yes, I see that.' He paused, then handed over the SOCO Report. 'Right. Last item on the agenda. Read this.'

Arrow took the document and scanned through it. As he did his face darkened. He read through it again, more slowly this time.

'What do you think of it?' asked Donaldson.

'Could mean nothing, could mean everything,' said the soldier grimly. 'Why the hell wasn't that window alarmed? According to this, all the others were.'

'I guess because it was so small, they thought they'd save a pound or two.'

'Could be. Anyway, you can find out the reason when you see the woman tonight. Go through the motions, and ask her if you can look over the system. See what they've got there, how it works, and how it was fitted.'

'Sure, we'll do that.' He turned to McIlhenney.

'Neil, have you had Crime Prevention training?'

The Sergeant nodded. 'Aye, about three years back. I'm reasonably up to speed about alarm systems.'

'Good,' said Arrow. 'Let's meet here at the same time tomorrow, yes?' The police officers nodded. 'So where is it now for you two?'

'Another fun day at the Old Bailey,' said McIlhenney. 'I only hope I don't wind up in bloody Aldershot again tonight!'

172

56

'You must be cooking in that uniform, Jimmy.' Sarah smiled faintly up at the silver-haired Chief Constable.

'I'm sorry, my dear. I have a Police Board lunch at twelve-thirty otherwise I'd have been more appropriately dressed. How is he today? I see the colour's back in his cheeks.'

'Don't let that fool you. That could be an infection. He's still critical, and the heart-rate keeps going up and down, despite the sedation. Mr Braeburn's coming in to check on him as soon as he's finished his surgical list. We'll see what he thinks then.'

Kindly and concerned, Sir James Proud looked down at her, and at Alex who was seated beside her, holding her father's hand. 'And how are you two?' he asked. 'How are you bearing up?'

'We're fine,' Sarah replied, for them both. 'Alex was great, the way she just took over looking after her brother.'

'Where's the wee chap now?'

'His nanny is looking after him.'

'And looking after the flowers,' said Alex. 'The house is full of them. They just kept arriving all day yesterday . . . some from very strange people, too. Do you remember that time earlier this year, the night Andy was hurt, when Dad had a huge fight with a man he was arresting for murder?'

The Chief nodded, intrigued.

'There was a bouquet from *him*!'

'*What!*' Sir James's voice rose for a split second, until he remembered where he was. 'He's in Peterhead now. He tried to kill Bob.'

'Yes,' said Sarah, 'and if you remember, Bob refused to charge him with that, or even with resisting arrest. He reckoned that one life sentence would be enough. The guy sent him a letter of thanks afterwards. The flowers yesterday came via his solicitor, with a Get Well note.'

Proud Jimmy shook his silver head. 'The world is a wondrous place! What sort of copper gets fan mail from a man he's put away for life?'

Alex grinned. 'Only my—' She stopped in mid-sentence, her mouth frozen open. Suddenly an expression of pain swept across her face. 'Ouch! Sarah, he's squeezing my hand, like he wants to break it! What do I do?'

'Squeeze back,' Sarah replied urgently. She looked up at the monitor and saw that the heart-rate was starting to climb again. 'Hard as you can. It's as if he's trying to make contact, as if he's trying to come round, despite all that sedative that Braeburn pumped into him.

'Kiss his hand, talk to him, let him smell your perfume – anything! Just try to let him know that we're here!'

57

He was back in the field, but the landscape had changed. No longer did it stretch away for ever. Instead it was encircled by high dark woods, reaching up towards the sky and blocking out most of the lights.

He was moving, but very slowly, looking around him at the filth and the carnage. Once again he saw the doll that was not a doll. He tried to avert his gaze, but his eyes moved slowly also.

At last it reached out beyond that fearful relic, to the centre of what had become an arena. There in the dreamscape, a dark looming shape rose up from the ground. In the distance, it seemed to have a face, twisted into a grotesque grin, leering at him, exulting in the knowledge that he was its captive. He tried to look elsewhere, but he was held firm, as if in a beam. He tried to squeeze his eyes shut, but knew as he did so that he was seeing not with any conventional sense. The dark vision remained.

He felt it call him onwards and he obeyed, although he did not want to go. This was a dream from which, he knew, there was no escape. In it he knew who he was. He remembered his run through the streets. He remembered the three men. He remembered the unnoticed girl. And he remembered the blow, and the pain; the sinking, the feeling of drowning, and at last his passage through the blackness that had delivered him to this place.

'Perhaps I am dead and in Hell,' he thought. *'Perhaps this is what Hell is: to be trapped for ever in your worst nightmare?'*

He was drawn towards the grinning shape in the distance; his movements seemed to gather pace. He fought against it, but it was no use . . . until suddenly he stumbled over something which had gone unnoticed as he looked ahead.

Managing to hold himself upright he looked down at his feet. There, collapsed on its back, lay the body of a man, a look of utter surprise on his face. He was in his early thirties, neatly dressed and clean-cut, with two small exceptions. Just right of centre in his chest, and through the centre of his forehead there were dark, ragged bullet-holes.

It was a face Skinner knew, from life and from a score and more of earlier dreams. As he stared down at it, the look of surprise faded, to be replaced by one of recognition. Slowly and stiffly the apparition began to rise from the ground with a mixed smile of welcome and anticipation. 'Well, hello again,' it began.

He recoiled from it in horror, feeling his hands clench with tension . . .

. . . and suddenly, upon his left hand he felt an answering pressure, something that was not of the dream. He held to it tightly, afraid to let go in case he was holding on to life itself, and as he did the apparition faded. He remained trapped in the dream . . . there was no escape from there . . . but he was held still and motionless, held back from the horrible grinning shape.

Other sensations came to him. In the distance he heard whispery voices. On the back of his hands he felt the softest of moist touches. A scent reached him, not one of the blood and oil and burning which filled the dream, but something fragrant, a scent that he knew.

There he lay, in his own private darkness, grasping the unseen fingers which had rescued him from the spectre, and another that had come to take his right hand. There he lay, suspended from life, dead but undead. There he lay, and held on.

58

'D'you ever notice how slow the pace of change is in London?'

Mackie looked at the acting Inspector, puzzled. 'What d'you mean?' he said. 'I'd have thought the opposite.'

McGuire paused on the pavement and shook his head. 'When I was a lad, I came down to Wembley once, with my dad and my uncle.' He raised an arm and pointed along Wardour Street. 'We had a pint in that pub there, and that one, and that one. They're all just as I remember them. You pick out three pubs in a row in the middle of Edinburgh, and if just one of them has the same name and paint-job that it had fifteen years ago, you'll be lucky.'

The DCI laughed. 'There's more to life than boozers, big fella.'

'So there is, and over the last ten years Edinburgh's had a new Conference Centre, a new Opera House, new cinemas, four big new retail parks, a new civil-service building, and umpteen big new office developments, in the city centre and out by the by-pass. Not bad for a city of under half a million folk.'

'Maybe so, Mario, but it could be that London is so big that change just isn't as obvious.'

Cyril Kercheval's nice little Italian place was opposite two of McGuire's fondly remembered ale-houses. Mackie gazed through the window and was pleased to note that it was much quieter than their Chinese meeting place. Kercheval was waiting for them inside, with a raffia-bound bottle of Chianti uncorked on the table.

'Hello again,' he began, rising to greet them. 'What have you been up to since yesterday . . . or can't you say?'

'It's all right. Special Branch isn't nearly as cloak and dagger these days. We leave most of that to your outfit. Mario's new to the section, so I've taken the opportunity to introduce him to some of our opposite numbers down here.'

Kercheval nodded in what seemed to be approval. 'Good, good. Not a wasted moment, eh?'

He looked at the menu, with a knowledgeable eye. 'Inspector,' he said, putting it down and filling their glasses with the dark red Chianti, 'you're a touch Italian, I think. How about choosing for us. On the MI5 tab, of course.' He sipped at his wine. 'Good stuff, this.'

'If you insist,' said McGuire, a good enough detective to know when he was being patronised. He spoke rapidly to the waiter in Italian. The man scribbled on his pad, reddening in the face at one point, and disappeared down a narrow staircase set in a corner of the dining room.

'Well? What did you order?'

'Scotch broth – that's soup of the day – and three Aberdeen Angus sirloins, medium rare, in a whisky sauce, with chips and peas. Sherry trifle to follow. My nose tells me that's all they're capable of cooking here. Oh yes, and I said to him that even without tasting it I could tell that the Chianti was shite, and could he please bring us a real bottle and uncork it at the table, otherwise there'd be hell to pay on account of us being coppers.' He smiled, showing all of his gleaming front teeth. 'That's only a rough translation, of course.'

Kercheval was as red as the waiter. 'Oh, I see. Glad to have you along in that case.' He turned quickly to Mackie. 'What news from the North? About Skinner, I mean.'

'None, either way. Mario phoned his wife an hour ago. They say that today will be crucial.'

'Mmm. Must be a worrying time for you both. Of course, you may not know him that well, what with him being Deputy Chief and all that.'

Mackie looked at him coolly, wondering at the sea change in his manner from the day before. 'Doesn't matter what rank he is. He's a copper and he's one of us. As it happens, Mario and I have both seen action with the boss. I was his PA before Maggie took over the post.'

'Oh,' said Kercheval, 'when you used the term PA yesterday, I assumed that Mario had married the boss's secretary.'

McGuire grinned meaningfully at the bachelor Mackie. 'A man could do worse,' he said, 'but my wife's a Detective Inspector. She outranked me until a couple of days ago.'

The waiter reappeared with a fresh bottle of Chianti, and opened it ostentatiously, handing the cork to McGuire as he poured a tasting sample into a clean glass. McGuire sniffed the cork, sipped the wine and nodded. The waiter filled three new glasses. As he withdrew, McGuire handed him the original bottle and spoke again in Italian. The waiter took the bottle with a thin, ungracious smile.

'What did you say then?' asked Mackie.

'I told him to take the first stuff home, put it in his car radiator and wait for a really cold winter.'

The DCI shook his balding head in mock despair. 'So Cyril,' he said to the MI5 man. 'What have you got for us?'

Kercheval sipped the replacement Chianti, eyes widening at the difference. Slowly he replaced his glass, then looked solemnly up at Mackie. 'Nothing, dear boy, I'm afraid.'

The two Scots stared at him, astonished. 'What?' said McGuire, his black eyebrows coming together in a heavy frown.

'As I told you, I went to see the DG, and asked if I could release the file on Davey to your investigation. He told me to give him a couple of hours. He called me back in last night, and said that we couldn't do that.'

'Why the hell not?' demanded Mackie.

'I don't question my DG, dear boy. Especially not when he's been to the PM about it.'

'You sure he did that?'

'Oh yes. I shouldn't tell you this, but it was the PM who stopped it. I'd have let the file go, especially since Davey's dead, and the DG always trusts my judgement.'

'So it seems that our fearless leader, the bastard, must have a short memory when it comes to people saving his life,' Mackie snarled.

'Either that,' said McGuire, who had stood behind the man as a human shield on that same rain-soaked evening, 'or he has a bloody good reason for keeping that file closed!'

59

'This husband of yours definitely wants to waken up, Dr Grace. It's a bit ahead of my schedule, but if you agree, then I think I'm going to let him.'

From her seat by the right-hand side of Bob's bed, Sarah looked up at Mr Braeburn. 'As far as I can see, he'd be less stressed off sedation. So yes, I agree. Take him off the drip.'

The tall, lugubrious consultant, dressed on this occasion in a white coat, beckoned to a waiting nurse. 'Disconnect Mr Skinner's IV sedative, please. Continue with the nutrients, but take him off the grog.'

The young woman did as she had been instructed, disconnecting the tube through which the drug had been flowing into Bob's arm.

'Given the dose he was on, I'd expect it to be about three hours before he's ready to come round, but with this fellow, God alone knows. Normally I'd take him off the ventilator in about an hour, but if we're both satisfied that he's ready to breathe on his own, I'll take the tube out now.'

Sarah almost blurted out her, 'Yes,' but stopped, forcing herself to think like a doctor, rather than a distraught, exhausted wife desperate to hear her husband speak. She thought back to his reactions over the last few hours, and looked at the steady, positive signs showing on the monitors. She glanced across at Alex, who sat on the other side of the bed, holding her father's left hand tight and watching her anxiously.

'I'm happy with that. Let's take the tube out before he wakens and chokes on the bloody thing.'

'Right,' said Braeburn. 'Would you like to assist me?' She nodded and moved round behind him. Gently, she raised Bob's shoulders slightly and tilted his head back, allowing the surgeon to ease the wet, mucus-strung ventilator tube from his throat. In spite of herself, she glanced at the monitor again, and saw happily that his breathing was continuing at the same steady pace. She held him up as the nurse, from the other side of the bed, pushed pillows under him to support his weight in a more normal position.

Alex's eyes glistened as she watched the beginning of her father's return to life.

'You stay with him,' Sarah said, 'and I'll get us some coffee. We could still have a wait until he's back with us.'

They finished two coffees as they sat by the bedside, watching and waiting. Alex continued to hold his hand as if both of their lives depended upon it. Occasionally, Sarah would stroke his forehead, to confirm that his body temperature was coming back to normal.

Gradually, as they studied him for signs of wakefulness, Skinner seemed to become less inert. Once or twice, his legs moved slightly beneath the cover, and his toes flicked and twitched.

'You want to shake him, don't you,' said Alex, 'to waken him.'

'That's the one thing we mustn't do,' said Sarah. 'He has to recover consciousness gradually.'

'Not that it was ever easy to shake Pops awake. I remember when I was a wee girl. I always wanted to go to the beach on Sunday morning, sun, rain, hail or snow – but that was the one day when he used to sleep late if he had a chance.

'I was always up and about early, waiting for him to surface. If he was taking too long I'd go into his room to waken him up. I used to shake him as hard as a seven-year-old could, but I couldn't budge him. He just lay there like a log. I knew he was pretending, but he could always wait me out.' She grinned. 'Eventually, though, I found the answer.'

'What was that?'

'I used to tickle the soles of his feet.' She reached down towards the foot of the bed, and slipped her free hand under the cover.

'Don't you bloody dare.'

It was a fuzzy, indistinct mumble, but it was intelligible. Alex and Sarah gasped in unison, rising to their feet. Bob's eyelashes flickered, ten, perhaps fifteen times, but at last his eyes opened. The women gazed down at him, struck dumb by their relief, until at last, Sarah leaned over him and kissed his forehead.

'Welcome back, my darling,' she whispered, her eyes swimming.

Alex sat back in her chair, hard, held his hand to her face and cried big, salt tears of relief.

'What happened?' Bob croaked. 'Heart attack?'

Sarah looked down at him in surprise. 'Heart attack? You? No way.'

'Wh' was it then? Don' remember.'

'You were jogging, darling, and you were attacked. You were stabbed. We've been worried about you for a while, but you're going to be all right.'

He smiled up at her and shook his head, weakly. 'Not jogging. Never jog. Running.'

She laughed. 'I stand corrected.'

He tried to speak again, but coughed, wincing in sudden pain.

'Easy, easy,' said Sarah.

'Throat's sore.'

'That's because you've had a tube down it for a day and a half. It'll ease. Want to try a sip of water?'

He nodded. She filled a glass from the jug at the bedside and held it to his mouth. He drank greedily, flicking his tongue over his lips to moisten them.

'A day and a half,' he whispered. 'That's how long I've been out of it?'

Sarah nodded. 'You've been under sedation since your operation. Standard recovery procedure.'

'What was the damage?'

'A pierced lung and a nicked artery. Other than that you're fine!'

He laughed faintly. 'Aye, I feel just great. Stabbed, eh. Of the two, I think I prefer being shot.'

Alex looked up at Sarah in astonishment. Like her father's colleagues, she had been told the alternative version of that chapter from his past. 'Let's hope you never have to make the comparison for real,' said his wife, trying to cover his gaffe.

Bob squeezed his daughter's hand. 'Hi, Babe. How're you doing?'

She smiled at him, her face still streaked with tears. 'Fine, now,' she said. 'Oh God, we were so worried about you.' She lifted his hand off the bed and pressed it to her moist cheek. As she did so, the diamonds on her finger sparkled with reflected light.

'Hey,' said Bob. 'What's this?'

She stared at him, startled. 'My engagement ring. Remember, we unveiled it on Saturday night.'

A shadow of confusion crossed his face. 'No,' he said, in the faintest of whispers. 'I *don't* remember.' He stared up at Sarah, frowning. 'What bloody day is this?'

She sat down on the edge of the bed. 'It's Tuesday. You were attacked early on Monday morning. But don't worry, honey. Traumatic amnesia is quite common. What's the last thing you can recall?'

He shook his head, frustrated.

'Okay then, tell me about the last meal you ate.'

He knitted his brow. 'Fresh pasta with a bacon, mushroom and tomato sauce,' he whispered. 'Chocolate mousse to follow. A bottle of Tyrell's Long Flat Red between us.'

'That was on Thursday,' Sarah said. 'A long time back, but don't let it worry you. You did have a pretty severe trauma. The memory gaps will fill up before too long.'

The corner of his mouth twisted. 'I don't know if I want them to. Here, did they get the bastards that knifed me?'

'Yup. Charged with attempted murder.'

'Pity. That means I won't get my hands on them.'

She laughed. 'You did already! But don't let's talk about that. Not yet anyway. You just relax and concentrate on getting better. You're still a sick puppy, you know.'

'Yes, Doc. Very good, Doc.' He tried to shift his position, and a spasm of pain crossed his face. 'Christ, I believe you.'

She reached out and touched his face. 'Easy now. They gave you quite a mauling in surgery. We'll get you some painkillers now you're awake.'

'I'm not going to burst open again, am I?'

'No, not now. There's been no sign of any more bleeding, so I reckon the arterial repair will be secure already. But you'll be in here for a while yet. Your body has to have time, and rest, to recover.'

He looked at her mournfully. 'If you say so.' Suddenly his face lit up. 'Hey, how's James Andrew Skinner?'

'Jazz is fine. I'll bring him to see you in a couple of days, when we've got you sitting up.'

'That's good. I miss the wee chap.'

'And he misses you, I think,' said Alex. 'Andy picked him up this morning, and his face lit up. But then he saw it wasn't you and he started to cry.'

Bob grinned at the thought, then gasped as another image of a baby flashed for an instant, unbidden, across his mind. 'What is it?' said Alex anxiously.

'Nothing,' he murmured. 'Just a memory flash.' Laboriously he reached up and tapped his head. 'All sorts of stuff going on in there, you know.'

'Yeah,' said Sarah. 'What was going through your mind when you were unconscious? In theory there shouldn't have been anything.'

'Can't remember that either.'

'Nothing at all?'

He paused, staring up at the ceiling. 'Yes. I remember someone holding my hand. And perfume. Are either of you wearing perfume?'

'I am,' said Alex.

'Then I remember that. Back in there . . .' he tapped his head once more '. . . I remember the smell of your perfume. Chanel No. 5 – I'd know it anywhere.'

Alex looked at him, puzzled. 'Your nose must be affected as well, in that case. You might know Chanel anywhere, but like always, I'm wearing Rive Gauche!'

60

'He bloody what?' Adam Arrow's eyebrows shot halfway up his high forehead.

'He said "No", Adam. The Prime Minister won't release the file on Davey.'

'Not even when he heard where the request came from?'

Andy Martin shook his head.

'I know that Kercheval character,' said Arrow. 'Bob might get on with 'im, but from what I've seen he's a real MI5 traditionalist. Know what I mean? Sees himself as the cream of the crop, and all the rest of us as bungling semi-pros, not to be trusted with the real stuff.

'I wonder if he mentioned to *anyone* that the request for Davey's file came from Bob.' There was a grim look in the little soldier's eyes. Wrinkles showed as they narrowed. 'Did he say anything else to the lads?'

'No. Only that the file was under wraps.'

'So they were wasting their time all along.'

A faint smile played around the corners of Martin's mouth. 'Not quite,' he murmured. 'He's not as smart as he thinks, is our man Kercheval.'

'No, he ain't,' said Joe Doherty, leaning back in his chair, grinning. 'I know him too. He's not so much a spook, more Caspar the Friendly Ghost.'

'Are you two going to let the rest of us in on the secret?' Arrow growled. Beside him, Merle Gower sat staring at Doherty: but beyond her, out of the soldier's line of vision, the light of comprehension was dawning in Maggie Rose's expression as she grasped the same implication that had occurred to her colleagues.

'Well,' said Doherty. 'For openers, he admitted to the guys from the start that there *is* a file on Davey. If he had told them that he'd have to find out whether one existed or not, he'd have left his options open. But being Kercheval he couldn't pass up a chance to impress two cops by letting them see that he's the sort of important guy who knows where the most important bodies are buried.'

'That's right,' said Andy Martin emphatically. 'And when the Prime Minister put a block on its release, there he was with egg all over his coupon. He couldn't turn around and say "Sorry, boys, I was wrong. There *isn't* a file," because he's told them for sure that there is. He couldn't even say that his DG stopped him, because he knows that Joe here wouldn't accept that level of refusal. So he had to come clean and pin the blame on the PM. He even compounded it by saying that if it was up to him he'd have released it.'

Doherty laughed out loud. 'That's old Cyril! No one knows better than him.'

'So it seems,' said Martin. 'Anyway, the upshot of it all is that Cyril has effectively told us not only that there *is* a file on Davey, but also that it contains material so sensitive that even in circumstances like these, with American interests involved as well as our own, our Prime Minister won't sanction its release.'

'Why not, d'you think?' asked Arrow.

The detective shrugged. 'I can only come up with two reasons, and they're both essentially the same. Either what's in the file would cost the Government Davey's seat in the by-election at a time when it can't afford to lose it, or it's so serious that it would bring it down altogether.'

The soldier shook his head and smiled. 'Know what, Andy? You've been around Bob so long, you're thinking just like him.'

The policeman grinned back across the table. 'That's the biggest compliment I've been paid in a while, mate.'

'So what would he do now?' asked Doherty.

'Why don't we go up to the Royal and ask 'im?'

'Christ, if we tried that, Adam,' said Martin, 'Sarah would cut our ears off. She said that he's out of immediate danger, but she's still worried about him. No . . . whether it would have been the boss's way or not, I'll tell you what we're going to do – assuming that you're game for it, that is.'

The soldier looked at him blankly.

'We're going to forget all about that file,' Martin told them, 'and conduct our own private investigation into Mr Davey and his background. Adam, I'd like you to run it, using your access through MoD security. I'll give you Brian and Mario as back-up, and young Sammy Pye, if you need him.

'We need to know whether there was anything in Colin Davey's ministerial life that might have compromised him, or made him serious enemies. At the same time, I want to know about the private person. Apart from his *Who's Who* entry and his party biography, we know sod all about him . . . and neither of those sources are famous for listing a man's less endearing traits.

'You look into things at the Ministry; dig as deep as you can. I'll have Brian and Mario ask some discreet questions around the constituency, and I'll go down myself with Pye to interview Davey's widow. Working together, we're going to find out what it was about

185

the late Minister that's so disturbing that it puts the wind up Prime Ministers.

'After that, we'll decide what we're going to do about it. Everybody happy?' Grunts of approval followed each other around the conference table.

Abruptly Martin sat up in his chair at its head. 'Right,' he said. 'That's one line of enquiry. What about the others? Most of them seem to centre around Maurice Noble, don't they? Adam, what can you tell us about his wife and her mystery man?'

Arrow hunched his disproportionately wide shoulders. 'We've identified him, without too much trouble. He's a Lieutenant in the Sappers, and his name is Stephen William Richards. Known to 'is mates as Short Wave, apparently. He's in the same line of work as our friend Major Legge, only from the other side. His speciality is demolishing, not defusing.'

'That kinda makes him number one suspect, don't it?' drawled Doherty.

'Not necessarily, sir. His work's all battlefield stuff. He's never been involved in anything covert, or even trained in it. I reckon I know more about the sort of device that took out that plane than he does.'

'Nonetheless,' interrupted Martin, 'he would have the basic knowledge, wouldn't he?'

'Aye, Andy, he would.' Arrow nodded in agreement. 'All that I'm saying is that we shouldn't make too big an assumption about him.'

'Fair enough; but right now he's the hottest lead we've got. What else do we know about him?'

'Basic background. He's twenty-six, educated at Westminster, then Sandhurst. His parents are both dead. He lost his mum when he was three, and was brought up after that by his old man . . . he was a vicar . . . and his housekeeper. The Reverend Richards popped 'is clogs two years ago. No siblings noted. The old vicar didn't get wed till 'e was fifty.'

'Interests?' asked Martin.

'Rifle shooting to near Olympic standard, cricket and squash. He represents the Army in all three.'

'Women?'

'Well, he's single, for a start. We don't keep tabs on every officer's romantic entanglements, but this lad's love-life has brought him to his superiors' attention on a couple of occasions. The first time was on his first posting after Sandhurst. Silly bugger got himself involved with his CO's sister.'

'What did the CO say to that?' asked Doherty smiling.

'A hell of a lot, according to Short Wave's file. The sister was ten years older than him, and 'ad just come through a very messy divorce. Our lad was told to cease and desist bloody quick, and he did.'

'The second time?' asked Martin.

'Just under a year ago. He was given a trial posting as an equerry to the Royal Household. He was hardly through the door before he was picked out for special attention by another lady some years older than 'im. Not even around this table will I say who he was involved with, but when it came to light, he was returned to his Regiment overnight, literally – on the direct instruction of the Secretary of State. Straight afterwards, Sir Stewart Morelli 'ad him on the carpet, personally, and put a note in his docket saying that his next promotion should be deferred by five years.'

'Why didn't they just kick him out?'

'I guess the J. Edgar Hoover principle came into play,' muttered Doherty.

'What's that?' said Arrow.

'Better to have him inside the tent pissing out, than outside pissing in!'

'Maybe so,' said Martin brusquely. He leaned forward across the desk, staring at Arrow. 'So what we've got here, Adam, is an explosives expert, with an established pattern of having it off with older women, who's been seen having a hand-holding dinner with Maurice Noble's widow three days after his death. On top of that, he could have held a personal grudge against Colin Davey. And you're telling me that I shouldn't make too many assumptions about him!'

Arrow chuckled ruefully. 'Well, if you put it that way . . .'

Around the table, Martin, Doherty, Alison Higgins, Maggie Rose, and even the invariably tense Merle Gower joined in the laughter.

'So how are you going to play him?' asked Doherty eventually.

'Carefully,' said Martin. 'We'll keep up observation on him and on Ms Tucker. Donaldson and McIlhenney are going to see her this evening to ask about these anonymous letters—'

'And about her alarm system,' cut in Arrow.

'Good. I'll tell them to play that up. If she and Richards did it, it'll do no harm to let her think that we're on the trail of a mystery intruder . . . Look, Adam, you couldn't fix something with Richards' Regiment, could you? Something that'll keep him tied up for a day or two.'

'Probably. But what good would that do?'

'It would ease the task of the watchers if they knew where he was. And it might force him to do something that would corroborate our theory. Make a phone call, maybe, that we could pick up through the tap you put on Ariadne Tucker's telephone. Ideally we should listen in on Lieutenant Richards' phone as well. Can you fix that?'

Arrow nodded. 'I can monitor the phone in his private apartment, but not the Officer's Mess. Mind you, he's hardly likely to use that to make a sensitive call.'

'There's something else I'd be grateful if you could do, Adam, and that's check the explosives stock at Richards' base. Is that possible?'

'Of course – but I'll tell you now, it'll be all right. He couldn't get his hands on official ordnance without someone knowing. If it were 'im, he'll have had another source.'

'Such as criminal, do you mean?'

Arrow shook his head. 'There's unofficial stock as well, Andy. The Special Forces have been known to be a bit lax in reporting material recovered from Ireland, or captured in overseas operations. There are other ways of acquiring explosives too, even for ordinary servicemen, if they have the know-how. If it was Richards, he's had access to some of that, but we'll have the Devil's own job proving it.'

'Do what you can, Adam. That's all I ask.'

'Sure.'

'Okay,' said Martin. 'Now our other line of enquiry. General Yahic.'

Doherty tapped the table, and shook his head. 'Closed off. We just found out – Yahic has been dead for ten days.'

Of those around the table, only Merle Gower did not look surprised.

'What 'appened?' asked Arrow.

'His own men shot him. The guy was as mad as a hatter, and he was getting too many of them killed, so his second-in-command, a Colonel called Brisnich, gave him a round behind the ear. Since then he's been closing down Yahic's operations around the world, until this morning, when he contacted the UN and said that he and his followers would hand over their weapons at Mostar tomorrow. He even faxed a photograph of Yahic's body in confirmation. So, other than in that mugshot, the General is very definitely out of the picture.'

Arrow whistled. 'That's a blessing. I'd reckoned that the next step would have been for Merle and I and a few of our pals to go in there and invite him for a chat. Now all we 'ave to do is hire a medium.'

Martin smiled, nodding. 'Yes. That's a big complication out of the way. Now we can concentrate on the real police work . . . unless of course, Adam, you're going to come up with Agent Robin.'

The soldier grunted. 'Believe me, mate, you'd be the first to know if I did.'

'I wish I *could* believe that, Captain. But after what we've heard about the Davey file, if you did catch Agent Robin, I wonder if you'd be allowed to tell anyone outside Downing Street about it, let alone a poor sad provincial copper like me!

'Right, that's it, everyone. Meeting adjourned.' He picked up his notes from the conference table and looked towards Doherty. 'When would you like to get together again, Joe?'

The American shrugged his shoulders. 'My orders are to offer assistance and to report regularly to the White House. If you need my backing in setting up that phone tap, you've got it, but otherwise I'll lay off for a while, and Merle, here, can get back behind my old desk in London. Let me know when you have something fresh to tell me from all these different enquiries, but for now, I've got enough for a solid report to the Oval Office.'

He caught a look of concern in Martin's eyes. 'On a Top Secret basis, of course. Don't worry, nothing will leak out of there. Nothing ever does . . . unless the President wants it to, of course. Just between you and me, I think he was hoping to have a chance to kick some Bosnian butt over the next few days, just to top him up in the opinion polls. He may be the only mourner at Yahic's funeral.'

Martin led Doherty, Gower and Arrow along the corridor and down the stairs to the draughty foyer of the headquarters building. All three climbed into a chauffeur-driven consular car, in which Doherty had volunteered to take his companions to the airport.

When the Chief Superintendent returned to his new office after saying his farewells, he found Alison Higgins waiting for him.

'Good news about the boss,' she began diffidently.

He nodded, and she could see the relief in his green eyes. 'Yes, but let's all still keep our fingers crossed. Sarah's still worried about him. She hasn't said, but I've got a feeling she's concerned about the long-term effects.'

'Nah! Not him. He's as hard as nails. He'll get over it.'

'Let's hope so.' He paused. 'Anyway, was there something else?'

'Yes,' she said slowly. 'I was wondering if you had any thoughts on how long I'll be without Donaldson.'

Martin shrugged his shoulders. 'As long as it takes. If we do get a result with Noble's wife and the soldier laddie, you won't see him again for a hell of a while. It won't be because he's going to Drugs and Vice either. No, he'll be preparing to be chief police witness at the Trial of the Century.

'Why are you asking? Do you want a replacement? With the boss out of action for a while, I can give you Maggie Rose on a temporary basis . . .' A recent memory came back to him '. . . or don't you two get on?'

Higgins shook her head vehemently. 'I've got no problem with Maggie. She's bright and she's a straight talker. If she's on offer, I'll take her, even if it's only for a few days. The truth is, I'd like to be free to give Leona as much help as I can. She's acting quite strangely, and I'm not certain how it'll end up.'

'What do you mean, strangely?'

'Well, over the last few days she's become almost euphoric. She's even having a supper party for a few of us tonight. She's on a high, when you'd still expect her to be in shock.'

189

'Is she on medication?'

'No. She wouldn't take any. I don't know what's driving her, but if it reverses on itself, she'll come down with a hell of a bang. If that happens, my godson might need me even more.'

'Mmm. In that case you can have all the time you need. Wee Mark's our star witness. In fact, he's almost our *only* witness!'

Martin settled into his chair, and indicated to Higgins that she should take a seat.

'What was his dad like? The late Roland. I wasn't here when he paid us a visit, but I got the idea that Bob didn't care for him.'

'What gave you that impression?'

'I think the fact that he called him an "insufferable little arsehole" may have had something to do with it.'

Higgins laughed softly. 'Yes, I could see that Mr Skinner and he might not have hit it off. Roly was a better talker than a listener, and an expert on everything. He found success in politics early, and it went to his head. He used to be okay, but lately, no, I'm afraid not. He always had time for Mark, but if he'd treated his secretaries like he treated Leona, then he'd have gone through about one a week.'

'Did he give you any hassle?'

'No, but only because I always made it clear that I would never talk to him about police work. But the truth is, if Leona wasn't such a close pal, and if Mark wasn't my godson, I'd have stayed away from them after he landed the Scottish Office job.'

'Aye, well, Ali,' said Martin. 'A week ago Roland McGrath was a power in the land. Today he's a pile of bones and ashes. You give your pal as much time as you can manage. From the sound of things, she needs it.'

61

'Just what could those bloody stupid letters have to do with this accident, Chief Inspector?'

Experiencing the full weight of Ariadne Tucker's frosty glare, Dave Donaldson found it easy to imagine how a hostile witness would feel in the box, under her cross-examination. A pang of relief passed through him as he remembered that English barristers were not admitted automatically to practice in the Scottish courts.

'Probably nothing at all, ma'am,' he said. 'But until we know exactly what the circumstances were, we can't discount the possibility of a connection. The letters, according to what we've been told by the investigating officers, accused you of infidelity.

'The relevant questions arising now are, who was the author, and what was the motive? Were they meant to harm your husband, or could they have been written by someone with a grudge against you? Your practice usually involves criminal cases, doesn't it?'

At once, her glare turned to a cool smile, which Donaldson found almost as unsettling. 'Yes, it does, Chief Inspector,' she said, in honeyed tones. 'But I am a very *good* criminal silk. In fact, I'm probably the best around at the moment. So my clients tend to leave court either by the front door, or in the knowledge that their sentence is a hell of a lot shorter, or less expensive than it might have been.

'Take the trial I'm on just now as an example. It's been going on for weeks. The Judge has just begun his summing up, and it'll take him another couple of days, but I know already and so does he that my client will walk. The chap's as guilty as sin, but my duty to the court is to demonstrate the weakness of the case against him. The Crown hasn't delivered enough material to the jury for a conviction, and the Judge's summing up should point that out.

'I tell all my clients that I'm there to prevent a miscarriage of justice, and they understand that. The fact is that in a good proportion of my work I actually *achieve* such a miscarriage, of natural justice at least.

'Therefore, Mr Donaldson, there are no grudges harboured against me as a result of my work. It's the bad barristers who have plots hatched against them in Parkhurst.'

'How about your private life, Mrs Noble?' Neil McIlhenney had decided almost at first sight that he disliked the woman. It was obvious in his tone. 'Any enemies there?'

The frost returned to her eyes. 'Not that I know of, Sergeant. Have you?'

McIlhenney smiled. 'That's a sure-fire certainty, ma'am. I think I'm making one even as I speak, which probably means that I'm good at *my* job, too.'

'No doubt you are, Mr McIlhenney, but I fail to follow your line of questioning. Why should my enemy want to kill my husband, or blow up a planeload of people?'

'Who says he did? Perhaps he wanted to kill you and didn't care whether he got Mr Noble.' He glanced around the drawing room. 'Maybe the bomb was meant to go off here, only it had a dodgy timer. Maybe your enemy assumed that Mr Noble would open the box at home, only he didn't.'

Ariadne Tucker was rattled. 'What enemy? I've told you, I don't have any.'

'How about someone who's mentally disturbed?' the Sergeant fired back. 'Emotionally stable people don't plant explosive devices. Any nutters in your life, public or private?'

'For the last time,' she shouted at the policeman. 'Sane or otherwise, I don't have any enemies!'

'So who would write those letters accusing you of adultery?' said McIlhenney quietly, managing, with a great effort, to keep triumph out of his tone. 'A well-meaning friend?'

She looked at him. The anger left her eyes. She nodded solemnly. 'Nice one, Sergeant.' She pushed herself out of her armchair and walked over to the bay window.

'All right, I'll tell you. There's no point in keeping it quiet now anyway. Maurice himself wrote the letters.

'From the earliest days of our marriage, he was paranoid about me. He was convinced that I had affairs. It started off as hints at first; nudge, nudge, wink, wink, sort of stuff, but gradually it became more serious. The hints became accusations.'

'We have to ask you this, ma'am,' said Donaldson. 'Was there substance in them?'

'No, there was not,' she said firmly.

'So how did you react to his suggestions?'

'I cross-examined him.'

'What do you mean?'

'I put him in the witness box. I made him set out his evidence, and I took it apart.'

'Did he have any evidence?' asked McIlhenney.

She sighed. 'No. Deep down poor Maurice, much as I loved him, was an essentially insecure personality, with little or no inner self-belief. He really could be quite inadequate.'

'Sexually?'

She looked sharply at the Sergeant. 'Well, if I'm being frank, he wasn't a superstud. But I was speaking in emotional terms. As I said, he was paranoid, a classic manifestation of low self-esteem. For example, if I met a colleague of his and exchanged even a few friendly words, it would fester, and I'd hear about it at some time in the future.'

'Did you ever meet Colin Davey?'

'Yes, I was introduced to him at a reception around two months ago. I took an instant dislike to him. Then about a fortnight after that I had a consultation with a solicitor who turned out to be his Constituency Chairman. As it was coming to an end, Davey called into his office. After we had each completed our business we talked for about twenty minutes, while he waited for his car, and I for my taxi.'

'What did you talk about?'

'Trivia. I didn't like him and I could tell that he didn't like me but it was easier to jabber about the weather than to sit in silence.'

'Did your husband know of these encounters?'

She nodded. 'He was in the room on the first occasion. The second time he was in the official car which came to collect Davey from the solicitor's office. When it arrived, Davey and I came out together . . .' Her voice trailed off as she saw the expressions on the faces of the two policemen.

'Oh no,' she said quietly. 'Surely not.'

'Later, did Mr Noble ever mention either of those meetings?' asked Donaldson.

She shook her head. 'No, he didn't. But after the letters, he wouldn't have.'

'What do you mean?'

'When Maurice showed me the first letter, I guessed at once that he had sent it to himself. I didn't accuse him at that stage. I just burned it, and I did the same with the second. But when the third arrived, I decided that I had to put a stop to it, so I called in the police.'

'Did you expect them to trace it back to him?'

'No. I was pretty certain they couldn't do that. I simply wanted to give him a scare and put a stop to the endless accusations. It worked. The arrival of the police gave him a hell of a fright. After they had gone, I sat him down and made him promise that the nonsense would stop. I told him that if he ever accused me again of having an interest in another man, then I really would leave him. That seemed to have done the trick.'

'So he said nothing to you about Davey?'

'Not in that context, no. All that he said about him was professional.

193

About his conduct, about the way he treated his staff, and generally about what a horrible man he was.'

'And you agreed with that?'

She nodded. 'Maurice was dead right about him. I thought that he was a typical politician. Arrogant, self-centred, and power-hungry sums up the way he came across to me.'

'You weren't attracted to him by all that arrogance?' asked Donaldson. 'It can happen, you know.'

She laughed, bitterly, in his face. 'Not in the slightest, Chief Inspector. But surely your argument is that my husband thought I was.'

'Not our argument, Ms Tucker. Simply a line of enquiry, a piece of potential evidence which we have to assess. From what you've told me and from what we've heard from others, it's a pretty strong possibility.' He paused. 'I'd like to record this discussion, ma'am. Would you give us a formal statement, please.'

'Of course,' she said. 'I know the drill. I'll set something down, sign it and let you have it. Could you collect it tomorrow evening?'

Donaldson nodded. 'Yes, but in the circumstances I'll have to ask you to write or type it yourself, rather than dictate it to a secretary.'

'Naturally.' She brushed her hands down her skirt. 'Now, will that be all?'

The DCI shook his head. 'No, there's just one other thing. The forensic people who looked over your house found signs of entry at a small mezzanine window. They said it was unalarmed.'

'Yes, it is, I'm afraid. The alarm system was in the house when we bought it. I expect that whoever installed it saved a few pounds because that window is so small. We'd been meaning to upgrade it, by installing movement sensors, but we never got round to it.'

'Have you noticed anything out of place since last Thursday evening?' asked Donaldson. 'Or did you hear anything that night? You said that you worked late.'

She pursed her lips. 'Let me think. I was in my study, off the second bedroom.'

'Would there have been lights showing?'

'Probably not. Anyway, let me think. Yes, I do recall hearing a sound, as if someone had tripped over something.'

'Were you startled?'

Ariadne Tucker looked at the Chief Inspector, as if to indicate that 'startling' was something which happened to other people.

'I just assumed,' she said, 'that Maurice had gone downstairs for some reason and had trodden on the cat. Which, almost certainly, is what happened!' She gathered herself and moved towards the door. 'Now, gentlemen, if that really is everything . . .'

Donaldson and McIlhenney followed her into the hallway. She held the door open for them, but as the Chief Inspector stepped outside she caught his arm. 'Look,' she said. 'This theory about Maurice thinking I was having an affair with the Secretary of State. It really is pretty far-fetched, isn't it?' For the first time, her voice sounded less than confident.

'Of course it is, ma'am,' said Donaldson soothingly.

'Aye,' said McIlhenney. 'The only trouble is, it fits the facts as we know them. When you get down to it, blowing a plane full of people out of the skies, that's pretty far-fetched too, yet that's exactly what happened last Friday!'

62

'Leona,' said Alison Higgins, as she hung up her overcoat in her friend's hallway. 'Are you sure you're up for this? How many people are coming?'

'I'm perfectly fine,' said the little woman. 'There won't be too many of us. Just you and Marshall Elliot, plus Roly's Constituency Chairwoman, Vice-chairman and Treasurer. Don't you worry, I can handle half a dozen close friends for supper. I'm cheating anyway. I've had a caterer send in a huge shepherd's pie and a big glitzy gateau.'

'Fine, but what's it all about?'

'It's just something I felt I had to do, in the circumstances. Go on, Alison, pour yourself a drink and relax. What would you like?'

Higgins shook her head. 'Ach well, as long as it keeps you occupied. Got any Swan Light?'

Leona laughed. 'The Sheila's Pint?' she said, mimicking an Australian accent. 'Of course I have, with you coming. Get yourself one, then give me a hand to set the table. They'll be here soon.'

'Where's Mark?' asked her friend, as she reached into the fridge.

'He's at his grandpa's for the night. I thought it might do the old fellow some good to have him around. My son's an amazingly resilient wee chap, isn't he?'

'So's his mother, by the looks of things.'

The two women had barely finished setting the table when the doorbell rang. Alison, in the hallway at the time, went to answer it, to find all four guests on the doorstep.

'Hello Marsh,' she said to the agent. 'All together, I see.'

'Yes, I thought it made sense for me to pick everyone up in the Rover.'

She smiled at him. Higgins had developed a secret attraction to Marshall Elliot. 'Tory staff still under orders to buy British, then?' she said lightly.

He returned her grin. 'If that was the case, my dear, we'd all be driving TVRs or Morgans or some such!'

His three companions smiled nervously. Alison thought that the Chairwoman looked particularly ill at ease.

'How is Leona tonight?' Elliot asked quietly as they entered the hall. 'I wasn't sure about this, but she insisted.'

'She's fine,' said Higgins, to the three constituency officers rather than to him. 'You have to remember that while she's been widowed, her son survived by some miracle. At the moment the relief seems to be outweighing the loss. This evening will do her good too. I know that it's important to her. So please – try not to feel ill at ease in her company.'

She opened a door off the hall and led the way into the living room, where Leona McGrath was waiting. Inside, Marsh Elliot completed the formal introductions of his three companions to Alison, who was meeting them for the first time.

Elizabeth Marks, the Constituency Chairman, as she insisted on being described, was a stout, tweed-clad woman in her early fifties, with severe iron-grey hair. Her husband Jeremy was the local Party Treasurer. He was a small mousy man, an inevitable seconder, Higgins imagined, of his wife's proposals in Committee. His main distinguishing feature was an incipient strawberry nose, which suggested that he and alcohol were frequent companions.

John Torrance, the Vice-chairman seemed the most assured and friendly of the trio. He was tall and slim, in his early forties, clad in a dark blue suit, with a cut which suggested private tailoring. Higgins knew him by reputation and by word of mouth from Leona, as a self-made millionaire with no desire for office, but with a clear vision of the way his country should be run.

'Superintendent,' said Torrance, with genuine interest as he shook her hand. 'Tell me, what's the word on Bob Skinner? I know him a little through the New Club. That was a terrible business the other night.'

'The news is fairly good,' she replied. 'He's conscious and the surgery has been effective. He's still in Intensive Care, in case of unforeseen complications, but he should be all right.'

He turned to Leona. 'And you, my dear. How are you?'

The little woman nodded her head, a touch nervously, Higgins thought, bouncing her brown curls. 'I'm fine, John. It was too much to take in at first, Roland's death and our child's survival. It was Bob Skinner who rescued him from the cockpit, you know,' she added, as an aside to Mr and Mrs Marks.

'You just have to come to terms with things. I have. Roly could have had a heart attack, cancer, been knocked down by a bus, anything. I couldn't have done anything about it. Whatever the cause, he's gone. I'll miss him for ever, but I'll do my crying in the dark. During the day I have to look forward, not back, for everyone's sake, for my son's most of all. I think I've found a way forward.'

She paused. 'First things first, though. What would you like to drink?'

She poured white wine for John Torrance, a Coca-Cola for Marsh

Elliot and whisky for the two Marks, who closed in on her with their private condolences.

'How's the investigation going, Superintendent?' Torrance asked as he and Marsh Elliot, flanking Higgins, gave them their moment.

'It's early days yet,' said Higgins. 'It's a difficult one altogether. I'm not heavily involved, but my Deputy is, and from what he's reporting back, there are a number of possibilities.'

'Presumably you're looking for international terrorists,' said Marsh Elliot.

'That's a natural assumption, but the fact is we're looking everywhere.'

'But Davey or Massey – or both – must have been the target, surely?'

Higgins, feeling cornered, shrugged. 'You can draw that conclusion if you like, Marsh. But you mustn't expect me to comment on it.'

Leona McGrath, seeing her friend's predicament, moved in to end the interrogation by summoning her guests to supper.

The Marks continued to surround their hostess during the meal, with elaborate Presbyterian concern which seemed as genuine as the Constituency Chairman's pearl necklace. Apart from the occasional glance to reassure herself that her friend was enduring the experience, Alison was left to enjoy the company and the attention of two attractive men, even if each was wearing a gold band on his left hand. The subjects of Bob Skinner's injury and the investigation were declared, tacitly, off limits; instead their conversation centred around sailing. Torrance revealed that he owned and sailed an ocean-going yacht, while Higgins confessed that her favourite recreation was crewing her brother's somewhat smaller vessel on the Firth of Clyde. Marshall Elliot registered his interest by admitting that before becoming a Conservative Agent, he had spent fifteen years as an officer in the Royal Marines.

At the other end of the table, far from being borne down by the droning Marks, whose only interest in life seemed to be their small accountancy practice, Leona McGrath seemed to be revelling in her surroundings, smiling and putting her guests at their ease. It seemed almost as if she had reversed the roles and was consoling them.

At last, she tapped her glass, interrupting, politely, John Torrance's account of a voyage around the Canaries, 'In the wake of Captain Bob,' as he put it.

'Friends,' she said. 'There are just a few formal things that I'd like to say to you. The first is to thank you all, especially you, Alison, and you, Marsh, for the tremendous support which you've given me since Roland's death. I hope that at the funeral you will all join the family in the reserved rows at the front of the church. The Prime Minister will sit beside Mark and me, and the family. I'd like you all to sit immediately behind us in the second row; with your wives of course, John and Marsh.'

All five guests nodded, heads bowed.

'Gentlemen,' she went on, looking in turn at Marks, Torrance and Elliot, her face showing strain for the first time that evening. 'For the burial, I would like each of you to take a cord at the graveside. Roly's father will be at the head of the coffin, with his brothers. Marsh, would you take the cord facing him, with Jeremy and John on either side of you. There are eight cords in all. I intend to ask Andrew Hardy and Sir James Proud to take the others. 'Would you all do that for me?'

'Of course, Leona,' said Elliot. Torrance and Marks nodded, mumbling thanks.

She glanced apologetically at Mrs Marks. 'Ladies, traditionally this is a man's task at a funeral. Roly's dad is very much a traditionalist and I wouldn't upset him.'

'I understand completely, dear,' said Mrs Marks.

'Good. Now to the last thing I have to say.

'The three things in life which my husband loved were his son, his Parliamentary seat and his Party.' Alison Higgins flashed a quick glance around the table, but none of the other guests reacted to her obvious omission.

'If, somehow, he knew last Friday that Mark would be spared, then he would have died happy. After that, he would have wished more than anything else for the seat which his death leaves vacant to be saved for his Party.' She paused and looked around the table once more.

'Although some of his colleagues have joined what the Opposition are calling the Chicken Run, and finding new, safer seats before the next election, Roly never entertained the idea of doing that. He believed that he owed it to the Party nationally and to you in the constituency to stay here, whatever the odds, and fight the next election. I know you all had doubts, but he was convinced that he would have held it.

'So was I.

'I've given this a lot of thought. I believe that I owe it to Roly to try to keep alive his determination to retain this as a Tory seat. As you all know, the Writ will be moved on Thursday, principally to give the Party the best possible chance of holding Colin Davey's seat, where they're going to slot the sitting MEP in as candidate.

'That puts you in a hole, does it not?' She looked directly at John Torrance, acknowledging what all the rest knew, that he was the real leader of the Constituency Party. Torrance nodded solemnly, but with a question in his eyes.

'Right. Let me help you out of it. John, in these circumstances can

199

you think of anyone who has as good a chance as I would have of holding this seat for the Party?'

He looked at her in astonishment for uncounted seconds. At last he said, slowly, 'No, Leona, I can not.'

She looked at each person around the table, one by one. 'In that case,' she said, 'humbly and sincerely, I offer myself to you as your Parliamentary candidate.'

Half an hour later, she waved good night from the front doorway to her four guests, each one still slightly shell-shocked from the experience of the evening. When she closed the door behind her and turned back into the hall, Alison Higgins was staring at her.

'Christ, Leona. Their faces! Mine too, I suppose, for I was as surprised as them. Are you sure about this?'

'Absolutely. I've never been more certain of anything in my life. It wasn't love that kept Roly and me together, you know. It was politics. You must have guessed that, surely.'

Almost reluctantly, Higgins nodded. 'I knew there was something. I have to admit that latterly it was pretty obvious that there wasn't any sexual chemistry left between you two.'

'Delicately put,' said Leona, with a bitter smile.

She led the way back into the dining room and picked up an unfinished glass of wine from the table. 'Poor Marsh. I really should have warned him in advance, I suppose.' She grinned again. 'God, the trouble he has with the women in his life!'

'What d'you mean?' said Higgins, puzzled.

'Margie Elliot gives her husband a very tough time. She's the talk of the coffee mornings, even in the presence of the MP's wife. They say she has a tongue like a navvy, and that she gives her poor husband the rough edge of it on a daily basis. They say also that Marsh, for all that he has a reputation as a man's man, can't do anything about it.'

'No? What about divorce, if it's that bad?'

'Not everyone rushes to divorce an awkward spouse. Take me for example.'

Higgins looked at her, frowning.

'Oh yes, Ali my dear. The coffee-morning gossips were quite specific about the MP too, although they didn't know I was listening at that point. There was a pretty young thing from BBC Television, then there was a rugby internationalist's wife, then a Judge's daughter. I could go on.'

She drained her wine glass, and Alison realised that her friend had crossed the threshold to the other side of sobriety.

'He didn't try it on with you, ever, did he?' Higgins shook her head, unsmiling. 'No, he wouldn't have. He was always wary of you. A little scared, almost. He covered it up though, with bluster.' She picked up a bottle of Fleurie from the table and refilled her glass. 'He used to say that you struck him as being sexually stingy. I told him that there were a couple of weekend sailors who could disprove that charge, but he stuck to his guns. I think he was pleased with the phrase. Sexually stingy.' She pronounced the words slowly and carefully, then burst into pealing laughter.

'Not something anyone would have said about Roly, though. He was sexually generous to a fault. To a very big fault, actually.' Carefully, and without warning, she replaced her glass on the table, sat down hard in the carver chair at its head, and burst into tears.

63

He shifted painfully against the pillows which propped him up, looking up at the lugubrious face of Mr Braeburn.

'Look, Mr Skinner,' said the mournful consultant, 'I'll grant that you have a remarkable constitution, to have survived a wound which would have finished off most people, and to be recovering from it so well. But I do wish that you would take my advice and accept more medication to ensure that you have a restful night.'

The big policeman smiled, but shook his head slowly. 'You've got me off the glucose and back on solid food. I even took a piss half an hour ago, albeit with the help of my good pal Andy over there. That means that my system's working normally again. In that case, when it wants to go to sleep, it will. I've got a thing about medication of any kind. Just ask my wife. I won't even take Rennies.'

'That's right,' said Sarah. She was still seated at his bedside, holding his hand. Andy Martin stood at the back of the room, beside the wall, laughing quietly to himself. 'He knows it all, my husband. His standard remedy for indigestion is a pint of milk, and his patented hangover cure is a six-mile run.'

Mr Braeburn nodded. 'Efficacious in both instances, I will allow. But surely, you will agree as a doctor with my recommendation in these circumstances.'

'As a doctor, of course I do.' Bob glowered at her. 'And as a wife, perhaps if you left us alone, I might try to talk him into it.'

'Anything to further the cause,' said the surgeon, throwing up his hands in despair. He turned and left the Unit, with Andy Martin following behind.

Sarah watched the door close and turned back to her husband. She squeezed his hand. 'Bob, don't you think we're being a bit difficult here? I mean, that guy just saved your life, and now you won't even let him give you a pill.'

His jaw tensed. 'Look, love, I just want to be able to sleep naturally, that's all. I hate the idea of sleeping pills.'

'No. There's more to it than that. After the accident on Friday, and before the attack, you were ... funny. Going out for a run in the middle of the night, for instance. That ain't normal behaviour even for you. What made you do that? Was something worrying you?'

'He shook his head. 'I can't remember.'

'Bob, I don't want to rush you into recalling things, but on Saturday night you had a nightmare. You didn't tell me what it was about, but I guessed it was a reaction to all the things you saw on Friday, much as I had immediately afterwards. Have you been having more dreams?'

'I don't know. I feel . . . I don't know how to say it. There's a sort of darkness in here.' He tapped his head. 'And a feeling of being trapped in it. I can't bring back detail, any of it. I just know that I don't want to take anything that will *make* me sleep.'

She rubbed his hand again, and nodded. 'Okay, I understand you. Bob, this isn't my expert field, as you know, but I'd say you were suffering from post-traumatic stress. Nightmares, flash-backs, even memory lapses, are all classic symptoms. I think I had some of the same last Friday night. But I'm different from you. I was able to cry myself through it. You might need some help.' She hesitated. 'Would you do something for me?'

'Depends,' he said slowly.

'Would you talk to Kevin O'Malley?'

'O'Malley? But he's a shrink! I don't need a head doctor.'

She grasped his hand, tighter than ever. 'Bob, he is an acknowledged expert in the sort of counselling which *you* inisisted should be available to every person on duty on the Lammermuirs last Friday. You're not immune, big guy. You need him too.'

He looked at her doubtfully. 'I can get myself through this. I just don't need drugs or quacks to do it.'

'Bob, this isn't the first time. When you woke up in a sweat on Sunday morning you told me that you'd had dreams like that before – after that business with the man in the cottage.'

Suddenly, he went rigid. He stared up at the ceiling, his eyes standing out. 'Him!' he gasped. 'He was in the dream; and a doll; and Chanel No. 5; and—' The words came tumbling out. He looked round at her, and for the first time in her life she saw panic in his eyes.

'Okay, okay,' she said firmly. 'That settles it. I'll ask O'Malley to see you tomorrow morning. For now, I'm going to recommend to Mr Braeburn that he gives you Prosac. And if he agrees, my dear, you *will* take it.

'That is not a request. *That*, Deputy Chief Constable, is an order!'

64

'Does Downing Street know about this visit, Chief Superintendent?' Although she was seated and he was standing, Laura Davey seemed to look down her long nose at Andy Martin.

The policeman gazed back at her in surprise. 'No, Mrs Davey. Nor is there any reason why it should. My force reports to the Crown Office, in Scotland, and to no one else.'

'That's a lofty principle,' she said, 'but a little naive, surely. My husband and Shaun Massey were the two leading Defence Ministers in the Western world. You don't expect me to believe that the investigation of their assassination is being left in the hands of a few Scottish detectives!'

Martin smiled down at her, as pleasantly as he could. 'Not a few, ma'am. We're a well-resourced Force in our own right, and of course we have help from other agencies as we need it. Let me assure you that your husband's death could not be investigated more rigorously. We will find his murderer,' he said with emphasis, 'but first we have to establish why he was killed.'

'Stewart Morelli told me that you were certain that he was the target, rather than Massey. Is that still the case?' said Laura Davey, her hostility lessening slightly in the face of Martin's unshakeable courtesy.

'That's a fair interpretation by Sir Stewart,' said the detective, 'even if it isn't one hundred per cent accurate. What we are certain of is that the bomb which destroyed the aircraft was hidden in your husband's Red Box.'

'What! You're sure of that?'

'Quite sure. We believe that it was detonated when the box was opened.'

'But how? Who . . . ?'

'Maurice Noble took it with him from the office the evening before the disaster. It was kept in his house overnight. That's what we know for sure. It was interfered with at some point between leaving Whitehall and being carried on to the plane.'

'Does that mean that you suspect Maurice?'

Martin grimaced. 'Let's just say it puts him on the list. Unless, of course, *he* was the target.'

Mrs Davey stood up from her fireside chair, and paced across the room past Sammy Pye, who stood, stiff and solemn in the window of the big Tudor drawing room, then back again towards Martin. She wrung her hands as she walked. 'But why would it have been opened in flight?' she said. 'That's most unusual.'

'We don't know the answer to that question. We haven't discovered yet whether it was Mr Noble or your husband who opened it, although we will know soon.'

'How?'

'I won't go into detail, but it involves DNA tests.'

'No,' said Laura Davey firmly. 'Please *don't* go into detail.' She sat down again, in her chair beside the blazing log fire, and looked up at Martin, no longer with disdain.

'What do you want to know, then, Chief Superintendent? Why have you come here?' She waved a hand towards a sofa. 'I'm sorry. I'm being very rude: please sit down, both of you.' Martin nodded his thanks and settled into the plush sofa, while Pye took a chair by the window.

'We need to know all about your husband, Mrs Davey. In particular, whether there was any . . . and I use the word in its broadest sense . . . domestic motive for his murder. Did he talk to you about his Ministerial work?'

She shook her head. 'No. Not at all. Colin hardly ever brought the Red Boxes down here, and when he did, we never discussed what was in them.'

Martin nodded. 'I need to ask you some fairly personal questions, Mrs Davey.'

'I understand,' she said. Still, the policeman thought, she seemed to tense slightly in her chair.

'Did you have a good marriage?'

'We got on well enough, if that is what you meant. Colin was away a lot, obviously, but when he was here, we didn't row, or anything like that.'

'Did he have any Constituency problems that you knew of?'

She laughed lightly. 'Not a chance. My husband ruled the place with a rod of iron, and the local Association loved him for it. A Constituency Party feels very grand when their Member of Parliament reaches Cabinet rank. He can do anything he likes and say anything he likes.

'All the office-bearers were Colin's placemen, and every one did exactly as he wished. The same was true of the local Council. The Tory administration there did exactly as it was told. As for George Russell, the MEP, he was as loyal and obedient as the rest. He'll reap his reward now as Colin's successor.'

'You expect him to hold the seat?'

'Of course he will! The flags will still be at half-mast on Polling Day, and he'll have the support of the local newspaper.'

'How can you be certain of that?'

She smiled again, almost sweetly. 'Because Colin bought it, before he came here as MP. We own a chain of local papers around the South-East, and all the editors have their orders.'

Martin grinned back at her. 'I suppose your husband refereed the local football team, too!'

'Not quite,' she replied. 'But he *was* the cricket umpire!'

They laughed together, gently, until the policeman's face grew serious once more. 'Now to the most difficult area,' he said. 'Was your husband faithful to you?'

Laura Davey drew a breath and swept her blue-blonde hair back from her right temple. 'I can say, categorically, that there were no other women in my husband's life. Is that a straight enough answer?'

Martin nodded. 'Couldn't be straighter. Did he ever mention a woman named Ariadne Tucker?'

'Maurice Noble's wife? Yes, a couple of times.'

'What did he say about her?'

She gave a brief laugh. 'He said that he had never met a lady who had her husband more firmly by the balls.'

'Mmm,' said Martin. 'What did he think of Noble?'

'Ah, poor little Maurice. Colin thought that he wasn't up to the job. Not totally committed, forgetful, too easily rattled, too easily bullied by the civil servants; those were just some of the things he said about him. Why, I recall him saying just last week, "I can't imagine why Morelli put that bloody man into that job!" He was going to fire him, at the first suitable moment.'

'And did Noble know this?'

'He must have had more than an inkling.' She stopped, and looked hard at Martin. 'You think Maurice did it, don't you?' she said quietly.

'The way things are shaping up, Mrs Davey,' he replied, evenly and frankly, 'it's difficult to see who else could have. The trouble is my boss up in Scotland, Bob Skinner. When he's faced with a situation like this, he reacts by looking all the harder for that someone else. He's ill just now, but I know that's what he would want me to do!'

65

'Look, Kevin. You are the only obviously sane shrink I have ever met, but I've just had my body carved up, so I'd like to keep my mind in one piece right now . . . if that's all right with you.'

O'Malley looked at the big figure in the bed. His face was drawn, pain lines were set around his eyes, and he looked frailer than the psychiatrist could have imagined, yet there was still something formidable about Skinner.

'You're the patient, Bob,' he said. 'So it's your choice at the end of the day. I'm not going to Section you, or anything like that. But in the past, when you've consulted me about suspects, you've always taken my advice. Why should it be different now that you're the patient?'

Skinner growled. 'Gerrout of it, man. Don't try logic on me – it won't work. I'll see myself through this thing. I slept fine last night, after Braeburn gave me that happy pill.'

O'Malley sat on the bed, and looked out of the window of the private ward into which the policeman had been moved. 'How do you know that you slept okay, Bob?' he asked quietly.

'I didn't waken up in a sweat. I had no dreams.'

'As far as you know, you didn't.'

'But I would bloody know, man; they're my bloody dreams!'

'Yet you can't remember them when you have them.'

'So who does, always?' He paused. 'Look, man, don't cross-examine me. I'm too old a campaigner for that. My memory of events is back. I recall every detail of what happened last Friday, every last victim.'

'So what? Your memory was working on Saturday night, but you still had the nightmare, to the point at which you were prepared to go out running twenty-four hours later, just to stay awake.'

The studious, bushy-haired O'Malley pushed himself to his feet and looked over to Sarah, who sat in a chair by the window, with a lively Jazz wriggling in her arms. 'This is my diagnosis, doctor. Tell me whether or not you agree with it.

'The patient is suffering from a form of mental toothache. There is an abscess in there, in the form of a suppressed emotional reaction. So far you've prescribed Prosac as a form of analgesic, and that has worked.

'But the abscess is still there, and it will not go away. It has to be drawn out and exposed to the light, if the patient is to be restored to a state of what passes in him for total mental and emotional equilibrium. The man, the doll, the perfume . . . we have to find out about them and to show Bob what they are and what they mean.' He leaned against the window frame and looked down at Sarah.

'My proposal is that the patient should be placed under hypnosis. However, this must be voluntary on his part and free from constraints on mine if it is to be effective. Do you agree, doctor?'

She nodded vigorously, smiling as Jazz, in her arms, tried to mimick the gesture. 'I couldn't agree more,' she said. 'Now tell me, without this treatment, what's your prognosis?'

O'Malley looked directly at Skinner. 'Without this treatment, the patient will form a dependence upon the palliative drug or will become a chronic insomniac, inefficient at work, and liable to fits of severe depression. Conceivably, these might require in-patient care. With my proposed treatment, the patient should make a full recovery. Without it, I am quite certain that he will never be the same man again.'

Sarah stood up, her child cradled in the crook of her arm, and came over to the bedside. 'There's no choice, Bob, really – is there? Come on, agree, for our sake.'

Skinner sighed, then winced as a shaft of pain from his wound shot through him. 'Okay,' he said. 'Let's do it. But on one condition, Kevin. There's something in my head that only Sarah knows about. The only other person who was in on the secret died two months ago. That story is dangerous in a way I can't begin to tell you, and it mustn't become public property. Therefore I will agree to hypnosis on the condition that only you and Sarah are present, and that you agree that anything I may say under hypnosis will be kept as secret by you as if it was a confession made to a priest. Will you give me that promise?'

'Of course. In this situation, anything you say will be in the context of a doctor-patient relationship. It'll be totally privileged. I'd be struck off if I ever breathed a word.'

'Right. I agree. When do you want to do it?'

O'Malley scratched his chin. 'As soon as Mr Braeburn says I can. That should be in a couple of days. Let's pencil it in for Friday. In the meantime, just rest up and keep taking the happy pills.'

'Can I start to look at some paperwork?'

'Absolutely no way,' said the psychiatrist, anticipating Sarah's open-mouthed protest. 'Listen to music, or read some of that Terry Pratchett on your bedside table, but do nothing associated with work. Don't even watch a crime show on television!'

He moved towards the door. 'See you on Friday, subject to Braeburn.'

Sarah settled Jazz into his push-chair and followed O'Malley outside. But when the door re-opened, it was Alison Higgins who appeared.

'Hello, boss,' she said with a smile, holding out a bunch of chrysanthemums. 'Sarah said I could look in for a minute.'

'Hi, Ali. Good to see you. How are things going?' he asked, weakly but eagerly. 'Has Andy got anyone in the frame yet?'

Higgins frowned. 'Boss, Sarah said that if I even whispered anything about work, she'd throw me out. So don't ask me.'

Skinner sighed. 'That's how it's to be, is it? Okay, how about wee Mark? You can tell me how he's doing, can't you?'

She smiled. 'I think that's allowed. Mark's great.'

'How about his mum?'

'She's fine too. She dropped a bombshell last night, all right.'

'Oh?'

'Yes. Did you know there's going to be a snap By-election?' Skinner looked puzzled. 'Yes, three weeks from tomorrow. Well, Leona had a few of us round for supper last night – me, Marsh Elliot and the Constituency big-wigs. Over the coffee she announced that she wanted to fight the seat in Roly's place.'

'What did they say?'

'After they recovered from the shock they agreed. There's a special meeting of the Dean Conservative Association tonight to adopt her as the candidate. It'll go through unanimously. She's already been granted leave from her teaching job, for the duration of the campaign.'

Skinner whistled weakly. 'Quite a woman, right enough. Will she win?'

'Bet on it!'

'I don't usually, but on this occasion I might. Just you keep an eye on her though, Ali. Don't get involved in the politics; just be a friend, and make sure she comes through it all right.'

Higgins smiled at him gratefully. 'Thanks, boss, because Leona dropped another bombshell last night, privately, on me – one that made me realise, as well as I know her, just how remarkable she is. But even at that, she's going to need me around, just in case.'

'Oh,' said Skinner. 'What was that?'

Higgins looked at him hesitantly. 'It's rather personal, sir. Oh, what the hell – I might as well tell you the story. You'll keep the secret, and it doesn't half bear out your dislike of Roly!'

209

66

'So what does a Tory Agent do, exactly?' asked Mario McGuire.

Brian Mackie looked at his colleague. 'Put that question to any ten of them and you'd probably get at least five different answers. But generally speaking they do what the title suggests. They act for the Party in the Constituencies where they're based. They recruit new members and keep the old ones sweet, turn out newsletters, run fund-raising events, collect subscriptions. The other parties might have a few salaried people on the ground in some local areas, but by and large full-time Constituency Agents are a Tory thing.' Mackie wrinkled his nose in what McGuire guessed to be disapproval.

'You seem to know a lot about them,' said the Inspector.

'In Special Branch we have dealings with them. You'll have to get to know them too.'

'Who pays them? The MP?'

'No,' said Mackie, 'the local Party employs them. A Constituency doesn't have to have a Tory MP to have its own agent, but the smaller associations can't usually afford one.'

'So what sort of people are they?'

'A mixture, as far as I can see. Some of them are ex-servicemen, like Marshall Elliot, the guy in McGrath's Constituency. Others have some sort of private income and can afford to live on the dodgy salary that the job pays. There are quite a few women among them, proportionately far more than you'll find in Parliament.'

'So what about this one down here? What's she like?'

'Miss Paula Whittingham? Haven't a clue. I could have asked one of our friends at Central Office to give us a pen-portrait, but I thought it'd be better to keep our enquiries discreet. You phoned her to make the appointment. How did she sound to you?'

McGuire grunted. 'Brisk. A bit like my wife, in fact, when she's got things on her mind.'

'Christ,' said Mackie, with a rare flash of humour, 'we'd better be on our best behaviour, then. Here, what's this about Maggie going to work for Alison Higgins?'

McGuire shot the DCI a glance. 'It's just for a few days, while Flash Donaldson's away. It was Mr Martin's idea, but no one was ordered, or anything.'

'Is she all right about it?'

'Sure. She rates Miss Higgins, even though they've had a couple of dust-ups in the past.'

Mackie nodded. 'That's good. How was Mags after last Friday? That was a pretty important job she did.'

'Ach, she was okay. Her job was co-ordinating recovery and keeping track of numbers, rather than picking up bits and pieces of people. She was a bit quiet at first, when she got home, but we poured a fair bit of drink into ourselves and were able to talk about it, just like we do after a normal day.'

'That's good. That sort of experience can affect different people in different ways. I heard that Major Legge's sidekick, the young Lieutenant, had to be packed off on sick leave on Monday.'

'Like I told Maggie,' said McGuire, 'as I see it, the only way to handle something like that is to say out loud what everyone says inside themselves, "Thank God that wasn't me or one of mine", and not to feel guilty about it.'

'Yes,' said Mackie, 'that's probably true. Anyway, where's this bloody office?'

They had reached the main street of Chindersford, the Berkshire market town which lay at the heart of Colin Davey's rural stronghold, and which gave the Constituency its name. There were no modern buildings in the thoroughfare. Most were half-timbered, in mock-Tudor style, and some looked as if they might even be authentic.

The Chief Inspector scanned either side of the street, as his Sergeant drove slowly along in a car borrowed from the local Force. At last he saw, fixed to one of the buildings on the left, a sign bearing the multi-coloured ice-cream cone which the Conservative Party uses as its logo, in the quaint belief that it resembles a torch.

'There, Mario. Another hundred yards on. Look – a space. Let's pull in here.'

McGuire pulled into the empty bay, and the two policemen climbed out. Autumn was turning into winter, but the weather was still mild, and neither felt the need of the overcoats which lay across the car's back seat.

The office of Chindersford Conservative Association was a double-fronted shop unit. In the window to the left a huge framed portrait photograph of Colin Davey sat on an easel, draped in black. He was smiling, yet McGuire grimaced at the picture, as something in him recognised a touch of cruelty, buried deep in those shining eyes.

A bell rang out as Mackie opened the door. Four elderly ladies, seated around a table at the back of the room, looked up as the policemen stepped inside. Each of them was sticking labels on envelopes taken from a huge box in the centre of the table, and replacing them in another on the floor. None of them spoke. They simply eyed the men up and down, then returned unsmiling to their repetitive work.

'Gentlemen,' boomed a deep, yet female voice from a dark doorway at the back of the office. 'I'm Paula Whittingham. Can I help you?'

As she stepped into better light, they could see that the woman looked around fifty-five. She was almost rectangular in shape, with the short neck of a rugby prop forward and a torso which seemed to by-pass her waist and merge directly with her hips. She was dressed in badly faded jeans, and in a sweat-shirt. Its sleeves were rolled up to the elbow, revealing thick, ink-stained forearms.

'Miss Whittingham: I'm Chief Inspector Brian Mackie, from Edinburgh. This is Inspector Mario McGuire, who called you earlier.'

She nodded – briskly, as if to confirm Mario McGuire's description a few minutes earlier. 'Sure. Come through here.' She ushered them into a back office, and closed the door behind them.

'Special Branch, I guess,' she said, waving blue-black fingers to deter Mackie's offered handshake. 'Looking into poor old Colin's past, right?'

The DCI gazed at her solemnly for a second or two, then nodded. 'Yes, you're right, on both counts. It's a routine part of a very large investigation, but it has to be done.'

'Of course it has,' said the woman, almost impatiently, as if she was letting them know that she was quite able to suck eggs. 'So, if Colin's public or private life might be an issue,' she went on, 'that rules out the mad Bosnian-Serb General we were all warned about a few months ago.'

'He's been ruled out permanently,' said Mackie quickly. 'No, there are no obvious links with terrorist organisations, yet we do have evidence that Mr Davey was the target. So we have to look for domestic motives.'

Miss Whittingham nodded. 'Understood. Look, before we go any further, I should tell you I'm ex-job myself. I was a Superintendent in West Mercia CID, before I took retirement a couple of years ago.'

'Mmm,' said Mackie, taken slightly aback. 'What brought you into this post?'

'It was vacant, I needed something to do, and I'm a Tory,' she said. 'Colin asked me if I would take it on. He said he needed somebody with a loud bark to herd the sheep. I haven't passed all my Agent's exams, so they call me Organising Secretary, but the job's the same.'

'I see,' said the DCI. 'You knew the victim, and you know this place. As one copper to another, should we look here for our murderer?'

Paula Whittingham shook her head slowly. 'Not a chance. Colin was a bullying, slave-driving son of a bitch, but they all loved him here.'

'How about Mrs Davey, Superintendent,' said Mario McGuire, directly but courteously. 'Did she love him?'

There was a pause, while the woman considered his question. 'In her way, I think she did. She certainly loved the prestige of being a Cabinet wife. She and Colin got on well enough. They respected each other, and she gave him the leeway he needed.'

'Leeway?' asked Mackie.

'The most suitable word, I think.' She looked the detective directly in the eye. 'The Secretary of State for Defence was homosexual, Chief Inspector. Not actively, at least not since he became a member of the Government, but it was a part of him, one which went right back to his days at public school.'

'Did he admit this to you?'

'He didn't have to. I was in Special Branch too, once upon a time, and before he was a Minister. We kept discreet surveillance on all our rising political stars, and we had a file on him.'

'You had? Do you know what happened to it?'

She smiled. 'At a certain point in his political career, it was, shall we say, "swallowed", by another part of the security apparatus. The fact that you two are here asking me questions, and in these circumstances, tells me that either it's been shredded, or that it's kept under lock and key by someone in a very senior position indeed.

'Congratulations, boys. You've unlocked Colin's secret, or at least the one I knew about. But if I were you, I wouldn't count on being allowed to uncover any more!'

213

67

'These should be enough to keep you going for the rest of the week.'

Shana Mirzana stood in the open doorway of Arrow's cramped office, carrying a small mountain of files. Her voice was muffled, as the heap was held secure in her arms by the point of her chin.

'Let's hope not,' said the soldier with a smile. 'I have to keep some time for you.'

She dropped the pile on his desk. 'In that case, can I help you go through them?'

'Not really, love; you wouldn't know what to look for.'

She pouted. 'You could tell me.'

'Not so easy, that. I don't know what I'm looking for myself, you see.' He reached up and took a file from the top. 'Are these all in date order?'

'Yes. It's what you asked for. Copies of every submission put before the Secretary of State since his appointment, with a note on his decision in each case. Good hunting . . . or whatever it is you're doing.'

'Thanks. I wish you could help me on this, honest.'

'What about Lieutenant Swift? Couldn't he?'

Arrow shook his head. 'John's on other duties just now, otherwise he would have.' She turned to leave. 'Hey, not so hasty!' he called. 'How was your concert last night?'

'Excellent.' She smiled. 'Wish you could have been there.'

'If you'd told me about it, I would have been. I haven't heard Van the Man in years.' He looked at her mischievously. 'What's my competition tonight, then?'

She tutted and pointed to the files. 'Looks as if that's mine!'

'Only until seven-thirty, after that I'm calling it a day. My place tonight?' She nodded. 'Stay over?'

She grinned at him, coyness and lust mixing in her eyes. 'Let me go home to pick up a change of clothes, then.'

'That's what I like about you London girls. You're so hard to persuade. Okay, you do that. But don't keep me waiting. I want to have a serious talk with you tonight.'

Shana stared at him in surprise. 'Serious, Captain Arrow? You?'

He stood up from his desk and came towards her, enfolding her in his arms. 'Why not? We've been seeing each other for a while now. Just to show you how seriously I take you, Ms Mirzana, tonight I'll be home by eight, and I'll even cook. Spicy sausage in tomato sauce, with pasta tubes.'

'Penne Picante. I love that.' She rubbed herself against him.

'That's good to hear. I got into terrible trouble, once, when I asked for that in a restaurant in Spain. It means "Hot Cock" in Spanish!'

She drew him close and kissed him, leaning over him slightly. 'I'm game for some of that,' she murmured. 'I like it Castilian style.'

'Later!' he said, turning her and propelling her towards the door. 'For now, woman, back to your silent office.'

She grimaced. 'Must I? It's like a morgue there. All the paper's going to the Minister of State. There's nothing for Joseph and me to do.'

'That'll suit Webber. He'll be able to put in more time in the Red Lion. Between you and me, I heard that Morelli was going to cut his notice period, and let him leave straight away.'

'I know. Joe told me this morning. He goes on Friday. Adam, have you heard any gossip about who the new Secretary of State will be, or even when he'll be appointed? All my sources have dried up.'

Arrow continued to ease her gently and very slowly towards the door. 'The hot tip was Andrew Hardy, the Scottish Office guy. But the problem is that they're short of Tories in Scotland, and McGrath's death made it worse. So it looks as if he's stuck there. Now the word is that the Minister of State in Northern Ireland is being lined up, but that his Secretary of State is battling to keep him. If he wins that fight, then Maglone, the Minister of State here, will get it. But however it goes there'll be no announcement until Sunday, after the memorial service for Davey in his Constituency. Now,' he said firmly, patting her bottom. 'On your way!'

He closed the door on her and went back to his desk, to start his scrutiny of the pile of submissions. The task was easier than he had feared would be the case. He began by eliminating those papers where the decision was purely administrative, where it was wholly routine, or where it was inevitable. This editing process left him with a small pile of contentious decisions.

The great majority involved the continuing battle with Her Majesty's Treasury to hold the Ministry's budget at a level which its establishment felt to be consistent with effective defence. A few involved troop deployments which were not in the public domain, including secret assignments in which Arrow's own SAS unit had been involved. An even smaller group involved purchasing decisions. Of these Arrow was drawn back again and again to one submission.

It involved the placing of a contract for air-to-ground missiles, to equip Harrier aircraft of the RAF and Fleet Air Arm. Arrow remembered the controversy which Davey's decision had caused at the time of its announcement. He had turned down the option of an English weapon with a revolutionary guidance system developed by a relatively small firm in the Cumbrian town of Workington, in favour of a conventional, work-horse, and, it was said, slightly outmoded missile, built in France by a consortium of European countries.

Arrow read and re-read the submission. Davey's decision had been taken against all Departmental advice, in the face of a field test which showed the home-based product to be far superior to the European concoction, and finally, despite overwhelming cost advantages.

'What the hell!' Arrow muttered to himself, as he read the Secretary of State's curtly delivered decision for the third time. 'If that isn't worth a bloody good look, I don't know what is.'

He picked up his telephone and dialled an internal number. John Swift, his colleague and number two, answered at once. 'Swifty,' said Arrow. 'You still got that SIS contact?'

'Yes,' grunted the Yorkshireman.

'Well, see if you can use it for me. I need a warts-and-all report on a European defence consortium called Aerofoil. They got a bloody big contract from us a few months ago, and for the life of me I can't see why!'

68

'You know, Neil, I never realised it before, but one of the advantages of being a copper has to lie in the fact that we never have to stay in court to listen to the Judge's summing-up. What a balls-aching bore of a day this has been! I'm thirty-six, a man in his prime. An unlimited spell on the loose in London should be my dream, yet here I am, just wishing I was back home with my wife.'

McIlhenney laughed quietly in the darkness. 'Listen, sir, I can think of worse days in my career than one spent sitting in the back row of the Old Bailey gallery watching the top of Ariadne Tucker's wig. And I'm sure that my Olive's enjoying her break from me.'

He shifted his body behind the steering wheel of the parked car. 'I remember after Tony Manson's murder, when Andy Martin and I had to interview all the tarts from those sauna brothels of his. You'd have thought that given their line of work, so to speak, they'd have had access to soap and water. But sweet suffering Christ did they hum. From the smell of sweat off them, ye'd have thought they did their business actually in the bloody saunas! Aye,' he said reflectively, 'after that, a day in a courtroom gallery's not that much of a chore.'

'So you didn't like the Drugs and Vice squad, then?' asked Donaldson.

'I didn't say that. It was about half and half. As far as the vice stuff goes, for a lot of the time we're regulators. The law says that prostitution isn't a social service, but we all know that it is. We all know what these saunas are, like, but if the councillors license them, which they do, then fair enough. All we can do is make sure that no one works there who doesn't want to, that those that do are old enough to know what it's about, and that they're clean. I think the Council should send the Environmental Health people in on regular inspections, but they're not that liberated – not yet, anyway.'

He paused, looking across at the DCI from the driver's seat of their car. 'No, it's the drugs side of it that gives you job satisfaction in D 'n V. Every time you break a supply chain, that's good. And it gets better the higher up the chain you go. The guys at the top are clever, and they've got a hell of a lot of firepower, but every so often one of them'll get careless, or someone becomes more scared of us than of him. Then we get a real result . . . there's no better sight than a big dealer going away for fifteen years.'

'In that case,' said Donaldson, 'how come everyone I spoke to was so worried when Tony Manson got the chop?'

McIlhenney shook his head. 'Ach, come on, nobody was worried about Manson. The thing was, he was the devil we knew. He was the only drug dealer I ever heard of with anything that passed for principles. He didn't sell to kids, and he only dealt in pure stuff, not crap. When he went, all sorts of cowboys moved in. That girl who stabbed the boss worked for one of them, I'm sure.'

'Yes, I know,' Donaldson interrupted. 'He was nicked early this morning, right in his factory. A bloke called Divers. Alison told me when I called her.'

'Vic Divers? The Squad's been after him for a while. How did we get him?'

The DCI chuckled. 'Somebody grassed him.'

'You're kidding!'

'No. Apparently, on Monday, after the Big Man was attacked, Our Andy came down on the city like a ton of bricks. Anybody with even the faintest suspicion of illegality about them was turned over. He was pulling people in for farting in the street, more or less! At the same time he put the word out that things would stay that way until we had arrested the guy behind the operation that the boss ran into. Yesterday he had an anonymous phone call putting Divers in the frame and telling him where to find him.'

'Great stuff,' said McIlhenney. 'I know that Divers. He'll be so pissed off about being shopped that he'll tell us tales about everyone *he* knows. I tell you, man, the jails will be full and running over by the weekend.' He laughed. 'Aye, you'll like D 'n V all right, sir.'

Donaldson's eyes widened so that the whites showed, even in the dim light of the Putney street-lamps. 'What d'you mean?'

McIlhenney smiled inwardly, knowing that he had scored a hit. 'Call it an educated guess. There are only two serious candidates for Andy Martin's old job. The way big Bob's played it in the past, the Head of D 'n V's always a DCI promoted into the post. Of all the runners, it'll lie between you and Brian Mackie, and Brian's too tied into Special Branch to be moved.'

'You're dreaming, McIlhenney. No one's said a thing to me.'

'Hah! You'll be the last to know!'

'You serious about this?'

'Aye. Only one thing can stop it, as I see it.'

'What's that?'

'If it turns out that Ariadne and her soldier boyfriend booby-trapped wee Maurice's lunchbox right enough, you and I'll be doing nothing for the next six months but working on the trial.' The big

Sergeant paused, considering the implications for his own career. 'After that, you'll be a Superintendent and I'll be an Inspector, and we'll both be in uniform. Our faces'll be too well known to be useful in CID for a while.'

'Bugger that,' said Donaldson vehemently. 'Let's get out of here then. When's the Met guy due on shift to relieve us?'

McIlhenney peered at his watch in the dim light, and looked back along the one-way street towards Ariadne Tucker's house. 'Five minutes ago,' he said. 'In fact, I think he's there now. More than that, Garen Price is heading in this direction.'

He had hardly finished speaking before the back door of their Peugeot, a step up from the undistinguished Vauxhall, opened and the Welsh Detective Sergeant slid in behind them.

'Hello, boyo,' said McIlhenney. 'What brings you here? Did you remember that it was your turn to buy the beer?'

Price's smile gleamed in the silver night. 'You lads will be in the chair when you hear what I've got here.' He produced a tape cassette from his jacket pocket and handed it to Donaldson. 'Drive on down the road, well away from here, then shove it in the player.'

McIlhenney switched on the engine and moved smoothly and quietly away from their observation point. 'What is it, then?' he asked, over his shoulder. Price leaned back in his seat, still smiling, but said nothing.

He made a sharp left turn, then a right. He drove for just under a minute until another right turn took them out on to Clapham Common, where he drew to a halt at the kerbside. 'Come on, Garen,' he said in exasperation to the wide-grinning Welshman. 'What the fuck is it?'

'We picked it up tonight off the telephone tap. I thought I'd share it with you right away . . . and then let you buy me that beer.'

'Let's see how many pints it's worth, then,' said Donaldson. He pushed the cassette into the player. A hiss came from the speakers as the tape started to run.

The white noise continued for a few seconds, until it was broken by the sound of a phone. It was answered on the fifth ring. 'Six-seven-eight-two,' said a soft, well-spoken male voice.

'Stephen!' At once Ariadne Tucker's voice sounded slightly petulant. 'Why didn't you show up in Court today? I put off a consultation this afternoon and stayed there, listening to boring old Ormrod's summation, all because I was expecting you.'

'I'm sorry, darling. It's all hell down here. We've had a no-notice inspection team in from MOD. Everyone's stuck on base until it's over. I *was* going to call you, but later, when I was sure you'd be home.'

Ariadne sighed softly. 'Oh! Poor darling. Imagine, being stuck in bloody Aldershot!'

'Aye, imagine,' echoed McIlhenney grimly.

Her tone changed yet again, taking on a sudden urgency. 'Are we still all right for the weekend?'

'Yes, of course, even if it means resorting to Plan B.' He paused. 'Listen, Ariadne darling, are you really sure that this is kosher, and all that, so soon after Maurice dying? Before the funeral?'

'Stephen, my poor little Galahad, if I didn't feel any guilt when Maurice was alive, why the hell should it bother me now that he's gone? As for the funeral, it looks as if he's been cremated already, in mid-air. I'll hold a memorial service at an appropriate time, in a couple of weeks perhaps. In the meantime, a woman's needs are many fold, as they say.' She laughed, suddenly, out loud. The sound rang round the car, startling at least two of the three detectives.

'How's this for a joke? I had the police round last night, wondering if I might be having an affair with Colin Davey. It seems that one line of enquiry is that Maurice thought I was, and might have been driven to kill him, and take himself out in the process. They've got the affair part right – too bad they're wrong about the name, eh? And about Maurice's murderous intentions.'

Her laugh deepened, becoming a chuckle. 'Imagine, me and Colin Davey. Every time I met the man he made my flesh creep! Oh no,' she said with a flourish. 'My tastes are much more agreeable than that.'

'Ohh!' Stephen Richards moaned in the dark. 'Well, my darling. You'll have the opportunity to indulge them at the weekend.'

'Yes, sweetheart. And you will have the object of your heart's desire. Sleep tight.' She blew a kiss into the phone and hung up.

White noise hissed around the car once more. The three men sat silent, until finally, Donaldson ejected the tape.

'She's a cold-hearted piece of stuff, is she not,' he said quietly, to himself as much as anyone.

'Not half,' said McIlhenney. 'I'll be extra nice to my Olive from now on.' He switched on the engine and drove off steadily into the night.

'So where does that put us, sir?' he asked, swinging away from the Common and heading off in the general direction of Chelsea Bridge.

'For a start,' said the DCI, 'although it doesn't rule out the possibility that the paranoid Noble might have *believed* that his wife was having it off with Davey, she seems pretty definite that he didn't kill him . . . Why is that, I wonder? Is it simply because she doesn't think he had the stuff to do it, or because she and the soldier boy killed *him*, themselves?'

'Tell you something,' said McIlhenney. 'If they did, and they can react like that after taking out a whole planeload, then these are two very dangerous people. What do we do now, sir? Pick them up?'

Donaldson tutted quietly. 'That's up to Andy Martin. I'll call him right now. But my inclination would be to play the thing out to the end. To tail Ariadne to wherever it is she's going this weekend, and then to take the two of them, together.'

69

Arrow was in the kitchen of his attic flat in Notting Hill when the buzzer sounded, a few feet from his ear. He took a pace to his right and picked it up.

'Hello,' he said brightly. 'Trattoria Español aqui. Can I help you?'

Shana laughed. 'Yes, you can open the bloody door!'

'Okay.' He pushed the button, replaced the receiver, and stepped out of the flat on to the landing to meet her. Shana was striding up the stairs towards him, past the first landing already, with a small rucksack bouncing on her shoulder. He jogged down to meet her halfway. She was wearing a plain grey cotton sweat-top and jeans, and looked, even in that simple outfit, very desirable indeed.

Adam looked down at the bag. 'You're travelling light. Hope I've got enough wardrobe space for all that lot.'

'I've got enough for one night. Once I've heard just how seriously you want to talk, I might consider bringing more.' She grinned at him. 'You're not having second thoughts about that, are you?'

He returned her smile. 'I never have second thoughts. Once I've decided on something, I see it through to the end.'

'That sounds promising.'

'It's my line of work. It's made me that way. Come on, love. Let's get upstairs.' He fished a key from his pocket.

She looked at him in slight surprise. 'You always lock up, even when you're only coming down to answer the buzzer?'

He nodded. 'It's the way I was brought up. We're very suspicious of our neighbours in Derbyshire.'

They climbed the stairs arm in arm. At the top, he opened the door and held it for her. Inside she went straight to the bedroom and laid her rucksack on a chair. She looked around, and nodded.

'I'm always impressed when I come into your flat. Compared to mine everything's so neat. Doesn't it frustrate you to be with someone as untidy as me?'

He grinned wickedly. 'I can use a little anarchy in my life.'

'Then you've come to the right place . . .' She bore down on him, and pushed him backward, on to the bed, kissing him, crawling over him, unfastening the buttons on his shirt.

'I should warn you,' he said. 'I've been handling chillies.'

'In that case, just lie back and keep your hands in the air.' Quickly she unfastened his cotton slacks, and leaned over him. 'Now, what did you say that you had on the menu tonight . . . ?'

It began with her tongue, licking, swirling, around him, and her hands, exploring, testing. 'Oh yes,' she hissed. 'I can see what you meant.'

He gripped the rails of his brass bedstead, and arched his back.

An hour and a half later, they lay there, naked, replete and dozing. Shana nuzzled her face against his neck. 'Hey,' she whispered. 'Now I've had the Penne Picante . . .'

'And extras!' he growled.

'. . . when am I going to see this pasta? I'm starving!'

'Soon,' he said. 'But there's something we've got to talk about first.'

'Mmm. Well, I suppose I could last for another half-hour or so.'

'No, I meant proper talk.' He propped himself up on an elbow, and looked down at her, his face suddenly serious, and she thought, anxious. A pang of fear grasped her.

'Shana,' he said. You know some of my business, but not all of it, not by a long way. Before I came into the job I'm in now, I was in the SAS. I did some pretty terminal things, and I managed to come through them all, by being a pretty callous little bastard. But I can't play that part any more.'

She looked at him, thoroughly frightened now. 'What are you leading up to?'

'Shana, love, all this Agent Robin stuff. We've got to put a stop to it.'

'What do you mean?' Her voice was brittle.

'I know about you. You've been feeding material to the Iraqis for the last three months.'

'Adam, that's not funny. Don't joke like that.'

'I wish I *was* joking. The SIS picked up information about the Iraqi network of deep-cover agents a few months back. They learned that Agent Robin, the English sleeper, was an LSE graduate working in the civil service, who had been recruited in Turkey, on a Muslim student summer-exchange programme.

'They learned too that Robin's purpose was to feed back sensitive information that would be of use to Iraq in planning Gulf de-stabilisation tactics. They didn't know which Department Robin was in, but it was a safe bet that it would be either Foreign, Defence or Cabinet Office. They didn't know either whether Robin was male or female, but when they fed all the data they held into a computer, it took about three seconds to come up with your name.'

She was wide-eyed now. She made a move to slip out of bed, but he grabbed her hand and held it until she stopped struggling. 'It's all right, love. I'm not going to hurt you. But just listen on.

223

'The MI6 people knew from their source that you were about to be activated. That's when they brought me in. You were under surveillance from that point on – phone taps at the office, at home, on your mobile, the whole works. When you were contacted we knew right away.'

Suddenly she glared at him. 'So all this, you and me, this was just you doing your job?'

'Listen,' he said fiercely. 'If I'd been doing my job properly, we'd be having this conversation in a cellar somewhere. Us getting involved wasn't on the agenda. Now we are, it's your one chance of coming out of this in one piece!' The fire left his eyes. 'Tell me why, Shana. You're no Muslim fanatic, and you're as British as I am. What did they use on you?'

Her gaze dropped from his, and she started to sob. 'They threatened to kill my parents.'

'Ahh,' said Arrow, matter-of-fact. 'That's pretty basic, and it's just like them. With someone young like you, it works nearly every time. Tell me, how did they set you up?'

She stifled a sob, and he wiped her eyes with a corner of the bedsheet. 'When I was in Turkey, on that exchange, I was approached by a man who said he had an employment proposition for me. I thought he was a Turk, so I had coffee with him. He was very matter-of-fact about it. He said that as a Muslim, the interests of the State of Iraq were my interests. He proposed that when I graduated, I should apply for posts in the civil service, with the Ministry of Defence or the Foreign Office as my preferences. Once inside, I should look for posts in sensitive departments. He gave me a list. The Foreign Secretary's Private Office was at the top. Defence was second.'

She went on: 'He said that once I was in a suitable post, I would be contacted and I would feed information back to them. When I was operational, money would be lodged for me in a numbered account in Zurich. He also said that if I refused or failed to co-operate in any way, then my parents would be killed first, and me next. You know all the rest. I've been passing information since I've been activated.'

She looked up at him desperately. 'What's going to happen to me, Adam? Are you going to put me away?'

He shook his head. 'Nothing's going to happen to you, love. You haven't done anything, you see.'

She stared at him, bewildered.

'You don't think I'd 'ave let you feed genuine secrets to the Iraqis, do you? Everything you saw, copied and sent was specially prepared. It was realistic enough not to compromise you with them, but written so that it would expose their agents in other Gulf States. We've shut down most of those within the last month. You're an international heroine, love, even if you did think you were a spy!'

224

She gazed at him, open-mouthed. 'Who knows about this?'

'Me, John Swift, Morelli, the PM and the head of MI6, that's all. Now what we've got to do is close *you* down, without the Iraqis suspecting that they've been stuffed.'

'How can you do that?'

'This is what Morelli, MI6 and I have worked out. Swifty doesn't have to know, and the PM doesn't want to. I've got a document photocopied and ready for you to hand over. It's from the director of MI6 to Morelli, saying that the Iraqi network has been uncovered in its entirety, and is about to be terminated. I've added in a note saying that you're cutting and running. You communicate through a safe house in Kilburn, right? You make a phone call, and take your material there, to hand it over to your contact. You see him, but you don't know his name. Am I right?'

She nodded. 'Yes,' she whispered.

'We know who he is, though. He's called Rafiq; he's a restaurant worker with a French passport. As soon as Rafiq transmits your message to Baghdad, he'll be picked up and charged. We'll announce his arrest, but we'll say that his contact in Whitehall has committed suicide. Unless we're all very much mistaken, the Iraqis will shut down the whole operation. They won't look for you, because our suicide announcement will make them believe that we've killed you. That's what they would do in our shoes; hold one for a show trial and execution, and just do away with the others.'

She looked up at him, her confidence returning. 'So what do I do?'

'Don't go to the office tomorrow. Leave here early and go home. Make your call to Rafiq, and set up a meeting for ten o'clock. Then pack your favourite clothes and take a taxi to Kilburn. Meet Rafiq at the safe house, and hand over the material. Let him leave first, then you go. But you don't go back to the Ministry . . . *ever*. Or to your flat. I'll see to it that it's cleared, and the rent and everything taken care of.'

'What do I do instead?'

He reached for his wallet, took out a piece of paper, and handed it to her. 'You go to this address. It's a flat in Godalming, in Surrey. But don't go straight there. Take a taxi back into London and catch a bus. That's nice and public and it'll make it easy for us to ensure that no one's following you who shouldn't be. There'll be someone there to meet you and to stay with you for the first few days – for your peace of mind as much as anything else. It'll all be okay.'

'And what about us, you and I? Do we have a future?'

'Of course, if that's what you want. I'll visit you as soon as I can be absolutely sure that the Iraqis have bought the whole story.'

She hugged him, quickly. Her body felt cold against his, and so he drew her down beneath the covers.

225

'Will I be able to see my parents, eventually?' she asked. She was still trembling, but her composure was returning.

'Not for a few months at the very least. Eventually, we'll arrange a meeting on neutral ground. But for now, they'll have to think you're dead too. For their own safety as much as anything. They'll be given a death certificate, and they'll have to hold a funeral. After a while, as soon as I judge that it's okay, I'll send a message to them.'

She took a deep breath. 'It'll be awful for them. But if you say so, then it has to be. But for how long, Adam? Will I have to live in hiding always? Will it be just like being in prison?'

He smiled. 'Not unless you insist on seeing it that way. As to how long, we'll move you out of Godalming after a while, possibly to Derbyshire, where I come from. It'll make it easier for me to visit you if you're there. You'll have a new identity too. We'll fix you up with a job . . . a lecturer, maybe . . . to let you build a real new life. After a year or so, you and I can begin thinking long-term . . . if you still want to, that is.'

She frowned. 'But won't people find out then, people from the Ministry, who'll think I'm dead?'

'Love, Swifty and I ain't in the office directories, remember. There are around twenty people in MOD who've ever heard of me. And none of *them* know my real name, or anything about my private life.'

She smiled, reassured. 'What *is* your real name?'

'Adam.'

'The other one, then?'

'What does it say on the doorbell downstairs?'

She wrinkled her brow. 'Feather, isn't it?'

'That'll do then. You can use it, if you like. After tomorrow, Shana Mirzana'll be no use to you. I'll get you a new birth certificate, NI number, passport and all that. Just you pick a name.'

She thought for a few seconds. 'Feather – yes, I like that. It's nice, even for a brown-skinned girl. As for a forename, do you think that Robin would be a bit cheeky?'

Adam laughed and gave her a quick hug. 'I think it would be perfect. I'll see to it tomorrow. For now let's eat, if you've still got an appetite.'

'I have,' she murmured, 'but not for food; not just yet.' She bit his nipple, gently.

'Hey,' he gasped. 'Tell me one more thing.'

'What?'

'When you broke into Maurice Noble's house last week, to photograph something that you hadn't had a chance to copy during the day . . .'

'You . . .'

'No, not me. I didn't follow you. Swifty did that. Anyway, when

226

you opened the Red Box, there was nothing, absolutely nothing unusual about it?'

'No, nothing at all.'

'Just as well,' said Arrow. 'Otherwise, right now a street in Putney would be missing one house, you'd be spread all over South London, and I'd be looking for a new girlfriend!'

70

She pressed the bell, three times in quick succession, then turned the plastic oval handle and pushed. As usual, the Yale was on the latch, and the dirty door, with great bare patches showing in its black paintwork, swung open before her.

'Hello!' she called out as usual as she climbed the narrow stair which led from the street directly into the small flat. Her ascent was made awkward by a huge nylon hold-all which she lugged by her side, grasped in both hands and held up to avoid it snagging on the wooden steps.

She was breathing hard as she reached the top of the flight and turned into what she imagined would be the living room, were the place occupied and not completely empty of furniture. She dropped the bag, which hit the floor with a thud, sending up a small cloud of dust.

'You're three minutes late,' the man said sharply. He was of medium height, and slim-built, with a complexion much browner than hers, and a thin black moustache. It came to her that after all their meetings, she was taking in these details for the first time.

He was poorly dressed, she noticed, in a crumpled suit and a shirt frayed clean through at the collar.

He nodded towards the hold-all. 'What's this?' he asked, with an edge of suspicion in his voice.

A cold chill ran through her. *Don't make him suspicious*, Adam had said. *We don't want him panicking.* She twisted her mouth into what she hoped was a rueful grin. 'Nothing. I was supposed to be going off for a break this morning, down to Devon with a few girlfriends. I was almost gone last night when this signal came in. I had a look at it and decided I had to pass it on. I'll have to catch the rest up on the train.'

'What's so urgent about it?'

The grin turned to a frown. 'You know better than to ask me that. I give you the information in a sealed envelope, you leave, I follow. We discuss nothing. That's the drill.'

He held out his hand. 'Okay, okay,' he said, in a guttural accent, 'so keep your hair on. Give it to me, and let me go, if it's so urgent.'

She nodded and bent over the hold-all. Unzipping a side pocket she drew out a brown A4 envelope, sealed and folded across the centre.

'Here. Take my word for it, it's urgent. Do what you have to do with it as fast as you can.'

The man took it from her, and shoved it roughly into a pocket of his jacket. 'Very well. I'm going. Remember, give me the usual ten minutes' start before you go to catch your train. Till the next time.'

'Yes,' she muttered, as he disappeared down the staircase towards the drab street outside. As she heard the creaking door close behind him, she breathed a huge sigh of relief. She realised she was shaking, and reached automatically into the deep pocket of her woollen jacket. Finding her Turkish cigarettes, she lit one and drew on it deeply, then, throwing the spent match into the nearest corner of the room, she exhaled, and sat down carefully on her tight-packed hold-all.

Only a few seconds later, she heard a sound. It came from directly above her head. 'Ugh,' she said aloud. 'Rats. Hardly surprising in a place like this.'

But then, the ceiling creaked once more, louder this time. She jumped bolt upright and backed against the wall, looking upwards. On none of her previous visits had she ever noticed the trapdoor to the attic. Now it caught her gaze and held it, as, slowly, as if someone's fingers were struggling for purchase, it began to move.

Finally the hatch was free. Where it had been, in the far corner of the ceiling, there was a black hole into nothing. But the doorway was empty for only a moment. First, she saw the ridged soles of a pair of heavy brogue shoes. Then short, stocky legs, encased in what seemed to be black, overall-style trousers appeared through the trap. They descended slowly, as if they were being lowered out of some awful dark cloud, until suddenly, with a rush, the rest of Adam Arrow dropped into the room.

'Oh! Adam, you shit!' It was almost a scream. 'What a scare you gave me!' She rushed towards him and hugged him. 'You might have told me you'd be hiding up there. If I'd known I had a guardian angel on the premises I wouldn't have been so bloody scared. I thought I wasn't seeing you again for weeks.' She hugged him again, tighter, and pressed her left cheek against his. 'Did you always mean to do this, or was it a change of plan?'

His arms were around her. The left clamped across her shoulders, returning her embrace. His right hand slipped round, and grabbed her jaw. He tugged, once, very hard. The crack filled the room, and in the same instant, she went limp in his grasp.

'No, Shana,' he said, in a voice as hard as the flinty expression in his eyes. He let the body go, watching as it crumpled to the floor. 'This was always the way it was going to be.'

71

'You look a bit tense, Adam. You all right?'

Lieutenant John Swift was one of those people who never beat about the bush.

'Eh? What? Course I'm all right.'

Swift nodded. 'That's good. You looked like shit for a second, that's all.'

'Just shut the fook up, Swifty.' He glanced up at his wall clock. It was just before midday. 'Now, what d'you want?'

Swift sat down squarely in the chair facing his desk. He was a big husky man, eight inches taller than Arrow. Like his colleague, he had come to MOD Security from the Special Forces, but in his case from the Special Boat Services, for which he had been selected after seven years in nuclear submarines.

'Got something for you,' he said, slapping a yellow folder with a red *Top Secret* classification down on the desk.

'What's this?'

'It's that report you asked for, on the Aerofoil consortium.'

'By heck, that was quick. Someone must have owed you a favour.'

'They did, but after this it's paid in full. That's the warts-and-all document you wanted. It's in there, all the detail, but for Christ's sake, Adam, be careful with it. You can't let any of what's in it go beyond this office, or neither of us will sleep easy.'

Arrow's eyebrows twitched upwards. 'Must be hot stuff then, Swifty. Summarise it for me.'

'Okay then.' He took a breath. 'The Aerofoil consortium has three main players. It was put together purely to develop and market a new air-to-ground missile called Reaper. The members are Fusil, a French company who build the rocket itself, Bartoli of Belgium, who special-ise in the payload, and SL, that's short for Société Lugano, a Swiss company, who provide the guidance system. The initiative behind Aerofoil came from SL. The company knew that it would have no chance of selling to any NATO member on its own, so it head-hunted partners from within the European Union. They designed and built their missile inside two years. The MOD order is their first biggie.'

'So what's so special about the missile?' asked Arrow.

'That's just it. If you've read our guys' assessment, you'll know that there's nothing special about it. Yet Davey gave Aerofoil the order, against what everyone said was a superior British product. You remember the flak that caused.'

The soldier nodded.

'Well, it seems that this was too much for MI6. That organisation is still its own master in some respects, and its D-G decided to make some enquiries off his own bat. What he found out made his hair curl.

'The investigation had a quiet look at Davey's bank accounts and investment portfolio but there was nothing there to indicate that he'd taken a back-hander. It had a look at the French and Belgian companies and found them squeaky clean. But when it tried to look at SL, it came up against a series of blanks.

'The people who fronted their technical input to the operation were unknowns, without any track record in the defence industry. The ownership of the company was obscure too, linked into a Swiss investment trust.

'Then someone had a bright idea. They had an expert look at SL's guidance technology and compare it to other systems in use around the world. And very quickly, they came up with an interesting analysis. The Reaper guidance system is similar in every important respect, and identical in some, to that used in its missiles by one major military power, and one alone.'

'And what's that?' asked Arrow impatiently.

'Russia.'

'Eh? We bought Russian technology from these people? 'Ow the hell did we do that?'

'Another terrific question, Adam, and another that MI6 asked too. They dug as hard as they could into Société Lugano, and eventually they came up with a name for its owner, one Martin Hugo, an immigrant to Switzerland at the time of the collapse of the Soviet Union. They even came up with a photograph. The D-G was out of control by this time, so he sent my pal over to Moscow with the picture, to show it to an old rival of his in the KGB. The Russian clocked it straight away. Martin Hugo's real name is Vassily Kelnikov, and he was a KGB General involved in Intelligence gathering. He was part of the coup against Gorbachev, but he vanished just before it went pear-shaped, taking a fortune in gold with him, plus, they suspected but couldn't tell for certain, a number of military secrets. The KGB have tried to find him ever since, but they didn't know where to look. Their best guess was that he had gone to America.'

'Okay,' said Arrow. 'So Davey bought recycled Russian missile technology, which was never brilliant in the first place, from a KGB fugitive. Why the hell would he do that?'

'MI6's last question. And the KGB gave them the answer. When

Kelnikov vanished he took items from files on quite a few prominent people, and one of them was . . .'

'. . . Colin Davey MP.'

'Spot on. It was blackmail. Davey was a poofter. Kelnikov compromised him when he was a junior Minister, and had the photographs to prove it. You can work out the rest. The Aerofoil submission landed on his desk, and a copy of a photograph arrived with his private mail. Davey had a straight choice. He picked the dishonourable way, and justified his decision with some bluff about us being good Europeans and not wishing to be seen to be insular.'

'I remember it well,' said Arrow. 'He took it to extremes though, buying Russian kit. So what did Six do with the report?'

'They took it to the PM, and he, true to current form, told them to lock it up tight in case the daylight got at it. The D-G begged him at least to shuffle Davey, but he refused. Said it was too close to the election. When I came asking questions yesterday, my contact went to the D-G, who said, quote, "Bugger the PM and his Government. Give MoD a sight of the file." So there it is.' Swift nodded at the yellow folder. 'They want it back by five o'clock, and I've promised, on your life, that it won't be photocopied.'

Arrow laughed. 'Thanks, pal. But I've no need to copy it. If Kelnikov was blackmailing Davey, all it tells me is that he didn't kill him. Mind you, it's a bit uncomfortable to think of him running around loose. How many other happy snaps does he have?'

'That's academic,' said Swift. 'Martin Hugo was killed in Switzerland three days ago. The KGB didn't even make it look like an accident, just blew his bloody head off on his front doorstep. They had a word with the French and the Belgians too, letting them know who their companies were playing with. The Aerofoil consortium will be wound up within the next few days, so score one for MI6.'

'But their opposition don't know that, do they?' said Arrow emphatically.

'Who?'

'Breakspear, the company up in Workington who *didn't* get the missile contract. Bryn Sawyer, their Managing Director, called in the Receiver a week ago last Monday. If anyone in this situation had a reason to get even with Davey, it was him. And with the sort of technology his company was into . . . I think I'd better go up and see my pal in Scotland. Then we may have to pay a call in Cumbria. You've done all you can for now, Swifty. Just make sure that you get that precious file back to MI6, well before five o'clock!'

72

'I agree with you, Adam. Sawyer has credentials as a suspect. But I don't want to go storming in there on the basis of nothing more than press cuttings quoting him as saying that he would "see off" Colin Davey.'

Andy Martin sipped his coffee and glanced around him, making sure that there was no one within earshot. They were seated at a corner table in the Edinburgh Airport Hotel, which was usually guaranteed to be quiet in mid-afternoon.

'Sawyer has possibilities, but as I see it, there are others. There's the notion that Noble believed that Davey was having it off with his wife. There's the fact, or so it seems, that she is having an affair with this young soldier, an explosives expert. We'll get to the bottom of that one when Donaldson and McIlhenney catch them on the job at the weekend. Remember this. Although you can promise me . . . and I won't ask how . . . that the Red Box was secure well into the night, it's still possible that Noble, or his wife, primed it first thing in the morning. If it was Sawyer, how would he get the bomb into Davey's box? Because that's where it was; and that's the only certainty in this whole bloody enquiry!'

'Maybe he swapped it for a dummy,' Arrow offered lamely.

'How? When?' The policeman shook his blond head firmly. 'No, mate. Before I go marching into another Force's territory, demanding search warrants, I have to have more to go on than supposition. You head back to London, and have Davey's office staff look back through all his mail, just to see whether there's anything from Sawyer that might have been even slightly threatening. I'll have Brian and Mario go back to Chindersford, to revisit Mrs Davey and the Agent, and to check out the same thing. If we get something from any of those that justifies it, then I'll ask for a search warrant and pay a call on Mr Sawyer. Okay?'

Arrow sighed. 'Fair enough, Andy. Hey, how about this for a thought. What if more than one person was planning to kill Davey?'

'Don't! Imagine a case where we've got someone charged with murder and someone else charged with conspiring, or attempting to commit the same crime. God, how I wish the boss was back in harness!'

'How's Bob doing?'

'Time will tell,' said Martin, 'but from what I hear from Sarah, he's got a battle to fight that could be as tough as ours.'

73

'I thank you all for the confidence which you have shown in me, and for the honour which you have done me by adopting me as your Parliamentary Candidate. I promise you, in return, that I will fight with every scrap of energy I possess to retain this seat for the Association and for the Conservative Party.

'When I have done that, and I will, I pledge also that I will maintain the exceptional quality of public service given by the Member of Parliament whom you have just lost, not simply as a gesture in memory of my husband, but in keeping with my own standards and beliefs.

'Surrounded by loyal friends and supporters, I look forward to renewing the Conservative mandate in this Constituency and to representing it for many years ahead.'

With a short bow of her head, Leona McGrath sat down, almost disappearing from sight behind the lectern on the blue-clothed table. As she did so, the 137 members of Edinburgh Dean Conservative Association who had just adopted her unanimously as their By-election candidate, rose to their feet, applauding enthusiastically.

The ovation continued until Leona rose again, bowing and waving her thanks, and until finally she gestured to her audience that they should sit down.

'Thank you once again,' she said, once order had been restored. 'After Roly's funeral tomorrow, our campaign will begin. If, as I am sure will be the case, your enthusiasm this evening is translated into effort in canvassing the support of the electorate, not only will you and I retain the seat, but we will do so with an increased majority.'

With a final wave, she turned and walked smartly off the stage of Edinburgh Academy Junior School hall, and into the wings, with John Torrance, who had chaired the meeting, by her side. Alison Higgins and Marsh Elliot were waiting for them. As soon as she was out of sight of the audience, Alison gathered her in a hug.

'Leona, you were terrific,' she said. 'You're right. You're going to retain the seat without a doubt. Don't you agree, Marsh?'

Elliot nodded emphatically. 'Yes,' he said seriously. 'Without a doubt. Those people out there respected Roly, and no mistake, but they never showed warmth or enthusiasm like that. The press will report that, and it will carry over into the opinion polls. You may have said a bit too much, though. If you hold the seat with a healthy majority, you'll have done your bit for the Party. If you decide then that on reflection you want to stand aside after a few months, your successor will be able to retain it at the General Election.'

Alison Higgins, looking at her friend, saw a frown begin to gather in her face, but Elliot went on. 'We're off to a flying start. If the first published polls show us in a healthy lead, in line with what our private soundings are telling us, then in a short campaign, the other parties will have no chance of catching us. Now,' he said, 'the Press, Leona. You must talk to them.' He stood aside, and she saw for the first time a man standing behind him. 'You know Sir Jerry Lacey, the Member for Upper Deeside?'

She nodded, surprised. 'Of course.'

'Well, Jerry has agreed, very kindly, to act as what we call Candidate's Friend, during the campaign. He'll be with you everywhere you go, as your adviser. When you're canvassing, on visits, at election meetings, all those; and he'll chair your press conferences. Central Office are giving us a Press Officer and a researcher, and the Scottish Director will be here full-time, advising on strategy, but Jerry will be your closest adviser. I've got a room set aside for a press conference now. Why don't we get on with it, to give you a little experience. The Press can be pretty tough on new candidates, you know. Shall we go?' He turned, as if ushering her onward.

Leona McGrath stood her ground. An awkward silence developed, until she broke it herself. She smiled at the ginger-headed Lacey. 'Jerry, it is very kind of you to volunteer, but I really don't want a minder.'

Elliot opened his mouth to protest, but she held up a hand, silencing him. 'Marsh, the one way I can lose this seat is if the electorate see me as the poor widowwoman, thrust forward by the Party to capture the sympathy vote. And that's how they will see me if I'm surrounded everywhere I go by minders and Party bodyguards. I know the game, Marsh. I was a Young Conservative before I ever met Roly, and I've worked at By-elections. So let's get something clear right now. I am *not* the poor widowwoman. I am here to win this seat, not dress up in my husband's clothes. I'll listen to advice, but this is my campaign, and I'll run it.' She paused. 'As for standing down in a few months, I meant it when I said that I'm here long-term.' She looked up at Torrance, who was still by her side. 'You can rely on that, John.'

She turned and took Sir Jerry Lacey's hand in hers. She could see that he was smiling, in what she took for relief. 'So, future colleague,' she said. 'Thank you very much, but no thanks. I've already got a Candidate's Friend, you see.' She nodded towards Higgins. 'Ali is going to give me all the time she can, in the evenings and at weekends. She'll make sure I get to my evening meetings on time and with my hair in place, and she'll be my shoulder to cry on, if and when I need one.'

He nodded. 'I quite understand, my dear, and I respect you for it. Any private advice you need, you can call me at any time.'

'Thanks.' She turned back to Elliot, who stood there, slightly bemused. 'Marsh, I'm grateful for the Press Officer and the researcher, and we'll have to give the Director her place. She's paying for most of the show, after all. But my inclination is that I want to take my press conferences alone, without a Chairman. You'll have to persuade me otherwise. What I *would* like you to do is set up a team to go through the morning's papers and spot likely questions, so that the researcher can brief me on the answers. I'll work myself with the Press Officer on the topics we want to raise each day.' As she spoke she emphasised each point with a stabbing finger, flashing in the Agent's direction. He smiled inscrutably, and nodded.

'Very good, Candidate,' he said. 'You're quite right, of course. You *are* the boss. But I really think that you should have a press conference Chairman, at least on the days when you have Cabinet support.'

'That's another thing,' said Leona instantly. 'Be as polite to the Cabinet as you can, but I don't want their support.'

'Oh really, Leona—' he burst out.

She shook her head, cutting him off. 'Marsh, think about it. How can it increase my popularity if every day I'm seen on television and in the Press surrounded by Ministers who are themselves deeply unpopular? They're a liability, and I don't want them. If I have supporters at public meetings, they'll be respected people from the Scottish community, not tainted politicians. As far as hecklers are concerned, if I could handle Roly across the dinner table, then I can handle them across a meeting room. Just you watch me.'

She hesitated. 'Look, I know this might be difficult for you, professionally, I mean. So I'll write to the Party Chairmen myself, in Scotland and in England, explaining my position, and I'll talk to the Scottish Director, when she's finished buttering up our Lady Chairman. I've already spoken on the phone with Andrew Hardy, and he agrees with me.'

Elliot smiled in defeat, the last of his protest seemingly spent. 'Very well, Leona, you do it your way. I'm here to support you and to make sure that your message gets to every elector. That's my job.'

'Good, because my objective over the next three weeks is to *meet* every elector, look them in the eye and shake their hand. The fewer minders I have around me, the better my chance of doing that. Now, where are the Press?' Elliot pointed to a doorway facing the steps up to the stage. He made to accompany her, but she put a hand on his sleeve. 'No, Marsh. I begin as I mean to go on.'

'But you're not prepared!'

She smiled. 'Don't worry, I'm not sticking my head on the block. I won't answer any serious questions. I'll simply repeat that I'm pleased to have been adopted, and that my first press conference will be on Monday in the main meeting room in the constituency offices at nine a.m. sharp. I'll be back in five minutes, at the outside.'

She was as good as her word. When she returned, Marshall Elliot had explained her decisions to the Scottish Conservative Director. 'Leona, my dear,' said Dame Janet Straw, a formidable broad-chested woman with iron-grey hair that might have been a wig. 'Are you sure about this?'

'Quite sure,' she said cheerily. 'Let me ask you something, Janet. How many By-elections have you and your colleagues in England won over the last ten years, doing it your way?'

'*Touché,*' said the Grandee. She turned to Elliot. 'Don't worry, Marsh. I have a feeling that this one's going to be all right!'

'I'm convinced,' he said. 'But there's something rather important before us all, before the campaign can begin. Alison, I think you should take our candidate home now, and help her prepare for tomorrow. It will be a difficult day, for Leona most of all.'

Higgins nodded, and the two women headed at once towards the door. 'My God, Leona,' said Alison, as soon as they were out of earshot. 'You really laid down the law to them.'

'I just took up where my husband left off. Roly was a great one for doing things his way, in every respect. But everything I told them was true. Can you imagine me sitting there surrounded by suits, having my every non-utterance pounced upon by the Press? No, thank you very much. I felt a bit sorry putting Marsh on the spot, though. After all, we know he has trouble enough from assertive women! I'll have to be extra gentle with him from now on.'

74

'You're new. What happened to that nice young Mr Martin who was here before?'

'He's in Scotland today, Mrs Davey,' said Brian Mackie. 'He sends his apologies that he couldn't come in person, but Inspector McGuire and I are here on his behalf.'

'Well, no matter,' Laura Davey replied. 'How can I help you today?'

'A couple of points have come up in the course of our enquiries that we need to ask you about. They're names; the names of people involved in the Reaper Missile controversy.'

Her face darkened. 'I wondered whether that would come up. So, whose are these names?'

'Maurice Hugo?'

She looked blankly at him and shook her head.

'Vassily Kelnikov?'

Something flashed across her eyes. She shook her head again, but briefly, without real conviction.

'Are you sure about that, Mrs Davey?' asked Mackie gently.

She turned her back on him and walked towards the window. 'That's a name I never wanted to hear mentioned in this house again. Yes, I've heard of Kelnikov. When I found the photograph that arrived in the mail, Colin told me all about him.'

She turned to face the policemen again. 'When I saw Mr Martin, I told him that there were no other women in my husband's life. That was true. Unfortunately, in the past, there was the occasional man. I knew about it, but he had assured me that those days were over. I believe that to have been true. He had a healthy fear of AIDS. But then, that damn photograph arrived, on a day when Colin was away, and when I opened his post, as we always did for each other. It showed him naked, with a man. I won't say what they were doing . . . There was a letter with it. "From the desk of Vassily Kelnikov", was the heading. I remember every word. It said, "You probably remember this encounter with a young friend of mine, in Vienna, in 1987. Most certainly I do. To remove it from my memory, at least for the time being, I will expect the British Government to purchase the Reaper Missile from the Aerofoil Consortium, in which I have a personal interest." That was all.'

'What did you do with the letter, and the photograph?'

'I gave them to Colin, of course, as soon as he returned home. I wasn't angry with him, I was sorry for him.'

'How did he react?'

'He broke down. He thought that his career was at an end.'

'And when it didn't end?' asked McGuire, very softly.

Her back straightened, and she turned to look at him. 'I saw that he had done what had to be done, Inspector.'

'Do you know what your husband did with the photograph and the letter, ma'am?' asked Mackie.

'I had assumed that he had burned them, but when I opened his safe, at the weekend, I found them, together with two other letters from Kelnikov, one thanking him for delivering the order, and the second, dated very recently, saying that there was some further business, involving a new anti-tank rocket, which he was sure they could do together.'

'What did you do with them, Mrs Davey?'

She glared at the tall, thin detective, down her long nose, as at first she had looked at Andy Martin. 'I burned them, Chief Inspector, I *burned* them. What else would you have expected me to do!'

'Nothing other than that, to be honest,' said Mackie. 'There's no harm done. You've confirmed for us that Kelnikov had no interest in having your husband murdered. Rather his interest was in keeping him alive. Now, another name. Bryn Sawyer. Mean anything to you?'

She looked at him blankly once more and shook her head.

'Okay,' said Mackie. 'That's all. I'm sorry that we had to raise this, Mrs Davey. I don't expect that we'll be bothering you again.'

'Good,' she said sincerely. 'Nothing personal, you understand.'

She walked them to the door. 'What about that awful man Kelnikov? What will happen to him?'

'It has already. His former organisation revoked his licence last week. He's out of business, for good.'

75

'Dust to dust, ashes to ashes . . .'

The undertaker tossed handfuls of earth into the open grave, in time to the Minister's words. Leona McGrath winced imperceptibly each time they smacked woodenly against the coffin six feet beneath the turf of the Dean Cemetery.

'. . . of resurrection and eternal life. Amen. Now go, and may God be with you all.'

The stocky, dark-suited clergyman stepped across to the head of the grave, and shook Leona McGrath's hand, then bent, solemnly to shake that of her son. 'Thank you,' said Mark solemnly. He was as white-faced as his mother, but held himself as proudly. Thirty yards away, where they had been gathered by the Conservative Party and police Press Officers, a score and more of media cameras clicked as the little boy looked the Minister in the eye.

The two stood there, with black-clad friends and relatives surrounding them. Chief Constable Sir James Proud, in full uniform and wearing a mourner's armband, stood a little apart, with the Secretary of State for Scotland by his side, and Jim Elder and Andy Martin behind. Beyond their little group, Marshall Elliot, with his weeping blonde wife on his arm, looked along at the tiny figures of mother and son, concern in his eyes.

'So long, Roly,' said Leona quietly, as she stood looking down into the open grave at the coffin, with its shiny brass nameplate and its eight cords, which lay discarded on its lid where their holders had dropped them. She wiped the last tears from her eyes with a small white handkerchief, then squeezed Mark's shoulder. 'Come on, young man. It's time to go.'

He took her hand and together they walked away from the burial place, towards the long black car, where Roland McGrath's father, and her uncle waited. Alison Higgins, in a dark suit and black hat, fell into step beside them.

'Mark,' said Leona, 'I want you to go back to the house with Auntie Alison. Grandpa, Uncle John, Uncle Billy and I are having a reception at the Constituency Office for the people who've come to the funeral. I'll be home as soon as it's over. Auntie Alison will make your lunch.'

'And maybe, just maybe,' said Higgins, 'after that, I'll take you to the zoo.'

Mark looked up at her, unimpressed. 'Couldn't we go to the UCI? *Home Alone Three* starts today. It's on at one-fifty and at two-twenty. Daddy would have taken me there,' he added, wistfully and persuasively.

His godmother looked down at him. 'If that's what you'd like, that's what we'll do. Tell you what – maybe we'll go to McDonald's for lunch.'

Mark nodded his head. 'Yes, please. Daddy would have taken me there too.'

His mother smiled at her friend. 'That's your day taken care of. In that case, I'll make a meal for you later, once the reception is over. Then we can crack a bottle and you can help me plan the next three weeks of my life. They will surely be busy!'

76

'Hello again, Superintendent,' said Brian Mackie.

Paula Whittingham looked up in surprise. For once she was alone in her glass-fronted office. 'Hello, there. I didn't expect to see you chaps again, at least not so quickly. Have you come to canvass for our candidate, or do you have some more questions?'

'It's business like before, I'm afraid, Miss Whittingham. We want to bounce a name off you.'

'Whose name?'

'Bryn Sawyer. He's Managing Director of a company called Breakspear, in Cumbria.'

In an instant the colour drained from the woman's face. 'Paula,' she muttered to herself. 'It's as well you retired from the Force. Why the hell didn't you think of him?' She looked up at Mackie. 'Yes, Chief Inspector. I've heard of Mr Sawyer. I wanted to set the local Force on him, in fact.'

'Why?'

'Because of a letter which Colin received. It was just after he had announced his decision on that missile, the one which caused all the fuss. We get quite a bit of hate mail through here, on a whole variety of topics. Most go straight to the dustbin, but we pass one or two on to the police, as a precaution. The letter from Sawyer was vitriolic, and it was threatening. Sawyer's company lost out on the missile contract, and he was not a happy man. I wanted to hand it over to our local CID, but Colin wouldn't. I suggested that he give it to the Ministry's security people, but he wouldn't do that either.'

'Did he say why not?' asked Mario McGuire.

'Yes, he told me that there had been enough fuss over the damn contract, and he wanted it just to die down and go away. He said that if Sawyer sent any more nasty mail he would do something about it, but that for the time being he would ignore it.'

'Do you know what happened to the letter?'

She nodded and started towards her private room. 'Yes. I've got it. It's through here. Come on.'

They followed her into the small back office, where she pulled open the second drawer of a huge wooden filing cabinet, and began to leaf through folders. At last she produced a sheet of blue notepaper, and waved it in the air. 'Here it is. Short, offensive and to the point.'

She handed it to Mackie, who took it from her and began to read aloud.

Dear Davey,

All politicians are slime in my book, but you are beneath that. In pursuit of what corrupt end I know not, you have sold out your country. By common consent of every specialist who has assessed it, including your own, the Breakspear missile which you have rejected represents a major advance in guidance technology and in battlefield capability.

The spurious reasons for your inept decision do not fool me for a second. It is quite obvious that you have either been bribed or bullied into putting Britain's interests aside.

Because of you, my company may well fail. Because of you, a substantial number of jobs may well be lost, in an area which can ill afford it. Because of you, servicemen's lives will be at greater risk than need be. I will not sit meekly and accept such treatment, especially not from a man like you. If my company goes under, then I promise you, sir, on behalf of all the people who will suffer, that I will stop at nothing to ensure that you are punished for your wickedness.

Yours very sincerely,
Bryn Sawyer, Managing Director.

He handed the letter to McGuire. 'That sounds pretty specific to me,' he said. 'In the light of that last part particularly, I don't think we've got any choice but to pay a visit on Mr Sawyer, when he's least expecting it.'

'What do you mean, about the last part?' Paula Whittingham asked.

'Bryn Sawyer called in a Receiver last week,' said Mackie. 'Four days before Colin Davey was killed.'

77

'I must tell you again, Bob. Without a willing subject, hypnotherapy is rarely successful. So, are you completely committed to this procedure?'

Skinner looked up into the eyes of Kevin O'Malley as they peered at him over gold-rimmed spectacles. 'Looking at the choices you set out for me on Wednesday, too damn right I'm committed.'

'Very good – then let's get on with it. Will it help, do you think, for Sarah to be present, or would you rather that she left us?'

He glanced round at his wife, and smiled. 'There's nothing that I wouldn't say in front of Sarah, conscious or otherwise.'

O'Malley raised a finger in a lecture-room gesture. 'Unconsciousness doesn't come into it. I don't propose to go in for deep hypnosis. I don't think that's necessary in this case. I want to use a technique that is really more like relaxation therapy, in which you are in a light sleep, or trance, but in which the memory behind the dream will be unlocked, stage by stage.'

'And will I remember, afterwards?'

'Yes, you will, but it will be a normal memory, not one which shock has made you repress. You will be able to recall it in daylight, and never again will it come back to haunt your dreams. I intend to progress slowly and carefully. Depending on what's in there . . .' he tapped Skinner's head lightly '. . . we might need two, or even three sessions before we've got to the bottom of this thing, and cured the mental toothache. Whenever I think you've had enough, I'll bring you back up.'

He pulled a chair up to the bedside and sat down. 'Let's begin. First of all, Bob, you have to be completely comfortable. Are you?'

Skinner settled even deeper into his mound of pillows. 'All things considered, I couldn't be better.'

'Good. Right, this is step one. I want you to look up at the ceiling, and pick out a single point on it. Found one?' Skinner nodded very slightly. 'Good. Now I want you to focus on it, completely. Close in on that spot, and don't let your gaze break away . . .

'That's it, that's it,' said O'Malley softly, in a gentle lulling voice. 'Now as you're doing that, I want you to begin to relax your whole body, as much as you can. Just let yourself sink into those pillows.'

He paused. 'Now, still keeping your gaze focused on that immovable point, I want you to bring into your mind the happiest moment of your life.'

Skinner felt as if he was floating, as if he was tethered to the ceiling by the single black dot at which he was staring. Unbidden, a time came into his thoughts, the moment when he and Sarah, both tearstained, had held their newborn son for the first time. Part of him wanted to call out to her, but he knew instinctively that at that moment they were sharing the same memory.

'Fine,' said O'Malley. 'Now as you look at that spot you're seeing that happy picture, and that's what you will keep in your mind as you fall lightly asleep. Relax, relax . . . that's it . . .

'Now, Bob, I'm going to count slowly to five. As I do, your eyes will close. When I want to bring you up, I will count back from five, and you will awaken, remembering everything that has happened. Carry on for a bit yet relaxing and gazing at the ceiling, at your happy picture . . .'

His voice fell away as he spoke and silence filled the hospital room. He waited for almost half a minute, then said softly: 'One. Two. Three. Four. Five.'

Sarah, watching from her chair in the corner, saw her husband's eyes close.

'Okay, Bob,' said O'Malley, in the same gentle voice. 'We're going to walk into the edge of the dream. You won't see me, but I'll be there. As we go, I want you to tell me what we see . . . Let me know when we're there.'

A few seconds passed. 'We're there now, Kevin, at the edge of the circle.' Skinner's voice was soft, and sounded almost melodic.

'What is in the circle?'

'Wreckage; the wreckage of an aeroplane. It's all over the place. Some of it is still smoking.'

'How far away is it?'

'A hundred yards or so, maybe a bit more.'

'We're going to walk towards it. And as we walk, I want you to describe the whole scene to me.'

As Sarah watched him, on the bed, she saw his eyebrow twitch.

'It's flat,' he said. 'As far as the eye can see, it's flat. And it's muddy. All muddy. Deep, deep mud. Everyone's wearing wellies. Except me!' Suddenly his voice rose in volume, and strangely, in pitch. It was as if suddenly, he had become younger, and was in distress. 'The mud's getting on my fucking uniform and they haven't given me any fucking wellies!'

The psychiatrist stared at him. He turned to Sarah, but when she looked up at him her eyes were wide and bewildered. She shrugged her shoulders. 'I don't know,' she mouthed.

'Okay, Bob,' said O'Malley. 'We're going to stand where we are for a while. I want you to tell me how old you are.'

'I'm twenty-two.' He sounded scathing, as if it were obvious. The anxiety had gone from his voice, but the youthful lilt remained.

'What's your rank?'

'Constable. Full Constable,' he added proudly. 'Finished my probation a few months back.'

'Are you married?'

'Not yet. Just engaged. We're getting married next year though.'

'What's your fiancée's name?'

'Myra, Myra Graham.'

'Tell me what the two of you have been doing lately.'

'We're just back from Estartit. Two weeks of San Miguel, sun and shaggin'!' The corners of his mouth turned up in a satisfied smile.

'Where are we just now, Bob?' asked O'Malley, quietly and carefully.

'It doesn't have a name. It's on the Solway Coast, in Dumfriesshire.'

'Why are you there?'

'Lots of us are here. The local Force couldn't cope. Some guys came down from Glasgow, and some of us from Hawick.'

'Why were you in Hawick?'

His tone became impatient. 'Because I'm stationed there for six months!'

'The plane that's crashed, Bob. Where was it coming from?'

'From Girona, in Spain. I can see the numbers on the tail, where it's stuck in the mud. I noted them down at the airport last week, just for fun! It's the same plane that Myra and I were on.' Suddenly his eyes wrinkled, and his face creased.

'All right, Bob. That's all for today. I'm going to bring you up now. Five. Four. Three. Two. One.'

Skinner's eyes opened, on the stroke of the last number. They were moist with tears. Sarah jumped to her feet and came over to the bed. She took his hand and pressed it to her breast. 'Bob, I never knew. You never told me.'

He looked up at her. His face was drained of colour and he seemed exhausted. 'I never told anyone, love. Not even Myra. Especially not Myra. I haven't spoken about it from that day on, not to a living soul. I find it incredible, but I'd blocked out even the fact of it. All my recollection of it had gone. And I still can only remember the parts that Kevin showed me just now.' He turned to look at O'Malley. 'I never imagined that the mind could do that.'

The psychiatrist looked down at him. 'There are no rules for the mind. It constructs its own safety mechanisms, and we don't have a bloody clue how it does it. In this case, I would say that it has

246

protected you ... or itself, whatever ... from harm by building an amnesiac wall around this entire incident, within a few months, even weeks of it. It's worked. You've functioned perfectly well over the years. Your career and your life haven't been damaged at all, when otherwise ... Who knows what the long-term effects could have been? I'd surmise that what happened to you last weekend is that the Lammermuirs accident knocked a couple of bricks out of the wall, and let through dream memories from deep in your subconscious.'

Skinner gazed up at him. 'What about the rest of it, Kev? Will it come back of its own accord?'

The psychiatrist ran his fingers through his bushy hair. 'Some of it might, given time. But I'm not going to allow that. We'll have another session tomorrow, if you feel up to it. I want to clean out all of this abscess as quickly as I can. Today was a remarkable beginning, astonishing even, but I have a feeling that we may still have quite a way to go.'

78

'So you're quite certain that we can take Agent Robin off our list of possibles, Captain Arrow?' drawled the American.

'One hundred per cent, Mr Doherty,' said the soldier coldly. 'That situation has now been resolved, permanently. I've had it under control for some time, in fact. I just couldn't say so earlier. Agent Robin has been neutralised, deactivated; whatever term you'd like to use, Robin is no longer functional.'

The sallow-faced man looked at him shrewdly. 'Sounds pretty terminal,' he said. 'Might I guess that it's tied in with that Iraqi your police arrested the other day in London, and to the civil servant they found dead around the same time? He's been charged with her murder, hasn't he?'

'I believe so,' said Arrow, looking him in the eye.

'Whatever,' said Andy Martin, interrupting. 'That leaves us with three open lines of investigation . . . live suspects you might say, if one of them wasn't dead. Joe, I'm glad you could make it up for this briefing. I promised to keep you in touch, even though this looks like staying a purely British affair. And Adam, I'm glad you're here too. I want MOD involved on two fronts this weekend.'

He looked across at Mackie and McGuire. 'You lads seem to have had quite a result in Chindersford. That letter shows Mr Sawyer in a pretty bad light. It's the sort of justification I need to ask for a search warrant.

'Brian, I'd like you to put that in hand at once with the Cumbrian magistrates. Secure two search warrants in fact, one for the Breakspear factory, where, so the local police tell me, Sawyer is still working alongside the Receiver, and the other for his home. We'll pay simultaneous visits each at nine o'clock sharp, under the authority of the locals who'll be backing us up. Oh yes, and ask our colleagues to go to a magistrate who can be relied on to keep shtumm. I don't want us asking someone for a warrant then finding out that he's a mate of Sawyer.'

He slapped the table. 'Right, division of forces. Brian, you and Mario hit the factory. Young Sammy here, and I, we'll interrupt Mr Sawyer's Saturday morning breakfast.' He turned to Arrow. 'Adam, do you want to come with us?'

The soldier shook his head. 'No, I want to follow the other one through. If you need an MOD presence, I'll send up my oppo Swifty. He's ex-SBS and you're going to the seaside. He'll like that.'

'Okay. Tell him to be at Police Headquarters in Carlisle at seven-thirty tomorrow morning.' He glanced at his watch. It showed 6.30 p.m. 'The four of us from here will go down in one car. We'll gather here at five-thirty sharp.' He glanced again at McGuire and Mackie. 'Mario, that gives you a few hours to be nice to your wife, and Thin Man, it gives you a few hours to find one!'

'Gee thanks, sir,' said the Inspector.

Mackie simply scowled. 'That's another home game at Tynecastle I'll miss.'

'Lucky for you, then. Now before we break up, let's update ourselves on the other enquiry. That could be under way already for all we know. Dave Donaldson and Neil McIlhenney are in place to track Maurice Noble's wife to her assignation with her fancy man.'

'Are you following him also?' asked Doherty.

'No need,' said Martin. 'We're assuming that they'll both wind up at the same place. Once they do we'll nail them.' He stood up, and the others followed his example. 'Tomorrow promises to be quite a day. When it's over, hopefully we'll have narrowed down our list of possibilities.'

'Let's hope we've got at least one left,' said Mackie gloomily.

'That's what I like about you, Brian,' said Martin. 'If there's a black side, I can always trust you to look on it!'

79

'Cheerful bugger him!' snorted McIlhenney as the night-shift watcher shuffled off, stiff and round-shouldered back to his team-mate in their car. He had reported, morosely and without a smile, on another uneventful night in Ariadne Tucker's narrow street, where unrestricted parking made it easy for the pair to keep up observation unnoticed by their subject.

It was just after 7.30 a.m., and the light of day was only just beginning to make its presence felt. Since it was Saturday, most of the curtains in the street remained drawn. Among the exceptions were those of Ariadne Tucker, in whose living-room window, seventy-five yards along on the other side of the street from their parking place, a light shone.

'Our girl's up and about already, then,' said McIlhenney, yawning and rubbing his eyes.

'Could be her mother,' said Donaldson.

'Doubt it, unless she's come back and no one spotted her. She left a couple of days ago, remember.'

'Aye, you're right. I'm at the stage on this job where all the days are beginning to merge into one. It's getting bloody cold, too. London can be hot in the summer, but it can be freezing in the winter too, especially when the wind comes whistling up the Thames.'

There was a quick knock on the back window, a door opened and Adam Arrow slid into the back seat. 'Morning lads,' he said breezily. 'No action yet?'

'Well, we're still here,' said McIlhenney, stating the obvious.

'Glad about that,' said the soldier. 'I wouldn't have fancied following you all in a taxi if she's got off 'er mark before I arrived.'

'No,' said Donaldson. 'But you weren't far off it. Look.'

His companions followed his pointing finger, along the street. Ariadne Tucker was standing at her front door, turning a key in the lock. She was dressed in black slacks and a cream jacket, and had a canvas rucksack slung over her shoulder.

'She isn't taking many clothes, then,' said McIlhenney. 'No, there's another bag lying in the path.' As he spoke she bent to pick it up. 'Bugger me, it's a cat basket. She's taking bloody Tigger on her dirty weekend.'

'It means this isn't a false alarm at least,' said Arrow. 'She wouldn't take the cat to Sainsbury's.'

As they watched, the woman glanced quickly up and down the street, then strode down the path, stepping over her low stone wall rather than opening the gate, and walked off down the pavement, away from their position.

McIlhenney made to start the car, but Arrow stopped him. 'Wait a bit. There are garages round behind the houses. Look, she's just turned into the access road. She's gone for the Mazda.'

'Hope we can keep up with it.'

'No problem. She won't want to be stopped for speeding. And anyway, those things aren't as quick as they look.'

They waited and watched the mouth of the access road, with their car engine running. Less than two minutes later, a red car pulled out, and turned right, towards the main road. McIlhenney put the car in gear. 'No!' said Arrow. 'That wasn't her. That was a Golf GTi. There's more than one garage round there.'

'I hope she hasn't changed cars,' growled McIlhenney. But at once, his fears were put at rest. A blue metallic two-seater, with black hard-top, swung out of the access road and followed the path of the Golf.

'Okay,' said Donaldson, 'that's her.'

The Sergeant pulled their borrowed Peugeot away from the kerb. 'Want to start a book on where she's off to?' he asked.

'Could be Aldershot,' said the DCI, 'to pick up her boyfriend.'

'Don't see it,' McIlhenney chuckled.

'Why not?'

'Because that's a two-seater. If she's picking up young Short Wave, she'd have to put fucking Tigger in the boot!'

'I don't see it being Aldershot either,' said Arrow, as they followed her through a sweeping right-hand curve. 'She'd have headed south for the M3 back there if that was the case. She's taking us over Putney Bridge. That probably means Hammersmith and the M4.'

'And where will that take us?'

'Depends. If she turns on to the M25 it could take us anywhere.'

'Great,' said McIlhenney, keeping two vehicles between their car and the Mazda as it pulled up at a red traffic light. 'I like a mystery tour.

'I remember a couple of years ago, Maggie and Mario were on an observation just like this. They got taken on a cross-country chase. The folk they were chasing went to ground in a house by the seaside in Fife, right on the beach. Brian Mackie and I were sent up to do the overnight watch. We spent the night freezing our balls off in the sand-dunes, while Maggie and Mario got to shack up in the local hotel. Bloody magic, it was. The Thin Man and I caught our deaths of cold, but those two have never looked back since.'

They headed along Fulham Palace Road, picking up the A4 in Hammersmith as Arrow had forecast. The traffic was light as they hit the motorway, but sufficiently thick for McIlhenney to maintain a concealing curtain of vehicles between Ariadne Tucker and her pursuers as they matched her gathering speed.

Before long they came to the signs for the M25. 'Place your bets, gentlemen,' said McIlhenney. 'I'll have a quid on the M25.'

'No bet,' said Arrow, 'that's where my money is. I'm hoping she's heading for Derbyshire. Then I can call in on my Aunt Ivy.'

'Okay,' said Donaldson, exasperated, 'I'll cover those. I say she stays on the M4.'

A minute later the DCI handed over two pound coins, as the Mazda swung on to the M25, heading north.

'Chance to get your money back, Dave,' Arrow laughed. 'She's got four choices here: M40 and the Midlands, M1 and the North, or M11 for Buckinghamshire and East Anglia.'

'What's the fourth choice?'

'Drive in circles round the M25 all fookin' weekend.'

The DCI laughed. 'Okay, I'll take the M11. Neil?'

'Give me the M1.'

'Fair enough,' said the soldier. 'I'll take what's left. M40.' Three minutes and three miles later he pocketed another two pounds.

'Right,' he grinned. 'Next bet. Where's she going to turn off?'

'Bugger off!' roared the two Scots, in unison.

As it transpired, Ariadne turned off at Oxford, around half an hour later. She took the A40, skirting the north of the City of Spires, and heading on towards Witney. 'Nice countryside this,' said McIlhenney, keeping her in sight, but in the distance on the single carriageway.

'It'll get nicer,' said Arrow. His companions looked at him, puzzled.

She bypassed Witney, where the road became dual for a few miles, and was sign-posted for Burford and Cheltenham. 'Oh Christ!' said McIlhenney. 'I've got a bad feeling about this. There's a jump meeting on at Cheltenham today. I think they're going to the bloody races!'

For a few miniutes, even Arrow's confidence was dented until, with barely any warning, the Mazda, 300 yards ahead, turned right off the A40 into Burford. McIlhenney accelerated to the turn and swung on to the dramatic, completely unexpected downward sloping main street of the Oxfordshire market town. He stared ahead. The road was empty. 'Where is she?' he snarled, thumping the steering wheel with one hand.

'Take that left turn down there,' said Donaldson, pointing. 'I think I just caught her tail as she turned in.' McIlhenney followed his direction. The road went nowhere but to a supermarket. On the far side of its car park, they saw Ariadne Tucker hurrying towards the entrance.

'Shopping,' laughed Arrow, as McIlhenney found a bay near the entrance. 'She's doing her fookin' shopping! We'll be here for an hour, anyway.' He glanced at his watch, which showed 9.13 a.m.

He was wrong, by fifty-nine minutes. Only Donaldson saw her as she emerged through the automatic door, still walking briskly, but no longer rushing. There was a faint smile on her face. He dug McIlhenney in the ribs and called to Arrow. 'Hey, that was quick: she's out. D'you think it was her turn to buy the condoms?'

McIlhenney eased out of the car park, following her but hanging back until he saw that she was turning left, heading down the main street once more. He slipped out of the junction, very slowly, driving as if he were a tourist, out early to beat the weekend traffic.

At the foot of the hill there was a set of traffic lights. The three pursuers saw the Mazda go through on green. As they made to follow on the amber, a tractor pulled out of an alleyway and blocked their path, just as the light turned to red.

McIlhenney exploded. 'You stupid bastard!' he shouted through his side-window, red-faced and waving his fist. The tractor driver was a young man, in his early twenties. He glared back at McIlhenney and dismounted from his cab. He seemed to climb out in stages. He was huge, at least six feet five, and built out of slabs of something very muscular.

He advanced on the Peugeot. 'Who are you calling—'

As Donaldson held the Sergeant's arm to restrain him, Arrow jumped out of the back seat and stepped up to the giant. They made a ludicrous sight, the little soldier gazing up at the vast young farmer, at least a foot taller than he.

'You,' he said clearly and loud enough for the pedestrians on either side of the road to hear. 'He's calling *you* a stupid bastard. You pulled right out in front of us there, without anything like a signal.' The ruddy young man glowered down at him. 'Now, sunshine, you're going to get back in your cab and move out of our way. If you don't, I'm going to leave you in a bloody 'eap by the roadside and shift it myself.'

The farmer laughed at him.

'Listen, mate,' said Arrow, crisply and evenly, in his finest Derbyshire, holding the man with a hard unblinking stare. 'This is your last warning. Move it or you won't be moving anything for about a month. And think on this. If someone my size says that to someone your size, it means only one thing. 'E can fookin' well live up to it! Get me?' To emphasise his point, he stabbed the hulk in the midsection, with the straight fingers of his right hand. The giant gasped and went pale. He bent over slightly, as if he was about to vomit. He looked at

253

his tiny tormentor again, then turned, and without another word, got in and reversed the tractor off the road.

As Arrow climbed into the back of the car, McIlhenney drove through the green light. 'Thanks, Captain A,' said McIlhenney. 'You saved that boy a right good tankin' there. I'd never have let him off as easy as that.' He smiled at Arrow in the rearview mirror.

'Never shout, Neil,' the soldier replied in a quiet emotionless voice, which brought a sudden chill into the car. 'Just tell them what you want, and show them what'll happen if they don't do it. Like a girlfriend of mine used to say, and like that lad just found out, size doesn't mean a thing. Now let's get Ariadne.'

Ahead of them, the road forked, becoming to the left the A424 to Stow-on-the-Wold, and to the right, the A361 to Chipping Norton. The Mazda was nowhere to be seen.

'Take a right,' said Arrow.

'You know where she's going?' asked Donaldson.

'I do now.'

From Burford, they had run straight into a village called Fulbrook. 'Right again,' said Arrow. McIlhenney obeyed.

The road grew narrow as soon as they turned on to it, with barely room for two cars. McIlhenney drove slowly and carefully along its twists. High hedgerows loomed on either side, until after almost a mile, they began to widen out and the searchers came to a small church, set on sloping ground to their right with a small parking area facing it.

'Pull in there,' the soldier ordered.

'What is this place?' asked Donaldson.

'Remember I told you that Richards' father was a vicar? When he retired he bought a cottage here, and when he died, he left it to his son.'

'You bugger,' said McIlhenney. 'You knew that when you took that bet off us on the M40!'

'Aye, but I couldn't be certain! Right, I'm going to see what's what. I'll wander into the church like a tourist. I should be able to see the village from here.'

He stepped out of the car, crossed the narrow road, and trotted up the few stone steps which led to the churchyard. The building itself was tiny, a place of worship dating from baronial days, best known in modern times for the graves of a famous literary family which lay around it.

Arrow wandered idly among the famous headstones, pretending to make notes with a pencil in a little book which he had produced from a pocket of his Barbour jacket. But all the while he was looking across at the hamlet of Swinbrook. There were barely a dozen cottages there, gathered round a little pond, which the narrow road skirted.

Four cars were parked on the grass on the other side of the water. A Suzuki Vitara stood off to the right, not far from a battered Austin Maestro. Ariadne Tucker's Mazda sat away to the left against a fence, drawn up as if in a rank behind a silver Renault. Beyond the two vehicles was a wide thatched cottage, with two attic windows, built in yellow Cotswold stone. A vine grew around and over the door. Arrow guessed that in the summer, it might bear blue clematis flowers.

Two chimney stacks rose up from the roof, and from each one, thick black smoke spiralled, as if from fires newly lit in cold hearths. He smiled quietly to himself and made his way, slowly and idly, back to the Peugeot.

'They're here,' he said, as he climbed in. 'It looks as if he beat her to it, although not by much. Two fires kindled; that's their smoke climbing.' He pointed above the hedgerow which bounded the parking place. 'One in the living room, one in the bedroom, I'd guess. His car's parked outside, and hers is behind it, jamming it in.'

'Should we do a DVLC check on the other car?' asked Donaldson.

'I couldn't see the number. Anyway, what's the point?' He paused, and looked at his companions. 'Okay, policemen. What do we do? Go straight in, or give them half an hour, just for devilment, and catch them on the job?'

'We've done all we've been ordered to do so far, and it seems as if we've got a result,' said the DCI. 'Before we do anything else, I'd better call Andy Martin and take orders from him ... But I'm like you. I can't wait to catch the Widow Noble sharing her grief!'

80

The Lakeland mountains loomed high around Seatoller, as Andy Martin, Sammy Pye and John Swift sat in their car. Despite Arrow's assumption at the briefing the evening before, they were a long way from the seaside.

Sawyer's home was in a village in the heart of the Lake District, past the southern tip of Derwent Water, overlooked by Great Gable and Glaramara, and beyond by towering Scafell Pike. The house was built of dark stone, almost the colour of the slate which formed its roof. It was an unimpressive rectangular villa, with a large garage outbuilding set well back from the road.

Martin checked his watch, and looked behind him. In the back seat, beside Swift, sat a Superintendent from the Cumbrian Force. The very sight of his thick serge uniform made the Scot begin to itch. For a few months, earlier that year, he had worn something similar, and had hated every moment of it.

'It's nine o'clock,' he said. 'Ready to go?'

Superintendent Hawes nodded. 'Yes.' He waved a piece of paper in the air. 'I've got the warrant.'

'Okay, on you go, Sammy.'

Detective Constable Pye slipped the idling Mondeo into gear and drove straight into and up the broad driveway of the villa. He noticed as he passed the sign at the gate that it was named *Aspatria*. A second vehicle carrying five uniformed officers, a Sergeant and four Constables, followed behind him. The car wheels crunching through the grey gravel path announced their arrival.

Chief Superintendent Martin stepped out of the front seat, with his Cumbrian colleague by his side, and pulled the handle of what he took for the doorbell. A boom sounded inside the house.

The woman who opened the door was in her early thirties. She was wearing a white top and a red skirt, to which a small child clung. 'Mrs Sawyer?' enquired Superintendent Hawes. She nodded, her eyes widening with fear as she saw the uniform and the men beyond.

'Is your husband at home?'

'Yes, he is!' The man's voice came from behind them, aggressively. They turned and saw him there, in the centre of the drive, wiping grubby hands on his overalls. He was of medium height, but strongly built, with greasy black hair. He looked to be around five years older than his wife. The gravel scrunched under his Timberland boots as he advanced towards them, purposefully.

'Mr Sawyer, I am Superintendent Hawes, from Carlisle,' began the uniformed officer. 'I have a warrant, granted by a magistrate, to search these premises. My colleagues here, Chief Superintendent Martin and DC Pye, are from Edinburgh and Mr Swift is from London. Mr Martin will explain the circumstances.'

'Search warrant?' Bryn Sawyer boomed. 'I thought you'd be here sooner or later, but to come ready armed with a search warrant, that's a bit heavy-handed. I think I'll call my lawyer.'

'I've got no objection to that,' said Andy Martin. 'In fact, I'd advise it. So call him by all means. We'll proceed with our search right away, but if you wish, I'll hold my questions until he arrives.'

Sawyer shook his head. 'No, let's hear what you've got to say first. It isn't as if I've got anything to hide.'

'But you were expecting us?'

'Yes, after that letter of mine to Davey, I suppose I was. Look, come on in here. Marian, take the kid out of the way, for God's sake.' He led the way into the house, and into a study, off the hall. Martin and Swift followed, while Hawes instructed his officers on the procedure of the search.

'That letter,' said the Chief Superintendent. 'Just bloody stupid, or a genuine threat, warning of consequences for Davey: which was it?'

'Come on,' said Sawyer, concern showing through his belligerence for the first time. 'Where was the threat?'

'You warned him that if your company had to go into liquidation, he'd be punished. Now you've got a Receiver in and Davey's dead.'

'Yes, but hold on a minute. He's an administrative Receiver, and I asked for him. I'm trying to recapitalise and restructure the business, to give me time to find new markets for our technology. As it is, I think I may have cracked it. I had a phone call from the MOD yesterday. Apparently Reaper bit the dust with Davey.'

'Who bit the dust himself,' said Martin evenly, 'as your letter promised, four days after your Receiver moved in. Surely in those circumstances, you have to expect us to take your threat just a wee bit bloody seriously.'

He sat on the edge of Sawyer's desk. 'Let me ask you something. What did you feel when you knew that Davey was dead?'

The man looked up at him, and smiled savagely. 'Immense satisfaction,' he said. Suddenly, guilt came into his face as if he had willed it there. 'Sorrow for the other people on board,' he added, 'but sheer delight that he had bought it. That bastard set out to ruin me, and my family. All his experts, every one of them, said to me, "Congratulations, Bryn, the Breakspear missile is a world-beater," then he turns

257

round and gives the contract to a piece of shit that couldn't hit a London bus. Let me ask *you* something, gentlemen. Don't you think the man was corrupt?'

'We know he was,' said Swift, '. . . now. But what the hell difference does that make? If every businessman who loses on a contract killed the guy who awarded it to someone else, we'd bloody soon run out of purchasers.'

Sawyer shook his black, tousled head. 'Just hold on a minute. I said I was glad the shit was dead. I didn't admit to killing him.'

'But you do admit to threatening to kill him, in that letter,' said Martin.

'No, I said I'd punish him. I meant that if it came to it I was going to expose him in the media, or something.'

'That's a bit tame for a man like you, isn't it? I mean, your business is making complex weapons of destruction. The one that killed Davey was a pretty simple device. And in the process you do have access to explosives, don't you?' The man nodded, slowly.

'Mr Sawyer, where were you on Thursday of last week, and last Friday morning?'

For the first time there was silence. 'Come on,' said Martin, 'it'll be checkable. And until you answer, I'm not going to let you see your wife, so you can cook up an alibi.'

'I was in London,' he said reluctantly, with resignation.

'Doing what?'

'I had a meeting last Thursday evening with the Australian Military attaché. They're shopping for missiles. It turned into dinner and went on till midnight. Next morning I got up and went home.'

'Which hotel were you in?'

'The Rubens, between Victoria Station and Buckingham Palace.'

'That's one more link in the chain of evidence. We've got motive, threat, access to weapons technology and hardware. Now you tell us that you were in the vicinity when the crime was committed. Be reasonable, Mr Sawyer; try to see where I'm coming from.'

Sawyer flared at him. 'I'll tell you where you can go, as well.'

Martin smiled. 'I'm sorry, I won't be going anywhere until you can persuade me that you didn't kill Colin Davey, or that you couldn't have had anything to do with his death.'

'How can I do that when you've made up your mind already?'

'No, I haven't, sir. I—' He broke off, as Sammy Pye's sombre face appeared in the doorway.

'Mr Martin,' said the young DC. 'We've found some things. They're out here.'

'Okay, Sammy.' He stood up from the desk. 'Mr Sawyer, you'd better come too.'

Pye led them in single file, through the hallway, out of the house

258

and round into the vast garage building; or rather into what was in part a garage.

The greater area was set up as a workshop; a very specialist workshop. In the corner there was a small forge, with an anvil beside it, and hammers hanging on a rack. Not far away stood an oxy-acetylene cylinder, a mask, and cutting gear. In the centre of the area was a workbench, on which were stacked several sheets of stainless steel. Scraps of metal lay all around the floor.

'Now if you'll follow me again, please, sir,' said Pye. He led Martin back out of the workshop and into the house, Sawyer, Swift and Superintendent Hawes following behind.

'When we arrived, sir, I couldn't help noticing the skirt that Mrs Sawyer was wearing. It's leather, and it's virtually the same colour as the stuff on the box that Mr Skinner recovered on Friday. So while the lads were searching the garage building, I had a look around in here.'

He led the way up a narrow stairway which led off the back of the hall. 'This could have been the maid's quarters, once upon a time,' said Martin, as they climbed.

'But not now, sir,' said Pye. 'In here.' He led the way into a small room, with a wide double window which overlooked the gardens to the rear of the house. Before it stood a wide table, with a heavy-duty sewing machine positioned at one end. The rest of the table was covered with thread spools and paper patterns, some of which were weighted down by a large pair of black scissors. To the right of the table there was a big divided stable-style door. Pye opened the upper half, to reveal a deep-shelved cupboard, packed with bolts of material. He reached in and removed one, unrolling it and holding it up for Martin and the others to see.

It was bright red leather.

Martin stared at the material, then at Sawyer. 'Jesus Christ,' he whispered, to no one. 'The man's made his own Red Box!'

In the dead silence, his mobile telephone rang.

81

'Yes, sir, I'll call you back as soon as we've got something to report.'

Donaldson switched off his phone. 'The Chief Super says we should go in. He's in the middle of his search just now, at the Sawyer bloke's place. He didn't go into detail, Adam, but he said to tell you that he's going to be busy there for a while.'

'Is he, indeed? Well, let's go and find out if we've got a couple of rival candidates in here.'

The trio climbed out of the car, and set off round the corner of the hedgerow. They skirted the pond on the narrow side and headed directly for the cottage, past the two cars.

'Lieutenant Richards's father must have left him a few quid as well as the cottage,' said Donaldson. 'That's a top-of-the-range Laguna.'

The wooden garden gate creaked slightly as Arrow opened it, but otherwise they approached the old house silently. There was no bell, only a huge, old-fashioned, blue-painted knocker. The little soldier seized it and rapped, as loudly as he could, once, twice, three times. They stood there for almost a minute, listening for sounds within, but hearing none.

'D'you think they might have gone for a walk while I was phoning Andy?' whispered Donaldson.

Arrow grinned at him, almost impishly. 'What would your priorities be in this situation?' He reached for the knocker again, but as he did so, the door opened. Ariadne Tucker QC stood there, holding it slightly ajar. Her pink satin robe was tied tight around her waist, but still she held it closed at the neck, with her left hand. Tigger the cat rubbed itself luxuriantly against her bare ankles. She looked at McIlhenney, who was slightly flushed with embarrassment, then at Donaldson, and finally down at Arrow.

She looked surprised, but a long way short of alarmed. 'Oh dear,' she said at last, in her long slow barrister's tone. 'This is very difficult. I think you'd better come in.' She turned and walked back into the cottage, with the cat padding along behind her. The front door led directly into a huge room, with plastered, painted walls and a shiny rug-strewn stone floor. There was a huge fireplace set in the gable wall, filled with blazing logs. Facing it, a staircase led up to the attic.

She walked over to it and put her foot on the first step. 'Darling,' she called out, 'I think you'd better come down. Some gentlemen are here to see us. Oh, and do put something on!'

The soldier and the policemen stood awkwardly in front of the hearth and waited.

'I'll make some tea,' said Ariadne brightly.

'I'd rather you stayed here, ma'am,' said Arrow.

'No, Captain, I think tea would be a good idea.' She turned and disappeared through a door in the far corner of the room. As the door closed behind her, Tigger ran across the floor and up the staircase. Arrow made as if to follow it, but stopped with his foot on the bottom step.

He called up into the attic. 'As the lady said . . . would you come down, please, Sir Stewart.'

Upstairs, a few seconds later, a door creaked. Slowly, and with as much dignity as he could maintain, Sir Stewart Morelli descended, his face a strange mixture of outrage and apprehension. He wore cavalry-twill trousers with a check Viyella shirt, but he was barefoot.

'How did you know?' Donaldson asked the soldier, incredulously.

'It was something Ariadne said, the first time we saw her. She mentioned my Army background, before I came to this job. She said that Maurice had told her, but he couldn't have. Nor could Colin Davey, even. In Whitehall, access to my file is restricted to Morelli and the Chief of Staff, and that old bugger doesn't gossip.'

'You never expected to find Richards here, did you?'

'Well, I couldn't be certain, but when I saw that flash car outside, I knew for sure it wouldn't be him. This house was all the vicar left his son.'

Morelli had reached the foot of the staircase. 'Arrow,' he barked, with a show of bluster. 'What the hell is all this about? What are you doing here?'

'I'm sorry, Permanent Secretary,' said the soldier brusquely, 'but those are *my* lines. I'm assisting these officers in a murder investigation, and we find you right in the middle of it. Like it or not, we'll have to ask you about your relationship with Ms Tucker . . . no, goddammit!' he snapped. 'With *Mrs Noble.*'

Morelli looked at Donaldson and McIlhenney. 'Very well,' he said. 'But I must ask the police to leave.'

'You're in no position to do that, sir.'

Donaldson put a hand on Arrow's shoulder. 'Adam, in the circumstances, we don't mind. We'll wait in the car.'

The little man looked up at him. 'Okay, but not in the car. I want you handy. Wait in the kitchen. I'm sure Ariadne'll give you tea.'

The detectives left by the door under the stairs. Arrow and Morelli faced each other across the room. They were silent for some time, as the soldier stared out the civil servant.

'How long, Sir Stewart?' he asked at last.

'Around a year,' came a voice from the doorway. Ariadne re-entered, carrying a laden tray. Automatically, Arrow stepped across and took it from her, placing it on a low table before the fire. She began to fill the three cups.

'We met at a Ministry evening I attended with Maurice,' she said as she poured. 'It was just one of those things. I had come to the end of my tether with Little Mo, as I called him. He was a lovely, intense chap . . . indeed, that was what drew me to him in the first place . . . but in the context of a marriage his intensity turned to possessiveness and pretty soon, as I told you, to paranoia.'

'So you gave the poor little bugger something to be paranoid about.'

She smiled coldly, taking a fireside seat facing her lover. 'I suppose you could put it that way.'

The look in his eyes stopped her smile stone dead. 'I just did,' he said. He turned to the Permanent Secretary, who had taken another seat by the fireside and was warming his bare feet.

'So, Sir Stewart, let me get this right. You two were having it off, before Maurice was given the Private Office job.'

'I don't like your turn of phrase, Arrow,' the man snapped.

'Tough. It suits the circumstances. Let me take it a little further. You two were having it off, but poor paranoid Maurice was giving Her Ladyship grief, making things difficult. So you came up with a wheeze. You'd give him the Private Office post, so that he would be away from home with the Secretary of State for long periods of time, leaving the field clear for you two to indulge in whatever it is you indulge in. All of us could see that the poor little bugger was never fit for the job, yet you shoved him into it, with promises of joy thereafter, and left him at the mercy of that shit Colin Davey.'

He glanced back towards the woman. 'If you'd reached the end of your patience with Maurice, why didn't you just leave him and set up home together?'

She peered at him coolly and smiled again. 'Because Lady Morelli would have been most upset. Because the Bar Council would have taken a dim view. Because neither of our careers could have stood the scandal,' she said.

'Get used to all those ideas now,' the little man growled.

'Arrow,' said Morelli, 'before we go any further, how did you trace us here?'

'Through young Richards, who owns this love-nest. We saw him with Ariadne, and then we heard her make arrangements with him for the weekend. My policemen friends thought we were going to find *him* here.'

'You tapped my telephone?' the woman blurted out indignantly.

'Too bloody right we tapped your telephone. You're an adulteress, and your husband's just been killed by a device planted in a Red Box to which you had access all of the night before it exploded. I reckon you'd rather appear for the prosecution than for the defence in those circumstances.'

She stared at him, and went very pale.

'Now, Stephen William Richards: where the 'ell does he fit in?'

'Your vetting procedures should be more thorough,' she said defiantly. 'Stephen is Maurice's half-brother. Their mother divorced her first husband, married Stephen's dad, had him, then died, all in short order. Maurice's dad, who was a really nice man, helped him through school and college, out of the goodness of his heart, because apart from this cottage, the Reverend Richards didn't have a bean.'

Arrow shook his head. 'And after all that generosity, the lad repays Maurice by helping you to cuckold him with Sir Knight, 'ere!'

'No, it wasn't like that. Stephen is devoted to me. He saw how unhappy I was with Maurice, so he helped us.'

'What was Plan B?' the soldier asked suddenly.

'If Stephen couldn't get up to town to give me the key personally, whoever got here first could pick up the spare from his cleaning lady Mary, on the check-out in the supermarket where she works at weekends. We've never had to do that before.'

'Why didn't he give you the key at Methuselah's?'

She looked at him in surprise. 'My, you have been nosy. Because he didn't have it with him, silly. He only came up to see me that day because he was devastated about Maurice, and wanted my shoulder to cry on. I asked him to come back up with the key, but he was trapped on base by an inspection.'

'I know that. I arranged it,' said Arrow. He looked across at her, in her chair. He could see that she was trying to keep her composure, but her hands were working unconsciously and nervously in her lap, and the lapel of her satin robe had slipped down, exposing most of her left breast.

'That's all very fine, Ariadne,' he said, 'but here's the prosecution case. Richards betrayed his brother because he'd do anything to have that black mark taken off his record, the one that Morelli put there, personally, after he and Davey crucified him for his indiscretions. A clean sheet and early promotion. That's what's in it for him. That's the object of his heart's desire, as you put it. That's how you two forced him to let you use his cottage, and his bed.'

His eyes flashed across to the Permanent Secretary. 'Isn't that right, Sir Stewart? And DON'T think of lying to me!'

'Yes.' Slowly Morelli nodded, looking down at his bare feet, now reddened with scorch-marks from the fire.

'Right. Now let me extend the case. You were supposed to be on that plane last week, but when Davey booked himself on, you

263

withdrew. Having done that, you told young Richards, an explosives expert, to make you a device. Just before Maurice left for the plane, Ariadne slipped it into his Red Box.

'Maybe it was meant to explode in the taxi, or perhaps later, when he and Davey were alone. Because Davey didn't fancy you either, Sir Stewart; everyone in the Private Office corridor knew that too. So maybe the plan was to take him and Maurice out together. But no . . . maybe the pair of you are just so evil that you didn't care where the bomb blew up. Whichever way, it all fits. Like a glove.'

To his immense, if private satisfaction, he saw that for the first time they both looked thoroughly frightened.

'We didn't!' Morelli protested, at last, while Ariadne sat, ashen. 'That wasn't why I withdrew from that trip. I pulled out only because Davey's decision to go meant that Maurice would be away for the weekend, and Ariadne and I could be together. And you'll never get Richards to admit to doing anything like you say.'

'How well do you know me, Sir Stewart?' asked Arrow quietly. 'I'll have a bloody good try. And anyway, how do you know he didn't do it? Even if you weren't involved yourself, how do you know that she and the lad didn't cook the idea up between them?'

'That's bollocks,' said the woman, recovering some of her assurance, 'but it's all irrelevant anyway. There are no witnesses to this conversation. You don't think we'll repeat any of this, do you?'

The soldier looked at her, pityingly. 'Don't be daft, luv. I had the spooks wire this whole place up last night. Every word of this, and every bump, grind and creaking bedspring from before we got 'ere, it's all down on tape.' He jerked a thumb towards Morelli.

'I've already got his admission that he used improper influence on a serving Army officer, to help him pursue a sexual relationship with a junior colleague's wife. Maybe you two killed Maurice, Massey and Davey and all the rest; maybe one of you did; maybe neither of you did. But you are a pair of treacherous bastards, and for you at least, Sir Stewart, it's the end of your career.'

He looked from one to the other. 'It's also the end of your dirty weekend. The two of you will come back with us to London, voluntarily, and you'll be interviewed, formally, by the police. After that, we'll decide what's to happen. If you don't agree, you will be arrested . . .'

'By whom?' asked Ariadne.

'By me, ma'am,' he replied formally, without a trace of his customary bantering accent. 'My position gives me that authority . . . as Sir Stewart will tell you. If I have to do that, you'll be taken directly to Scotland, where you'll be interviewed by the officer in charge of the investigation. So tell me. Where are we going?'

'London,' said Morelli wearily. 'We'll go to London.'

'Good. We leave as soon as Her Ladyship's dressed and you've got your bloody shoes on. Until then, neither of you will be out of my presence.' His glare stopped Ariadne's protest, even as it formed on her tongue. 'I'm not having either of you getting on your mobiles to warn the boy Richards.'

He called out towards the kitchen. 'Dave, Neil! Find the bloody cat, if you can, then get in here. We're all heading back to London.'

82

'Yesterday was quite a stunner, Bob, for me as well as for you. But I see that sort of thing every now and again in a patient; a deeply-suppressed memory forced to the top by a recent trauma.

'I'm not surprised you kept the recollection hidden from yourself all these years. It must have been bad enough for a twenty-two-year-old to be thrust into something like that, but to find that you had been on the same plane just a few days before . . .'

He shook his head. 'Tell me, were you given any counselling after the experience? Were you even offered any?'

Skinner laughed softly. 'Don't be daft, Kevin. We didn't have things like that back in the seventies.'

'Then God alone knows how many damaged people like you we have wandering around. You wouldn't care to sue your Force, would you? I'd be happy to give expert evidence on your behalf.' In the corner, Sarah spluttered with suppressed laughter.

The DCC shook his head. 'Times have changed, man. As a Commander there's no one more in favour of stress counselling than I am. If I'm learning anything from this experience, it's that it should be compulsory from now on.' He paused and grinned again. 'But before I can do anything about that, I have to get myself back to work. So let's get on with curing that mental toothache.'

O'Malley nodded. 'If you're absolutely sure you're ready. That was quite a session we had yesterday.'

'Kev, after that, I can't wait to bring the rest out. I'm not just ready, I'm impatient.'

'Okay, but let's slow down. You're too pumped up just now. I want to start with five minutes of relaxation and meditation. Just sink into those pillows, pick out that spot on the ceiling again, think your happy thought, and concentrate on them both to the exclusion of everything else.'

Skinner was almost asleep before O'Malley counted him into his trance.

'Hello, Bob,' said the psychiatrist gently, once his patient's eyes were closed. 'I want you to take us into the dream again, at the point at which we left it yesterday. Let me know when we're there.'

He sat upright in his chair and waited. After a few seconds, Skinner spoke, drowsily. 'We're in the big, flat field. Oh Christ, but I wish they'd given me wellies. I'll never get these boots cleaned.'

'We'll worry about that later. Let's go forward now, and as we do, you describe what we're seeing.'

Skinner took a deep sighing breath. For a few seconds silence hung in a pall over his bed.

'Bits of the plane are still smoking,' he said slowly. 'There's wreckage all over the place. It looks like a hurricane I saw on television a while back. Everything's smashed to pieces.

'There are suitcases and rucksacks, all over the place. They're all burst open; the things that were in them are spread around. Look over there, Kevin. It's a big sombrero. And there, a big black fan, like they sell in the markets. There's someone's stuffed donkey. Oh, look at it, the way it's standing up in the mud.' His voice was incredibly young and sad. 'It's looking around like a lost dog.'

His limbs moved slightly on the bed. 'Over there, Kevin,' he said suddenly. 'What's that? It's a hell of a big donkey, surely. Come on.' His legs twitched, as if in his dream he was trying to run through the mud.

'What the hell is it? Is it someone's dog?' He fell silent again, his legs thrashing now.

'*Ahh!*' The sudden cry filled the room, making Sarah's blood run cold. 'Aw no, look at that man. Oh Christ, look! You can see his bones; you can see his guts, lying out there in the mud. And he's burned, poor bastard.

'Oh my, look over there. It's another, and another, and another. Jesus, Kevin, can you imagine the last thirty seconds or so, when they all knew they were going to crash! What it must have been like in that plane! And that could have been Myra and me. Just a week ago.'

'Yes, Bob,' said O'Malley, very gently, 'but it *wasn't* you. Nothing you can do about it. That's the way the dice rolled. Now let's move on. Keep talking to me, as we go, describe for me what we're seeing and what you're doing.'

'Okay,' said the young Skinner. His legs began to labour once more. 'The mud's thicker here. There are more bodies over there, in front of us. They're not burned, or as badly smashed up, but some are sunk right into the muck.'

'Okay, Bob, now carry on, don't stop. Are we heading for anywhere in particular?'

'For the far end of the field.'

'And what's there?'

'The cockpit. I can see it, where it's ploughed right into the ground. There's no one there yet. The firemen and the ambulances are all stuck.'

'Who's with us?'

'Inspector McGuinness, from Hawick, and a bloke called Pender, another Constable.'

'And we're all going towards the cockpit?'

'That's right.'

'Okay, let's just head for it.'

The thrashing of Skinner's legs grew more violent, as if the mud was turning to glue. All at once it stopped. 'Over there, Kevin. That thing – it looks like a doll. I'm going to look at it. That's what it is. It's a doll. See? The arms and legs are all out of their sockets the way dolls go when you twist them. The head's all turned round, too. Wait for me a minute, I'll just put it right.'

He paused, as if concentrating on something. To O'Malley and Sarah, watching him, it was as if the air in the small room began to tingle. And then he screamed.

A pitiful heartrending scream.

'What is it, Bob, what is it?' asked O'Malley, his voice shaking in spite of himself.

'It's wee June, Kev, it's wee June!'

'Who's wee June?'

He was sobbing in his sleep, uncontrollably. 'My pal Dougie Fiddes, from Motherwell. He's only a couple of years older than me. He and his wife, Shona, arrived in our hotel a fortnight ago, at the end of our first week; them and their baby, wee June.

'Aw, Kev, I was playing with her in the pool last week, on the day we left. She's only two, and now look at her, look at her. Oh man, it's just no' fair!' He paused, his voice catching on his sobs.

'And look at me, Kevin. I've pissed myself!'

O'Malley looked down and realised suddenly that Skinner was speaking the truth, past and present.

'Bob, we're going to come up now. That's more than enough for this session. On one: Five. Four. Three. Two. One.'

Skinner's eyes snapped open, staring at the ceiling in horror. His hand clutched at his sodden groin.

'God,' he whispered, trembling. 'In my life I've been shot, stabbed and half-strangled, but I've never had an experience as awful or as terrifying as that. I remember it now, as clear as a bell, yet . . .'

'Yet you've been having the experience, subconsciously, for half your life,' said O'Malley. 'Your way of dealing with something that for most people would be too awful to contemplate has been to shove it right down into the depths of your mind, and as I said yesterday, to build a wall around it. I've had other patients who have done that, but they've all been dysfunctional personalities. For you to have suppressed it all and achieved what you have is remarkable. In fact, it suggests—' He stopped. 'No, I'll keep that thought to myself, until we're all through.'

Sarah was still shaking as she came to stand beside him. 'Do you want to go on, Bob? We know about the doll now, but we still have to confront the man in the cottage. Are you strong enough for that?'

He smiled up at her, weak, white-faced, but determined. 'I have to do the rest of it, love. But in one more session. Next time, I promise to stay continent. That wasn't just an awful experience. It was very embarrassing . . . then *and* now.

'Yet,' he said, 'at the time, neither McGuinness nor Pender mentioned that part of it. I think it was because they'd done the same themselves.'

83

'That's a bit of a turn-up, Adam,' said Andy Martin. 'It must be a bit awkward for you, finding your boss right in the middle of the situation.'

'I work for the Ministry,' said Arrow, 'not for the individual. It doesn't worry me a bit. In fact, I'm pretty pleased with myself. The idea of having such a corrupt bastard at the heart of the country's defence: I tell you, it would curdle any soldier's blood. What I'd really like to do is offer him a pearl-handled revolver and the key to the library – except he wouldn't have the balls to do the decent thing. Mind you, if I didn't have your two coppers around, I might be inclined to help him. But no, we'll go back to London, we'll pick up the tapes from the spooks and play them to the pair of them, and then your lads can interview them formally.'

Standing in the Swinbrook churchyard, with Donaldson's mobile phone in his hand, Arrow heard Martin suck in his breath. 'I don't know about that, Adam. Morelli's very heavy duty. I don't think it's fair to lump that on Dave's shoulders. If Bob was fit he'd be on the first plane down. As for me, I'm a bit tied up here with our other live prospect. I'll have to consult the Chief. I suspect he'll want to handle this one himself.'

'One knight to another,' chuckled Arrow grimly.

'That's right. Anyway, for now, you get your prisoners back to London. I'll be in touch.'

Martin pushed the 'End' button and strode back into Sawyer's study.

'Right, sir,' he said. 'Let's go over this again.'

The man was seated in a hard-backed chair, with Sammy Pye standing, stern-faced, behind him. He was still wearing his oily, grimy overalls.

'How many more times?' he snarled. 'Metal-working is my hobby. I'm a blacksmith. My wife is into leather.' A chortle welled up in young Sammy Pye's throat, but was choked off short by a single glance from the Chief Superintendent.

'She's a tailor by training, and she runs a dress-making business from the house. Lately she's been designing her own range. She's always worked in spun fabrics, but a few weeks ago she came up with a concept in leather. She bought that length to try it out.'

'*Red* leather, Mr Sawyer? That's pretty garish for clothing, is it not?'

An eyebrow rose as he looked up at the detective. 'Colour selection is not my wife's greatest asset as a designer. You saw that skirt she was wearing. A bit bright for morning wear, you'll agree.'

'Is that all she's made in that material?' asked Martin. 'There's quite a bit missing from the bolt.'

Somehow, Sawyer managed to shake his head and shrug his shoulders simultaneously. 'She did make something else, but it was a disaster. She found that it's too difficult to work with the bloody stuff on anything more complex than a skirt. She was supposed to be making a tailored top, but it wound up looking like a red bag with holes in it.'

'How about your metal-work? What sort of things do you do?'

'Anything. Sculptures in steel, wrought-iron gates, furniture . . .'

'Cabinets?'

'Yes,' said Sawyer warily. 'I could do . . . but I haven't.'

'You haven't made a steel box,' Martin signed with his hands, 'about this wide, this long, this deep?'

'No.'

'And you haven't bound it in red leather?'

'No!'

'Nor decorated it with gold paint, of the type we found in the lower part of the cupboard in your wife's studio?'

'No!'

'Okay.' Martin paced across the small room, and back again. 'Let's leave that for now. Let's talk about explosives instead. Your company uses them, doesn't it, for live missile tests?'

'Yes.' Sawyer shifted in his chair.

'And you admit that you are thoroughly experienced in handling and priming them?'

'Yes, I am,' he said grudgingly.

'You have to keep a meticulous record of their use, of course.'

'Of course.'

'In that case, can you explain why, at your factory, which my Chief Inspector has just searched, there's a discrepancy in those records? Why you actually have about three kilos less explosive there than your stocksheet says?'

'We had a live test firing from a Harrier a couple of weeks ago. My stock controller probably hasn't entered that withdrawal as yet.'

'Come on,' said Martin, 'he should have entered it as soon as it was taken out.'

'Yes, I know, but Griff was off with flu around that time. We probably slipped up. Look,' he said, standing up with his jaw stuck out aggressively, 'what have we got here? What do all these questions add up to? What's your allegation?'

'I haven't alleged anything yet, Mr Sawyer. I've just established with your help that you have metal-working and munitions skills, that you're in possession of certain materials, and that you were in a certain area of London at a specific time. That's all I've done so far.

'But now I'll tell you what those circumstances suggest you might know already; that Colin Davey, a man you threatened, was killed by a bomb placed in his Ministerial document case – a steel box, bound in red leather, decorated with gold paint.'

Sawyer stared at him. 'I think I want my lawyer now,' he said.

'Yes,' said Martin. 'In fact, at this stage, I insist that you call him. I will have certain things to put to you formally, under caution, and he should be present. But you'd better tell him to engage a Scottish solicitor as well, and to head for Police Headquarters in Edinburgh. Beause that's where you and I are going.

'Come with me, please, Mr Sawyer.'

84

'What's this all about, sir?'

'Well, Lieutenant Richards,' said Adam Arrow lazily, 'it's about you, really. You're a very important soldier. You could give my friend and me the answer to some questions that 'ave been troubling us.'

Stephen William Richards sat, straight-backed, immaculate in his brown uniform, gazing slightly anxiously across a desk, in an interview room in the basement of the Ministry of Defence building in Whitehall. Two Military Police Sergeants, who had escorted him from his base in Aldershot, stood to attention behind him, the peaks of their caps casting crescent shadows across their faces.

'My friend here,' the little man nodded to his right, 'he's a policeman, from Scotland. His name's Detective Chief Inspector Donaldson.' Suddenly he smiled. 'Bloody long ranks, these coppers 'ave, don't they?' he said conversationally. 'No wonder they must use initials. DCI Donaldson and I are involved in the investigation of the murder of the Secretary of State and all those other people who were killed in the plane crash last week. Those people included your half-brother Maurice, I understand.'

The Lieutenant nodded, a shadow of pain passing across his face.

'Mr Noble kept quiet about your relationship when I vetted him for the Private Office job earlier on this year. I wonder why? Maybe it was because 'e was embarrassed about your run-in with the Minister and the Permanent Secretary, and about your problems as a trainee equerry. Could that have been it, d'you think?'

'Perhaps,' said Richards quietly.

'You're quite an athlete, aren't you, Lieutenant?'

'A bit.'

'Sexual athlete too?'

'Hardly.'

'You like older women though, don't you?'

'Perhaps.'

'You like your half-sister-in-law, Ariadne. You fancy her something rotten, don't you?'

The young man flushed.

'Come on, admit it – you've always fancied her.'

He nodded, eyes downcast.

'Tell me, Stephen,' Arrow asked, 'what did she see in Maurice? They must have been an odd couple.'

'No,' said the Lieutenant, 'not always. When he met Ariadne, Maurice was a different guy. Sure, he was serious, but he was confident, outgoing. He had had plenty of girlfriends, but they'd always been quiet types, never his equals in personality terms. Ariadne was different. He looked up to her, and as her career progressed, the higher he had to look. They married very quickly. Maurice began to change shortly after that. He became possessive, to the point of being boring about it. From the earliest days, I knew they were headed for trouble.'

'But you didn't resent Ariadne for it,' said Arrow slyly. 'You leched after her instead!'

'No, I didn't. I adored her but she was my brother's wife. End of story.'

'For as long as your brother was alive,' said Donaldson quietly.

Richards looked at him, with sudden apprehension. 'What do you mean?'

'With your brother dead, the field might be clear for you.'

'If it weren't for Morelli,' Richards interposed. 'Anyway,' he added, with a touch of defiance, 'she's still my sister-in-law.'

'Come on, Richards,' Arrow snarled. 'Your moral code's a load of crap. You did everything for Ariadne except fook 'er, but that was only because she never asked you. If she 'ad, you'd have been in there like a rat up a drainpipe, you two-faced little bastard. You betrayed your brother just as surely as if you'd slept with her. You knew about her and Morelli, but rather than put a stop to it, you helped them by letting them use your cottage as a fuck-pit.'

He stopped and glared across the table at Richards. The young man's face was white, and a study in panic.

'I know all about it, Short Wave. We've been trailing Ariadne; this morning we picked her up in Swinbrook, and him. They're upstairs now, in separate rooms, with colleagues of ours, listening to some pretty fruity tapes and waiting for some very big brass to come down from Scotland to interview them.' He paused, letting his words sink in.

'Tell us, Lieutenant,' said Donaldson, picking up his cue, 'when did Morelli first learn of your relationship to Maurice Noble?'

The Lieutenant's head slumped towards his chest. 'At the time of the fuss last year,' he muttered. 'I had to fill up a personnel form for the Palace, listing next of kin. I put down Maurice's name. My MoD file hadn't been updated since my father's death.'

'I see.' The policeman nodded. 'Let's talk about something else now. When Morelli put that mark on your record, didn't you think he was being harsh?'

'Yes. I threatened to appeal to the Chief of Staff, but Sir Stewart said that if I did that he'd see that the appeal resulted in my being kicked out.'

'How long after that did you find out about him and Ariadne?'

'Not long. Ariadne told me about it.'

'And when were you first asked for the keys to Swinbrook?'

'About the time that Maurice was given the Private Office job.'

'Who made the approach?'

'Ariadne asked me.'

'Were you offered any inducement?'

The young officer nodded. 'Yes. She said that Sir Stewart would be grateful, and that after a while he would remove the note from my record, and push my promotion through. She said that she had persuaded him to agree to review it after a year.'

'About now, in fact.'

'Yes. When we met the other day, she said he'd promised to do it next week.'

Donaldson smiled sadly at him. 'Didn't you ever make the connection – that Morelli had got you under his thumb for the very purpose of furthering his relationship with your brother's wife? Or are you the sort of poor innocent who can't conceive of people being that devious?'

'Yes,' said Richards, after a while. 'I suppose I am. But I'd still have done anything for Ariadne.'

'Okay,' said Arrow suddenly. 'This place is reeking of hearts and fookin' flowers. Which one of them asked you to make the bomb? Morelli or the woman?'

The Lieutenant looked across at him in blind fear. 'What do you mean?'

'You know what I mean. That plane was blown up by a device hidden in Davey's Red Box. We think that *you* made it. Now did Morelli ask you, or did Ariadne?'

'Neither. I don't know what you're talking about, Captain.'

'Bugger this,' barked Arrow roughly. 'Dave – Sergeants. Leave us alone.'

The Military Policemen turned, unquestioning, and marched over to the door. Donaldson looked doubtfully at his colleague for a second, then followed them.

Left alone together, the two soldiers sat in silence for a while, Arrow staring directly across the table at Richards.

'I've been in places like this before,' said the little man eventually, in a quiet, matter-of-fact tone. 'With people like you. They all expected me to beat seven different colours of shit out of them. Some of them even wanted me to. But I 'ardly ever had to. I'll grant you, there have been some cases when both of us knew that someone wasn't going to walk out of the room. But either way, even when some bugger thought he was too tough for me, I always wound up hearing what I needed to hear. Now Stephen, look me in the eye.' He fixed his gaze on the young officer, and held it there, unblinking.

'Did Stewart Morelli ask you to make a device for him?'

'No.' The voice trembled slightly.

'Did Ariadne?'

'No.'

'Did anyone?'

'Where would I have got the explosives?'

'That isn't an answer. Your regimental records are okay, but that doesn't mean anything. You could have pulled our Special Forces trick and taken the HE out of a heavy shell, for use in covert operations. The shell gets marked down as a dummy on the live firing range.' He paused. 'Now, did anyone else ask you to make a device?'

'No, sir.'

'Not Maurice?'

'No, absolutely not'.

Arrow nodded. He broke his gaze, as if allowing the young man a few moments rest then fixed it on him once more.

'Let's talk about your brother. Did you get together often?'

'As often as we could.'

'Did he ever talk about his job, since he moved into Private Office?'

'No, he didn't like to. It depressed him.'

'Did he ever talk about his wife?'

'Yes. All the time. From the earliest days, he would go on about her affairs.'

'That must have been very difficult for you, when you knew that it was true.'

'Yes, it was. But I regarded it as a sort of self-fulfilling prophecy.'

'And you lusted after her yourself, anyway.' Arrow gave a short laugh, with no humour in it. 'Did Maurice ever ask you about your work, about the technical side?'

'Occasionally.'

'Did he ever ask you about assembling devices.'

Richards's eyes narrowed, but he did not turn them away from Arrow's stare. 'Yes, he did'

'And what did you tell him?'

'It was all conversational. I just told him the basics, that you take your HE, stick in detonators and set up a wiring circuit, to be completed either by a timer or a mechanical trigger.'

'Was Maurice a technically-minded man?'

'He wasn't an idiot; as I recall he had Physics A-level. But he always had people in to do jobs around the house.'

'What did Maurice think of Colin Davey?' Arrow asked suddenly.

Richards blinked. 'He thought he was a shit. That's the thing about Maurice. He was never really cut out for MoD. Shits all over the place in the Services. Like Davey, like you – like me, I suppose. But you can't be wholly nice and still be efficient in a business where the ultimate speciality is killing people.'

With the speed of a striking snake, Arrow's right hand flashed across the table and slapped Richards, open-palmed, across the face. 'True, that is. You can't be,' he said coldly. 'And don't you ever call me a shit again.'

The younger man's head snapped sideways with the force of the blow. He stared at Arrow, in surprise and fright, a red weal growing on his left cheek.

'Did Maurice think that Ariadne was having an affair with Davey?'

'Maurice thought everyone was having an affair with her,' said the Lieutenant, his voice shaking. 'Except Morelli and me, that is.'

Arrow's left hand flashed out. A second slap cracked around the small room. This time Richards howled.

'That's very neat,' said the little man, with a smile that was not in the slightest amused. 'You've really put your brother in the frame for it, haven't you? And you reckon I'll believe that because it's the easiest option. But Ariadne still had complete access to that box.

'Now,' he said, still smiling, grabbing the younger man's right hand in his and beginning to squeeze his knuckles together. 'Who asked you to make the device? *Was it Morelli, or was it her?*'

85

'What about this Sawyer fellow, Andrew? What do you make of him?' Sir James Proud looked odd on the monitor screen, his form made even squarer and his uniform even bulkier by the video link.

Martin wondered for a moment about his Chief, dressing officially for a trip to London to interview two suspects, but realised that it was entirely in character. Proud Jimmy needed his uniform like a medieval knight needed his armour, or a Judge his wig and red robe, to show who and what he was, and to help him impress his authority. *Still,* thought the detective. *It doesn't make him any the less of a copper.*

'I doubt, sir,' he replied, 'whether I've ever seen a stronger chain of circumstantial evidence pointing to a person's guilt. He has motive, expertise, materials, and we've established his presence at the scene. He hasn't wavered once in his belief that the world's a better place without Colin Davey. There's only one problem. He won't admit it.' He looked into the small camera above the screen. 'What about the people you have down there?'

The Chief shook his silver head. 'That's the second problem, Chief Superintendent. Everything you've said about Sawyer, I can say about them. Morelli and Tucker are paramours. Morelli now admits that he promoted Noble into a job for which he wasn't competent to increase his access to his wife. Then there's Noble himself, a very depressed and unstable man. It's confused, Andy, very confused.'

'What about the soldier?'

'Arrow gave him a good going over. He didn't bash him about or anything ... well, not too much ... but he didn't incriminate anyone, other than by implication, his brother. I tell you man, we could go on all bloody night!'

Martin nodded. 'So what will we do, sir?' he asked.

'The sensible thing,' replied the Chief. 'I'm bringing all three suspects—'

'Morelli too?'

'Aye, Morelli too; I'm playing no favourites! ... up to Edinburgh. I'm going to have them all interviewed, and Sawyer too, by the Procurator Fiscal. We'll give him a hatful of possibilities. It's his job to decide which one he's going to charge.'

'If any,' muttered Martin.

'Aye, Andy lad. If any!'

86

'One. Two. Three. Four. Five.' Skinner's eyes were closed on 'Three'.

'We're moving on, Bob,' said O'Malley in a voice not much above a whisper, 'from where we found the doll. There's Inspector McGuinness, Constable Pender, and you. Where are we headed?'

'We're moving towards the nose section of the plane,' said the young man's voice. 'Towards the cockpit, where it's crumpled into the mud. There's been no fire there, only wreckage. The smoke is all behind us now.'

'How far is it to the cockpit?'

'About a couple of hundred yards.'

'What do you see between here and there?'

'Bits of the aeroplane; wreckage; luggage and duty-free bags. There's a bottle of vodka over there, sticking in the mud, and it's not even broken. The people are, though. There are bodies, lots more bodies; some of them in bits. Oh look, there's a girl over there, one of the stewardesses. Aww, no, no, no, that shouldn't be.' His voice was high, almost whimpering.

'Aren't you stopping to help any of them, Bob?'

'No. I don't think they can be helped. Anyway, McGuinness says no. He says other people will do that. He's leading us on towards the cockpit. I don't want to go, though.'

'Why not, Bob, why not?'

'Because I don't want to see what's inside. But he's making us go anyway.' On the bed, wrapped in his dressing gown this time, Skinner's legs began to twitch, then writhe.

'Are you there yet?' asked O'Malley.

'Nearly.'

'Describe the wreckage for us, please.'

'It was white, but it's dirty now, as if it had rolled over. The part behind the cabin, where the plane ripped apart is crushed into the ground, and the nose is sticking almost straight up into the air. There's a man's body caught underneath it where the fuselage goes into the ground. I can only see his head and shoulders. His face is all yellow.'

His forehead creased. 'Who, sir? Me?'

'Who are you talking to, Bob?'

'Inspector McGuinness. He's telling me to climb up there and look in the cockpit, just to make sure.'

'To make sure of what?'

'That everyone in there's dead!' he snapped back at the psychiatrist.

'Okay, Bob, okay. Just keep telling us about it.' The entranced body on the bed began to move once more, jerkily. 'What are you doing now?'

'I'm climbing, up towards the windows. There are torn bits in the outer casing. I'm using them as hand grips and footholds. It's not too difficult: I'm nearly there now. Bugger! That was sharp: I've cut myself.' His right hand jerked suddenly, but his legs continued to move.

'Right, I've made it. I'm going to look in the window.'

Skinner fell silent. O'Malley, sitting beside the bed, and Sarah, in her corner seat, watched his face intently. And as they did it changed. Where it had been that of someone in a deep, if troubled sleep, it took on the appearance, even with eyes closed, of a man confronting something dreadful, something too awful to be contemplated.

The sound, when it came, was one of grief. Pure, deep, inconsolable grief.

'*No!*' he keened, he wailed. '*No! No! No! Please, you bastard, don't let this be.*'

As they listened, the wife and the counsellor realised that, apart from its misery, there was something else that was different about his voice. It sounded rougher, and more mature, as if the last innocence of youth had been rubbed away.

'Bob,' said O'Malley, very quietly. 'How old are you?'

'Twenty-eight.' He was sobbing, tearlessly.

'Where are you?'

'Luffness Corner. Between Aberlady and Gullane.'

'And what are you doing?'

'I'm looking through the window.'

'Which window?'

'Of the Mini. The window of the Mini.'

'What do you see inside? You must describe everything.'

On the bed he shuddered, and shook his head.

'Yes, Bob, you must. I'll keep you locked in there until you do. Tell me, and release yourself.'

In his trance sleep, he began to whimper. Sarah was appalled by the sound, and terrified.

'The car's against a tree,' he moaned, at last. 'The front end's smashed in. I see the engine, inside the body compartment. That's the thing about Minis. That's what happens to them if they hit something hard enough. I see wires and cables all over the place. There's one of them almost under my eyes. It's the brake-fluid pipe. It's got a nick in it. Not a tear. A cut. D'you see it?'

'Yes, yes, I see it,' O'Malley responded urgently.

'Do you understand me? It's been cut, by a blade. About a third of the way through. The fucking thing's been sabotaged.'

'I see it. I understand. Now, what else do you see?'

He shook his head again. 'No, please. I can't look any further.'

'We must finish it, Bob. You must finish it. Look through the window!'

They waited, but not for long. His mouth opened in another long, howling cry.

'Myra! I see Myra. The steering column is through her chest. There's glass in her hair. There's blood on her hands, and on her face. I can smell the blood, and the oil, but above it all, I can smell her perfume. It's Chanel No. 5. She always wears it. The bottle's in her handbag, on the passenger seat, and it's smashed.

'And she's dead. Oh, God help us, my wife is dead!'

Down to his right, in the corner, O'Malley was aware of Sarah, her face buried in her hands and her shoulders shaking.

'Bob,' he said. 'You will leave the dream now.' As he watched, Skinner's face relaxed. 'But I'm not going to bring you up yet. I want you to sleep calmly, for fifteen minutes, to recover.'

He stood up, lifted the weeping Sarah from her chair, and led her from the room. Outside in the corridor, it took some time for her to compose herself, but eventually, her sobbing subsided. A passing Sister saw her and looked at the door of Skinner's room in alarm, but O'Malley waved her away.

'Has he ever mentioned that to you before?'

'No,' she whispered. 'He told me that Myra had been killed when her Mini went off the road and hit a tree, but he never said that he'd been there, that he'd seen her. Why couldn't he share that with me?'

'Sarah, my dear, if he couldn't acknowledge it to himself, how could he tell you? Come on, let's go back in. I'll give him a few minutes more rest, then I'll bring him back up. But I warn you – I wasn't expecting anything like this. I've no idea how he's going to react to the memory.'

87

'Five. Four. Three. Two. One.'

Skinner's eyelids flashed open, wide. His eyes seemed to stand out slightly as he stared at the ceiling, but they did not seem to be focused on anything in the present.

'Think your happy thought, Bob,' said O'Malley. 'Concentrate on your present happiness, and let it drive everything else to one side. Concentrate, and talk me through it as you do. What are you thinking about right now?'

'Sarah and Jazz,' he said at last. 'In Spain, by the side of the pool. The sun's going down, and I've got a beer in my hand . . . Alex, on the day when she came back from Europe and took us all by surprise. Sarah again, and me, on the day we got married.'

'Good. That's your reality, remember. That's your life today. The memories that we've unlocked over the last three days might be terrible, but they are things in the past, and they can't hurt you any more than they have already.'

Bob pulled himself up to a sitting position on the bed, drew Sarah to him, and hugged her, hard enough for him to wince from the pain of the healing wound in his ribs. 'I know that,' he said, looking over her shoulder at O'Malley. 'But it amazes me that I was able to keep them so deeply suppressed, and for so long. Imagine, for all those years, I didn't have the balls to face the truth of my own experiences.'

'No,' said the psychiatrist. 'In *my* experience your reaction is a sign of exceptional strength of character, and of very strong mental control. You should never have been put in that position at that air crash all those years ago. You were still a very young man, you had been on the same plane a week before; then to find the body of your friend's child . . . To expose you to that was inexcusable behaviour by your commanders.'

Skinner smiled at him. 'Give them a break, Kevin. They really weren't to know, and I didn't say anything. Mind you, it explains one thing. Eddie McGuinness went on to become Deputy Chief Constable, and latterly I worked quite closely with him. Yet I had this in-built dislike of the man, that I could never explain to myself. I can now. The fact is that any half-fit man could have climbed up to look in that cockpit window. Eddie ordered me to do it because Pender was throwing up, and because he didn't have the bottle himself to face what might have been in there.'

'What was in there, Bob?'

'Nothing. The crew had run to the back of the plane before the impact. It was the Captain's body that was trapped under the fuselage.'

'Yet when you looked through the window, in the dream...' O'Malley stared at Skinner. 'That was quite remarkable,' the psychiatrist said. 'In fact, I've never encountered anything like it. First, as a very young adult you had an experience which would have left most people mentally scarred for life. You coped with it by taking all the detail of it, walling it up, entombing it in the depths of your mind.

'But then, a few years later, you had an experience that was even worse. Infinitely worse, in fact. You dealt with that by taking it and hiding it, for extra security, actually *inside* your first terrible memory, behind the wall, in that tomb in your subconscious! Remarkable, quite remarkable. Bob, if you'll allow me, I'd like to publish a report of your case, on a Mr X basis, of course.'

'I'll need to think about that!'

'Naturally, but I hope you'll agree. You know,' he went on, 'it's pretty obvious how those locked memories were disturbed.'

'Sure, through me being called to a second air crash.'

O'Malley shook his head. 'No. Not just that. I'm aware that you rehearse situations like these – but that hasn't been enough to trigger any memories. The crash itself might have knocked a couple of bricks out of the wall, but it would have repaired itself pretty quickly. It was the cockpit, and especially the moment when you had to break into it to rescue the child. That's really what knocked down all the mental barriers. Not only were you smashing into that cabin, but also into your own subconscious!'

'The man in the cottage,' said Skinner slowly. 'He appeared in the original dream, the one I had when I was under sedation. Why didn't he reappear under hypnosis?'

'I think he was probably just a side-effect of your sedation. You obviously knew who he was, so I'd say that he relates to a separate experience, but one that you've come to terms with to an acceptable degree.'

The two men looked at each other in silence until Sarah squeezed her husband's arm. 'Bob, how did you come to be at the scene of Myra's accident? Surely they didn't send for you?'

'No, love. I was driving home after my shift. It was as simple as that. I got there a minute after the Fire Brigade and before the ambulance. The car was so smashed up that I didn't even realise it was her ... until I looked inside, and caught the scent of Chanel No. 5.' His voice tailed off.

'But . . . what you said about the brake-fluid pipe. Why would anyone want to do that to Myra?'

He swung his legs over the side of the bed, and stood up, then took a few steps towards the window. She watched him as he turned back to face her.

'That's the whole point, love,' he said quietly. 'Myra was driving *my* car that day. It was a souped-up Mini GT job, and it went like shit off a shovel. Hers was an elderly Triumph 2000, a big genteel thing that she took to work, and that the pair of us used to take Alex around in. One of the police mechanics did homers in his lunch-breaks, and he looked after it for me. So I had the Triumph in town that day, being serviced. Normally, I'd have been driving the Mini.'

'Was the cut pipe investigated?'

'I'm sure it wasn't. I have to assume now that it was only me who saw it, and I was in no state to talk to anyone about anything.'

'No,' said the psychiatrist, 'nor to face up to the realisation. That's why your defence mechanism clicked in again.'

'I guess so,' said Skinner. 'Anyway, after the accident, our traffic guys found some mud on the road. They assumed that Myra had been travelling too fast . . . which she usually was when she drove the Mini . . . and that she'd hit it. The Fatal Accident Inquiry verdict was accidental death, end of story.'

He turned and with a warm smile, leaned across to O'Malley, and shook his hand. 'Thanks Kevin, for the last three days, and for draining the mental abscess.'

'How do you feel now?'

'Cleansed. The toothache's gone for good. All of a sudden I feel physically stronger too. I'm almost ready for action again. Know what? I'm looking forward first of all to a natural sleep, then to getting out of this place.'

'Woah, hoss,' said Sarah. 'This is your physician speaking. She, and Braeburn your surgeon, are telling you that you have another week in here.'

He glowered at her, in real annoyance. 'Well, if I have, I'm buggered if I'll spend it reading magazines. I want to see Andy tonight for an update on the crash investigation . . . AND I want him to set up a team meeting in here for tomorrow. We've got to get a result from this investigation, and fast.'

She smiled. 'How do you know Andy hasn't made an arrest?'

'Come on, if he had, not even you could have stopped him from telling me all about it.'

'Ah, but you forget. He's not just dealing with your wife now. He's dealing with a potential mother-in-law. In fact, he hasn't just made one arrest. He and Jimmy have made *four*.'

Skinner's eyes widened in astonishment.

88

'You don't know how good it is to see you looking yourself again,' said Proud Jimmy. 'I don't mind telling you now that it scared me silly, looking at you lying there with that bloody great tube down your throat.'

'It didn't exactly fill me with a hell of a lot of confidence,' said Skinner wryly.

'But you were out of it all, weren't you?'

'Aye, most of the time, but once or twice I was aware of it. The memories are all coming back now, and one of them is of thinking, "Here, Skinner, this is not too clever." Still, as you say, it's all okay now, or it will be once my lung and my battered ribs heal up.'

For the first time in a week, Skinner was dressed in a shirt and slacks, and seated comfortably in a chair. On the television in the corner, the cronies of *Last of the Summer Wine* wandered soundlessly through their dales.

'Can you remember the attack?' the Chief asked him.

He flashed his silver-haired friend a slightly scathing look. 'Oh aye, only too well! Those three clowns!'

'The one you hit in the throat; he's still in Ward 23, you know.'

'Life's a bitch, isn't it?' said Skinner. 'The girl isn't still here, though, is she?'

'No. She's on remand on an attempted murder charge.'

'Mmm. I can't make up my mind whether she was more scared than vicious. I'm sorry I broke her wrist, whichever it was.'

'Listen man, if you hadn't, she'd have stuck that knife in you again, and we'd have been burying you on Friday, as well as young McGrath.'

'Aye, I know, but . . . D'you not think we could drop the charge to serious assault?'

Sir James looked at him sternly. 'Absolutely no way. Whether it was premeditated or not, she was carrying a blade. You know the policy on that. She's going down for attempt to murder, and the Advocate Depute is going to ask for an exemplary sentence. That's cut and dried.' The frown was replaced by an amused chuckle. 'From the sound of you, this experience seems to have changed you. Is it going to be Gentle Bob, instead of the Big Man, from now on?'

'Hah!' Skinner snorted. 'I've come out of this with a new set of objectives, Jimmy. And when I achieve them, you'll see just how soft I've become.' He stared grimly at the wall for a few seconds.

'Talking about McGrath,' he said suddenly, 'Ali Higgins told me about Leona surprising them all, and putting herself up for the seat. She's a great wee woman, that one. Edinburgh Dean will do better with her than it did with her late husband, that's for sure!'

'Now, now Bob. Ill of the dead, and all that.'

'You mean it ill becomes me in the circumstances?'

Proud Jimmy laughed heartily. 'Something like that, I suppose. Here,' he said, 'I'll tell you of someone who didn't share your enthusiasm for the Widow McGrath as a candidate: her agent, Marshall Elliot.'

'Eh?'

'Yes. I was speaking at the funeral to Dame Janet, the Tories' head cheerleader in Scotland. She told me that Elliot had been spitting blood about it to her, on an Agent to Agent basis, last Friday afternoon before her adoption meeting. He said that he felt she was doing it from the wrong motives.'

'And what did Janet feel?'

The Chief chuckled again. 'She said that deep down, every Agent feels that he can do it better than the candidate, or the MP. She said also that Elliot is the most fanatical Tory she's ever met, and that he'd been going out of his mind with worry because he was convinced that Roland McGrath didn't have the stuff to hold the seat at the next election.'

'No matter,' said Skinner. 'From what I've seen of Marsh Elliot, he's a good bloke. Whatever his private view, he'll give her his very best in her campaign, I'm quite certain of that. Remember that guy I nicked last summer?'

'The one who tried to kill you? Who could forget him?'

'Well, I quite liked him, but I still put him away for life.'

Proud Jimmy laughed out loud. 'Yes, and he sent you flowers and a "Get Well" card.'

Skinner stared in astonishment. 'You're kidding,' he gasped.

'No. Sarah has all your cards at home. You'll find it among them. Anyway, to go back to Elliot for a moment, I think you're right in your judgement of him. I chose my word carefully when I said that he didn't share your *enthusiasm* for Leona. Dame Janet went on to tell me that they watched her together at the adoption meeting, and Elliot changed his mind on the spot. She won him over, convinced him that whatever her motives, she'll hold the seat.'

'Too right she will,' said Skinner. 'That's not me revealing my politics,' he added, 'it's just a statement of fact.' Smiling to himself, he stood up and stretched, gingerly. 'Anyway, enough of the side-show.

What about you, eh? Tell me, Chief Constable, when was it that you last arrested someone?'

'God alone knows,' said Proud Jimmy. He grinned at his Deputy. 'But at least when I arrest them they're taken away in a car, not a bloody ambulance!'

'Still. Sir Stewart Morelli, and the whole surviving Noble family, save the cat: that's quite an afternoon's work. Andy told me all about it when he and Alex were in earlier. He brought me up to date on the whole investigation. I rather think we've got a problem – an embarrassment of suspects. You were dead right to pass it on to the Fiscal.'

Sir James grunted. 'Morelli. Bloody man! I don't really think he had anything to do with the bomb, but the circumstances indicate that he could have. You know, when I got down to London, he'd got some of his courage back and tried to bluster his way out. Tried to treat me like some backwoodsman. Talked to me as if I was one of his tame Generals!'

'Must be the uniform, Jimmy!'

'Maybe. He's got more respect for it now, anyway. I wound up telling him that he was a suspect and that I was a copper, and that whether or not we were both knights of the same order he was getting no fucking favours from me, and that he and Mrs Noble would be putting their weekend travel bags to good use by travelling up to Edinburgh, under arrest.' Suddenly he gave a wicked smile. 'You're wrong about the cat, too. The woman insisted on bringing it with her.'

Skinner laughed out loud. 'So what did you do with them last night?' he asked. 'Lock them up in cells in St Leonards?'

'Hardly. I wasn't that tough on them. In fact, I was probably too bloody kind in the end. I put them in rooms . . . *separate* rooms . . . in the Ellersley, with Donaldson and McIlhenney as baby-sitters. The soldier, Noble's half-brother, spent the night in Redford Barracks, with Arrow and his sidekick.'

Idly, Sir James strolled across the room and picked a handful of green grapes from a bunch on Skinner's bedside cabinet. 'Morelli was a deal less bumptious this morning,' he said. 'Arrow sent copies of the tapes of their conversation at Swinbrook to the Cabinet Secretary, as soon as they were transcribed. They can move fast when they like, those buggers in Whitehall. The new Secretary of State for Defence was appointed this morning . . . a man from the Northern Ireland Office . . . and at the same time they announced that Morelli had taken early retirement, because of shock over the murders of Davey and Noble and over his own narrow escape.'

He paused. 'The two lovebirds didn't seem too friendly today, either. She had formed the impression, justifiably, that he was trying to wash his hands of all responsibility, at her expense.'

'Is there a Lady Morelli?' Skinner asked. 'And is she aware of any of this?'

'There is, and she is now,' said the Chief. 'He's an evil little bastard, that Arrow, you know. Before we left London, he went to see her, explained the whole situation, and suggested that she should brief the family solicitor!'

'Hah!' said Skinner, cutting short his sudden exclamation as his wound gave him a twinge. 'That's Adam behaving reasonably. Believe me, Jimmy, you really wouldn't want to know what happens when his evil side shows itself.'

89

'It's nice to see so many friends coming to visit me, all at the same time.' Skinner smiled as he looked at the faces gathered around the big table. 'I'm still amazed that my wife allowed it.

'I must thank the NHS Trust Chairman for letting us use his Boardroom.' He turned to Detective Constable Pye. 'Sammy, ask Ruth, my secretary, to type a letter for my signature, please. She'll know what to say.'

He looked from one to the other: at Andy Martin, and on to Brian Mackie, Mario McGuire, Dave Donaldson, Adam Arrow, John Swift, Neil McIlhenney, Sammy Pye and finally to Joe Doherty, who had flown up both to attend the update briefing and to visit Skinner as an old friend.

'Well . . .' he went on, with a smile. His face looked drawn, still, but he was regaining his colour, and all the old vitality shone from his eyes. In fact, Martin thought, it was as if there was something extra there: a new certainty, a new assurance, something, perhaps, that came from having lain at the doorway to eternity, and taken a look inside.

Did you have any out-of-body experiences, Bob? he had joked, when he had visited his friend on the previous evening. *Not quite,* Skinner had replied, entirely seriously, *but I did have an out-of-mind experience. When I'm ready, and it'll be fairly soon, I'll tell you about it.*

'. . . you lot seem to have been pretty busy, while I've been having my mid-life crisis. The Chief Constable and Chief Superintendent Martin . . .' the references were formal, as if to emphasise that the DCC was back in business '. . . have brought me up to date with every aspect of the investigation.

'The first thing I have to do is to congratulate you all on some terrific work. Quite honestly, I thought we'd be grinding away at this one for months, years even. Okay, I know we still don't have a conclusion, but as I keep on thumping home, especially for our military pals at the end of the table, that isn't our job.

'My dad used to say that there are two sorts of people in the world, the thinkers and the labourers. We're labourers, to a great extent. We go out there gathering in the bits and pieces of evidence and dragging them all together into a bloody great pile. Once that's done, we hand it all over to the Crown Office, to let them do the thinking and take the final decisions on prosecution. I can't recall an operation in my career where the labouring, the gathering-in of evidence, has been done more effectively.'

He paused, and looked round the table once more. 'In fact, you've been so efficient that I don't begrudge the Fiscal his job. Up to now, all the pressure, all the international attention including the heavy breathing from friend Joe here, has been focused on you lot. Now it's on poor old Davie Pettigrew, and I don't envy him one small piece.

'By now, he should have held the press conference at which he was going to announce his decision on action, after interviewing the various suspects. That's where the Chief is just now.' He pointed between Donaldson and Arrow, to the corner of the room. 'We'll switch the telly on in a few minutes, and catch what he's said. I don't know any more about that than the rest of you.'

'Yes, Bob,' said Arrow, 'but what do you *think* he'll do?'

Skinner shrugged his shoulders, but carefully. 'It's all about options. I gather that the international possibilities we identified at the start have all been ruled out.'

'That's right,' said Doherty. 'Yahic is dead, and the Iraqi network seems to be in full retreat.'

'And Agent Robin?'

'Agent Robin has been traced and deactivated, Bob,' said Adam Arrow carefully. Skinner nodded without comment, but made an unspoken assumption.

'In that case,' he went on, 'Pettigrew and the Crown Office have got five suspects on their hands.' Around the table, one or two faces looked at him curiously.

'In custody, or at least co-operating with them, they have Morelli, Ariadne Tucker, Lieutenant Richards and the guy Sawyer. They're all heavily implicated by their own actions, and they all qualify in different ways, so let's look at them, one by one. Okay?'

Nine faces looked back at him, expectantly. Several heads nodded.

'Let's take Morelli first. Frankly, gentlemen, there's as much chance of him winding up in the dock, for this crime at least, as there is of me winning the next Miss World. The fact that he was having an affair with Noble's wife, was if anything an incentive to keep the man alive.' Out of the corner of his eye, he caught sight of Sammy Pye's puzzled expression.

He elaborated. 'Morelli and Ariadne were both enjoying a substantial bit on the side, neither asking any more of the other than sex. That was fine as long as they both had partners to deceive, but if one was single, especially if it was a demanding, selfish person like I'm told Ariadne is, the balance of power would change.

'Morelli cleared the way for their out-of-hours nookie by putting

Noble into the Private Office job. If Davey had fired him, as he intended, he could have dealt with that by posting him somewhere far away, like the Falklands, or Hong Kong, as part of the hand-over team. Even if he was a serial killer, rather than just a serial shagger, doing away with Noble would be the furthest thing from his mind.'

Dave Donaldson raised a hand. 'What about the thought that Morelli might have been under threat from Davey?'

'Again,' said Skinner, 'why kill him? Davey was under pressure himself after the Reaper decision, and there's going to be a General Election before too long. The odds were all against him being in office in six months' time. Even if he was after Morelli's scalp, there was no chance of him lifting it. So let's set Morelli aside for now. Quite frankly, if I'd been interviewing him, I'd have taken a statement, handed him over to the CPS for prosecution for extortion, and left it at that. But he pissed off the Chief, and that is always a mistake.'

'Extortion?' queried Mackie.

'Something along those lines, Brian. He used his position to force young Richards to let him use his house in the Cotswolds for the purposes of screwing his half-brother's wife. What sort of verdict d'you think a jury of *Sun* readers, or *Telegraph* readers . . . or even *Guardian* readers . . . would bring in on that one?'

'Will that case be brought?'

Skinner looked at Arrow. The soldier laughed softly, and answered for him. 'No danger. Too messy. The deal's already done. Morelli retires early and collects his full pension in the process. His punishment is having to spend the rest of his days with Lady Morelli, who struck me as a woman with a long memory and a bloody good recipe for humble pie.'

'Let's look at Ariadne now,' said the DCC. 'She's in the same boat as Morelli. Why should she want Maurice dead? She earns three or four times the money he did, so she's not tied to him financially. He was obsessive about her, but if it bothered her all that much she'd have walked out on him long ago. Her punishment for his suspicion was to let Morelli into her knickers, and that seems to have suited her fine. As for her wanting to kill Davey, she hardly knew the man. There were loads of people in the queue before her.'

He paused, as if to gather more air into his recuperating lung.

'But let's say she, or she and Morelli together, did want Maurice dead. How would they do it? There's only one realistic way. They forced young Richards to make them a device, then either Ariadne planted it in the Red Box during the night, or she let the boy in and he rigged it for her.'

'I checked,' said Arrow, interrupting. 'Richards was on an exercise that night.'

'Okay, delete that option. It would have to be Ariadne who planted the bomb. Now Adam, you say that you can be certain that the box stayed intact for at least part of the night. Can you put a time on that?' The little soldier glanced to his right, at his colleague.

'It had to be clear still at three-thirty,' said Lieutenant Swift. 'I followed Miss Mirzana . . .' His face fell, as Arrow glared at him, enraged.

'I'm sorry, Adam,' he said desperately. 'It just slipped out. But we're all friends here, aren't we?'

'So Robin was the girl who was found dead,' drawled Joe Doherty, 'not the guy who killed her. You had Agent Robin tagged from the start, and you were running her. You fed her phoney information and they swallowed it, until finally, you scared the Iraqis into folding their tents. Hey, I'll bet even the detailed CIA information on our Agent Eagle came from your source, not from their investigation.'

Arrow nodded, glowering again at his colleague. 'Yes, you're right. Agent Robin was a double all along, only she didn't know it. Neither did the Iraqis. The prosecution case against the man Rafiq will be that he read the final message and killed her when he saw that the network had been rumbled, rather than leave her to face possible arrest.' Along the table, Skinner, struck by his choice of words, shot him a quick, but impassive glance.

Dave Donaldson leaned forward. 'Could she have planted the bomb, then?'

'No way,' said Arrow. 'She wasn't trained as a saboteur or an assassin, only as a spy. She didn't have the knowledge, or the materials. She broke into Noble's house to photograph a document in the Red Box that she couldn't copy during the day, and she passed on her film at an evening meeting in the safe house two days before she was killed. The box was clean when it left the office, and Mirzana didn't carry anything into the Noble place other than her camera. We know that because Swifty was watching her every step of the way. He sat six rows behind her at a Van Morrison Concert, then watched a late night showing of *Reservoir Dogs*, before trailing her out to Putney. No, Dave, Agent Robin was not our bomber.'

He turned back to Doherty. 'Your last guess was right, though. Our people did pass on the identity of your sleeper. I'm surprised it took you so long to pick him up.'

'Thank you,' said Doherty grimly. 'Those bastards at Langley have been shielding their budget on the strength of that arrest. Wait till I tell the President.'

'But no names, Joe, eh?' interposed Skinner, seriously.

'You have my word as a Southern gentleman on that, sir.'

'Good. Now to go on,' said Skinner, 'we know for certain that if a bomb was planted in that box, it was done after three-thirty. Now, I ask you all. Noble had an early start, and Ariadne knew it. Wasn't that cutting it fine?'

He pressed on. 'But let's say she did. From what we've learned, the device could only have come from Lieutenant Richards, although he couldn't have planted it. Adam, you've interviewed this guy. Vigorously, from what I hear. Whatever the motive, could he have helped to kill his brother?'

Arrow looked up the table at him, from under hooded eyebrows. 'The lad's besotted by Ariadne,' he said. 'He'd do almost anything she asked. But he didn't do that. No fookin' way.'

'Which leads us on to Mr Bryn Sawyer. Andy, you said that he didn't seem surprised to see you.'

'He wouldn't, after that letter to Davey.'

'In that case,' he said, emphasising his points with a stabbing forefinger, '*if* he's our man, *if* he made a dummy Red Box, filled with explosive, and managed, somehow, to arm it and swap it for the one with which Maurice Noble left his home in Putney, before he got on the plane, *if* he's that bloody clever . . . how does he suddenly manage to become so bloody stupid that he lets you find all the gear in his workshop and in his house?'

'Because he *is* an artist blacksmith, boss,' said Martin, 'so he would have the steel. And his wife is a dressmaker, and *did* buy that red leather. He knew that if we started asking about him those details would come to light, and we would trace those purchases, so he left them there for us to find, and relied on his cover story.

'Plus, he had access to the military high explosives that we know were used, and there is a stock discrepancy. Possession of all those items, and his skills, offer strong circumstantial evidence that he made the box and the bomb. He was in London at the time the switch would have to be made. He was even in Heathrow at the same time as Davey and Noble. And he had made a physical threat to Davey.'

Skinner shook his head. 'No, Andy. He wrote a letter which can be interpreted as a physical threat.'

'Okay, but it is still a very positive case. What more can Pettigrew ask for?'

'He can ask us to show beyond a reasonable doubt that Sawyer was in a position to make the switch. With everything else, that would do it for sure. But without that piece of evidence, and with the existence of the Tucker-Richards theory, which no one can actively disprove, and which could open up a defence of impeachment to confuse the jury, it would still be a dodgy prosecution; especially when the Crown Office has a far safer scapegoat at its disposal.'

'You're right there, I suppose.' Martin nodded resignedly.

'Who's that, sir?' asked Dave Donaldson.

'Maurice Noble,' said Skinner. 'He's the fifth suspect. The Crown Office could simply lead evidence before a Fatal Accident Inquiry in the Sheriff Court to show that Noble was in a disturbed state of mind, and that he suspected Davey of having an affair with his wife. Pettigrew could even put Ariadne in the witness box and force her to admit that he was right, in everything but the name of her partner. Then he could introduce Richards's evidence that Maurice asked him how you made a bomb, and that he gave him the basic information.

'In a criminal trial, the Crown would have to prove access to the explosives, but not in an FAI, at least not beyond too reasonable a doubt. They wouldn't need the same level of proof, and although Noble would effectively be on trial posthumously, there would be no opportunity for defence evidence to be introduced. There are only seven jurors, a simple majority verdict is enough, and the Sheriff has wide powers of direction.'

He spread his hands wide. 'I ask you, gentlemen. What would you do?'

Martin leaned back in his chair and stared at the ceiling. Joe Doherty smiled. Arrow looked glumly along the table.

'Still,' said Skinner breezily, 'that's all guesswork and bullshit. Let's switch on the telly and hear what Pettigrew had to say himself. Dave.'

Donaldson, who was seated closest to the television set, leaned over and picked up its remote unit. He pushed the Start button several times, but no picture appeared.

'Come on, man, we'll miss the bloody thing!'

'Sorry, boss, the battery must be low.' At last, the screen lit up, to show a crowded room. Sir James Proud was seated at a table, before a blue backcloth. Beside him, a stocky, bushy-bearded man was on his feet.

'... ten days, exhaustive enquiries into the Lammermuirs disaster have been made, led by a team of detectives under the command of the Chief Constable, on my left, working with colleagues in other Forces and agencies.

'On Saturday, four people were detained in various parts of England and brought to Edinburgh to assist the police with their enquiries. I have now had an opportunity to interview them all. Our investigation is continuing and is reaching a stage at which I expect proceedings to be considered. In the meantime, the four individuals have been released on police bail, until Friday, when they will report to me for further questioning.

'That is all I have to say at this stage. I would caution you all to exercise restraint in your reporting. Any attempt either in Scotland or England to interfere with witnesses in this case will be viewed very seriously by Crown Office.' As Sir James rose to his feet beside him, the Procurator Fiscal picked up his papers and bustled out of the room.

The picture cut back to the newsreader. 'Campaigning began today in several By-elections which have arisen as a result of the Lammer-muirs disaster,' she began.

'Turn it off, Dave,' said Skinner. The DCI pressed a switch several times, but without success. A street canvass in Chindersford came on screen, showing the Tory candidate with the newly appointed Defence Secretary at his side. 'Kill the sound, then, if you can,' said the DCC. Donaldson pushed the mute button. The set fell silent at once.

'What was your Fiscal saying, do you think, Bob?' said Doherty.

Skinner grinned. 'I'm not often wrong, Joe, but I'm right again. He's leading up to taking the Noble option. He'll have the Fab Four up again next Friday, and then he'll announce that no charges have been made, and that he's holding a Fatal Accident Inquiry as soon as possible. That is not a guess, my friend. That is a fucking certainty.'

At the other end of the table, Arrow was frowning. 'The trouble is, Bob, Maurice didn't fookin' do it.'

'No,' said Martin. 'I still fancy Sawyer.'

'Then while I recuperate, you've got five days to prove it!'

'Who do you fancy, boss?' asked Neil McIlhenney.

Skinner eyed him curiously. 'I thought you were being unusually quiet, Sergeant. But I don't answer your questions, I throw them at you. So you tell me . . . who do *you* fancy?'

'Me, sir?' The Sergeant put on his best 'simple detective' expression. 'To be honest with you, and I know I haven't met Sawyer, but I just don't fancy any of them. Apart from the boy Richards, who's just a love-struck eejit, they're all a bunch of shites, but that's all they are. Noble's too easy an option, but so's Sawyer in a reverse sort of way.

'If you're going to shove a red-hot poker up someone's arse you're not going to write to him giving him advance warning. That's why Davey knew he was safe in filing that letter. If Sawyer *hadn't* sent it, I'd go for him, but because he did, I don't . . . if you see what I mean.'

'Yes, I see, Neil, and I agree with you. Truth be told, I don't fancy any of them either. You can have as many options as you like in this game, but there's always only one solution. So until the Fiscal says, "that's it – I'm picking him, or her, or them," we've got to keep on looking.'

He paused. 'If I've learned anything this week, it's that it's possible to sit right on top of something, without even knowing that it's there. Sometimes, with a crime as big-scale as this, the tendency is to look for big-scale solutions. So over the next few days, I think we should set aside all the assumptions that we made at the start, pick up some of those we discarded, and—'

He stopped in mid-sentence and gazed down the table. 'Lieutenant Swift, have I lost your attention?' he said evenly.

The Yorkshireman, who had been staring at the silent television, jumped in his seat.

'I'm sorry, sir,' he said. 'It's just that . . .' he pointed back at the screen '. . . I know that bloke.'

90

'I'll tell you something, Andy,' said Skinner. 'You've only got one fault left as a detective. You're too open-minded.

'I've got a great team around me. You've all got your own strengths, and together you're unbeatable. But you know, of all of you, the one who thinks most like me is your pal McIlhenney. He's not nearly as quick a thinker as you, or as analytical, but he's a devious bastard. That's what he and I have got in common.

'He knows when to set logic aside and say "Bugger it, what's the real story here?". Basically, he's got a criminal mind. I think the best detectives probably have. So you take him on to your personal staff and use him, shamelessly, as your personal sounding board . . . along with me, of course.'

It was early evening, and they were in Skinner's hospital room. At the Ward Sister's insistence he had rested for a few hours after returning from his Boardroom meeting. In fact, he had been exhausted, and had not put up a moment's resistance. Now he sat up in bed, connected with the outside world by the mobile phone which he had persuaded Sarah to allow him. It sat on the bedside cabinet.

'So, has Adam finished that check you asked him for?' asked Martin, coming to business at last.

The DCC nodded. 'He called in half an hour ago. There's a report on the shelf, there. Have a look.'

Martin picked up the paper and read through it. He whistled as he finished and put it down. 'Bloody hell,' he said. 'Could we have been heading up the wrong street all the tlime?'

'If you were, I'll take most of the blame. I set it all in motion. I overlooked something pretty obvious. Let's hold our horses, though. That's a coincidence, but it's no greater than your missile engineer in Cumbria having those materials in his workshop. We need a few more pieces in place before we get too ex—' He was interrupted by the harsh tone of his mobile phone. Martin, who was closer to it, reached across, picked it up from its charger and took the call.

'Yes?' he said cautiously. His tone changed at once. 'Of course, sir. Here he is.' He handed the instrument across the bed. 'It's the Secretary of State, calling from the Scottish Office,' he whispered.

'Thanks. Good evening, sir.' Skinner held the receiver to his ear, and listened for a few seconds. 'There's no doubt about that? You're one short?' He paused. 'Oh yes, sir, it's significant. Very significant. All I need now is one more fact to fit, and I think we might have the answer. Yes, I'll keep you in touch. Goodbye.'

He reached across and behind himself and dropped the phone back into its cradle. 'Another piece. Once we hear from our star witness, it could be that we'll have the whole bloody jigsaw. You did bring that tape recorder, didn't you?' Martin nodded, dipped a hand into his pocket, and produced a tiny electric notebook.

'Come on, Maggie, where are you?'

'They had been sitting in virtual silence for five minutes, before the door opened and Maggie Rose's red head appeared. 'Hello, boss,' she said, with a smile. 'I've brought that witness you asked to see. Come away in,' she said to a figure behind her as she threw the door wide.

Mark McGrath stepped into the room. He was wearing his Police Cadet cap.

'Hello, young man,' said Skinner. 'It's a bit strange seeing me here, isn't it?'

'Yes, Mr Bob. Are you all right now?'

'I'm getting there, son, thanks very much. Andy, lift our guest up and let him sit on the bed.'

He pulled himself upright, adjusting the pillows at his back.

'Mark,' he began, 'your Auntie Alison told me, and I think I've probably heard for myself too, that you've got a terrific memory. You remember just about everything you see and hear.'

'That's right,' said the boy, puffing out his chest proudly.

'That's good, because we want you to do some remembering for us. I want you to talk into this wee tape recorder here, and tell us everything about the morning of the accident, from the moment that you and your daddy got ready to leave your house in London, to the moment that you got on the plane. Will you do that?'

The child nodded, solemnly. Martin switched on the recorder. 'Anytime you like, Mark.'

'We were at the flat in Dolphin Square,' he began. 'I had honey-coated Sugar Loops for breakfast. Mummy and Daddy had toast.'

'Can you remember what you all talked about?'

'Mummy and Daddy talked about her going to the dentist. She had lost a big filling the night before and had a 'mergency appointment in the morning. Daddy and I talked about Celtic. Then Victoria ... she was Daddy's secretary ... arrived, with the Red Box.' He gave the words great weight, as if he were pronouncing the capitals.

'And after that?'

298

'After that the buzzer rang. Victoria picked it up and said that it was the Government car to take us to the airport. Then she and Daddy and I all went downstairs. Only it wasn't . . .'

91

'Well, my friend,' said Skinner to Martin, as the door closed behind Maggie Rose and little Mark. 'In all my years I don't think I have ever heard a better or more reliable witness. That's it. The whole story. Markie even gave us a motive, only thankfully he didn't realise what he was saying. There's a public meeting tonight, I believe, in the assembly hall at Stewarts Melville. Our murderer will be there for sure, rather than at home. So, right away, send Mackie, McGuire and young Sammy to search those premises. They'll know what they're looking for.'

'What about a warrant?'

'They can call in on Sheriff Sinclair on the way there. He lives in Arboretum Road.'

'If he isn't at home . . . ?'

'Then find him, Andy – him or any other bloody Sheriff. I want that place searched tonight, and if the troops uncover anything, I want to know right away. Once that's in motion you take McIlhenney, and Adam Arrow, go along to Stewarts Melville, and as soon as Leona's meeting is over, make the arrest. But take all precautions, and be very, very careful.

'From what we've heard today, and seen earlier, Marshall Elliot is a very dangerous man.'

92

'You see, girls, it was the wrong box.' Skinner sat in an armchair in his room, playing happily with his gurgling son. 'We found Roly McGrath's Red Box at the crash scene in the Lammermuirs, and when we found what was left of the other one, we assumed that it must have been Colin Davey's. Only it wasn't.

'I tell you, he's some chap, is wee Mark McGrath.' He lifted Jazz high above his head. 'I hope this one turns out like him. He's as bright as a button, and he has a tremendous memory for even the smallest detail. Listen to this.' He picked up Andy Martin's electric notebook, which was lying on the bed, and switched it on. Sarah and Alex sat in silence as the clear, piping voice rang out.

'. . . Only it wasn't the lady from the Government Car service. It was Uncle Marsh, with his big Rover 820 SDi.'

'That's very good, Mark, knowing the model,' said Skinner.

'I know the number too. L 511 QFT,' he recited. 'I always remember things like that.'

'You weren't expecting Uncle Marsh, then?' asked Martin.

'No. Daddy said to him, "What are you doing here?" and he said, "I was in London for a meeting at Central Office, so I thought I'd surprise you, and take you to the airport myself." He took the Red Box from Victoria and he put it in the boot of the Rover. Victoria got in the car, in the back seat. Then he asked Daddy where Mummy was, and Daddy told him about her toothache.' The child interrupted his torrent of words to take a deep, gasping breath.

'I was getting in the car when I heard him say something else to Daddy. He said, "You . . ." He called Daddy a Bad Word. "You *something*. I know about you and Margie." That's my Auntie Margie,' he interposed confidentially. 'He said, "I know all about you two, you little *something*, and I'm going to finish you. It's not just that you had her," he said. What does that mean, Mr Bob?'

301

'Never mind, Mark. Just go on, exactly as you remember it.'

'All right. Uncle Marsh said, ". . . but what you've done to her." He said that, then my Daddy pushed him away.'

'You're sure he said all that, Mark? You haven't made any of it up?'

'I never make things up, Mr Bob. I just remember them.' The little voice sounded offended.

'I'm sorry, Mark. Go on. What did Daddy say to Uncle Marsh?'

'He didn't say anything. He saw Mr Davey . . . he lives in Dolphin Square, too . . . and he shouted across to him. He was getting into his car. Daddy asked if he was going to Heathrow, and Mr Davey said he was. So Daddy said to him to send his car away, and come with us. Mr Davey said, "Are you sure you've got room?' and Daddy said, "Of course. Mark can sit on Victoria's knee. He'll like that." So Mr Davey and the other man came with us.'

'Did the other man have a Red Box like Victoria's?'

'Yes, Uncle Marsh took it from him and put it in the boot with ours.'

'Who was in the front seat beside Uncle Marsh on the way to the airport?'

'Daddy was. He was the fattest.'

'Did they speak much?'

'Yes, but I couldn't hear what they were saying.'

'When you got to Heathrow what happened?'

'We were stuck in the traffic, so we were late. Mr Davey was getting angry, because he thought we would miss the plane. We got there in time, but we had to hurry. Uncle Marsh got the boxes from the boot and gave them to Victoria and the other man, and we all rushed away to check in.'

'At the check-in, did the boxes go through the X-ray machine?'

'No. The airport men just waved us through, past the queue.'

'And did you go straight on to the plane?'

'Yes. Mr Davey's man phoned from the car, and told them that we were coming.'

'Right, Mark,' said Skinner's voice from the tape machine. 'I want you to think very carefully about this. During the flight, was anything said about the Red Boxes?'

'Yes. Just when April was taking me in to see Mr Shipley and Mr Garrett, in the cabin, I heard Mr Davey's man say to Victoria, "Miss Cunningham, I rather think we've got our boxes mixed up." Then the door closed, and I didn't hear any more. Not long after that . . .'

'Okay, Mark,' they heard Skinner say, quickly. 'We won't go into that.'

He switched off the tape and rewound the cassette.

'Wow,' said Sarah. 'Some kid.'

'What set you on the trail of Elliot?' asked Alex.

Skinner looked at her and shrugged. 'Luck. I was just starting to think, *What if* . . . but the thing that triggered it was Adam's mate Swift. The telly was on in the corner, without the sound, and he was watching it when he should have been listening to me. There was a By-election report on at the time, and they showed a picture of Leona, out canvassing, with Marsh Elliot by her side. Swift pointed at him. He said, "I know that bloke. He was my CO in the SBS and a right evil bastard he was too!" The whole room suddenly went as quiet as a tomb.

'At first, we had worked on the assumption that someone had planted the bomb in Davey's box, while it was in Noble's keeping. Then when Andy's raid turned up the leather and the steel in Sawyer's workshop, we turned to the idea that he had made a dummy, and had got close enough to them somewhere to make a switch.'

He stood up, carefully, with Jazz sprawled across his left shoulder. 'But when Swift spotted Elliot, and said what he did, all of our thinking swung right around. *What if* . . . we all thought at once, and some of us said, ". . . the bomb wasn't meant for Davey at all, but for Roland McGrath!" When Swift told us that Elliot had been a Marine before joining the SBS . . . as he'd told me earlier, and that his unit had been involved in mainland sabotage operations in the Falklands and elsewhere, the thing just took wings. I called the Secretary of

State and asked him to check on all the Red Boxes in his Office, to see if they were all accounted for.'

'Why?' asked Alex, fascinated.

'Because the boxes are sometimes sent to constituencies with week-end work for the Ministers. And sometimes, there will be more than one box. Hardy often has three or four of the things at one go. He did the check and phoned me back to say that one of the Junior Ministers' boxes was missing.

'At the same time, Adam Arrow was checking Elliot's military record. That's his report there.' He pointed to the document which Martin had read earlier. 'Summarised, it says that he was indeed in the SBS, but that he was removed from the active list after an operation in Africa, where he and his men were surprised by a family of civilians. Elliot ordered them killed – mother, father, grandmother and three children. His men refused to touch the children, so Elliot killed them himself.

'After the operation, his young second-in-command . . . Arrow's chum Swift . . . complained about the incident. There was an investigation. Elliot was retired, but the whole thing was covered up.

'Major Marshall Elliot is still in the Territorial Army, in the Artillery. Periodically, he goes on live firing exercises on the range in Northumberland. On the most recent session he attended, there was an unusually high incidence of faulty shells. Arrow is certain that they were faulty because Elliot removed their explosives. Apparently that's a trick his people used to pull in Ireland if they wanted to take care of someone in an untraceable way.'

'My God,' said Sarah. 'And this man became a political Agent.'

Bob raised an eyebrow. 'You don't think they vet them, do you? They'll take just about anyone who'll work for the money.'

'So you think that Elliot killed McGrath because . . .' Sarah began, until her husband interrupted, with a shake of his head.

'Not "think". We're bloody certain.'

'Okay, whatever . . . killed him because McGrath had been having an affair with his wife? And blew up the plane in the process.'

'As for his motive, bonking his wife would certainly be a main reason for Elliot deciding to kill him, but there was another. We know how zealous he was as a soldier, but according to Dame Janet Straw, he was just as big a fanatic as a Tory Agent. He was convinced that McGrath was going to lose the seat, and desperate about it. Finally, there was something else Dame Janet said to the Chief – that every Agent thinks he can do better than his MP.

'Add them together: a cold-blooded killer, a politically driven fanatic and someone who believed that Roland McGrath was a loser. My guess is that Elliot is so unbalanced, that those three things alone would have tripped him into deciding to kill the man. Then sexual jealousy . . . which the Fiscal was ready to accept as Maurice Noble's motive . . . was added in. We've got Mark's clear evidence to vouch for that.'

He paused. 'But there's something else. Think back to the tape. According to Mark, Elliot said, "It's not just that you had her, but what you've done to her." Remember?'

'Yes,' said Alex. 'I wondered about that. What do you think he meant?'

Skinner glanced across at her. 'I hesitate to discuss this subject with my daughter, but it ties into something that Leona told Alison Higgins. About five years ago, Roly McGrath went on a swansong rugby tour of Europe with his old team. They were away for a couple of weeks, and when they got back, Roly brought Leona a nice wee present, just the thing for a chap to give his wife . . . genital herpes.'

'Oh God,' said Sarah. 'That's awful. I've had patients whose lives have been ruined by that complaint. In terms of pain, incapacity and embarrassment, it's the worst sexually transmitted disease of them all. It's incurable, and when it flares up it's crippling for the patient. It's soul-destroying for a doctor, too. You feel so helpless in the face of your patient's suffering, because there's so little you can do. If Leona McGrath has that, she's marvellous to be doing what she is.'

Skinner nodded. 'Leona has it, and so has Margie Elliot. She admitted it to Brian Mackie this evening. Roly McGrath was generous enough to pass it on to her. That's how Marsh found out about them. When it broke out, she had to tell him.

'For all his other motives, I reckon that's why he decided to kill McGrath rather than just wait for him to lose Edinburgh Dean then stand for it himself at the first opportunity.'

He paused, letting his pronouncement sink in.

'It isn't necessary to ask a jury to believe that he meant to cause the accident. Ministers don't work on their papers on public aircraft. He would expect that the box would travel safely to Edinburgh under McGrath's seat, and would have been opened later, either in the car that picked him up from the airport or back in the office.

'And that's what would have happened, had he not switched the wrong box in the rush at Heathrow and had Maurice Noble not noticed it during the flight. But I reckon, even if he had considered the possibility, he'd still have gone through with it.'

Alex stepped up to him and lifted her brother from his cradling arms. 'Look, Pops,' she said quietly, breaking the enveloping silence which filled the room. 'I don't want to put a damper on things, but after all, I am a lawyer, even if I'm still wet behind the ears.

'Your whole evidential chain is predicated upon the word of a five-year-old, okay a remarkable one, but a five-year-old nonetheless, and one who has just survived the trauma of an air accident.

305

'Do you think you'll get him to peform in the witness box like he did for Uncle Bob, Uncle Andy and Auntie Maggie? And even if you do, that defence Counsel will not be able to plant a reasonable doubt in the mind of the jury? You won't be allowed to lead evidence of Elliot's SBS atrocity, you know.'

Bob nodded, looking sombre. 'Daughter, if this is you as a trainee, what are you going to be like once you start to practise?' He reached up and ruffled her hair. 'I'd be as worried as you if Mark was all I had, for his sake. But fortunately he isn't. There's the Government driver Elliot sent away, and the driver of Davey's car. They'll put him at the scene.' Suddenly he smiled up at her. 'And then, of course, there's Davey's Red Box.'

'Eh?'

He nodded. 'I was getting to that. Brian Mackie phoned me just before you arrived. He, McGuire, and the boy Pye found it, locked in a cupboard in Elliot's house. With that lot, I'd expect even such a murderous bastard as him to see sense and plead Guilty.'

'Let's hope so,' said Sarah vehemently. 'If part of his motive was to take over McGrath's constituency, and Leona has frustrated that, couldn't her life be in danger?'

'We have to assume so. That's why I sent Andy in, mob-handed, to arrest him even before I knew the outcome of the search. Dame Janet said that Leona had won him over. I don't believe that for one second.'

He squatted slowly down on one knee beside Sarah's chair. 'Love', he said, taking her hand in his and kissing it, 'Doctor. With all this sorted, please can I go home? Now.'

She frowned at him. 'Bob, Mr Braeburn said you should stay in until the end of this week.'

'Yes, I know, but Braeburn doesn't know me. I'll grant you I've got a way to go, but I'm getting better by the minute. I promise I won't go running for a while, at least not after dark, and I won't go back to the office until you and he say I can. I'll recover quicker and better around the wee chap there than I will in this room. There are times when I feel that I'm locked in here with all the stuff that Kevin O'Malley pulled out of my head. I can cope with it, all right, but I'll handle it more positively in the real world than in here.

'Please,' he said.

She looked at him with the eye of a headmistress assessing a remorseful pupil. 'Well,' she said finally, 'I'll ask Mr Braeburn.'

'Good,' he said, releasing her hand and standing up. 'While you're doing that, I'll be packing my shaving kit.'

93

The throng in the Assembly Hall of Stewart's-Melville College was far more attentive, and appreciative, than any that ever gathered there for morning prayers. It was, also, significantly larger.

The majority of the listeners were ladies, but there were a substantial number of men present. This pleased John Torrance as he looked down from the platform, particularly since he knew that the Liverpool versus Manchester United match which was on live television that evening represented a substantial counter-attraction.

He was pleased too with the age-spread of the people in the hall; but most of all, he was delighted by his candidate's confident, assertive and thoroughly pleasant performance.

As they had done at her adoption meeting, her audience rose spontaneously to their feet in applause as Leona finished her speech. As on that earlier occasion, she allowed them to express their enthusiasm for a few minutes before settling them and sending them home with her thanks and a few words of encouragement, to make them feel certain that a vote for her in seventeen days' time would not be wasted.

'Leona,' said Alison Higgins, greeting her friend as she stepped down from the stage, 'no one could have done better than that. Not Roly, not Andrew Hardy, not any of them. That was a terrific start.'

'Thanks,' said the little woman brightly, gathering up her notes and shoving them untidily into her briefcase. 'Now all I have to do is keep up that sort of momentum for two and a half weeks.'

'And you will, my dear,' said John Torrance, coming down the steps behind her. Higgins turned to look at him, urbane and handsome in his dark blue tailoring, and felt a crush coming on.

The Vice-chairman linked arms with the ladies, and walked them through the departing crowds towards the exit. As they went, they returned the nods and smiles of Leona's potential constituents.

'Where's Marsh? I didn't see him around,' said Alison, as they neared the double doors leading to the school's wide, floodlit yard. They were standing open.

'He nipped out halfway through the speech,' said Torrance. 'To count the collection, I expect. I imagine that he's taking down the posters now, and tidying up the hall. That's the Agent's lot. Anyway,'

307

he went on, 'I'm glad that Marshall isn't around, or our worthy but tedious Chairman and her husband, because I want to be very rude.'

'Do you indeed?' said Leona, smiling.

'Yes, I do. To celebrate our first meeting, I would like to invite the candidate to join me in a little supper at Rafaelli's. You too, Superintendent, of course.'

'That would be lovely,' said Leona, 'but I have to go home for Mark.'

'No, you don't,' said Alison, at once. 'I'll go back and relieve Maggie. This nice man wants to feed you, dear, and you've bloody well earned it! So go, or else. Here, gimme the keys of your car. We came in it together, after all. I'll take it home and John can drop you later.'

The Candidate sighed. 'I don't seem to have a choice, do I?' She fished the keys of her Alfa Romeo 164 from her bag and handed them over.

'Cheers,' said Higgins. 'See you later.' She turned and walked smartly off through the double doors and turned right, to the spot where Leona had parked earlier. They would have followed her at once, to Torrance's Jaguar which was parked alongside, had they not been stopped by two elderly fur-wearing, pearl-strung ladies who had sat in the front row during the meeting, hanging on the Candidate's every word.

Andy Martin, Adam Arrow and Neil McIlhenney saw them, bent in conversation, as they strode into the yard, between the heavy iron gates. They saw Alison Higgins climb into the driver's seat of the black Alfa and pull on the seat belt. And to the right of the double door they saw Marsh Elliot running towards his brown Rover 820 SDi, registration number L 511 QFT.

'Stop, Major!' Martin's command cut through the evening air. The Agent halted in mid-stride, looked around, then broke into a renewed sprint, his car key extended before him.

As John Torrance glanced up in surprise at the commotion, the detectives and the soldier began to run too, like hunters towards their prey.

They were sixty yards away, but the blast from the Alfa still took them off their feet, and its heat seemed to sear their lungs.

They picked themselves up, staring in horror at the roaring fireball. At its heart, they could see the outline of the car's skeleton, and of the dark, twisted shape behind the wheel. The Jaguar, which had been its neighbour in the park, lay on its side, with flames licking at its undercarriage.

'Alison!' Neil McIlhenney screamed, high-pitched. He broke into a lumbering run, but Andy Martin floored him with a rugby tackle before he had gone ten yards. As they hit the ground, the petrol tank of the Jaguar gave a dull, muffled *'Crump!'* and a second column of flame shot fifty feet into the air.

The two policemen lay on the tarmac yard, with the Sergeant still struggling in the Chief Superintendent's iron grip. Still deafened by the first explosion, they did not hear the sound of Elliot's Rover as its heavy diesel engine barked into life. With eyes only for the horror of the inferno, they did not see it as it bore down on Adam Arrow, standing in front of the gateway.

The little soldier stood his ground, an automatic pistol in his hand as if from nowhere. The Rover, roaring in second gear, picked up speed across the yard. It was almost upon him when he fired three shots, *'Crack! Crack! Crack!'* in less than a second.

They were perfectly grouped, just above the centre of the windscreen, to its left, directly above the steering column.

At the last instant, Arrow threw himself to one side, feeling the rush of air as the car swept past him, and rolling over to see it crash into one of the huge iron gates, tearing it from its hinges, and hurling the dead driver over the wheel and through the windscreen, to lie, shapeless, across its twisted hood.

94

'Why, for God's sake, Andy?' Skinner stared at his friend across the living room at Fairyhouse Avenue. Sarah sat beside him on the couch, her face still white with shock.

The knees of Martin's flannels were dirty from the tarmac of the quadrangle. A bump had risen on his right cheek, where McIlhenney's flailing elbow had caught him.

'We'll never know for sure,' he answered. 'But John Torrance said something that could well have a bearing on it. He told me that at the adoption meeting, Elliot suggested to Leona that once she'd made the seat secure, she could step down. She cut him off short, and said that she was there for the duration.'

'That would do it,' said Skinner emphatically. 'He must have decided that he couldn't wait any longer, whatever the risk. No doubt he thought that with the investigation having picked up suspects we'd try to nail a second explosion on one of them. Or maybe he decided that we'd go looking for a terrorist solution.'

'But what good would it have done him with the By-election under way?' asked Martin.

'Read your electoral law, Andy. If any candidate dies once the campaign is under way, the writ is void and the process has to begin all over again.' He leaned back in his seat, and dropped his head on to his chest. 'It's all over for the person, but politics, after all, is more important than life and death. In this case the show goes on uninterrupted. Sure, the candidate's in shock, but that doesn't matter. The other parties needn't bother turning up. They'll have to weigh Leona's votes, rather than count them. But our poor Alison. It's all over for her. And she had plans, Andy, she had plans.'

'She never knew a thing, Bob.'

'That's a small mercy,' he said. Although still not back to full strength, suddenly his voice was savage.

'I tell you, boy, you should steer clear of me. I am a walking jinx. I put Roy Old on that plane. I told Alison to spend as much time as she could with her friend.' He gazed at the ceiling and murmured, '"Death stands above me, whispering low, I know not what into my ear." Know that one, Andy? It could have been written for me. For Roy Old, and for Alison, being around me was very dangerous . . .

310

fatal, in fact. But not just them. For someone else, years ago . . .' His voice tailed away. As it did, Alex, who had been kneeling on the floor beside Martin, stood up and came over to sit on the arm of the couch, beside her father.

'Pops,' she whispered. 'Sarah told me. About what you went through with Kevin O'Malley, and about the things he uncovered. She told me about Mum, and the accident.' She looked at him solemnly, and took his right hand in both of hers.

'You mustn't feel guilty about the fact that she was driving your car. There isn't a day of my life goes past when I don't miss her, or wonder what might have been. But what might have been wasn't, and that's that. It's all in the past, and over the years we've coped, you and I. Pretty well, I'd say.

'So while I'm glad that you've spilled all those unhealthy suppressed memories out of their box, promise me that you won't torture yourself over Mum's death. In fact promise me that you won't think of it any more.'

Bob smiled at her. 'Sweetheart, you're asking me to do the impossible. O'Malley made me face a truth so awful that I've been hiding from it for sixteen years. Your mum was murdered, by mistake, instead of me. There's no way I can just set that aside.'

He glanced across at Sarah. 'But don't you two worry about me being tortured by remorse. I might feel that way over Roy and Alison, but I feel none at all about Myra. I'm a copper, and I can focus all the guilt on the person who cut that brake pipe.

'I'll tell you what I am going to do, Alex. I'm going to find out who that person was, and if he, or she, is still alive, I am going to make them wish most earnestly that they were dead! I'm not going to do it for you, or for me, but for your mum. Because like every victim, she deserves justice, and that's what she's going to get . . . even if it *is* sixteen years late. If I just set aside what I know now, I might as well take early retirement.'

'Bob,' said Sarah quietly. 'You won't turn this into a mission that will dominate your life, will you?'

He frowned at her. 'No, of course I won't. You know damn fine that my life belongs to you two, and to the wee fella upstairs. Anyway, don't start on about it being a mission. Like I said to Alex, there was a crime and I'm a policeman.'

'But, honey, that isn't your job any more.' Her voice rose. 'You're Deputy Chief Constable. Delegate it to Andy, and to CID, just like any other crime.'

The coldness of his sudden stare pierced her, and made her stomach flip over.

'Just like any other crime!' he repeated, softly and incredulously. He shook his head.

'That's my wife you're talking about, Alex's mother – *and she was murdered.* If you believe I'm capable of passing it down the line like some bloody shoplifting offence, then you don't really know me.

'And if you're selfish enough to *expect* me to do that,' he said, with a heavy sadness, 'well, Sarah, I'm not sure that I really know you either.'

She drew a sudden gasping breath, as hurt and anger, mixed together, flashed in her eyes. Suddenly, the silence in the room was almost palpable. Andy and Alex stared at them in consternation, as a retort formed on Sarah's lips, ready to burst out . . . and, at that moment, the telephone rang.